The Journey of Ban

Journey of Ban

Published by Rockjack Books

Printing History

Rockjack Books
First Printing 2007

Cover illustration and book design by
Mark Kashino

Text Illustrations by
Mary Blackeye

Rockjack Books
6631 Glacier Drive
Boise, Idaho 83716

ISBN: 978-0-9719567-2-3

Printed in Canada

To Alex
10-27-07
James Harshfield

The Journey of Ban

James B. Harshfield

Rockjack Books
Boise, Idaho

Acknowledgement

I offer thanks to Pat Duncan, Miriam Depew, Jeremy Bateman, and Barbara Harshfield for their special assistance in helping make the Journey of Ban a reality.

With pleasure, I extend to Mary Blackeye the honor of being the first recipient of the Trilogy of Ban Award of Excellence. The quality of her artwork goes beyond average and mingles with distinction.

- JAMES B. HARSHFIELD

Dedication

I dedicate this book to Jack Carlsen
and Everett Swayze.

It has been my privilege to have these
fine gentlemen as a part of my life.

ANCIENT BOOK OF LANDS
ROGA OF TANZ
2321 BK

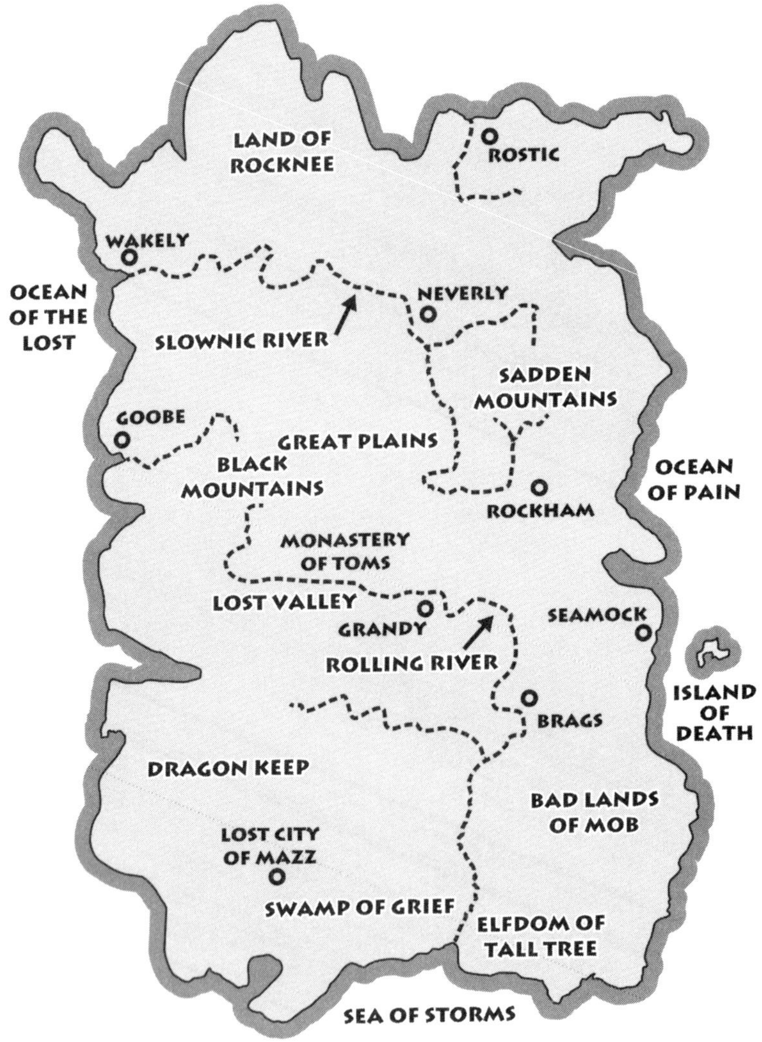

Contents

Part 1

Part 2

Part 3

PART
1

PROLOGUE

Coaldon hiked up the steep, rocky trail for most of the day. The warm sun, pleasant breeze, and majestic scenery filled him with contentment. Even though his feet hurt and his legs burned with fatigue, he pushed himself with unusual determination. A long hike into the wilderness of the Sadden Mountains was the challenge he needed to release his pent up energy. This recess from his daily routine offered him a way to be immersed into the beauty of nature. The young prince wanted this journey to be a time of peace.

After paying the appropriate wages of sweat and fatigue, he finally reached the summit. From this vantage point, he felt like a king surveying the unrivaled magnificence of his kingdom. He was mesmerized by the majesty of creation spreading out before him. Coaldon's inquiring eyes scanned the far off lands with curiosity. With the wonderment of a child, he desired to discover their hidden secrets. His youthful mind fantasized about visiting these mysterious places, meeting exotic people, and solving fascinating mysteries.

Yet, in spite of the rush of good feelings, the shadow of an unknown presence lurked under the surface of his mind. This was like an itch that could not be scratched or an intuition that could not be identified. The hint of an impending disaster drifted like a foul odor in the young warrior's mind. He tried to reach for it, but only detected a fleeting whiff of its presence. Down deep he knew something was wrong, yet he could not detect its nature.

Coaldon was a half-elf of the royal family of Rocknee. He had recently found himself thrust into a war between the forces of evil and the quest for justice. After a quiet life as a youth in the Outlast wilderness, he had been cast into a war of epic proportions. The innocence of his youth had been ripped away by the polluted substance of iniquity. He struggled to understand why violence could be found in such a beautiful world.

As Coaldon's eyes wandered over the vast landscape, he considered the events that were dominating the Empire. The ugly deeds of Crossmore the Wizard violated the standards of decency taught to him by his grandparents. Crossmore used death, pain, and torture to help expand his power. With the cunning of a fox and the dishonesty of sin, he assumed the role of emperor. To gain control, the wizard summoned an army of vulgar creatures from the Chamber of Oblivion. Trogs and geks were preparing to invade the empire from remote sanctuaries. Crossmore used these foul creatures to create fear among law abiding citizens.

Through great pain and agony Coaldon learned that:

evil creates evil;
wickedness poisons goodness;
terror ferments fear;
hopelessness consumes confidence.

He realized that the forces of righteousness were facing the nearly impossible task of conquering the evil creeping across the land.

Coaldon awoke from these thoughts to face the end of a long day. The young prince abruptly became aware of the encroachment of the cold night air. He had to shift his attention from Crossmore to finding shelter for the night. The cool evening breeze chilled his body as the memories of the trog army dampened his spirit.

Pleasant Expectations

The violent battle with the trog army was slowly becoming a distant memory for the dwarf community. Several months earlier the dwarves of the Hardstone Clan and Coaldon's companions had escaped the trog army, finding safety in the caverns of Rockham. The Long Beard Clan of Rockham had welcomed their relatives from the north with open arms. The Long Beard Clan had lived many centuries in Rockham, building an elaborate maze of tunnels and rooms deep in the Sadden Mountains. The dwarves found security and peace living in the roots of the mountain.

For the past several weeks, Prince Coaldon had the desire to find relief from the suffocating boredom of confinement in the underground dwarf city of Rockham. He had craved to smell the fresh air of the high mountains and to sit in the cool shade of giant pine trees. The young warrior wanted to spend several peaceful days enjoying the grandeur of nature. He needed to clear his mind from the sadness infecting his soul. The memories of war clouded him with grief. In addition, his confinement in the underground city had created a reserve of energy in his youthful body that needed to be released. Even though he had been discouraged from making this journey by his grandfather Brad, Coaldon's stubbornness determined his decision. He could not imagine facing danger on this innocent trip into the wilderness.

With his body full of excitement, his faithful dog at his side, and the Blade of Conquest strapped to his back, he was ready for a most delightful hike. The half-elf departed Rockham at sunrise to allow himself ample time to reach the high mountain Pass of Rosco before nightfall. He planned to spend several days searching for the peace he had experienced as a youth on the farm in the Black Mountains.

The cool morning air greeted Coaldon as he left the caverns of Rockham. The trail to the north was regularly traveled by dwarves gathering roots, berries, and herbs in the high meadows. The path was steep, which only added to Coaldon's enjoyment of the physical challenge. Sid, Coaldon's wolf-like dog, raced ahead of him, romping and playing in the wide open spaces. The trail angled up a long, tree-covered ridgeline, passing over a rocky knoll, and dropping into a green, lush meadow. A narrow river of cold, clear water flowed down the valley at an unhurried pace.

Coaldon wanted to stay in this wondrous place, but decided he needed to continue his journey. The northern end of the valley was bordered by a tall, rocky cliff with a waterfall cascading down its sheer face. The mist from the falls drifted upward, forming a cloud sliced by a rainbow. With eager steps, he followed a narrow trail angling up the face of the cliff. At the top, the trail led up a narrow rocky canyon. A noisy stream surged down the ravine with robust energy.

As Coaldon trudged up the vague outline of the ancient path, a hint of anxiety shadowed him. The young prince became concerned when Sid's behavior changed from carefree frolic to watchful attentiveness. Sid slowed his pace, sniffed the air, and watched the trail with increased vigilance. A rock falling down the canyon wall alerted Coaldon to his repressed uneasiness. He literally staggered when he realized he had dropped his guard in a reckless manner. The first survival lesson he had learned from his grandfather was to be aware of his surroundings at all times.

Intuition told the young warrior that something foreign was occupying the wilderness. He searched the trail for signs of danger, but found nothing to indicate a problem. A feeling of anxiety continued to haunt him, but he found nothing to justify the anxiety.

Guided by over-confidence, he repressed this subtle warning and enthusiastically hiked up the trail. The path left the canyon walls behind and crossed a steep, rocky, barren mountainside. The sun was setting in the west when Coaldon finally arrived at Rosco Pass. The Sadden Mountain range dominated the north and south features of the eastern segment of the continent. To the west of the mountains, the Slownic River divided the broad expanse of the Great Plains into two distinct regions. To the east of Rosco Pass, the coastal plain sloped to the Ocean of Pain.

As the sun dropped below the horizon, Coaldon began to search for adequate shelter. The rocky surface of the summit offered little protection from the harsh weather at this elevation. Coaldon remembered passing a small meadow on the east side of the summit. With long strides, he loped back down the path and reached the meadow before darkness consumed the last rays of day light. The young prince discovered a stream flowing from a tapered cut in a stone wall. The channel was just wide enough for him to crawl through. This narrow fissure opened into a small, protected area wide enough for him to set up camp. It was not long before he had consumed a hearty meal and found the comfort of his sleeping blanket. As he lay staring at the stars in the sky, his mind reviewed the events of the day. Sadly, his sense of peace was clouded by a subtle feeling of discord and tension. Coaldon

decided to sleep with his sword next to him in case he was besieged by unwelcome guests during the night.

The dim light of early morning flooded Coaldon's campsite, offering a door into the new day. The cackling call of a bird abruptly drew his attention. Coaldon sat up in a state of disorientation. As Coaldon's mind cleared away the sluggish residue of sleep, he felt a hint of evil touch him. Deep in his spirit, he knew great danger lurked near by. He again heard the cackling sound. Both Coaldon and Sid looked up to see a large bird sitting on a rock over their heads. To Coaldon's surprise, Sid sat quietly staring at the bird with indifference. The bird looked directly at Coaldon with intelligence and understanding. The young warrior had never seen or heard about a bird with such unusual characteristics. The large creature was about the size of a young war eagle, dressed in dark brown feathers, and characterized by bright red eyes. White wing tips offered an unusual contrast to the rest of its body.

The bird gave several cackling calls, looked up the slope toward the summit, and flew into the stillness of the morning. Coaldon rekindled the fire and ate a hurried meal. He did not want to waste time in the trivial pursuit of food while the adventures of the day waited for him. With the skill of a seasoned traveler, Coaldon loaded his pack and adjusted the straps to gain the greatest comfort. As he grabbed his sword, he felt a familiar warmth radiating from the hilt. Yesterday's anxiety suddenly returned!

In a quiet voice he muttered, "Oh, No! This could be a bad day."

Coaldon knew the Blade of Conquest would vibrate and give off heat when evil was present. Sid gave a deep growl and raced out of the sheltered campsite. Coaldon followed him with sword in hand to discover the reason for the dog's excitement.

Unwelcome Visitors

Coaldon had only taken several steps before an unpleasant committee greeted him. Surrounding him was a large group of trogs, smiling with grotesque faces. Trogs were tall, ugly beasts that had been summoned, by Crossmore the Wizard, from their imprisonment in the Chamber of Oblivion. The large and muscular beasts had leathery, black hides. Their round, flat faces were adorned with several small horns curving downward from their foreheads. Two large, yellow eyes protruded from their faces, giving them the appearance of being dull-witted. The beasts' large, gaping mouths revealed greasy, brown teeth. A steady stream of green slime dribbled down their chins. Behind and off to the right of the trogs stood a tall beast with the appearance of intelligence and authority. This creature, a gek, had a long, narrow face with large green eyes, big ears, wide mouth, and a broad forehead. The ugly head stood on top of a powerful, hairy body with long legs, and gangly arms.

The gek pushed his way through the line of trogs with violence and contempt. As he stopped in front of Coaldon, he laughed in a loud, arrogant voice.

He snickered, "What do we find here, maybe the lowest scum of the earth? You humans are so pathetic and miserable. Oh yes, my master, Crossmore, sends his greetings and best wishes for a wonderful day. You are now my prisoner and will provide me with many hours of entertainment."

By this time, Coaldon had overcome his initial shock at being in such a dangerous situation. He rolled back his shoulders, assumed a false front of courage, and smiled. Coaldon said in a loud, clear voice, "Your bogus words only mirror the foul intentions of your master. You are enslaved to Crossmore's corrupt mind and empty destiny. You are nothing and to nothing you will return. "

The gek looked at Coaldon with stunned disbelief. The powerful beast was accustomed to the trogs cowering to its authority. Coaldon's defiance caused the gek to lose face in front of its subordinates. In order to reestablish control, it rushed at Coaldon with sword in hand. The gek's face was bright red with rage and its teeth slashed the air. The beast planned to show this wretched human its real power.

Coaldon had not expected such a violent reaction. In desperation, he pointed his sword at the charging creature. A bright flash of light erupted from the end of his sword, striking the gek in the chest. The gek turned into a cloud of smoke. Without hesitation, Coaldon attacked the slow-thinking trogs before they had the opportunity to move. His sword swept with the speed and accuracy of a weapon on a sacred mission of purification. Half the trogs fell to the ground while the remainder rushed up the slope toward the summit in a state of panic. Trogs were created to be subordinate to their gek masters. Once the gek master was destroyed, the trog slaves lost their power to act as warriors.

The air around the battle site was clouded with the black smoke of vaporized trogs. Once trogs and geks died, they returned to the emptiness of their original source, nothingness. Coaldon watched as Sid returned after chasing the escaping trogs up the mountainside. This moment of victory was only a small triumph in the war against the trogs' invasion. From past experience, Coaldon knew the trogs would pursue him until he was either destroyed or he had escaped from their unending pursuit. Without waiting for another attack, he started running down the trail. The rough, uneven path made it difficult for the half-elf to keep his footing. He was feeling good about his progress until he heard a dreadful sound. He stopped in a wide area in the bottom of a rocky ravine to make sure he was not imagining it.

With growing anxiety, he confirmed his suspicions. A deep, resonating sound echoed back and forth in the narrow canyon. The boom of a trog war-drum throbbed its dreadful beat in a steady and familiar rhythm. The drum's slow, deep thump, plus the sound of trog voices, created an image of pending doom in Coaldon's mind.

With rapid and terrified beats, he could feel his heart rattling inside his chest. A grip of fear raced through his body with an unrestrained rush. His stomach churned with nausea and his mind froze in a state of paralysis. A deep sense of loneliness clouded Coaldon's spirit with the realization of total isolation. He knew that he had to conquer the enemy within himself before he could possibly challenge the trog army racing to destroy him. Like the approach of a bad dream, he heard loud voices screaming in the distance. Coaldon knew he could not remain in this state of paralysis if he was to survive. The Empire was depending on him to be a rock of strength. The people of the Empire needed his leadership and courage to help in the struggle against Crossmore. As Coaldon stood on the desolate path, he began to search for a way out of this treacherous situation. His mind seemed to work in slow motion as trog voices drew closer.

Then, from a deep alcove in his mind, a wave of peace gently washed against the fear gripping him. Like a flash of light, Coaldon remembered receiving the knife, Strong Edge, as a birthday present from Starhood, his elfin grandfather. With the clarity of the original event, he distinctly heard the words of commission stated by his grandfather. Coaldon remembered Starhood placing the knife in his hand, stating, "This knife will help protect you on your journey in life. Its name is Strong Edge. If you allow the power of the knife to assist you, it will connect your will to the One Presence. It will bind you to me in times of great danger."

As Coaldon reached down and grabbed the knife, a surge of indescribable power flowed into his trembling body. Peace soothed his jumbled, confused thoughts with strokes of calm. Coaldon felt as if he had been resurrected from a pit of hopelessness. He slowly raised his head from dejection.

It would only be moments before the scourge of the trogs would trap him. Coaldon realized it would be impossible to fight the large number of trogs and geks. After studying the surrounding area, he determined that the only escape route was to climb a steep canyon wall to the south. With sudden grief, he realized Sid would not be able to escape with him.

In a commanding voice, Coaldon declared, "Sid, run for your life! The trogs will be so intent on capturing me they will not be interested in you. Sid, go!" Sid stood watching Coaldon, then ran down the trail and out of sight.

Coaldon took a deep breath and began to climb the steep cliff. Hand over hand, he pulled himself up the first section of the rock wall. Coaldon had to probe with his fingers in order to find adequate hand holds to pull himself up. He had progressed up the first half of the cliff when the trogs arrived below him. It was not long before the trogs spotted the young prince climbing up the cliff face. At this discovery, shouts and laughter erupted from the beasts. As he looked down, he saw trogs start to climb the wall, aided by the cheers of their fellow soldiers. With a burst of energy, Coaldon rapidly climbed the remainder of the cliff. His fingers were bleeding and his body ached as he pulled himself onto the ledge at the top of the cliff. Coaldon could tell by the voices below him that his pursuers were quickly overtaking him.

Coaldon decided to attack the trogs rather than attempt an immediate escape. The trogs were so close at hand that he was uncertain if he could escape without first slowing their advance. He had to gain time before the mass of the trog army arrived. He would risk the possibility of death in order to gain precious minutes.

He decided to fight the trogs at the top of the cliff on a wide stone plateau. Coaldon waited in anxious anticipation as the first trog emerged over the top of the wall. To his displeasure, four trogs climbed on to the stone shelf at the same time. Coaldon's quick attacked destroyed the first pursuer. This success was swiftly followed by near disaster. A large, powerful trog attacked him with a club in a slow, awkward motion. The weapon struck Coaldon a glancing blow across his shoulder.

The agonizing pain from the blow caused his knees to weaken. With staggering steps, he fell near the edge of the cliff. With his head hanging over the rim of the cliff, he saw the trog army, watching from below, celebrating his seeming defeat. As the trogs took delight at his impending death, a bolt of anger pulsed through the Prince.

Coaldon, ignoring the excruciating pain, rolled to his left just as the trog's club hit the ground where he had fallen. Dangling over the edge, he crawled to his knees, gathered his strength, and gave a wide swing of his sword. The sword dug deeply into the massive legs of the trog. The forward momentum of the blade helped Coaldon regain his footing. With a burst of energy, Coaldon climbed up a rocky knoll and rushed through an opening in the trogs' attack formation. This move shattered their concentration and caused a slow, uncoordinated response.

By this time, five more trogs had climbed onto the top of the cliff. The trogs lumbered up the slope, one at a time, allowing Coaldon's swordsmanship to quickly reduce the odds by two. Yet, before he was overwhelmed by the five remaining trogs, he leapt from the knoll and into a gully that opened over the face of the cliff. Coaldon tried to escape up the small ravine but was blocked by two trogs. Even though he attacked with aggressiveness, he was not able to strike a lethal blow. Coaldon realized he was going to die if he did not retreat, so he turned and rushed down the gully towards the edge of the cliff. At this point the five trogs roared with satisfaction when they realized Coaldon was trapped between them and the edge of the cliff.

When Coaldon turned to face the trogs, he understood his critical situation. Two trogs lumbered down the ravine toward Coaldon while the remaining beasts stood above him on the wall of the gully, blocking his escape. In a tranquil manner, Coaldon faced the two trogs, dropped to one knee, held the Blade of Conquest in his right hand, and lowered his left hand to his side. As the two trogs approached Coaldon with relaxed swaggers, they were delighted to see Coaldon's submissive posture. Honor and glory would be theirs if they destroyed this enemy. When the trogs were several strides away from Coaldon, they stopped their advance in a state of bewilderment. Coaldon knew the trogs would be confused by this strategy. The trogs carefully watched Coaldon, waiting for his next move. As Coaldon stared at them, the weak minds of the trogs were lulled into a passive state of uncertainty. Once the trogs relaxed their guard, Coaldon took immediate action. In one swift motion, he grabbed a handful of dirt with his left hand, throwing it into the faces of the two trogs. As the trogs raised their hands to protect their eyes from the flying dirt, Coaldon leapt forward, swinging his sword in a sweeping motion. As the sword flashed through air, it inflicted deep cuts into the midsection of the trogs' bodies. Coaldon did not wait for the trogs to respond before he rushed between his two wounded opponents and ran up the gully toward freedom.

Coaldon ran with the determination of a trained athlete. He swiftly escaped into the maze of gullies that dominated the landscape. For the rest of the morning, he heard the distant noise of the trogs as they followed him up the tree-covered mountainside. When Coaldon crossed the top of a ridgeline, he took a short rest. In order to leave no tracks, he walked down a rocky outcrop that extended down the side of the ridge. Upon reaching the canyon floor, he found a stream of ice-cold water tumbling down a narrow, rocky ravine. To cover his escape route, he walked up the stream, even though his feet were numbed by the icy water.

Coaldon heard trog voices when they crossed the ridge line high above him. This helped motivate him to push beyond the limits of his endurance. He continued to struggle up the stream until he found a steep rocky hillside with a northern exposure rising from the streambed. Coaldon took advantage of this escape route to leave the stream and gain some distance from the advancing trog army. He climbed up the rock face which hid him from the enemy. He spared no energy or time in scrambling up the hillside. It was late afternoon when Coaldon reached the snow-covered ridge.

Coaldon collapsed on the ground in total exhaustion. He knew he could go no further, but needed to find a place to hide. With the practiced eye of an experienced woodsman, he noticed a layer of flat, open depressions on a cliff face that had been hollowed out over the centuries by the wind and weather. At the risk of being seen, he climbed out onto the stone formation and crawled into a shallow, flat cave.

Coaldon lay under the shallow, rocky overhang with sweat dripping from his body, his back cramping from the pain, and exhaustion tormenting every muscle. In the distance, the sound of loud, guttural voices echoed in the rock canyon, creating a terrifying sense of entrapment. His memories of beautiful trees, majestic cliff, and green meadows had been replaced by the possibility of a violent and grotesque death. Yesterday's vision of peace and happiness had been ripped away. As the half-elf reflected on the events of the day, his mind churned in anger. The magnificence of nature had been polluted by the foul incursion of evil.

Memories

As Coaldon rested, he felt the security of his small, stony hiding place wrap around him. He found the paralyzing impact of fear melting away. Even though the young prince had successfully survived the day, loneliness soon descended upon him. He missed the gentle smile of Grandma Ingrid, the firm hand of Grandpa Brad, and the cheerful radiance of his twin sister, Noel. He closed his eyes to find slumber, but the excitement of the day would not allow him to sleep. Memories of his escape raged through his mind in an unending circle of repeated events. Over and over, he smelled the foul odor of trogs, saw their ugly faces, and remembered the day-long rush to escape from their pursuit.

Then, a sudden shift of thought caused Coaldon to refocus his attention onto the major events of his life. It seemed the brush with death had opened a door into his past. He saw his life passing before him in a rapid progression of memories and images.

Coaldon saw his childhood home in Lost Valley, among the towering Black Mountains. The small, productive wilderness farm of his grandparents spread out across a lush green meadow. He observed his grandparents, Brad and Ingrid, working at different tasks around their wilderness farm. Gardens were grown, livestock tended, and a warm family life had been maintained.

As a child, he remembered learning that his mother had been an elf, and his father, a human. They had been killed when Wastelow, with the help of Crossmore the Wizard, conquered the Empire.

On his eighteenth birthday he learned that his grandfather had been deposed as emperor by Wastelow; he was the rightful heir to the throne; and he had a twin sister, Noel. Among the gifts he received on his eighteenth birthday were the Blade of Conquest, Strong Edge the knife, and the Gem of Watching.

The shock of these discoveries had forced him to leave behind the carefree life of a youth, and to be launched upon a most unusual adventure. Coaldon remembered when the Council of Toms decided to rescue his twin sister, Noel, from her captivity in Neverly. For him the successful rescue of Noel reopened a wonderful relationship with his dynamic and caring twin sister. He had clear memories of the violent battle between the dwarves and trogs. The images of death and great suffering, by the dwarf community, were vivid in his mind. It was with joy that he remembered the dwarf community escaping to the city of Rockham.

Coaldon's thoughts returned to the present when he heard the voices of trogs directly above his hiding place. The trogs had arrived as the long shadows of the evening introduced the impending arrival of nightfall. The blanket of darkness covered him in the secure shade of obscurity. At this moment he was not concerned about the trogs, but instead, ate his evening meal and drifted into an agitated sleep.

Cackles

As the light of the new day washed over Coaldon, he found it a relief to awaken from his troubling sleep. His night had been plagued by an unpleasant encounter with a night terror. The half-elf had a difficult time shaking off the residue of a violent dream. '. . .people were living in the midst of a churning black cloud. They leisurely walked around a village, oblivious to the storm. The people were not aware of the lightning, thunder, and rain. Coaldon knew the storm was only the prelude to a hurricane, soon to descend on the helpless village. The villagers smiled, laughed, and went about their daily activities, unaware of the storm. Coaldon kept telling the villagers to seek cover from the storm before it was too late. They only looked at him as if he was crazy, pushing him away with threatening remarks. They kept telling him to go away. Hatred was directed at him for interrupting their quiet lives. He covered his head to protect himself from their blows. He ran away, feeling the sweat of hopelessness dripping from his face. Loneliness and despair choked his mind. He did not know what to do. . .'

Upon awakening from his unsettling dream, he became painfully aware of sore, aching muscles. This discomfort added to the frustration of being trapped in the prison of his hiding place. The shallow cave had saved Coaldon life, yet he agonized at being forced to lie inactive for so many hours. As the light of the new day greeted him, he could not detect any signs of the enemy. While Coaldon considered what to do next, a large shadow descended over his hiding place. Coaldon's whole being froze with panic at the thought of being trapped. He assumed that the trogs had discovered him and would attack at any moment. Coaldon knew that if he was to fight, he would need to climb across a wide rocky face to find enough footing to defend himself.

Yet, when he was not attacked, he looked out of the cave to determine what had cast the shadow. On a nearby ledge, Coaldon saw the bird he had seen the day before at his camp site. The large brown bird had rumpled feathers, white wing tips, and a crown-shaped tuft of gold colored feathers on its head. Even though the creature's body drooped under the weight of an aged life, its red eyes gleamed with intelligence and alertness. The bird gave a loud, cackling call as it shifted its weight from one foot to the other. It paid no attention to the young prince, but rather, peacefully basked in the warm morning sun.

At first, Coaldon was unsure of what to do. He asked himself, "I wonder if the bird's reappearance is an unusual coincidence? Should I attack, do nothing, or talk to it?"

Finally, Coaldon spoke, "Can you understand me?"

The bird tipped its head to one side and responded, "Yes, I understand you. By the way, you look funny trapped in this cliff. Ha! Ha! You are a most naive young man. You must feel humiliated at your present circumstances. It was great fun watching you run like a rabbit from the hounds of Hell. I am impressed you were able to escape. There is still hope for you. At least you did something right."

Coaldon was shocked by the open and frank criticism of yesterday's escape. Somewhat defiantly, he asked, "What is your name? Why are you following me?"

The bird hopped closer to Coaldon with a sense of authority. It continued, "My name is Cackles. Topple asked me to watch over you while you wander like a lost sheep amongst the wolves. Your friends decided it was time for you to learn about the importance of heeding good advice. I think you are learning nicely."

Coaldon closed his eyes in embarrassment. He knew he had failed to listen to the advice of his grandfather. The searing criticism by Cackles burned into his mind like a hot iron. He had failed miserably, yet thankfully, no one was hurt besides himself. Coaldon closed his eyes to allow the pain of his failure to pass into the category of 'learned experiences'. This was no time to dwell on failures; rather, he needed to find a way to escape the trogs.

Coaldon commented, "I accept your criticism with an open mind. Yet, I must leave behind yesterday and survive my current situation. Escape is my first priority."

Cackles gave a loud cry, spread his large wings, and flew into the sky with stately elegance. Coaldon watched as the bird soared with long, graceful turns over the surrounding area.

Coaldon decided to wait for evening before he took any further action. He spent the rest of the day reviewing his current situation and trying to develop a plan of action. In truth, he did not have the slightest idea of what to do next. As the hours of the day passed in agonizing slowness, Coaldon decided he had to do something soon or he would explode from boredom and frustration.

During the day, Coaldon did not hear any trog voices. With this in mind, he decided to leave the cave at nightfall. At dusk, he carefully wiggled out of the hiding place and climbed stiffly to the ridge top. As he stood next to a snow bank, Cackles flew over his head and landed on a rock. Again, the large bird seemed to ignore Coaldon. In a state of tranquility, Cackles peacefully surveyed the landscape. As the cool night air flowed off the tall mountain peaks, the large bird closed his eyes to take a nap.

Coaldon's impatience finally got the best of him. In frustration, he demanded, "Would you be willing to help me!?"

At this interruption, the bird erupted from its snooze in frustration and anger. Giving a loud squawk, he looked at Coaldon with amazement.

It finally responded, "My, you are most impetuous and impolite. It has been a long time since I have dealt with the impatience of youth. For some ghastly reason, I assume this encounter with you will somehow be good for me."

Coaldon was dismayed at his breach of etiquette. His grandmother would have scolded him for such a display of rudeness.

Coaldon followed, "I am sorry for disrupting your sleep, but I need to escape from the trogs. Would you please help me?"

Cackles looked at Coaldon for a long time before responding. "I also apologize. I am not used to being around humans. I should understand your need to escape. Oh, of course I will help you. I advise you to fly away with me. Ha! Ha! Grow wings and take pleasure in the freedom of flight."

At this point, Coaldon understood the bird's dry sense of humor. He decided to enjoy this moment with his new friend.

Coaldon injected, "I must depend on my two long, gangly legs to provide transportation, unless you are willing to carry me?"

Cackles gave a loud screeching cry, leaped into the air, and landed on top of Coaldon's head. The young prince was surprised as he staggered under the weight of the large bird.

Cackles commented, "I have a better idea, you carry me."

With a giggle, Coaldon said, "All right. I will walk. You will fly. I do not want to carry you on my head all night. I promise I will listen to your advice. I have learned my lesson."

Cackles hopped to the ground and stared into the distance with intense concentration.

He then said, "The Trogs are guarding every escape route from the area."

Coaldon questioned, "Do you have any suggestions how I might get out of here?"

Cackles responded with a croak of annoyance in his voice, "As a beggar, you need to learn to respond to me with more humility."

With a twinkle of delight in his eyes, Coaldon fell to his knees and bowed to the bird in mock submission.

With a smug look of majesty, Cackles replied, "Much better. You have assumed the proper position to honor my true greatness. Ha! Ha! Ha!"

Looking up from the ground, Coaldon said, "Oh, great Cackles, I beg for your guidance! I depend on your great wisdom to protect me!"

The large bird fluffed its feathers and spread its wings in a stately manner.

After strutting around the area in an elegant fashion, the bird stated, "I, Cackles of Dumpford, declare you a loyal subject and under my safeguard. The grand and noble Cackles must ponder this problem with regal contemplation."

Coaldon bowed three more times to Cackles. "You are most impressive, great Cackles!"

With a satisfied look on its face, the bird directed, "The only way to escape from your present dilemma is to go over the Pass of Regrets. You must walk up this ridge, carefully pass a trog outpost, and follow the trail over the summit. I will help if you need assistance. Go now, humble servant, guided by my magnificent wisdom. May peace and prosperity be your companions."

With a look of obedience and cowering, Coaldon bowed saying, "You are most impressive and honorable. I give tribute to your impressive character. I bid you farewell, most noble bird."

With slow, pompous steps the ancient bird swaggered to the edge of the cliff, spread it wings in a grandiose fashion, and flew away with the dignity of a great lord.

The Summit of Regrets

Without waiting for further dialogue, Coaldon began his climb up the ridge. Even though darkness limited his ability to move rapidly, his elfin night vision helped him walk with confidence. It was midnight when he saw the flicker of a fire against the backdrop of a tall mountain and narrow ravine. With the skill of a seasoned scout, he crawled within a short distance of the campfire. One trog and gek stood guard while three trogs and one gek slept near the fire. Coaldon decided the beasts were guarding the only route over the summit. He studied the location of the camp to determine how to get past it safely. After evaluating all possibilities, Coaldon decided there was no way to get around the camp without being detected.

He thought, "Since I cannot go around the camp, I must go through it. I will make a direct attack on the guards. Surprise will be my ally."

With the impulsiveness of youth, Coaldon crawled within several strides of the guards before attacking. He rushed forward and destroyed the surprised trog with one swift stroke of his elfin sword. Next, he pointed the sword at the gek, releasing a blinding flash of light. Screams of death awoke the remaining soldiers. As Coaldon's sword flashed in the fire light, he attacked the sleepy trogs. With deadly accuracy, he slew two of the beasts. After his initial assault, he stepped back to catch his breath and observe the camp site. Out of the corner of his eye he saw a trog rushing toward him swinging a large club. Before he could defend himself, Coaldon received a blow to his rib cage twisting him to the left. As his body finished a full turn, he prepared his sword to attack. Coaldon noticed that the trog's roundhouse swing had pulled its arms behind its back. At that moment, the trog had no way of protecting itself against Coaldon's counter-attack. In spite of his pain, Coaldon's sword ripped into the trog's vulnerable midsection with savage revenge. The beast collapsed to the ground with a critical wound.

Coaldon regained his balance, but the overwhelming pain in his side caused him to lose grip of his sword. As he gasped in agony, the last gek swaggered out of the darkness with overbearing confidence.

The beast roared with robust laughter, "So, you have a little sore on your side. This should be like taking candy from a baby. You have caused enough problems. I will put an end to your childish mischief."

Coaldon regained his poise, pulled out his knife, and painfully dropped into a fighting position. The giant gek leapt forward, swinging its massive sword. Coaldon jumped backward just as the sword cut a slice across his leather jacket. With the grace of a newborn calf, Coaldon tripped over a rock and tumbled to the ground. The gek towered over him with its sword raised over its head. As Coaldon prepared to draw his last breath, a savage screech penetrated the night. A black shadow flew out of the darkness, attacking the gek's face with long, sharp talons. The gek stepped back in shock, dropped its sword, and swung both hands at the black phantom. This hesitation allowed Coaldon time to crawl to his feet and strike. Using this interruption to his advantage, Coaldon dove forward, burying his knife deep into the gek's chest. Only a cloud of smoke marked the ending of the gek's existence. The fight was over.

Coaldon's body drooped forward in exhaustion and pain.

Cackles, with the grace of a ballerina, landed near the fire. The bird's croaking echoed off the surrounding rock walls as he stared at the sagging warrior.

Cackles finally scoffed, "You are one of the most naive people I have ever met! Nobody in his right mind would have attacked such a formidable foe. I guess you did not know you could lose the battle. It is now time for you to return to Rockham, that is unless you can find a new way to create more problems for yourself. Go over the pass, follow the river to the Great Plains, and wait for someone to meet you. I look forward to receiving your homage in the future. Until then, good bye."

Cackles flew into the darkness like a passing dream. The old bird had arrived and departed so quickly that he seemed like a figment of Coaldon's imagination.

Without hesitation or looking back, Coaldon hiked over the summit with short, painful steps and a dejected spirit. The pain in his side was a constant reminder of this unwelcome adventure. He set a steady pace until midmorning of the next day. The young warrior took an extended rest when he arrived at a large river flowing south out of the Sadden Mountains. He would later learn that this was the headwaters of the Slownic River.

Coaldon instinctively knew that he had made the final transformation from youth into adulthood. The horrors of the past few days had crushed the innocence of his adolescence. This would allow his budding adulthood to successfully confront the challenges of life. His terrifying initiation was both a reward and a burden. By accepting the gift of adulthood, he also received an increased responsibility in the defense of the Empire.

Since Coaldon had not detected any signs of trogs by midday, he decided to slow his pace to take the stress off his bruised body. At sunset, he found a protected campsite, lit a small fire, and ate a peaceful meal. The flickering flames of the fire reached into his mind, bringing back memories of Pacer the Warrior. He remembered Pacer always talking about a campfire being the 'traveler's friend'. Pacer would say, "A campfire warms, dries, cooks, greets, heals, and protects the weary voyager in life."

Coaldon slept soundly and awoke with renewed energy.

With a persistent pain in his side, Coaldon slowly walked down the valley. By mid-afternoon, the narrow valley opened onto the broad expanse of the Great Plains. The river turned west, disappearing into the distant haze of an approaching storm. In response to the growing threat of rain, Coaldon searched for suitable shelter from the storm, but had to finally accept the limited protection of a large tree. Black clouds rushed from the west, attacking everything in its path with blustery winds and a steady downpour of rain. The storm clouds rumbled and raged like angry, fighting giants. The downpour of rain and cold wind intensified Coaldon's dark mood. He pulled his coat over his head to find protection from the rain.

The storm quickly passed, leaving large puddles of water and purified air. The warm afternoon sun bathed Coaldon's hiding place with the cleansing power of new hope. Coaldon spent the remainder of the day enjoying the gift of life. He found this reprieve a time of rest and recovery. The young warrior had no desire to wander off on another adventure. Enough was enough.

The Great Council of Rockham

Coaldon's return to Rockham was a happy event for friends and family. Yet, his near death experience was treated with alarm by the dwarves. The citizens of Rockham were deeply concerned about trogs being so close to their home. Grim tones of anguish filled the halls of the city. Light hearts of the past were replaced by hush voices of fear.

Several weeks after Coaldon's arrival, the sound of horns echoed in the vast maze of tunnels and caverns that formed the City of Rockham. At the sound of the trumpets, the dwarf community migrated to their enormous meeting hall, the Room of Harmony. Legend tells stories of how thousands of skilled dwarf stonemasons built this heritage of magnificence. Rare gems had been set into the walls and ceiling to allow light to be refracted into facets of beauty. Holes had been cut in the roof to allow sunlight to fill the room with a warm glow. Seeing this room for the first time was like experiencing a fantasy come true. Dwarf engineers designed the cavern to have perfect acoustics in spite of the stone walls. Even though the room was massive in size, any speaker, talking in a normal voice, could be heard from any location. It was rumored that elfin magic permeated the walls of the carven, enriching the splendor of the room.

As dwarves filed into the large room, they sat in rows of comfortable seats carved from the natural stone of the cavern. The immense size of the cavern allowed the entire population of Rockham to attend at one time. The dwarves from each clan sat in designated areas. The Rockham clans sat on the right side of the cavern while the Hardstone clan, from the northern Homekeep, sat on the left.

After the Hardstone clan arrival at Rockham, several months earlier, its members had become an integral part of the city. The citizens of Rockham had greeted their long lost relatives with open arms. It only took several weeks for the two communities to blend into one united effort. The bond of blood had overcome the separation of time. It forged the dwarves into a unified force.

As the crowd settled into their seats, the blast of a single horn announced the beginning of the Great Council of Rockham. A sudden and respectful hush replaced the robust discussions about this anticipated meeting. The history books would later note this council as one of the most important gatherings in dwarf history. Every person in the room felt a chill of excitement as the grand procession entered the cavern.

The audience stood in respect for the council members and dignitaries. Deposed Emperor Brad and Queen Ingrid led the procession with noble poise. Prince Coaldon, Princess Noel, and Starhood followed with slow stately grace. Shortshaft and Rolfe, the two dwarf leaders, lumbered forward with heavy steps and grim faces. Pacer, Brother Patrick, Earthkin, Topple and Cando followed with much less formality. The council members were last to enter.

Two rows of seats on the stage had been reserved for the dwarf ruling council and guests. After the dwarf leaders and guests were seated, a drum roll announced the beginning of formal deliberations.

Shortshaft stood up in an awkward manner and stated in a gruff voice, "Let the council now begin the work of saving the Empire from destruction. You are reminded to remain silent during the meeting. This will allow the council to complete their work quickly and efficiently. I encourage the council to be quick in making its final decisions. So, let it begin."

Emperor Brad was the first to talk to the community. He explained how he had been deposed as emperor by Wastelow. The audience hissed when the old warrior explained how Crossmore gained the power of the imperial throne by poisoning Wastelow. He then presented the events of Coaldon's life and Noel's rescue from Neverly.

Brad finished by saying, "The Key of Ban is an ancient elfin book containing powerful magic. During the First Quarter Age of the Empire, a violent war was fought between the forces of Good and Evil. The Key of Ban was used to cast the vile army of Doomage into the Chamber of Oblivion. Crossmore has found a way to reenter the Chamber and release the evil creatures from imprisonment. He is using them for his own foul purposes. The Key of Ban must be found in order to control Crossmore and his army. It will be the responsibility of Topple the Wizard to use the Key to once again throw the power of evil back into the bowels of the earth."

Rolfe then detailed the escape of the Hardstone Clan from their Homekeep and the great battle with the trog army.

Coaldon then shared his experience with trogs on his recent trip into the wilderness of the Sadden Mountains. The audience gasped in dread as Coaldon shared the details of his encounter with the enemy.

After these introductions were completed, Emperor Brad assumed the role of moderator of the Council meeting. Standing before the audience, he projected the image of royal authority.

He stated, "It is obvious, after Coaldon's recent encounter with the trogs that the invasion of the south has started. Time is short and heroic deeds will be required from each of us. The future of the Empire depends on the decisions made at this meeting. So, let us ponder each action with great care. Starhood will now assume the role of Grand Advisor to the Elfdom of Talltree and open the metal tube assigned to your care?"

Starhood gracefully stood and stepped forward. With eternal patience, he paused before beginning to talk.

In a slow and deliberate voice, he stated, "While Noel's rescue party was in Neverly, the imperial capital, they experienced a rare event. The group discovered a room protected by magic. After a short period of investigation, the warriors found a way to enter the room. Inside, they found a trunk containing a small metal tube. The rescuers were able to grab the tube from the trunk and escape before the room was destroyed by Crossmore. Coaldon carried the tube to Rockham and gave it to me for safe keeping. It is written on the tube that the Grand Advisor to the Elfdom of Talltree was the only person who could read the message found in the tube. Therefore, I now complete the assignment given to me many centuries ago. The voice of prophecy will speak through me."

With reverence, he slowly removed the cap from the tube and withdrew a rolled piece of parchment. He carefully unrolled the scroll and placed it on the podium. A cloud of anticipation covered the audience. The contents of the mysterious document had been the topic of discussion by the people of Rockham for many days. The dwarves knew their very survival might depend on the contents of the tube.

Starhood was in no hurry to reveal the information on the scroll. He took a long time to read and reread the message before he looked at the audience. In a dignified voice he read,

The Verse of Fate

"By fellowship broken, the need to stand alone;
By friend anew, the task to grasp;
By the waters of pain, to float in fear;
By the journey of sacrifice, the path to take;
By courage of self, the mountain to face;
By steps of trust, to door of hope;
By hand on the sword, the key to gain;
By act of love, the slaves to free;
By waves of sea, the ancient will speak."

When Starhood finished reading the verse, he paused to allow the words to reveal their own message. He reread the prophecy to the audience several times before sitting down. Brad approached the podium with uncertainty etched on his face. The simple words of the verse clouded his mind with confusion.

He stated, "I had hoped the message would provide clear direction to our future actions. Yet, mystery clouds the essence of the prophecy. I believe it is best to end the meeting at this time. The council needs time to evaluate the message. The prophecy has many hidden meanings that need to be investigated. We will gather here tomorrow, at the same time, to discuss the results of the council's meeting. Go in peace, my friends."

The dwarf community felt a growing sense of urgency about the impending invasion of the trog army. For weeks, they had been preparing to defend the city against attack. They understood that the meaning of the Verse of Fate could affect not only their community, but the future of the Empire. The results of the council deliberations offered hope to what seemed like a bleak future.

In order to expand the expertise of the discussions, Brad's company joined the council meeting. The group was responsible for completing a difficult task. It needed to plan for the defense of Rockham, plus find a way to recover the Key of Ban. At the meeting, each person on the council presented their own interpretation of the Verse of Fate. Disagreement, rather than harmony, dominated the debate. Arguments and frustration threatened the purpose and tenor of the meeting. After extended talks, the members of the Council could only agree upon the meaning of several verses of the prophecy. This grim realization cast a dark shroud of doubt over the gathering.

Finally, Brad decided it was necessary to focus the group's attention on what they had achieved.

Speaking with the compassion of a kindly leader, he stated, "We, as a Council, need to draw some conclusions. We could debate this prophecy for days without gaining any better understanding. The great minds who wrote these words wanted to give us enough information to provide significant direction. We need to trust in the conclusions we have agreed upon. We are to use what has been given to us. I believe we have enough information to make immediate plans. So, I will summarize our discussion. The 'hand on the sword' is Coaldon. The 'water of pain' means the Ocean of Pain. The 'key' means the Key of Ban. The word 'trust' defines the character needed to complete this quest. Now, what conclusion can we draw from this information?"

Starhood had remained silent during all of the discussions. His quietness was not an act of uncaring, but rather a time of reflection. He knew it was more important for him to study the prophecy in peace, rather than enter into the group dialogue. Brad's invitation to speak coincided with the culmination of his meditation. From deep in his spirit, he perceived the core meaning of the message.

He slowly stood with august confidence. In carefully chosen words, he slowly stated, "What I say will be short and to the point. I find no reason to color my presentation with a flood of words. I believe Coaldon is to go to the great city of Seamock. He will need to gain access to a boat in order to sail on the Sea of Pain. He will experience fear during his voyage. The only destination he could possibility go to is the Island of Death. There are no other islands off the coast of Seamock. He will be offered a choice of following an easy or difficult path. Through the power of his sword, he will gain the Key of Ban. The events of the rescue of the 'Key' will require him to show trust in the providence of life. With our current knowledge we can not interpret the remainder of the Verse of Fate. It will be up to Coaldon to use this information to help guide his journey. I offer this summary for your consideration."

The group remained quiet for a long time. Admiring eyes were focused on Starhood. The quality of his presentation was not cluttered with excessive rhetoric, but showed clarity of thought.

It was Pacer the Warrior who broke the silence.

He stated, "Starhood, thank you for your statement. You have pulled together scattered ideas into a realistic interpretation. I whole-heartily agree with you. It all makes good sense. What is the consensus of the group?"

A chorus of agreement made it easy to get past the quizzical stumbling block. The council then proceeded to consider the general strategy for war against Crossmore. The meeting went late into the night before a plan-of-action was developed.

At the appointed time, on the following day, the horns once again called the community together. The dwarf community eagerly anticipated the outcome of the meeting. They were confident the council would develop a plan to put an end to Crossmore's vile campaign of suffering and death. Silence greeted the bleak faces of the council members as they entered the cavern.

Topple was the only person who radiated an excited smile and carefree attitude. As he walked down the aisle, he greeted the children in his enthusiasm. Earthkin, the dwarf, was forced to swallow his frustration at Topple's disrespect for the seriousness of the present situation. Earthkin often wondered if Topple's carefree attitude was a sign of senility, or spiritual maturity.

As Council Members assumed their seats on the stage, Brad approached the podium with his usual noble poise. He looked at the audience with compassion as he spoke in clear distinct words, "We are facing one of the greatest crises in the history of the Empire. Only by heroic actions can we expect to win the battle against unbelievable odds. Each person must confront the challenges of tomorrow with courage."

With this said, Brad yielded the Podium to Shortshaft, the Head of the Rockham Council of Elders. Shortshaft's rough appearance deceptively covered the depth of his wisdom. His gentle nature had been acquired through a long life. His deep brown eyes scanned the audience. The old dwarf wondered if the community would accept the plan with enthusiasm. After a close look in the faces of the community members, he knew he had been granted the authority to guide them in these difficult times. Their unspoken trust in him washed away his hesitation. His spirit ached in knowing the price many people would pay to create a future for the Empire.

He spoke slowly, saying, "It has been the job of the Council to decide how to rid the Empire of Crossmore. My friends, we have lived many years in isolation and peace. We are now called by fate to assume a major role in the life of the Empire. Please open your hearts and minds to the discernment of the Council. "

Emperor Brad then returned to the podium and shuffled through a pile of parchment. Finally, with a look of satisfaction, he found the desired document. He glanced down the page before turning to look at each Member of the Council.

Facing the audience, he stated, "The Members of the Council have carefully reviewed the hidden meanings of the Verse of Fate. We worked until late last night to develop the following plan of action."

Brad saw nods of understanding from all locations of the chamber. The dwarves sat in quiet trust of Emperor Brad's evaluation and leadership.

Brad followed, "The plans developed by the Council put into motion events that will create death and suffering. The members of the Council decided it was necessary to face the future with decisive attitudes and actions. We believe it is important to aggressively implement our plan for the defense of Rockham. If we pause in doubt, we will beg defeat. It is necessary to confront the enemy head on."

With his stomach twisted in knots and heart throbbing in sorrow, Emperor Brad cleared his voice.

He continued, "Many months ago I decided it was time to begin the quest to remove Wastelow from power. On Prince Coaldon's eighteenth birthday, I set in motion the first steps for conquest. The results of the Council of Toms have blossomed into a bright beginning. At that time, I did not anticipate your involvement, but by the guiding hand of the One Presence you have been invited to spearhead a major counterattack. Today, you are encouraged to join our small band of warriors, wizards, and supporters to reclaim the Empire. Do you have any questions?"

A lack of comments indicated it was time to go to the next order of business.

Brad then declared, "It is the consensus of the members of the Council to present the following recommendations."

"First, we direct Coaldon to go to the Island of Death to retrieve the Key of Ban, as foretold by the Verse of Fate. Pacer and Topple will accompany him. It will then be the responsibility of Wizard Topple to use the Key of Ban to conquer Crossmore's army."

"Second, you, the citizens of Rockham, will immediately implement the plans to defeat the trog army. The dwarves will make hit-and-run attacks against the Trogs in the mountains to create confusion and doubt. We believe it is possible to drive the trogs from the wilderness. This will require a large expenditure of resources and manpower. It will be important to keep the enemy off balance as long as possible. We recommend Earthkin and Ripsnout be commanders of the dwarf army under the guidance of the clan elders."

"Third, Hilda (Topple's sister), her apprentices, and Bobby (formerly Badda) will remain in Rockham to help with war against the trogs."

"Fourth, Ingrid, Noel, Starhood, Brother Patrick, and I will go to the Monastery of Toms. It will be our duty to gather support for the rebellion and prepare the local people for the fight against Crossmore."

"Fifth, Cando the Wizard will return to Neverly to keep an eye on Crossmore and muster local support."

"Are there any comments for the Members of the Council?"

The members of the audience asked many questions and offered suggestions to the Council. After an hour of general discussion, Brad called for a vote of support for the Council's plan. A vote of hands indicated 100% acceptance.

After the vote was completed, Rolfe and Shortshaft stood before the community and led the dwarves in an ancient war chant. The war chant was repeated over and over, creating an unusual response from the audience. An instinctive, ancestral warrior state-of-mind was awakened within each dwarf. The need for the dwarf community to survive became the motivating force. The war chant was as follows:

"Crush, crush by will to fight,
  the threat to stony home.
Crush, crush as mighty rock
  to be bone of stone.
Crush, crush the foe to earth,
  by rock of hands to hone.
Crush, crush for the sake of clan,
  the need to stand as one."

As the gruff voices of the dwarves rumbled with enthusiasm and excitement, a new power of determination captivated the whole community. The dwarves marched from the cavern with loud cheers of victory. It was as if a wall-of-stone was moving out of the cavern, ready to crush the enemy.

Change in Plans

The Council's plans were immediately put into operation. Rockham became a bee hive of activities as citizens offered their unique talents to the defense of the city. Additional barriers were constructed around the city; soldiers practiced strategies for mountain fighting; women prepared field rations; and older adults made bandages.

Coaldon was no exception to this burst of activity. His mood greatly improved as soon as he had been assigned his new mission. The boredom of living in the cavern had taken a heavy toll on him. He became increasingly irritable at being confined to the underworld city. He was a person of big skies, tall mountains, open fields, and fresh air.

Coaldon accepted the burden of his new errand with enthusiasm. Even though he was intimidated by an overwhelming responsibility, he was also excited by the new challenge. The prince was ready for an assignment that would push him to the limits of his ability. He was highly motivated to rid the Empire of Crossmore's vile presence. It was necessary to find the Key of Ban, no matter the cost to him.

Coaldon, Pacer the Warrior, and Topple the Wizard, left Rockham with hopes of an easy journey to Seamock. The team departed during the night to hide their departure from trog spies. A small group of friends and family held a brief ceremony. Brother Patrick led the service with the pomp of a skilled liturgist. The rite was short, with Brother Patrick asking the One Presence to guide their journey to a successful completion. With mixed feelings, Coaldon said good-bye to friends and family.

In spite of a warm glow of high expectations, the companions faced opposition every step of the way. As they traveled across the canyon country, it became necessary to constantly scout passable trails. The group faced an unending series of rocky canyons, densely covered areas of scrub trees, and thickets of thorny bushes. Bruises and scratches symbolized their passage through the vast barrier. They finally resorted to using their swords to cut through the underbrush. Fatigue and sweat seemed to be the only tangible results for all their hard work.

Pacer commented, "It seems unusual that the dwarf maps did not indicate the difficulties we would be facing."

Topple responded, "I agree. Something odd is taking place."

The adventurers had traveled several days from Rockham when a cloud of despair descended upon Coaldon. His mood had changed from that of high hopes to outbursts of anger, hostility, and sadness. Pacer kept a close eye on the prince as his mood slowly dropped into black depression. By the end of the third day, Coaldon's fatigue and discomfort were so intense Pacer decided to stop and allow him to rest. Normally, Coaldon could easily walk many days with a heavy pack without showing fatigue. The young prince looked at his companions with expressions of helplessness. Even though he tried, something unusual was affecting his ability to travel. When they stopped to rest, Pacer watched Coaldon sag to the ground into a lethargic heap of muscle and bones. The young warrior drifted into a deep sleep.

Pacer finally said to Topple, "We cannot continue this way. I do not understand why we are having such a difficult time. It is like a wall has been placed before us. First we are blocked by impassible foliage, and now Coaldon is infected by an unknown ailment."

Topple responded, "I agree with you. Maybe we need to reevaluate our plans."

Pacer followed, "At our present rate of progress it will take us many weeks to arrive at Seamock. We are wasting time. I do not believe things will get any better, but only worse. The future of the Empire depends on Coaldon finding the Key. What can we do?"

The wizard looked at Pacer with a curious expression. "Maybe Coaldon will need to go on alone. I have the energy to transport him to Seamock, but not us. Can he handle the mission by himself?"

Pacer answered, "We do not have a choice. The young lad will need to do it. I guess it's time for him to prove himself."

The old wizard concluded, "I will send him to Seamock while under the influence of a trance. We will return to Rockham. I believe a special mission will be waiting for us."

Pacer concluded, "Our young friend will be surprised to wakeup in Seamock without us. I wish I could be there to watch him."

The Harbor

As Coaldon slept, an eerie sensation enveloped him. Bewilderment crept into his mind. The contrast between reality and fantasy grew into a nebulous maze. He could not distinguish the difference between himself and the power that was slowly consuming him.

He found it easier to yield to the force, rather than to fight its encroachment. As the haze of confusion cleared away, Coaldon found himself drifting into a comfortable trance. He felt his body floating freely like a feather in the air. A soft wind grasped him with gentle hands, carrying him away. He found himself skimming over the landscape, feeling no resistance to the forces of nature. Through clouds, around mountains, over rivers, and under the water, he surged forward as a rushing wind escorted him to a new destiny. On and on he traveled, flowing in complete harmony with life. He felt as if he was traveling on a magic carpet.

Suddenly, the shock of an unexpected reality erupted like a hot breath. His enjoyable jaunt across time and space was transformed into the sights and sounds of a strange place. At first, he thought he was awakening from a pleasant dream. Then, the contrast between his last memories and the reality of the new surroundings created mind boggling disorientation. Desperately, he struggled to fend off bouts of dizziness.

He was not in the canyon country, but rather, found himself sitting on a wooden dock, looking at a large harbor with many ships at anchor. Coaldon could only respond to his present situation in quiet disbelief. He had never seen an ocean, smelt the odor of salty sea air, or seen large sailing ships. Confusion was replaced by the awe of a curious child. He found his new surroundings to be a sensual delight of sights and sounds. He was so mesmerized by the harbor and ships that he ignored the presence of a large city off to his right. In a daze, he watched the large ship gracefully sway back and forth as the wind moved across the harbor. Squawking seagulls flying overhead added to the splendor. The cool sea breeze, blowing off the harbor, refreshed his body and spirit. He no longer felt nauseous.

The sound of loud voices awoke Coaldon from his dream-like spell. It was as if he had been splashed with a bucket of cold water. He realized the excitement of the moment was only a passing enchantment. The reality of the present situation demanded his full attention. Where was he? Where were Topple and Pacer?

Turning toward the voices, he saw three men approaching him. They were dressed in colorful, cotton work clothes and talking with an unfamiliar accent. The men passed him with no interest. He heard the men talking about the arrival of a merchant ship from a foreign port. From where he sat, he could see several ships being unloaded by a large crew of workers. As Coaldon looked down the dock, he could see carts loaded with merchandise starting to roll toward large warehouses lining the oceanfront. One cart after another passed behind him, being pushed by large, burly men. Their gloomy faces indicated a life of hard work and misery.

In a whisper, the young prince finally stated, "Maybe I am in Seamock. Yet, how did I get here? What do I do now?"

The young warrior knew he had been given the responsibility to recover the Key of Ban. For some reason, he was now alone in a strange place without support or guidance.

As the long shadows of evening began to creep across the harbor, Coaldon decided it was time to take action. He was hungry and needed a place to spend the night. Since Pacer carried the money for the journey, Coaldon assumed he was without funds. He decided to check his pouch to see if, by chance, he had any money. To his surprise, he found 100 stomas and a note. Coaldon stared at the note with mixed feelings. He knew he had to read it, but he did not want to. He was afraid that tragedy had befallen Pacer and Topple. With hesitation, he slowly opened it.

The note was written in ancient elf script by Topple's graceful hand. The note stated, "I discovered that an unknown force was limiting our progress. The only way to escape the assault was to return to Rockham. I decided to send you to Seamock. You must now complete the task by yourself. Go with courage, wisdom, and common sense. Do not be fooled by deception. Go in trust and peace. Your friend, Topple."

After reading the message Coaldon cried in a shaky voice, "I am in Seamock! I am alone! I am a stranger in a foreign land!"

Hanging his head in despair, he continued, "Am I capable of completing the mission by myself? I did not realize how much I depended on the guidance of my companions. I feel like a little child."

Self-doubt paralyzed him. The young prince sat on the dock with a battle raging inside of himself. The fear of failure claimed dominion over his thoughts. Yet, he realized he could not allow uncertainty to control his life. Panic had to be controlled or all was lost.

In desperation, Coaldon began to repeat the following phrase over and over, "Trust not doubt. Trust not doubt. Trust not doubt."

His mind gripped these words with total abandonment. As the meaning of the phrase became real to him, anxiety slowly melted away.

Seamock

After conquering the demon of doubt, the pangs of hunger began to dominate his thoughts. With a pouch full of money, the prospects of a good meal and a comfortable night's sleep had greatly improved. As he walked down the dock to the warehouse district, it was like going through a right-of-passage into a new life. Coaldon felt a surge of confidence growing. In order to maintain this feeling of success, he kept repeating, "I can do it. I will be successful."

As Coaldon walked through the streets of Seamock, looking for acceptable lodging, he observed dirty, poorly dressed men and woman populating the seedy taverns near the harbor. The streets in the harbor district were lined with a wide variety of shops, offering services to the sailors visiting the city. Coaldon was fascinated by the clothing worn by the sailors. He was aware of the distinct difference between the rugged, earth colored clothing worn by country folks and the bright, colorful attire worn by sailors. He also noticed that the sailors seemed more easy-going than the hard working people who lived on farms.

The streets near the harbor were occupied by many people who sat quietly, observing the flow of shoppers. Coaldon wondered how these inhabitants earned money. Then it occurred to him that these individuals might not make an honest living. He remembered his grandparents telling stories about the thieves, pickpockets, and murderers who resided in the streets of every seaport. Coaldon soon noticed that the vagrants paid no attention to him and his long sword. They were looking for helpless victims.

Later that evening, he found a clean, quiet boarding house named River Run. The guests were mostly businessmen dressed in dark wool pants and light colored cotton shirts. The front door of the inn opened into a large community room. The fireplace was located to the right and the dining area at the far end of the room. A huddle of chairs was arranged around the front of the fireplace, offering guests the opportunity to stay warm and pass the time in conversation. The location of the dining room permitted guests to dine in peace, away from the robust chatter near the fireplace. The bar, kitchen, and registration desk filled the wall on the left side of the room.

Coaldon's entrance into the room created a stir of discussion and comments. His backwoods clothing and long sword were uncommon in the big city. Coaldon ignored his sudden notoriety, paid for several nights lodging, and purchased a meal. He found a table at the far end of the room next to the wall. Sitting with his back to the wall, he was able to watch the people and protect himself from any possible attack. He ordered a large plate of roast pork, potatoes, and green beans with a piece of pumpkin pie. The meal was just what Coaldon needed to satisfy his youthful need for an ample volume of food.

After finishing the meal, he ventured to the fireplace to join in the conversations that continued at a nonstop pace. It was common for lonely businessmen to spend the evening talking, with fellow travelers, about their journeys and business dealings. Coaldon sat down next to a fat, bald headed man wearing the look of boredom. The man responded to Coaldon like a hungry dog going for meat. After many lonely days on the road, the merchant was a reservoir of pent-up words.

He erupted, "It is not often we find a backwoods warrior visiting this wicked little city. What brings you to this den of intrigue? By the way what is your name? I am known as Revore the Fat."

Coaldon responded, "I am glad to meet you. My name is Hands the Blade. I have been sent by my master to pick up supplies and to look for new business."

With this introduction, Coaldon only had to sit back and listen to the man's explosion of words. Coaldon learned the merchant had recently visited Neverly to buy hats and shoes. He explained that the city was under heavy military control after the rescue of Princess Noel. It was rumored that Emperor Crossmore was angry over the escape of Noel.

Coaldon found it enjoyable to listen to his acquaintance vividly describe his travels through the broad expanses of the Empire. The encroachment of the cool night air into the lodge forced the guests to huddle closer to the fireplace.

Coaldon was abruptly shaken from his peaceful state when the door into the boarding house was opened with a loud bang. A group of grimy, foul smelling men swaggered into the room. They glanced around the community hall with a look of false authority. The leader was a tall man with long, oily hair and a hollow face covered with a straggly beard.

In a loud voice the surly man declared, "We are Crossmore's vigilantes. We have been sent to maintain order and prevent rebellion against our beloved leader. Any talk of mutiny will be answered with death. Join us in honoring Crossmore the Great."

After this introduction, the vigilantes walked through the crowd observing each person with careful scrutiny.

When the leader came to Coaldon, the leader roared, "What brings a country dunce to Seamock?"

Coaldon rose to his feet and bowed. "My name is Hands. I visit your fair city in peace. I recognize your authority and honor the name of your great leader."

He then sat down with his head lowered in humility.

With tobacco juice running down his chin, the leader laughed in a haughty voice. Without warning, he gave Coaldon a shove. Coaldon fell backwards onto the floor.

The leader barked, "Do not try any funny business while in Seamock. If you challenge our authority, you will die."

Coaldon stood up in a slow painful manner, bowing his head in submission to the vigilantes. He had much more important things to do than create a conflict. He did not want to draw attention to himself.

Yet, the young warrior could not help but smile at the phony arrogance of the group of men. The vigilantes looked like insecure children trying to act as confident adults.

The Old Sailor

After this encounter with the vigilantes, Coaldon retired to the recesses of his room for the night. It had been a long, unusual day. His full stomach and tired body invited him to enjoy a long night's sleep. As he lay down on the soft bed, he fell into a deep comfortable sleep.

He awoke to the light of a new day, ready to fulfill his assigned task. After a large breakfast he walked to the taverns on the water front. He entered one tavern after another, seeking information about the Sea of Pain and the Island of Death. To his surprise, nobody was willing to talk to him. It seemed the topic of the island was not open for discussion. Coaldon learned people had a fear of the mysterious piece of landscape to the east.

After a long, fruitless morning, Coaldon entered a tavern called the Do Drop Inn. The foul, dark tavern had the smell of rancid ale and sweaty bodies. The bar was piled with empty glasses and the remains of uneaten meals. The floor was covered with sawdust; the walls were layered with centuries of memorabilia; and the ceiling was black with the deposit of smoke and grease. His stomach turned with revulsion at the very thought of entering the room.

Coaldon stated to himself, "This is truly one of the most depraved places I have been, but maybe this is where I will find my answers."

He sat in the back of the room to rest and watch people. He ordered a tankard of ale but did not drink it because of the unclean nature of the inn.

Coaldon's attention was drawn to an old man entering the tavern through the front door. The open door allowed bright sunshine to blind the eyes of the individuals sitting in the dim room. The people inhabiting the tavern acted like rats hiding from the light of day. They behaved like victims seeking protection from an unknown adversary. The dwellers lowered their heads in resentment against the intrusion of the light flowing into their sheltered domain.

The old man walked into the room with ritualistic reverence for the Holy

Sanctum of the Ale. He walked lightly and with proper respect, not wanting to violate any unwritten rules honoring the holy ground. Over time, the Congregation of Ale Drinkers had developed guidelines allowing them to worship the sacred drink in peace and solemnity.

The old man, entering the tavern, had a long gray beard, hair combed into a ponytail, and a patch over his left eye. His brightly colored clothes were in contrast to the modesty of his character. The gentleman's shuffling steps indicated many years of hard work. Rolled shoulders and a hanging head offered submission to the trials of his life. The old man's appearance brought back memories of stories told to Coaldon about sailors.

The old gentleman did not hesitate, but walked directly to Coaldon's table and sat down. Coaldon could smell the heavy scent of smoke and garlic drifting from the old man's garments and body.

With a twinkle in his right eye, the old gentleman said, "You must be more careful. You are creating an unhealthy stir of curiosity in the community. Why do you ask about the Island of Death?"

Coaldon smiled with satisfaction at the possibility of gaining information about the Island of Death.

With hesitation he responded, "I am a man of adventure and good times. I want to visit the island to satisfy my inquisitive nature. It would be an exciting adventure to face the unknown dangers of the island."

With a wicked look of understanding, the old man gave a sarcastic chuckle.

He commented, "The Time of Change is ripe with the legends of ancient prophecy and current revelations. It is a strange coincidence that you arrive looking for information about the Island of Death just as the Empire falls under the spell of Crossmore. Nobody has inquired about the Island of Death for centuries. I asked myself, 'Why today?' Then I said, 'I must hurry to warn this young warrior before the depths of Hell greets him with certain death.'"

He paused, before continuing, "You must leave here immediately!"

Coaldon sat in stunned disbelief at the insight of this old gentleman. Had he really been so transparent?

Then, loud voices could be heard outside the tavern. The door of the tavern was opened with such violence that it swung off its hinges. A group of six vigilantes burst into the room with swords in their hands. The old man suddenly jumped to his feet and raced to hide in the shadows of a doorway. The vigilantes rushed up to Coaldon's table, stopping several strides in front of him.

Coaldon casually stood to greet his visitors.

In a calm voice he stated, "Good morning. What brings you to the Do Drop Inn on this bright and wonderful day? May I buy each of you a tankard of ale to wet your parched mouths?"

The leader of the vigilantes was the same individual who had confronted Coaldon at the River Run Inn the night before. The leader's body rippled with anger and his face bulged in agitation. His eyes flashed with fury while saliva foamed on his lips.

He raged, "Why do you go around town asking about the Island of Death? Only people with rebellious intentions would want to know anything about that wicked place."

In a calm voice, Coaldon stated, "I am an adventurer who is interested in exploring dangerous and intriguing places. The Island of Death is my next conquest."

With a pathetic gesture of authority the leader raised his sword high in the air, commanding, "You are under arrest for suspicious behavior. You will be questioned to find out the real truth. We cannot allow you to corrupt the fine people of Seamock with your seditious ideas. Now, yield your sword and follow me."

At this challenge, Coaldon's smile radiated the confidence of a seasoned warrior. He did not follow the vigilante's orders. When he did not yield his sword, the vigilantes stood in confusion. The leader snarled in contempt at Coaldon's passive resistance.

Then, with blustering authority, the leader yelled, "Attack him, you pack of fools. You can now practice the fighting skills I have taught you."

Two vigilantes stepped forward with their swords in a ready position. Coaldon had the impression the swords were too heavy for the strength of the vigilantes. With lighting speed, Coaldon drew his sword and challenged the vigilantes with expert control of his blade.

He casually said, "Please do not advance any further. You might pay with your lives."

The vigilantes laughed with delight to think anybody would challenge their authority. They believed that their allegiance to Crossmore would offer them magical strength and skill during battles. Moving with swaggering conceit, the pitiful group of vigilantes circled around Coaldon with awkward steps. The leader stood back to observe the attack. His retreat covered his cowardly nature.

Before the vigilantes could position themselves to begin their attack, Coaldon inflicted his first wound. The flick of his sword left a shallow wound on the sword arm of the tall man to his right. The wounded vigilante screamed in agony at the sight of blood running down his arm. He dropped his sword, threw his arms in the air, and ran from the tavern in a state of hysteria. Two vigilantes, ignoring their wounded companion, stepped forward to claim the title of hero. Coaldon noticed they handled their swords like children playing with wooden sticks. He felt ashamed to fight such a pathetic group of unskilled fighters. Coaldon decided to use a technique taught to him by his grandfather. With several quick flips of his sword, two of the vigilante's weapons spun from their hands. This left the two men standing before Coaldon, weaponless. With several more twists of his sword, Coaldon cut the belts of the two men, causing their pants to fall to the floor. In a comical act of clumsiness, the two men tripped over their trousers as they tried to escape.

The humiliated vigilantes crawled out of the tavern, happy to be alive. Coaldon then quickly rotated his position to confront the two remaining attackers. The two vigilantes acknowledged Coaldon's superior swordsmanship and rushed out of the tavern. The leader stood in wide-eyed disbelief at the turn of events. Before the head vigilante could retreat from the room, Coaldon blocked his escape.

Coaldon said in a quiet voice, "I did not come to Seamock to play childish games with you and your miserable followers. I came in peace. Now, I will leave you with a reminder of my visit."

In terror, the vigilante stood paralyzed as Coaldon brought his sword to the man's face. With a clean stroke, Coaldon drew his sword across the vigilante's cheek, shaving the hair off the right side of his face. Unknown to Coaldon, a beard was a sign of status among vigilantes. By shaving the vigilante's cheek, Coaldon had given a great insult to the self-image of the leader. After the leader raised his hand to his face, he fell to the floor, howling in grief at his loss of honor. Humiliation would follow this poor fellow for months.

Crossmore

Far from Seamock, the walled city of Neverly basked in the hot summer sun. Neverly, the imperial capital of the Empire, was located on the banks of the Slownic River. It lay on the boundary between the Great Prairies to the west and the hill country spreading out to the east. Its central location made it the natural site for the seat of power.

Under the cruel leadership of Emperor Wastelow and Crossmore the Wizard, the once beautiful capital had been transformed, over the past twenty years, into a dilapidated city. The tall, thick walls of the city showed signs of poor maintenance. Sections were crumbling into piles of disintegrating bricks and mortar. Streets had become cesspools of garbage and a never ending series of potholes. The clean and pleasant buildings of the past had fallen into disrepair and abandonment. All aspects of the city, except the palace, showed the neglect of defeated people. Crossmore made sure the palace was preserved and furnished in the grand image of his own self-importance.

Neverly's prominence as the center of power in the region went back before recorded history. A long string of compassionate rulers had formed a tradition of benevolent leadership. It was unusual for an emperor to take advantage of power for personal gain. The citizens placed complete trust in their sovereigns. For many centuries, peace and prosperity characterized the Empire. This drastically changed when Wastelow and Crossmore assumed power. Recently, a tax increase drained the Empire of its prosperity and forced many citizens into poverty. The vitality of the past was drained to support a large army and the luxurious life style of the two emperors. Lawlessness and depravity characterized the Empire.

Every day, large crowds of homeless people gathered in front of the west gate of the city, waiting for the daily rationing of food. Soldiers closely monitored the crowds of homeless people, ready to crush any sign of unrest. Spies constantly reported rebellious activities and were rewarded with extra food and clothing. Rebellion was answered with immediate death.

The city was dominated by two stately towers. The East Tower had been Noel's prison before being rescued by Coaldon, her twin brother. The West Tower symbolized all that was evil in the Empire. Crossmore practiced his sorcery in the West Tower with insidious results. It was common for red, yellow and greens lights to flash from the tower windows during Crossmore's sinister practice of magic. His devotion to the use of the dark sciences allowed him to grow in power. Crossmore would stop at nothing to assure his absolute control of the Empire. Terror and fear were the tools of his trade.

On this particular evening Crossmore sat in front of his mirror of power, contemplating the next step in his plan for conquest. He laughed with wicked glee at the memories of the dwarves' pathetic retreat to Rockham. This jovial mood changed when he reviewed Coaldon's recent escape from the trogs in the Sadden Mountains. The wizard glowered in anger at the thought of his troops failing to capture a dangerous opponent.

Even though the sting of failure haunted his mind, Crossmore stated, "My, I do enjoy creating terror in the lives of my enemies. More fear! More fear! I think it is time for a little mischief. I will do something to keep the dwarves off-guard. They will just hate my new scheme! I want to touch their hearts with the horror of my wickedness. I will do anything to claim what is rightfully mine. It is my destiny to gain full power over the Empire."

Crossmore's Scheme

The dwarves were surprised when Pacer and Topple returned to Rockham without Coaldon. Yet, the community was so busy, it did not have time to be concerned about Coaldon. They trusted Topple to make the right decision.

The community had been preparing for an assault by the trog army. On a daily basis, small groups of women and children, under military escort, were sent to collect food from the nearby hills. The necessity of gathering supplies out-weighed the risk of an encounter with trogs. Besides, no signs of the trogs had been seen in the area.

On the evening of Topple's and Pacer's return to Rockham, a tragic wail arose in the cavern of the city. Several groups of food gatherers had not returned from the hills. The cry of sorrow was soon followed by a penetrating silence. Hushed voices wept at the loss to the community. A Council of War meeting was called to discuss how to deal with the disaster.

Shortshaft opened the gloomy council meeting with somber words, "Women, children, and warriors are missing. How could this have happened? Are the trogs responsible?"

Earthkin responded in a firm, yet respectful voice, "I wonder if any of the missing dwarves are still alive? I hope so. When dealing with Crossmore, we must not be surprised by anything. We have been expecting a direct assault, yet he may be trying something different. He may want to weaken us by using fear and terror."

Topple was tired after a long day of traveling, but he felt it important to contribute to the conversation. With uncharacteristic seriousness, he stated, "This might be one reason why I have been brought back to Rockham. We must first find out what has happened to the missing dwarves. I will search Crossmore's mind to find the out what is happening. I suggest we meet after I have had a chance to investigate. So, if you will excuse me, I must prepare for an encounter with a dangerous opponent."

After leaving Rockham, Topple ventured to a rocky knoll on the south side of Rockham Valley. Ancient lore claimed this location possessed hidden powers buried deep in its foundation. Topple found an alcove to shelter him from the cool night breezes. He built a fire and rested his back against a rock. The warmth of the fire massaged his body. The flickering flames touched the core of his soul. Staring into the fire, Topple relaxed into a state of peace. He felt a stream of energy flow into him from the earth.

Only on rare occasions did he enter into Crossmore's world. If detected, he would be in danger of attack. He wrapped himself with a protective shroud of magic. His body tingled as bands of magic flowed around him in tight circles. He slowly opened himself to the stream of Crossmore's communications. At first, he only heard the distant mumble of voices. These voices grew into clarity as he released himself deeper into the void of the cosmos. It was essential for him to be only a mouse in the corner of a large field.

Finally, the fuzzy words became understandable. Topple heard several voices laughing in celebration.

The first voice declared, "Ah! Ah! Oh, Great Master, we have captured a large group of dwarves as you have commanded. This has been a special day."

Then the voice of Crossmore rejoiced, "Very good! Very Good! Royal Leader, I am most pleased. Where have you taken the prisoners?"

The Royal Gek answered, "As you commanded, we have taken the creatures to the large cave located in a narrow ravine at the head of Meadow Valley."

Crossmore followed, "Protect them well. They are valuable to me. Send the following message to the sniveling rats in Rockham. 'I have captured many dwarves. They will die unless you cooperate. They will be released once you depart from Rockham. The little children will be the first to suffer if you do not cooperate. As your Emperor, I command you to leave Rockham immediately!'"

The leader responded, "It will be done as you have commanded."

The evil wizard answered, "The dwarves have such a strong sense of caring for friends and family. We will use this strength as their weakness. I find pleasure in knowing they will suffer."

Topple withdrew from his trance at this point. Even though his face showed the stress of the encounter, a confident smile rolled across his face.

In a quiet voice, he said to himself, "This should be a most challenging adventure. Crossmore walks such a deceitful path. I must be ready for him at all turns."

It was late into the night when he arrived back at the city. He decided to wait until morning to share his revelation. By sunrise the ransom message had been mysteriously delivered to the doors of Rockham. The War Council held an early morning meeting to receive Topple's report. In an unhurried fashion, Topple shared the details of what he had heard in the conversation between the Royal Gek and Crossmore. A glimmer of hope radiated through the dwarves' bleak disposition when they learned the captives were still alive.

Shortshaft was the first to speak, "What can we do to rescue the captives? Could we actually be bribed into leaving our home?"

Earthkin, the dwarf warrior, erupted in blazing anger at these questions. He boomed, "We will rescue our family members at all costs! There are no options. We can not surrender Rockham! Do you actually think we can bargain with Crossmore? He will never release the captives alive! His words can never be trusted! So, the question is not, will we leave, but rather, how will we rescue the innocent victims?"

Earthkin's emotional statement was not challenged. His ideas represented the consensus of the council members. Admitting defeat to Crossmore was totally unacceptable. After a short pause to allow the anger of the members to dissipate, the group began to plan for the rescue.

Pacer opened the discussion, "I wish to clarify several facts. Crossmore is both cunning and deceitful. The location of the cavern in the meadow is too close and convenient for my liking. Crossmore will expect a rescue attempt. I believe an ambush will be prepared for us when we enter the valley. Therefore, we must be well prepared. I am afraid this will be a game of cat and mouse."

Shortshaft followed, "We can make wonderful plans, but if we do not know what is happening in the meadow we are wasting our time. I believe it best to send scouts into the valley through the north entrance. We need accurate information before we can make realistic plans."

A rumble of voices agreed.

Earthkin summarized the feelings of the group, "My first impulse is to rush to meadows with a large army and crush the trogs. Yet, it is best to use common sense. Crossmore is waiting for us to do something stupid. Our strength, against such a large army, will be to use cunning and wisdom."

Each member of the council departed the meeting with a heavy heart, but radiating a glimmer of hope. Topple, out of respect for the somber mood in the cavern city, refrained his usual burst of excitement. Anyway, there were other things that needed his attention.

Battle of the Meadows

The War Council held a hastily-called meeting to receive the reconnaissance reports gathered by the spies returning from the meadows. The scouts revealed that there were three large groups of trogs in the valley. The first was located on the ridgeline leading from the city into Meadow Valley. This group would ambush any rescue attempt from Rockham. The second army was concealed in the narrow canyon leading to the North Cave. The last group of trogs guarded the dwarves held in the cave.

After a long meeting, the War Council developed a plan that would draw the trogs' attention away from the cavern holding the captives. Unknown to the trogs, the North Cave had a secret entrance in the rear of the cavern. While a diversion was created by the dwarf army in Meadow Valley, a small group of warriors would enter the cavern through the concealed entrance to rescue the captives. The plan was simple, but required a high degree of coordination.

The War Council decided to secretly place a large army behind the trogs on the ridgeline above Rockham. These warriors would be transported to the battle site through ancient tunnels. A small contingent of warriors would approach the ridge from Rockham, triggering the trog ambush. Once the trogs had attacked the approaching warriors, the army hidden on the mountain side would attack from the rear.

After defeating the trogs on the ridge line, the dwarf army would approach the ravine through Meadow Valley. The trogs' attention would then shift from the captives to the approaching army. It would be the responsibility of the rescue team to enter the cavern and free the captives.

Timing was a critical element in winning the battle. A quick response would catch the trogs off guard and help protect the captives. The slow-witted trogs would require additional time to respond to changes in the battle. After considering all the factors, the War Council issued assignments. The dwarves needed to repair seldom-used tunnels, distribute supplies to the army, disperse warriors in the proper locations, and establish a means of communication.

It took several days to make arrangements for the first phase of the battle plan. On the morning of the attack, a large army of dwarf warriors lay hidden in tunnels behind the trog army on the ridgeline. A small contingent of dwarf soldiers left the city, making no attempt to hide their advance. The warriors sang war songs while they climbed the steep trail leading up the mountain side. As they approached the ridgeline they left the path and ambled along a rocky knoll, away from the point of the ambush. This casual movement gave no indication of their awareness of the trogs' presence. When the dwarves had advanced into the middle of the trogs' position, the enemy burst from their hiding place. With loud, hysterical screams the trogs rushed forward in long, lumbering strides. When the attack was launched, the dwarves had ample time to find defensive positions in the rocks. The thundering pack of trogs looked more like a stampeding herd of buffalo than warriors in a military maneuver. The trogs' strategy was to overpower the enemy with the element of surprise and by sheer numbers.

By moving quickly through the large rocks, the dwarves were able to use boulders as shields. Several dwarves were killed in the initial assault, yet the delaying tactic allowed the hidden army to begin its surprise attack on the trogs. The dwarves' attack, from the rear, was executed with such skill and violence that the trogs were thrown into chaos. Even though the dwarves were out-numbered ten to one, they were able to compensate for this difference by absolute determination. The trog brigade was quickly decimated and thrown into panic. After receiving many causalities, the remaining beasts made a mad dash toward Meadow Valley. The victorious warriors followed the escaping trogs with unrelenting pursuit. The enemy was allowed to escape into the canyon to help create a sense of panic and doubt in the remainder of the trog army. The dwarves had successfully kept the trogs attention on the advancing army.

It did not take long before the dwarves set up defense lines in front of the canyon leading to the cavern. Small scouting teams were sent into the canyon to probe the trog defenses. Returning scouts reported heavy resistance to the warriors' advances. By evening, all scouting parties had arrived from the ravine. The dwarf army set up camp and prepared for an attack.

Unnoticed by everybody, wizards Topple and Cando followed the dwarf army up the mountain and into Meadow Valley. They made a camp on a hilltop overlooking the dwarf camp. The two men talked late into the night. Several times Topple looked over the valley to estimate distance between their location and the cavern holding the captives. At daybreak, leaving Topple, Cando hiked across the valley floor to a position on the opposite hilltop. The dwarves were aware of the two wizards but treated their activities with indifference. They assumed the men were waiting to watch the battle.

A beautiful sunrise of yellow and orange greeted the new day. The majesty of the sky was contrasted to the silence in the valley. The usual sights and sounds of the local wildlife were missing. This silence cast an eerie sense of forewarning. The presence of evil pulsed in the meadow. The dwarves had to push away feelings of foulness infecting their hearts.

It was midmorning when a flash of light was seen coming from the mountainside overlooking the cavern. The signal indicated that the soldiers in the tunnel were ready to begin the rescue. The battle plan called for small, heavily armed units of dwarf warriors to assault the trogs in the ravine.

The attack units carefully moved deep into the ravine, engaging the trogs. At first the trogs retreated, drawing the dwarves deep into the canyon. The hit-and-run tactics by the dwarves lasted several hours. The trogs finally mounted a large counter attack, driving the advancing dwarf army out of the ravine.

Then, bleating horns announced an assault by the dwarves. The front line of the trog army was crushed by methodical waves of rotating weapon deployment. The dwarves attacked with a row of pikes; followed by longbows, and then, hand-to-hand combat. The first row stepped back, allowing the next group of warriors to attack. This created confusion among the ranks of the trogs. The warriors defeated the churning mass of beasts with relative ease. When the dwarves approached the entrance into the cavern, many additional trogs were brought from the cave to reinforce the retreating beasts. At this point, the attack stalled and the dwarves were forced to move back into a defensive position. The fighting stopped when both sides formed stationary lines. Across the no-mans-land, the enemies looked at each other with animosity.

Meanwhile, the attack within the cavern had begun. The rush of beasts from the cavern, to reinforce the sagging trog defenses, had depleted the number of trogs in the cave to a skeletal force. Pacer, Earthkin, and Rolfe lead the assault from the rear of the cavern. The trogs were caught by surprise and provided little resistance. The dwarf rescuers freed the prisoners from their bindings and were prepared to leave when a shock wave knocked everybody to the cave floor.

In the sky above the canyon, Crossmore's image appeared from a dark cloud. An earthquake rattled the area and a deafening roll of thunder forced the dwarves to hold their ears. The trogs and geks screamed with joy at the appearance of their great leader. The trogs started a slow advance toward the dwarf army under the cloud of Crossmore's power. As the trogs reached the dwarves' defenses, an overpowering surge of energy froze both armies. Unable to move, combatants looked into the sky to see bolts of electricity pulsing through the air. The energy originated from two locations in Meadow Valley. Topple and Cando were challenging the power of Crossmore.

Crossmore turned to confront his two rivals. He had once again been stymied in attempting to destroy his enemies. Absolute hatred blazed from his eyes. Using all his magical powers, he released massive surges of energy at the two wizards. By splitting the energy of his assault between the two destinations, the strength of his strike was reduced by half. His assault was met in midair by opposing blasts released by the two wizards. The collision of these forces created a shock wave that knocked over trees, produced avalanches, and threw both armies onto the ground. The immense pressure created by the battle between the two opposing powers caused a deluge of rain, hurricane force winds, and intense bursts of light.

Crossmore soon realized that if he continued splitting his power between the two wizards, he would not win the battle. He detected that the wizard to his left was the weakest opponent. He decided to shift his full power to this enemy. He assumed he could destroy the weaker wizard and also withstand the attack from the wizard on his right. Shifting the direction of his assault, he blasted Cando with his full power. Cando resisted for several moments, but soon withered under the assault. He collapsed to the ground in defeat.

When Crossmore transferred his attention to Cando, it allowed Topple to attack unabated. Topple dipped deep into his life reserves to create a massive pool of energy. The old wizard had never challenged himself to this level. He believed he had no alternative. Crossmore needed to be stopped.

Topple's blast of energy lit the meadow with the brilliance of the sun. The ball of blinding light hit Crossmore before he had a chance to switch his attention back to Topple. The attack struck the evil wizard with such force that his image melted into a shower of red and white sparks. His power dissolved into wisps of vapor.

Topple's attack had forced him to go beyond safe levels of self-preservation. After releasing his assault, he collapsed into a quiet void. He no longer had physical form, but floated in a loose collection of particles. After the collapse of his life form, he drifted into a random cloud, devoid of human characteristics. The remains of the old wizard shot into the southwest sky in a stream of dust.

The dwarves took immediate advantage of Crossmore's defeat by attacking the confused trogs. It only took a short time for the savage dwarf warriors to destroy most of the enemy. Trogs and geks ran into the mountains in panic.

The rescue team and the hostages exited from the entrance of the cavern. A joyful reunion was held between the warriors and the captives. A search of the area discovered the semiconscious body of Cando, but Topple was not found. The long procession back to Rockham was a time of celebration and grief. The community had survived, but at a terrible price.

Tipsy of Seamock

After watching the vigilante rush from the room, Coaldon turned to locate the old man standing in the shadows. The ancient gentleman signaled Coaldon to follow him out the back door of the tavern. Both men rushed from the building and ran down several alleyways until they reached a forested area. The old man smiled at Coaldon with a glow of pride and respect.

He stated, "My name is Tipsy. Welcome to Seamock."

Smiling, Coaldon responded, "My name is Hands. Thank you for intervening. I must say, you have a most interesting name. I am sure your mother did not give you this title."

The old man looked at his new acquaintance with a twinkle in his eye. "When I was a seaman apprentice, I accidentally tipped over a row boat full of seasoned sailors. These good natured fellows were looking for a way to initiate me into the ways of the sea, so this event caused a stir of good times. I was tried by a kangaroo court for endangerment of life. The judge wore an old, black blanket and a chamber pot for a crown. Each member of the jury was draped in colorful pieces of cloth. I wore only my underwear. My face was painted red. During the trial, I was forced to sit in a chair on the gang plank. Each witness told unbelievable stories describing my crimes. The crew hooted and howled at each additional fictitious story. For my punishment, I had to ride, for several days, in a small boat pulled behind the large ship. The boisterous crew nick named me Tipsy."

Coaldon laughed, "Your name has a unique history. Some day you will need to tell me the full story."

Tipsy followed, "You have done us a great service. The community will pay for your deeds, but it will be worth it when we celebrate the Day of the Half Beard. You need to be careful because the soldiers will be looking for you. I believe you have something more important to do than play games with the local militia. The imprimatur of fate is branded on you. If you need help, I offer my assistance. Whatever you do, I recommend you quickly leave from the city."

The young prince responded, "I am honored to accept your offer of aid. We should go our own ways and meet later. I need to gather my belongings from the inn before leaving the city. Where shall we meet?"

The old gentleman replied, "We can meet at the old lumber mill on the west edge of the city."

Coaldon casually walked to the inn. The young warrior's carefree image did not reflect his true desire to escape from the city. He knew the inn would soon be visited by an unhappy group of vigilantes. His mission was too important to be compromised by an unnecessary confrontation. Without seeming to hurry, he gathered his possessions and left for the rendezvous.

As he walked out of town, he detected someone following him. In order to escape his pursuer, he left the road and turned into the woods. After a short distance, he hid in the brush and waited. It was not long before he saw a tall, thin man sneaking through the forest. When the stranger drew near, Coaldon leaped from his hiding place, knocking him to the ground. The man had a weasel face, scraggly beard, and cowering presence.

In a whiny voice, the man pleaded, "Please, do not harm me. I was only on a walk in the woods. Why are you attacking me? I am no threat to you."

With a quick sweep of his arm, Coaldon grabbed the man, lifting him to his feet.

Coaldon demanded "You are lying! Either tell me the truth or face the consequences."

"No! No! No!" the man moaned, "I know nothing!"

Coaldon continued, "I am a stranger in this fair city. I want to go on my way in peace. I know you are following me. Why?"

In breathless words the pursuer answered, "I am a city official. It is my duty to investigate threats to the Empire. You are a warrior. You could be dangerous."

Relenting, Coaldon released his rough grip on the man.

In a quiet voice Coaldon stated, "I thought you were a bandit. Yes, I have been trained to use a sword, but only to protect myself. I am a loyal citizen. You can be at peace in knowing that I am a simple farmer searching for adventure. I am sorry to cause you a problem."

With self importance, the official boasted, "I could imprison you for resisting arrest. I will let you go because the loyal guards often act impulsively. You may go, but do not return to the city. I want no more trouble."

The official turned and walked away with an arrogant saunter. Coaldon watched him until he disappeared. He followed at a safe distance to make sure the man departed for the city.

By nightfall he found the mill and reunited with the old sailor. It was late evening when the two men sat in front of a warm fire in a deserted building. They said little as they shared a simple meal of boiled trail food and dried meat.

The old man finally said, "I know the man who followed you. He will not send the army to look for you. Yet, you must not return to the city. Now, let's talk about your situation. How can I help you?"

Coaldon thought about the question. Being careful not to reveal anything, he responded, "I need to go to the Island of Death."

With a look of concern, the old man stated, "This is a most unusual request. Why would anybody in their right mind want to go to that dreadful place? You must have an important reason to take such a risk."

After a pause, he continued, "I will make arrangements for you to be taken to the island. We have a long distance to walk if we are to reach our destination by sunrise. We will need to travel most of the night."

Coaldon commented, "Thank you. I will remember your kindness."

Coaldon was happy to get started. It was time to take the next step on his uncharted journey. He trudged through the night with a growing appreciation of the help offered by the old sailor. He realized that in the future, the unexpected would be the expected. A parade of unanticipated events would be his constant traveling companion.

Their trek across the countryside was uneventful, offering time for casual conversation. Coaldon was fascinated by the stories told by Tipsy about his adventures at sea. Coaldon tried to visualize what it would be like to survive raging storms, fight pirates, and endure months of isolation.

The moon provided enough light to guide their stumbling feet. They moved at a steady pace south of the city into an area of farms and orchards. Barking dogs were the only harbingers to announce their passage through the moonlit night.

As they walked over the countryside, Coaldon's mind swam in disorientation at the rapid pace of events. Last week, he was in Rockham; several days ago, he was fighting his way through dense underbrush; and now, he was traveling in a strange land with an old sailor. After fruitless attempts to put order to puzzlement, he finally admitted to the unexplainable mystery of his life. As he yielded trust to the Spirit of Life, peace crept into his mind.

Ting

In the early morning light, the prince's thoughts were interrupted when the old man led him into a clearing where he saw a farm house in the distance. Coaldon heard the distant thunder of the ocean waves crashing onto rocks. His attention shifted when he heard the violent barking dogs. The young warrior felt uncomfortable as the howling dogs grew near. Without thinking, he projected thoughts of friendship into the minds of the fast-approaching canines. The dogs suddenly stopped barking, causing an uneasy silence.

The old gentlemen commented, "These are vicious dogs. It is unnatural for them to stop barking while pursuing trespassers. I believe the dogs' master will be hunting for us."

Coaldon responded, "I let the dogs know that we are friends."

Then out of the silence of the night, Coaldon was surrounded by the rush of six large dogs. Coaldon gave a loud laugh as he looked into the dogs' eyes. The dogs surged forward to greet him with robust enthusiasm. Coaldon fell to the ground under the weight of the pack of frolicking canines.

In the distance, furious yells were accompanied by the noise of somebody crashing through the underbrush. As Coaldon stood up to investigate the noise, a giant man rushed at him with sword in hand. The large man had a bushy, black beard, a round face, and long curly hair stacked wildly on his head. He attacked Coaldon without hesitation. Coaldon only escaped death by falling among the dogs. He crawled into the brush to find cover and regain his footing. Without pausing, he drew his sword, and walked into the clearing to confront his attacker. The huge man turned to face Coaldon with the intention to kill him. The man rushed forward, taking an uncontrolled swing at Coaldon with a large two-handed sword. Coaldon feinted to the left and raised his sword just as the heavy weapon hit his blade. With an upward thrust of his sword, Coaldon forced the opponent's weapon to fly harmlessly over his head. This move exposed the enraged man's right side. Not wanting to kill his adversary, Coaldon placed the tip of his sword on the man's throat.

In a controlled voice, Coaldon declared, "Friend, drop your sword. I do not want to harm you."

The big man paused to evaluate his situation. He knew he could easily kill Coaldon by making a return swing of his sword, but in the process he would also die. Then it occurred to him that his opponent could have killed him without offering him the opportunity to surrender. Making a wise choice, he dropped his sword without making any threatening movements. As the big man's eyes shifted to the right, he saw the old sailor standing on the edge of the forest clearing. All tension drained from his body when he recognized his friend. He realized he had again acted without thinking. The large man knew his quick temper had almost cost him his life.

With his emotions in a heightened state of readiness, Coaldon was surprised to see his opponent sag in grief. Coaldon remained in place until he saw the old man signal for him to stand down. Instinctively, Coaldon leapt backwards, ready to continue the fight if his opponent made any hostile moves. In response to Coaldon's retreat, the big man fell to his knees and placed his head on the ground.

Tipsy, with a look of disgust on his face, walked up to his friend kneeling on the ground.

Tipsy declared, "Tiny, aren't you the great warrior and good citizen? I have never seen such a pathetic display of stupidity in my entire life. No wonder a reasonable woman will not marry you. Now get up and apologize to my guest."

With a red face, the big man stood and faced Coaldon in complete humility. The bearded man lowered his head, kicking the ground with a nervous foot.

He looked into Coaldon's eyes, saying, "I apologize for my rude behavior. Thank you for sparing my life. I have the bad habit of acting without thinking about the consequences. By the way, what happened to my dogs? They have never acted like this."

Coaldon bowed and offered a gesture of greeting by the sweep of his left arm. Coaldon said, "My name is Hands the Blade. I accept your apology, but I find your welcome most novel. I hope this is not the traditional manner in which people greet each other in this land. By the way, you have friendly dogs."

At this comment, Tiny only shook his head in wonderment, "Welcome to my farm. I was preparing breakfast when you arrived. Would you please join me?"

Tipsy and Coaldon eagerly accepted the offer. The three men walked to the farmhouse, ready for a hot breakfast.

Coaldon and the old man added their primitive cooking skills to help Tiny prepare breakfast on a large wood stove. They ate, with zest, the traditional farm breakfast of ham, eggs, and wheat cakes. Tiny spent the morning working around the farm. This allowed Coaldon time to sleep and enjoy the ocean-front scenery. Upon returning from his chores, Tiny entered the farmhouse like a shy mouse trying to avoid being seen. Coaldon was fascinated by the obvious contrast between

Tiny's raging temper and his very gentle nature.

The old man invited Coaldon and Tiny to join him on the front porch of the house. From the porch, they could observe the ocean, rugged cliffs, and beaches. Through the ocean mist, the distant outline of Seamock could be seen. Many birds turned in lazy circles, dipping, and diving in their never-ending search for food.

Finally the old man said, "Tiny, our new friend wants to go to the Island of Death. Would you please take him? I would go, but I am too old for such a journey."

Coaldon could see doubt and hesitation pass over Tiny's face. Tiny sat for a long time staring at the ocean without saying a word.

He finally erupted, "Why should I do such a foolish thing!? The ocean around the island is treacherous and full of demons. Any person landing on the island will be destroyed by the evil spirits. Few men have ever come back from that terrible place. The ones who did return were forever mentally disturbed by strange dreams and bizarre behaviors. Victims have been known to scream and rage for days. I want to live a full life, not die in the throe of a demon possession."

Coaldon was surprised at Tiny's explosion of fear. He was uncertain how to respond to Tiny's doubts. He finally decided to tell Tiny the truth and offer him a display of power.

Coaldon responded, "I am on an important mission affecting the future of the Empire. I have been sent by Emperor Brad to go to the Island of Death to complete a special assignment. I carry special tools to protect us in case we encounter adversaries."

Coaldon pulled the Blade of Conquest from its scabbard and held it high in the air. At his command, blue and red streams of energy flashed up and down the blade in dancing surges of light. Coaldon then pointed the blade at Tiny, releasing a small pulse of power. Tiny's long hair stood on end, his face puckered like a dried prune, and his arms stretched out in front of his body. As the power of the blade possessed Tiny's body, his eyes opened wide in terror. Once the energy evaporated, the big man leaped into the air and fell to the ground, trembling in shock. Tipsy rocked with laughter at Tiny's reaction. Tiny slowly raised his head to check himself for any lasting damage. Finding none, he sat up and gazed in awe at Coaldon's blade.

Coaldon said, "I only released a small amount of energy. I did not want to be detected by forces of evil. Hopefully, this demonstrates to you that we will be traveling with special powers."

Still trembling, Tiny collapsed into his chair. Loud gasps of air filled his lungs. He finally said to Coaldon, "I may regret this decision, but I will go with you. When do we leave?"

The old man interrupted, "I recommend you leave tomorrow before the weather changes. I will remain on the farm to take care of the crops and animals while you are gone. I wish I could go, but this is not my burden."

H

The Strait of Void

Tiny was so busy getting ready for the trip across the Strait of Void he did not have time to think about his decision to go with Coaldon. If he had taken the time to reconsider, he would have run screaming into the woods and hid until the temptation had passed. He was large in size, big in heart, but small in courage.

By mid morning the boat was prepared, supplies stowed, and Tipsy ready to take over the operation of the farm. The young prince approached the vessel with hesitation. The boat looked small and insignificant in comparison to the vastness of the ocean. As he climbed into the bobbing craft, a bout of anxiety gripped him. The to-and-fro rocking of the boat caused him to reel in apprehension. With both hands gripping the sides of the vessel, Coaldon watched Tiny leisurely push the craft into deep water. With a leap, Tiny jumped into the boat causing it to roll violently from side to side. Coaldon knew he was going to die. Yet, to his great relief the boat did not sink, nor did death claim his life. It was not long before Tiny set the two sails and the boat was gliding smoothly across the water.

After an hour at sea, Tiny commented, "Relax and enjoy the ride. We should arrive at the island by late tonight. We may meet several ships in the next few hours, but after that, we will be very much alone. No ship's captain in his right mind would go near the island."

The bright sun, steady breeze, and quietness lulled Coaldon into a sense of peace. He slowly gained confidence in the ability of the boat to stay upright. The prince soon admitted to himself that there was hope in safely reaching the island. By early afternoon a dense fog bank loomed on the horizon. Tiny did not say anything, but his large body twitched with nervous tension at the prospect of sailing in dense fog.

As the fog bank drifted toward them, the air became uncomfortably still. The sails drooped and the boat bobbed lazily on the smooth sea surface. The sun became unbearably hot and the air intolerably heavy. The first sign of peril occurred when the boat began to shake. The gentle vibrations slowly increased into violent shock waves. Without warning, the craft jerked forward, then backward. Both men had to hold on to the boat or be thrown overboard. This continued for several moments before the boat once again became motionless.

The two travelers had just started to relax when the craft suddenly jumped forward. The speed of the boat increased without any apparent cause. Tiny soon discovered he could not control the boat's direction. As the vessel skimmed over the water, panic gripped both men. It was not long before the vessel was completely swallowed by dense fog. Coaldon sensed the boat was being pulled, not pushed toward the island. And suddenly, the craft stopped just as abruptly as it had started. An eerie silence assaulted their minds with agitation. They felt as if something was sucking the air from their lungs. Reality was slowly being distorted by unrecognizable images of impending disaster.

Coaldon saw distress on Tiny's face. The large man was a homebody, uninterested in the excitement of any adventure.

At this point, Tiny was seriously reviewing his decision to go on the trip. He wanted to be home in the safety of his quiet house. He reminded himself that he had made this choice by following the whim of his emotions, not the power of logic. He believed he had been tricked into this ill-fated disaster by his old friend.

In a loud voice, Tiny declared, "There was no wind. We are trapped in dense fog. I am uncertain of our location. And worst of all, I believe the boat is surrounded by demons."

Coaldon reassured him, "Everything is alright. We will get through this difficult situation."

Tiny never heard a word. He began to create, in his mind, sights and sounds that did not exist. His eyes darted back and forth as he waited for a foul creature to reach into the boat, pull him into the sea, and nibble on his toes. Even though the sea air was cold, Tiny's body was covered with sweat. Panic limited his ability to think and act rationally.

Coaldon decided he needed to do something before Tiny burst into an emotional rage. With the dramatic flair of a great actor, Coaldon drew his sword and swung it back and forth over his head. He wanted Tiny to place trust in the power of the sword. Using the boat's compass as a guide, Coaldon pointed the sword in the general direction of the island. He released a small pulse of energy through the blade, creating a flowing pattern of red, blue, and yellow lights. In the dense fog, the blade offered a beautiful display of colors. The boat began to move in a straight line under the power of the blade. Tiny firmly gripped the sides of the boat and closed his eyes. The speed of the boat increased until it was cutting a large wake.

After traveling for many leagues, the boat stopped. It began to turn in slow circles, first in one direction and then in the opposite. This rotation stopped when the boat began to violently jerk from side to side. Coaldon had the feeling they were the victims of a war being waged between two opposing forces struggling to determine which direction the boat would go.

As the vessel danced wildly in the water, Tiny's body became rigid. His facial muscles twitched uncontrollably. He began to gasp for air in irregular gulps. A deep rumbling sound grew in his chest. His body trembled with uncontrollable fear, and his bulging eyes stared into emptiness.

Coaldon decided, against his better judgment, to once again use the power of the Blade of Conquest to reach the island. He was ready to risk being detected by Crossmore. With the sword extended in front of him, Coaldon closed his eyes and conjured an image of the boat arriving at the island. When the mental picture was complete, he released the vision into the blade. He remembered hearing the muffled sound of a voice and feeling spasms of pain, as energy drained from his body and he lost consciousness.

The Beach

Coaldon opened his eyes to discover that the fog had disappeared and bright sunlight bathed his cold, exhausted body. The boat was rapidly moving across the water, heading toward a broad sandy beach. As Coaldon tried to move, he found an empty space between his mind and body. Coaldon could sense events going on around him, but he was unable to physically respond. He soon realized he was paralyzed in a sitting position in the front of the boat. He heard Tiny's voice, but was unable to answer. Tiny soon realized Coaldon was not moving or responding to his words. The large man did not have time to deal with Coaldon's problem because the boat was rushing toward the beach.

Tiny landed the boat with the grace of an expert seaman. With Coaldon still sitting in the boat, Tiny tried to pull the heavy craft across the beach towards a grove of trees. After making little progress, he lifted Coaldon from the boat and laid him on the beach. By removing Coaldon, he was able to drag the boat into the shelter of the trees. He then carried Coaldon into the dense foliage and propped him up against the boat.

Coaldon was as helpless as a baby, yet had the ability to understand what was happening around him. He felt completely humiliated when a bird perched on his head and bugs crawled over his body.

In helplessness, Coaldon watched his companion prepare the campsite for the evening. Tiny continued to chatter at Coaldon about the trip across the Strait, yet showed no concern about his condition. The prince decided the large man was exhibiting the characteristics of shock and disorientation. After eating a large meal, Tiny fell into a deep, restless slumber near the camp fire. While sleeping, the large man began to yell about monsters chasing him. His skin had the waxen pallor of death, rather than the warm glow of life.

As Coaldon sat next to the boat, he began to view the world from a different perspective. He discovered his five senses had been greatly enhanced by his state of paralysis. He had never seen or felt nature in such a powerful manner. The light of the moon stroked him with gentle waves of peace. The night sounds were like an orchestra playing a beautiful song. The pulse of the earth spoke to him of the power of creation. The chill of the night air surrounded like a protective blanket, and the dignity of the forest shared with him the enduring strength of life.

Coaldon's new awareness of nature filled him with renewed courage to face the trials of the present moment. As he allowed these different voices to speak to him, he felt an evil power reaching to locate him. He knew Crossmore was searching to find the source of the energy that had disturbed the normal flow of magic. Crossmore's black power covered the light of the moon, casting a sense of dread.

In a deep, melodious voice, Crossmore spoke to Tiny, saying, "Who are you?"

Tiny erupted from his sleep with a burst of terror. In desperation, he looked around to find the origin of the words.

Then Crossmore said, "I sense your presence. Who are you? Why are you on this island?"

Tiny responded in a weak, uncertain voice, "I, I, I hear you, but I do not see you."

The raging voice of the wizard yelled, "Answer me, or face the painful consequences of your disobedience!"

Tiny quickly answered, "My, my, my name is Tiny from Seamock. My, my, my boat was driven ashore by a strange surge of waves. Where am I?"

The hidden voice laughed with great humor, "You are on the Island of Death. This is most unfortunate for you. You will soon die a miserable death. Ha! Ha!"

The large man trembled, "I am just a poor farmer. Please help me."

The evil wizard laughed with glee at Tiny's request.

He declared, "Oh, I will help you alright. I will leave you here. Your death will end your worthless, miserable life."

After a pause, Crossmore continued, "I am looking for the power that disturbed my magic. It is obvious your simple mind is not the source. I now leave you to bask in the horrors of your wretched life."

Crossmore's presence then dissolved into the mist of the night.

Coaldon was fascinated that Crossmore had not detected him. Maybe the paralysis had prevented Coaldon's power from being noticed. Crossmore's visit had once again triggered Tiny's uncontrollable anxiety. The large man desperately looked at Coaldon, searching to find refuge from his hopeless state of affairs.

Coaldon knew he had to gain control of the situation. He could not allow his mind and body to remain separated. He had important things to do.

He decided to reach out from the core of his being to examine the wall separating his mind and body. As Coaldon pushed a probe of energy from his consciousness, he soon discovered a wall of crippling pain blocking him from conversing with his body. He also detected an energy field of anger flowing around his consciousness.

He questioned himself, "What am I to do?"

Coaldon realized the anger and pain were not his own. He assumed that the use of the blade had allowed an unknown presence to attach to him. Out of desperation, he decided to communicate with his invader. As Coaldon once again probed the turbulence, he sensed the energy of two forces supporting each other. Anger and pain were intimately intertwined as cause and affect. Coaldon determined that the pain was an outward manifestation of anger.

Without thinking Coaldon asked the question, "Why are you angry?"

His mind reeled as the image of a wizard formed into a clear picture. The evil presence caused the Blade of Conquest to vibrate. The image of Doomage the Wizard hissed with hatred from the wall of agony.

Coaldon pushed the image of the wizard back into the mass of pain. He assumed the anger was the product of an evil event inflicted on the suffering soul. Coaldon speculated that the tormented person had attached to him while searching to find relief from its terrible agony. The young warrior decided it was better to heal the lost spirit, rather then attack it.

Coaldon realized he did not have the power to cure such a profound wound. In confidence, he reached out to Starhood, his elfin grandfather.

He begged, "Grandfather, I need your help. Please heal an ancient wrong."

Coaldon did not have long to wait before a warm glow entered his body. A small flame radiated like a beacon throughout his whole being. As the force of healing grew, it slowly pushed outward from Coaldon's core. When the power encountered the wall of suffering, it gently bonded with the torment. The grace of healing gradually soaked up the anger and pain. Coaldon could feel the stir of goodness and peace. It was only moments before the wall of separation melted away. As Coaldon released a deep breath, a cloud of blue smoke flowed from his mouth. The infected soul had been released from its bondage.

Tiny nearly fainted when he saw the smoke flowing out of Coaldon's mouth. He believed an evil spirit had escaped from Coaldon, searching for a new victim. Tiny froze under a blanket of trepidation. His body would not do what his mind commanded – run.

At this point Coaldon opened his eyes and gave Tiny a smile. Coaldon declared in a firm voice, "It is good to be back. I have missed you."

Tiny leaped to his feet in excitement. He grabbed Coaldon as if he was a rag doll. Coaldon gladly endured Tiny's embrace.

Coaldon projected a thought to his grandfather, "Thank you. You were successful."

A Choice to Make

Coaldon awoke to rain pounding on the tarp covering their sleeping area. An unwelcome rainstorm had descended on the island during the night. Coaldon and Tiny were forced to stumble around in the dark to put up a makeshift tent. In spite of the storm, Coaldon slept soundly through the rest of the night and half the morning. He opened his eyes in a state of confusion, searching to find clues to his present location. His mind struggled to put order to the blur of events of the past few days. As the dreamlike fog cleared from his mind, Coaldon remembered Tiny, the ocean, and the battle within himself. Yet, these memories seemed like a fantasy. Sometimes, the unusual is so unusual it takes time for it to become real.

Coaldon saw Tiny tightly rolled in his sleeping blanket. His chest rose and fell with the steady rhythm of deep sleep. After a brief survey of the camp, he decided to close his eyes for a few more minutes of rest. Eventually, the smell of cooking ham and pancakes wafted through Coaldon's layer of sleep. He abruptly sat up to see Tiny huddled over a small fire, preparing breakfast.

Coaldon sleepily mumbled, "Good morning. I am hungry."

Tiny turned towards Coaldon with a look of surprise, "You mean, good afternoon. You have nearly slept the whole day. Our afternoon breakfast is just about ready."

The men ate the meal with relish.

Tiny commented, "The past few days have been difficult for me. I am not a man of great daring. There were many times I believed I was going to die. I just knew monsters were after me. I am glad to be alive and to have a special companion."

Coaldon responded, "Yes, it has not been easy. It is now time for you to make a decision. Do you wish to return to Seamock? Do you desire to wait here until I return from my expedition? Or, maybe you would like to go with me?

Tiny did not hesitate in responding, "I will go with you. I do not want to leave your side until we return to Seamock. I am afraid of being left unprotected on this accursed island."

Coaldon laughed in relief, "I was hoping you would go with me. It will be my pleasure to be accompanied by such a fine fellow. We will make a grand team."

The rain slowed to a gentle mist by early evening. The two adventurers happily greeted the outline of the sun as it immerged from the overcast sky. Coaldon decided to spend the rest of the day exploring the area around the campsite. He did not find the presence of magic. He had anticipated that the whole island would be an active matrix of magical energy.

On the following morning, the warm sunshine elevated the men's spirits. Eager to begin their journey, Tiny and Coaldon loaded their packs with extra provisions and started hiking toward the south end of the large island. By early afternoon they found an ancient road constructed of finely cut and fitted stones. The quality of the stonework indicated that a high level of civilization had once flourished on the island. After following the road for the remainder of the day, they arrived at a junction. One road continued south and the other turned to the east.

After a long pause, Coaldon commented, "I think it is best to spend the night here. I have no idea which road we should follow. Let's find a sheltered campsite and prepare dinner. I need time to think."

Dark clouds covered the setting sun, offering the prospects of rain by morning. The advent of darkness created a sense of uncertainty. An unseen world lurked just beyond the edges of the fire. The movement of large and small creatures in the brush stirred the men's imagination. The presence of the unknown challenged them to push away thoughts of doubt and insecurity.

Clouds soon obscured the light of the moon, leaving only a residue of darkness as rain descended on the campsite. With the steady pounding of the rain on the tarp, Coaldon drifted into a deep, but restless sleep. Unrecognized images skirted the perimeter of his dreams, leaving only vague hints of substance. The hidden flow of shadows created a state of ambiguity in Coaldon's mind. Many voices tried to speak to him at the same time, causing a jumble of gibberish. In a state of bewilderment, Coaldon's subconscious mind tried to find meaning in the barrage of words directed at him.

Then out of the nebulous flow of his dreams, two voices took the shape of two giants, each standing on different roads. The giant standing on the road to the south was dressed in brightly colored clothes and radiated a warm, pleasant smile. The sound of his gentle voice offered the sweet, alluring quality of sensual bliss. Coaldon had to fight the temptation to follow the seductive attraction of the giant. He could feel the draw of pleasure inviting him to yield to the temptation of ecstasy. The enticing pull of self-satisfaction drew his awareness like an inescapable fulfillment.

Then the thunder of a deep voice drew the prince's attention away from the magnetism of pleasure. He protested loudly when his focus was diverted away from the warm caress of physical elation. Anger flashed as he was forced to face the giant standing on the road to the east. This giant stood with his massive arms crossed, looking at Coaldon with expectation. He was dressed in warrior's clothing, had a round bearded face, and possessed a penetrating gaze. As the giant opened his mouth, Coaldon heard a rumbling sound. The penetrating voice sliced through Coaldon like a sword cutting through air. This assault opened a hole in Coaldon's chest, allowing the young prince to look deep into his own soul. Coaldon reeled backward when he saw the stain of darkness in his life. He heard the black spot inviting him to live a life of selfish pleasure. Coaldon watched in horror as a finger reached out of the darkness, touching his spirit. Coaldon realized he had been infected with the human disease of self-gratification.

The booming voice of the second giant then declared, "Do not pass by me unless you are willing to pay the price for wholeness. The journey down this road will challenge you to conquer the tempting call of evil. You are invited to follow the difficult path of sacrifice."

Coaldon's dream created such agitation, he forced himself to awaken. He discovered the rain had stopped and the first light of dawn was forcing the night to retreat in submission.

Coaldon said to himself, "Follow the path of sacrifice. I remember hearing these words from somewhere."

As the web of confusion cleared, he heard the words echo in his mind. They were from the Verse of Fate, 'By the journey of sacrifice, the path to take'.

Coaldon realized the road to the south was a trip into self-indulgence, while the road to the east would demand self-discipline and suffering. Without any further thought, Coaldon knew he had to take the road to the east.

Tiny, being a farm boy, was up at the break of dawn to prepare for the day. Coaldon did not share his dream with Tiny, but only stated his decision to take the road to the east. Tiny accepted this decision without concern or question. After breakfast, they loaded their packs and started down the narrow road. As they traveled, a lurking sense of apprehension churned in the pits of their stomachs.

The road wandered in a southeast direction over wooded hills, down a green valley, and past a foul-smelling swamp. Mid-morning, Coaldon noticed a tall, desolate mountain looming in the east. At first, it was only a hazy image in the distance, but as the day passed, its stark outline grew in definition. Its bleak, rocky appearance offered an unpleasant image.

ᚢᛦ ᚴᚦᚺ ᚨᐱᐱᛏ ᐱᚹᚺᛘᛦ

As the Door Opens

Tiny and Coaldon decided to push ahead until they reached the mountain. It was early evening when the companions arrived at the foot of the large peak. They discovered that the road ended directly in front of the mountain. A small river flowed from the north, separating them from the peak.

The mountain's rocky base supported steep, treeless slopes that rose sharply to a tall, pointed summit. It was void of life from top to bottom. Many large channels sliced down the sides of the barren peak. High mounds of dirt and rocks were deposited at the bottom of each gully. Coaldon looked at the landscape with growing discomfort. He knew magic somehow supported the lifeless mountain.

The surrounding forest teamed with the sounds and activities of life. Birds, furry animals, and insects darted back and forth in an endless parade. Yet, the presence of life ended at the edge of the mountain. Emptiness dominated its bleak landscape.

The two men looked at each other in a state of indecision. The road they had been following ended at the river.

Coaldon said, "What do we do? We can try to go around the mountain, or maybe the mountain might be of interest to us. I suggest we set up camp and make the decision in the morning."

Nodding in agreement, Tiny stated, "I do not like this place. I never imagined any part of nature could provoke such negative feelings."

Like a tower of demise, the mountain dominated the view from their camp. The beauty of a small stream, lush grass, and the dense forest did not brighten their spirits. After dinner Coaldon said, "Since you are now part of this adventure, it is important for you to understand our mission. We are searching for the Key of Ban. It is a book that was created by elfin magic, during the wars of the Second Quarter Age, to imprison the forces of evil in the Chamber of Oblivion. It takes the power of a benevolent wizard to activate the magic."

Coaldon paused before continuing, "Crossmore the Wizard has found a way to penetrate the Chamber of Oblivion and release the forces of evil from their bondage. He is using them to fulfill his plan of conquest. The Key of Ban is the only power that can return this scourge back to the Chamber. Legend states that the Key of Ban will be found in the Cave of Hope in the Land of Westmore, by rolling waters. I have been sent by the Council of Rockham to open the Gates of Conquest with the power of the One Sword and retrieve the Key of Ban."

Coaldon completed the story by discussing the events of the Council of Rockham. He recited the Verse of Fate in a somber and serious tone.

Tiny was quiet while Coaldon told him the story.

In a meek voice Tiny stated, "I did not realize I had been invited to participate in such an important event in the history of the Empire. I feel humbled and unworthy to join you on this quest. Yet, I am here for some reason. What do we do next?"

Coaldon responded, "We need to decide if we are in the Land of Westmore, facing the Gate of Conquest."

In a confident voice, Tiny said, "You stated that the One Sword will open the Gate of Conquest. I suggest we return to the mountain and challenge it with your blade. If the sword does nothing, then we are in the wrong location."

Coaldon smiled, "I agree with you. Let's allow the sword to fulfill its mission. Tomorrow may offer us a most interesting adventure."

Both men spent the night in deep slumber. They were awakened by the pleasant sounds of singing birds.

While eating breakfast, Coaldon turned to Tiny stating, "I have never described a mountain as being good or bad. I have always used words like tall, steep, rocky, or rugged, but never in emotional terms. Grief and misery seem to be a part of this peaks nature."

After a moment of reflection, the young prince continued, "Well my friend, are you ready to take the next step on our journey?"

Tiny nodded with enthusiasm. This was the first time since leaving Seamock that the large man had looked forward to confronting the challenges of their mission.

The two men casually walked down the road, talking about the events of the past few days. In a mysterious sense, they knew the encounter with the peak would offer them a door into their future.

The mountain's stark reality greeted Coaldon and Tiny with its cold and depressing aura. The road they were following abruptly ended at the river. Coaldon first looked at the river then at the peak. The peak did not seem to belong. It was out of place in relationship to the surrounding countryside. He had the impression that the river existed long before the peak had appeared in its present location.

Tiny broke the silence by saying, "I see the outline of an old bridge foundation on this side of the river. I wonder if the road once went directly into the mountain?"

Coaldon commented, "We need to find a way across the river to examine the area at the base of the peak. The river is too deep and narrow to cross at this location. If we are to cross the stream it will be necessary to either make a raft or find a place to ford the river on foot."

After exploring up and down the river, they found a wide, shallow section. The rushing water made crossing it difficult, but not beyond the physical strength of the two men.

Upon arriving on the opposite side, they returned to the remains of the bridge foundation. They estimated the old road was buried under the mounds of debris. The area between the river and the mountain was a lifeless wasteland of barren rocks and dirt. Coaldon examined the hillside where he estimated the road would be located, but could not find any signs of its presence.

Tiny began searching south along the hillside. Working with the persistence of a bird dog, it was not long before Tiny found faint outlines of writing on the surface of a cliff and signs of an ancient road entering into the mountain. Coaldon joined Tiny to help inspect the area.

After a thorough search, Coaldon declared, "This is amazing! I cannot believe this! The road on this side and the other side of the river do not match. The ground has moved at least one hundred strides over time."

Out of curiosity, Coaldon shifted his attention to the marks on the face of the cliff. Most of the marks had been worn away by centuries of wind and rain, yet in a sheltered area the ancient script was readable. Coaldon grabbed a handful of white dust from the ground and rubbed it onto the surface of the writing. When he brushed away the dust, the outline of the letters was visible. Coaldon looked at the long, wavy characters from different angles to detect the pattern of the writing.

During his childhood in the Outlast, Coaldon's grandmother had taught him to read the common language, plus many dialects of high and low elf. After a close examination he was able to decipher the script. Coaldon determined the words were written in a corrupted form of the common language used during the Second Quarter Age. This was the period when Doomage the Wizard controlled most of the Empire with his vile power.

Coaldon read the words several times with growing disbelief and agitation. He looked at Tiny then back at the words.

He finally said, "This mountain was truly built on grief and pain. You will find the meaning of these words disturbing."

Tiny commented, "There is no reason to protect me. I need to know if I am to help you."

Coaldon began to read, "Enter at the price of death. This mountain has been built with the souls of my precious slaves. I thirst for the energy of their spirits. I grow strong from the wails and moans of their voices. Long live Doomage the Great."

Coaldon's voice cracked with emotion as he quoted the words. After regaining his composure, he added, "I wish I had never come to this horrible place. Is it possible that this mountain is alive with the souls of many innocent people? I have no idea what to do next. Is this the Gate of Conquest? Tiny, do you have any suggestions?"

Tiny could tell Coaldon was having a weak moment. He needed to show strength, not the spineless example he had demonstrated over the past few days.

Tiny responded, "We cannot allow this to cloud our mission. We must do what is right. If the mountain is built on the pain of many poor souls, then we must try to reconcile their suffering. We also must find the Key of Ban. The Verse of Fate states that 'by hand on sword, the key to gain'. I suggest you raise your sword to the mountain to determine if it will open a door."

Coaldon looked at Tiny with growing respect. "Thank you for your encouragement. You speak with the eloquence of an educated man. Maybe there is more to you than meets the eye. Tell me about your past."

Tiny looked at the ground in shy reservation. "I was educated and taught at the Academy of the Masters in Neverly. I was not happy wearing the robes of a teacher or playing the games of the Academy. One day I challenged the masters concerning their self-serving dedication to Wastelow the Emperor. At a Meeting of the Masters, I bluntly told them they were selling their souls to Wastelow's evil intentions. For these words, I was banned from the Academy for life. In hurt and anger, I decided to retreat from the academic world to the simple-life of a farmer. I wanted to search for the real meaning of life, not just strive to gain understanding as defined by words. I believe actions best define and express the power of creation. So, for many years I have struggled to find peace."

Coaldon was delighted to discover a complex mystery in what appeared to be a simple man.

Coaldon laughed as he said, "As each new page of your life is revealed, you offer me a challenge."

Smiling, Coaldon continued, "It is time to get back to the issue at hand. We need to do something. Your suggestion sounds good to me. So, let's put the Blade of Conquest to the test."

Coaldon pulled the sword from its scabbard and pointed it toward the face of the cliff. The instant he touched the sword, deep rumbling came from inside the mountain. The ground under their feet began to sway back and forth. From top to bottom, the face of the mountain ruptured in many places creating giant rock-slides. Large avalanches began to tumble down the side of the mountain. Coaldon and Tiny watched in horror as an avalanche raced down the mountain towards them. It seemed impossible for them to escape the inevitable crushing power of the landslide.

Coaldon was so focused on the avalanche hurling down the slopes, he forgot about the sword in his hand. Tiny was first to notice a small opening in the face of the cliff. In a state of panic, Tiny yelled at Coaldon. When Coaldon heard the shout, he turned to discover the hole in the cliff. With only seconds to spare both men dived through the crack just as the weight of the landslide hit the spot where they had been standing. The massive rush of rocks and dirt quickly covered the passageway they had just entered. Darkness surrounded them as the mountain continued to rumble.

Tiny yelled, "Coaldon, take your hand off the sword before we are killed."

Coaldon responded by returning the sword to its scabbard. The moment he removed his hand from the blade, the mountain stopped quaking and shifting.

Enter at Your Own Risk

Coaldon was surprised at the enormous power stored in his sword. The touch of his hand on the blade had shaken the very foundation of the giant mountain. Coaldon had never considered the possibility that such power was available to him. He felt a growing sense of responsibility to use it for the purpose it had been created.

The rumbling noise of the avalanche soon stopped and the darkness of the tunnel surrounded them like an unwelcome tomb. The two men stood in shock at being trapped in the passageway without any way to escape. It took several moments for their minds to comprehend their new situation.

Coaldon finally asked, "Tiny, are you all right?"

In gasping breaths, Tiny answered, "It is good to hear your voice. I am only bruised and scratched. I am happy to have escaped. How are you?"

The prince answered, "I am fine. I believe we have just experienced the old adage of 'jumping from the frying pan into the fire', but at least we are alive and in good health."

As Coaldon pulled the Gem of Watching from his pouch, the light of the stone penetrated into the darkness of the tunnel. The surface of the passageway was constructed of a hard, black substance. The tunnel extended straight into the mountain as far as he could see.

Coaldon inquired, "Do you hear a humming sound?"

Nodding his head, Tiny responded, "I hear the sound, but cannot identify its origin. I feel misery flowing from its penetrating resonance. It must come from some unholy act of magic."

The noise pressed into Coaldon's mind with inescapable distress. It permeated every cell of his body with a demand. The elusiveness of the query challenged Coaldon to search for resolution to the agitation that was tearing at him. It was not a straightforward expectation, but rather a complex certainty begging for an answer.

As Coaldon reached for understanding, a vision flooded his consciousness. The humming sound appeared as waves radiating from the walls of the tunnel. These waves blended together to form a collage of unrecognizable, interwoven shapes. A rush of movement then transformed these vague images into a visible reality. He saw a mass of humans pressed tightly together into a collection of grim faces, grasping hands, and open mouths. Coaldon soon realized the drone was the communal cry of many voices pleading for help. The young warrior struggled to image the source of such misery. He never thought it possible to behold such gloom.

In gasping words, Coaldon told Tiny about the grotesque images he had seen. Upon finishing the story, he stared quietly into the Gem of Watching.

The light from the stone penetrated the prince's spirit with curative power. The healing did not remove the burden of the current situation, but rather offered hope. In a mysterious way, the restorative light of the Gem helped provide him with the courage to take the next step.

The sound of Tiny's breathing drew his attention back to the present moment. Coaldon looked at his companion, then at his own fingers. He knew the mission could only be completed by the work of hands. It was now time to confront the impossible and make it possible. It was time to go beyond the limits of his mind and allow providence to guide his steps. He would only allow the picture of success to control his thoughts.

Coaldon smiled as he looked at Tiny. The gentle giant had more talents than he had ever expected. Tiny was a man of destiny. His outward appearance did not accurately reveal the inner-man.

In a soft voice, Coaldon said, "We have crossed the threshold of the mountain, yet where will we find the Key?"

Tiny responded, "You ask a most interesting question."

After a long pause, Coaldon continued, "I just realized that the prophecies of the Verse of Fate are revealed in an orderly sequence. Verse 6 states that 'By steps of trust, to door of hope'. We have faced the mountain, but now we are to have trust. It is time to allow hope to be our guide."

Nodding in agreement, Tiny responded, "We must also discover the meaning of the words 'By act of love, the slaves to free'. What slaves? Where are they? "

With a nervous twitch, Coaldon abruptly declared, "I believe the slaves are the souls somehow trapped in this evil mountain."

Tiny stated, "I assume the Key of Ban was hidden here by the elves."

Coaldon questioned, "I wonder why they placed the Key in this foul place?"

Tiny reflected, "I believe the elves realized the Key was too powerful to float freely in the world. It had to be hidden in a safe place until the appointed time."

Coaldon followed, "Why didn't the elves free the souls when they visited the mountain? I wonder if the Blade of Conquest is the answer? Is it possible the sword is the only instrument that can break the bondage of the slaves and retrieve the Key?"

Coaldon added, "The elves did not possess the One Sword at that time. The Sword of Conquest would arrive at a later date. They had to yield to the providence-of-time to complete both tasks."

The two men quietly sat in the warm glow of the Gem of Watching.

They slowly began to understand the reality of their present situation.

Coaldon broke the silence by saying, "It is apparent to me that we only have one direction to go, down the tunnel. We can sit here and wait for something to happen to us, or we can make things happen. I say, 'Let it begin'!"

Tiny commented, "As a historian, I have read about individuals who go beyond the ordinary to fulfill a momentous task. I have waited many years to use all my talents to do something worthwhile. I do not want to hide behind books and ideas. I want to accomplish honorable deeds. I am ready!"

Coaldon led the way down the tunnel, lighted by the Gem of Watching. The light from the Gem only reached a short distance before it was absorbed by the darkness. The black tunnel was in stark contrast to the passageways constructed by dwarves. Dwarf tunnels radiated a warmth of caring, while this black passageway emitted the grim cast of misery. The passageway followed a straight line directly into the core of the mountain.Adding to the uncertainty of the moment, Coaldon experienced a heavy weight pressing down on him. He sagged under a burden of unknown origin.

After they walked for what seemed an eternity, Coaldon decided to call a halt. He immediately dropped to the floor in exhaustion.

He looked at Tiny saying, "How are you doing? I feel as if I am carrying the weight of the world."

Tiny, being aware of Coaldon's fatigue, responded, "I am doing great. I do not feel anything out of the ordinary except for the frustration of being trapped in this unclean mountain. Do you need help?"

Coaldon answered, "No, but I might need some assistance later."

For Coaldon, the rest was much too short; yet, he knew it was necessary to continue the hike.

After plodding along for many hours, Tiny announced, "I believe it is early evening. We should stop for the night." The large man possessed an uncanny sense of time.

Coaldon enthusiastically agreed with Tiny's suggestion. The unknown load carried by Coaldon increased the farther he moved into the mountain. The past few hours of walking had forced Coaldon to go beyond his normal limits of endurance. He took one heavy step after another."

After a meal, Coaldon stated in a groggy voice, "I am afraid we will walk forever if we do not find a way out of this unending circle of magic. Is it possible this tunnel will never end? I am beginning to believe the Gate of Conquest is something much different than what I originally envisioned. It might not be an actual door. "

Tiny responded, "The answer to your questions will be revealed to us. We must be patient. Haste will only block the discovery of the truth."

Coaldon slept soundly throughout the night, but Tiny, on the other hand, was about to be introduced to the reality of the mountain. Up to this point, he had not heard the voices or felt the burden of their misery. As the large man wrapped himself into his sleeping blanket, he heard a sniffing sound. At first, he ignored the noise because he assumed it was a figment of his imagination. As the sound of the sniffing grew louder and louder, he began to believe that something was searching for him. He felt exposed and vulnerable to whatever was probing the tunnel.

Tiny reeled in horror when he felt a chill touch his soul. The large man was suddenly assaulted by an endless stream of grief. The gloom was not his own, but had been imposed upon him. The more Tiny tried to resist the invasion, the more he fell under the control of the infectious sorrow. After a long struggle, he realized it was useless to fight its incursion, but best to accept the enveloping power of suffering.

Throughout the night, Tiny tossed and turned, but could not find peace with the voices of the mountain. Coaldon and Tiny awoke at the same time.

Before departing the following morning, Tiny said, "Last night I was touched by voices. The burden of their misery is profound."

With tired eyes, Coaldon looked at Tiny with compassion. "I believe the voices are reaching out to us in anguish. They do not want to destroy us, but are searching for help. I suggest we accept their despair with sympathy. If we become pessimistic, we will lose ourselves within this ocean of grief. I suggest we nurture positive thoughts. I am anxious to get started, so let us find whatever is awaiting us."

Tiny followed, "Let's walk as if the sun is shining on our faces."

They continued their journey, determined to conquer the hostile environment of the tunnel. But Tiny and Coaldon soon discovered it was much easier to talk about being positive than to actually be optimistic. They found the negative influence of the mountain constantly slipping into their minds. Only by monitoring their thoughts were they able to remain positive.

Coaldon continued to experience the weight of carrying a heavy burden. Yet, the struggle of monitoring the attack of negative thoughts took his attention away from his physical discomfort.

As the day progressed, their mental battle went on, hour after hour. They found the grieving voices constantly attacking their minds. It was mid-day before Coaldon decided to rest. They had become so intent on controlling their thoughts that they lost track of time. A quiet meal, a drink of water, and a moment of relaxation were greeted with relief.

As Coaldon relaxed, an idea burst into his mind. With eagerness, he declared, "I am convinced that the Gate of Conquest is not a physical place, but a state of mind. It is possible that I must conquer something in order to rescue the Key of Ban."

Tiny quickly followed, "If this is true, what do you need to overcome?"

Coaldon continued, "If I remember right, a passage in the Verse of Fate states:

"By steps of trust,
    to the door of hope.
By hand on sword,
    the key to gain."

"This indicates to me that I must trust in the power of the One Presence, as well as place my hand on the sword. Yet, I am afraid to touch the blade. The last time I held it we nearly died."

With a smile, Tiny stated, "What else can you do? So far, the Verse has correctly guided us. So my friend, I challenge you to go beyond fear, firmly grab the hilt of the sword, and let the show begin!"

Nodding in agreement, Coaldon prepared for action. He cleared his mind and reached for the sword. As his hand stopped just inches from the handle, he looked at Tiny for encouragement. Tiny's smile gave Coaldon permission to fulfill his obligation. Without further delay, he firmly gripped the hilt of his sword. Upon contact, bands of energy encircled Coaldon in rotating streams of light. Coaldon looked outside the light to see Tiny either asleep or in a coma. He tried to move, but was bound by the circular motion of the energy surrounding him. With sudden intensity, he felt an uncontrollable desire for revenge searing through his whole being.

Without thinking, Coaldon swung the sword around his head in wide circles. Energy pulsed up and down the sword, seeking to strike out with vengeance. Hatred surged through Coaldon in ever-tightening circles. Blood demanded blood!

Coaldon felt like an outsider observing his own destruction. He had to gain control or face his own death. Yet, blackness slowly possessed his soul. Coaldon reached out for help.

He requested, "Somebody, please help me!"

Then out of the shadows of his being, he heard Topple's familiar voice, "My! My! My! You look so silly waving the sword around your head! Ha! Ha! Around and around you go and where you stop, nobody knows. Ha! Ha! You need to realize that this anger is not your own, but an extension of the slaves' hatred passing through you. You are illuminating the captives desire to strike out at Doomage. So, my good friend, I recommend you let go of the anger, hold on to the rod of faith, sing a happy song, and pet an ant. Or should I say, let go of the lion's tail, sit on a rock, dance in the rain, and kiss a duck. Oh well, something like that. Have a great day and say hello to Tiny for me. As always, your good friend, Topple."

Topple's ancient insights touched Coaldon. The spell of vengeance broke when Coaldon burst into laughter. Topple's bombastic nature, childish innocence, and scorching humor blessed Coaldon. As he yielded to the Truth, he found the Gate of Conquest opening before him.

A rupture in the fabric of the mountain was created. That which was solid before became a nebulous cloud of fluid colors. As the cloud began to throb in agitation, Coaldon found himself and Tiny being transported through the mist into a twisting and spiraling pattern. As if shot from a catapult, they were hurled through time and space at blinding speed. The rush ended when they were thrust into a small cavern. Upon entering the room, they landed on the floor of the cave as if they were feathers floating to the ground.

The Stone of Joining

At first, Coaldon and Tiny stood in the middle of the cavern struggling to comprehend their new environment. It took several minutes for them to regain their sense of orientation. The dark brown walls of the small cave were dimly lit by a mysterious glow. Wooden furniture, books, papers, and assorted debris were scattered around the room in disarray. Coaldon had the impression that a violent event had occurred within the cavern, tossing the contents in all directions. On the opposite side of the room a black, shiny box sat on a white, stone table. The room did not have a speck of dust anywhere; it was as if the last event had occurred only minutes ago. Coaldon knew this room was the core of the mountain. From here, the peak was constructed and the souls held captive. He detected the pulsation of the enormous web of energy that held the mountain in a stable network.

Coaldon was the first to comment, "Surprise! Surprise! We have finally arrived at our destination. The crossing into here was unbelievable. I thought I was going to explode when we entered this room. Wow!"

Tiny laughed, "That is what I call a real trip."

Coaldon followed, "Now that we are here, I recommend we search the room. We might be tempted to rush ahead without full understanding."

Both men slowly moved through the cavern, examining each document, book, and object. Most of the items they found were junk. The name Doomage was a common word, but little of value was found. Doomage had not kept many records or notes. At the end of their search, Coaldon gave a yelp of excitement. He held up a piece of paper covered with notes.

He erupted, "I think I have found some important information. These are comments by Doomage about this room and its powers. Most of it is irrelevant to us, but the last few lines are revealing."

Coaldon read, "The axis of control was unstable today. A defect in the Stone of Joining allowed the vortex to shift the mountain about 100 strides to the south. When the power grid flickered, I almost lost control. During this pause, not one soul escaped. I feel such relief. This event has helped me appreciate my gorgeous slaves. Just the thought of losing their wailing and hatred causes my heart to feel sadness. I gain such strength and warmth from their pain and resentment."

Coaldon paused before he continued to read, "I find delight in my power to separate their bodies and souls. By keeping their bodies and souls separated, I utilize the energy of their struggle to be reunited. Their soulless bodies are held in suspension by my great power."

With contempt, Coaldon threw the document onto the floor. His eyes turned to the black glass box sitting on the table.

He projected, "The mountain is held in equilibrium by the power of the Stone of Joining. I wonder where it is located. Maybe it is found in the black box."

Tiny's eyes kept surveying the room as Coaldon talked. The black box ended up as the focus of his attention. The box was about six hands wide and five hands tall. The blurry outline of a round object appeared through the semi-transparent material. The general appearance of the box indicated it was a shell covering the mysterious contents. When Coaldon finished talking, Tiny walked over to the box to examine it more closely. Without thinking, he reached out and touched it with the tip of his index finger. Coaldon gasp at Tiny's impulsive behavior, but to his delight nothing happened.

In a guilty voice, Tiny said, "Why did I do such a stupid thing? Oh well, no harm done."

Coaldon approached the box with confidence. After a careful examination, he found nothing unusual. Following Tiny's example, the prince decided to also touch the cover. As Coaldon reached out, a surge of power shot from the box, knocking him backwards onto the floor. At this very moment, a shudder passed through the mountain. A large crack appeared in the wall behind the black box, exposing blood red material. Coaldon struggled to his feet in a state of perplexity. He looked at the box with renewed respect.

In a shaky voice, he said, "I feel as if I was kicked by a mule. I think we have found the Stone of Joining. I wonder why you can touch it and I cannot. Maybe it has something to do with the sword."

In spite of the danger they faced, Tiny burst into loud laughter. Tiny's uproarious laughter caused tears to run down his face. Coaldon could only stand in a state of uneasiness, wondering what the large man found so humorous.

Between bursts of giggling, Tiny said, "Touch your hair!"

Coaldon raised his hand to his head to discover his long hair was standing on end. Coaldon ran his hands over his head to push his hair down, but the hair only popped back up. Of course this caused Tiny to continue his bout of mirth. It took several minutes of stroking before Coaldon could train his hair to lay flat on his head.

Once Coaldon realized how silly he looked, he joined Tiny in celebrating the comical circumstances of his outstanding hair. The humorous event broke the spell of anxiety clouding the two men.

Coaldon responded, "It is so easy for us to loose track of the simple joys of life while in the midst of danger. Oh well, I suggest we get back to the task at hand. I believe the Stone of Joining and the Key of Ban are inside the black cover. Maybe I could use the sword to open or move the black box."

By this time, Tiny had regained his composure after Coaldon's hair-raising experience. In spite of the danger, he was in a pleasant mood.

Tiny commented, "I agree with you, the Key is probably found inside the box. I do not think it would be wise for you to touch the box with the blade. You might unbalance the power holding the mountain together. I suggest I lift the box off the table."

Coaldon's attention was divided between listening to Tiny and looking around the room. The jolt he received created a lingering image in his mind. He saw a large ball of fire with many beams extending from it. At the end of each ray was a small, red cell wrapped within a transparent shield of magic. Long tentacles extended from each cell connecting them into a solid network. A red substance flowed from each cell, streamed down the beam, and into the ball of fire.

As the image of the ball-of-fire swam in Coaldon's mind his attention returned to their present circumstances. With a burst of clarity, his mind made a direct link between his vision and the Stone of Joining. The Stone of Joining was the central source holding the mountain together. The energy flowing from the captive souls provided the power to maintain the mountain.

The prince was jerked back to reality when he heard Tiny ask, "Coaldon, are you all right? Wake up! We need to make some decisions."

Coaldon responded, "Sorry. I just had a strange vision. I will tell you about it later. Right now we have work to do. Go ahead and lift up the black box."

Tiny approached the box with great respect. With trembling fingers, he firmly grabbed the cover with both hands and slowly lifted upward. Tiny was surprised to find the box was not heavy, but almost floated into the air. He removed the black cover and carefully placed it on the floor. When Tiny returned his attention to the table, he saw a small, blue book lying next to a black stone. A beam of pulsing yellow light flowed between the book and the stone. Tiny noticed a red, transparent mist flowing through the walls of the cavern into a black stone and a corresponding black light radiating from the stone outward into the mountain.

Coaldon stared in disbelief at the simple appearance of the stone and book. The façade of simplicity cloaked the real power lurking in the two objects. He noticed the red mist and black light formed the intricate balance. Doomage's genius for evil was majestically wicked. Coaldon was particularly interested in the bond between the stone and the blue book.

Coaldon finally said, "I wonder why the benevolent wizards allowed the Key to be attached to the stone? Look, there is writing under the title of the book. Can you read it? I do not want to get too close to the stone."

As Tiny lowered his head over the book, he felt the two forces pushing through him. He knew if one force was more powerful than the other, he would be torn to pieces. He strained his eyes to read the small letters scrolled on the book's cover.

Tiny read out loud, "Key of Ban: Bondage to Freedom and Evil to Captivity."

He looked at Coaldon with a puzzled expression on his face.

The big man questioned, "Now, what does that mean? Do the words of the subtitle provide an indication of the book's purpose?"

Coaldon responded, "I am surprised the book has a subtitle. No one ever told me about these words. The book must have two different functions. We already know the meaning of the 'Evil to Captivity'. This power will cast the forces-of-evil into the prison of the Chamber of Oblivion. The meaning of 'Bondage to Freedom' must relate to the slaves of the mountain."

While listening to Coaldon, Tiny became mesmerized by the inner-life of the stone. He could see small specks of light flashing as incoming energy was transformed into an outward flow of power.

Tiny injected, "I believe the elves wanted to kill two birds with one stone. By attaching the Key of Ban to the Stone of Joining, it would be necessary to free the slaves in order to gain the Key. This was their way of forcing us to deal with both issues at the same time. In other words, it is impossible to deal with the rescue of the Key without also confronting the bondage of the slaves. This adds an interesting wrinkle to an already complicated situation."

Coaldon nodded in agreement. "It is now time to decide how I should use the blade. Should I direct the power of the sword at the black stone or confront the stone through the Key of Ban? Right now, I believe it is best to go through the book. What is your opinion?"

Tiny reflected, "I believe the Key is more powerful than the blade. The book might have the power to control the Stone without directly assaulting it. The Key would act as a buffer."

The young warrior suddenly stepped back in hesitation, as he felt a stab of uncertainty flood his mind. A moment of weakness shadowed his mind with doubt.

Closing his eyes, he struggled against the desire to walk away from his responsibilities. It was as if two opposing forces were battling to control his decision. The persuasive influence of his human-side offered words of fear and insecurity. In contrast, his higher-self challenged him to risk death for the good of the Empire. He felt a slight shutter of anticipation shimmering through the sword and the mountain. It was as if time was standing still waiting for him to complete his task.

Finally, Coaldon's focus returned to the cave and the moment of decision.

Coaldon smiled at his companion, saying, "There is an old fisherman's verse that states, 'You can either fish or cut bait'. It is now time for me to go fishing. The results of my actions might cost us our lives. Yet, this is a small price to pay for the good we will accomplish."

Tiny followed, "You have procrastinated long enough. Do what must be done."

Ceremonially, Coaldon drew the Blade of Conquest from its scabbard in a slow, dignified motion. The sword suddenly burst into life. The energy in the blade did not manifest itself with the usual display of light, but rather its color changed from silver to dark brown. The blade throbbed with immeasurable energy. It possessed the knowledge of what was about to take place.

Coaldon grimaced as he struggled to hold onto the pulsing sword. He looked up to see Tiny staggering to the far side of the room, panic contorting his face. He became immobilized by the magnitude of the power in the room.

With all his strength, Coaldon tried to move the point of the sword toward the Key of Ban. The massive clockwise movement of the energy flowing around the sword held it firmly in place. Coaldon strained every muscle in his body to direct it closer to the book. Slowly, ever so slowly, the tip of the sword dipped closer to the book. Sweat rolled down his face as his body rippled with strain. When the tip of the blade was a short distance from the book, a surge of power from the Stone of Joining pushed the blade away. The battle of opposing forces caused the walls of the room to tremble.

He once again pushed downward onto the blade. At first, the blade did not move, but when the resistance of the black stone collapsed, the tip of the sword suddenly leaped forward striking the Key of Ban. As the Blade of Conquest sliced into the book, the sword released a flash of light so intense, it burned Coaldon's face and hands. The energy of the sword was magnified a thousand times by the magic contained in the Key of Ban.

The Stone of Joining suddenly exploded into a cloud of sparkling dust. The collapse of the stone's control over the captive allowed the soul to float free. Coaldon assumed the mountain would crumple, but he was wrong. The liberation of the souls was followed by an outward explosion of energy.

R

Let's Get Out of Here

After his victory, over the Stone of Joining, Coaldon collapsed into a deep sleep. He was unaware of anything until a cool breeze penetrated his senses. Coaldon reached past the curtain of slumber to awaken himself. He tried to open his eyes, but found them matted shut. With both hands, he gently rubbed away the dried mucous. Both eyes finally opened to see the long shadows of evening.

Turning his head in all directions, he saw a vast, barren land where the mountain had once stood. Furniture and the remains of the room were scattered around him. The Blade of Conquest lay on the ground next to him, its point still sticking into the Key of Ban. To Coaldon's relief, he saw Tiny sleeping on the ground. Coaldon pushed himself to his knees, then to his feet. With a brush of his hand over his head, he became aware of a change in his hair. His once long, black hair was a mound of curly locks.

Forcing his stiff muscles to move, Coaldon stumbled toward Tiny. As he approached his new friend, Tiny opened his eyes. The giant man looked at Coaldon with an admiration reserved for heroes.

With enthusiasm, Tiny said, "I was unsure if you would ever wake up. How do you feel?"

Coaldon smiled at Tiny, "I guess I am all right. I never thought I would ever see you again. It is wonderful to stand here."

With a straight face, Tiny said, "Your appearance has greatly improved. I need to give you a name to match your new hairstyle, a name that reflects your distinguished appearance. How about Fuzzy? Ha! Ha! Ha!"

While Tiny laughed, Coaldon responded, "I will accept my new name with honor and pride. Now, I need to capture a meal lurking in my backpack. I am hungry."

The rumble of an earthquake abruptly interrupted Coaldon's celebration.

Tiny commented, "The ground has been shaking ever since I awoke. If you look to the east you will see where the ground is starting to split into deep trenches. I wonder if the whole island has been destabilized by the actions of the Blade of Conquest. Maybe we should hastily depart this accursed place."

Coaldon first looked at Tiny, then at the trenches in the east.

He responded, "This does not look good. We have a long walk back to the coast. Let's eat a quick meal and get started. The boat is our only means of escape."

In a sweeping motion, Coaldon retrieved his sword. As he pulled the tip of the blade from the Key of Ban, a green vapor flowed around the book. Coaldon tried to hold his attention onto its wavering appearance, but the image of the book drifted in and out of view. It then rematerialized. Coaldon closed his eyes to allow his mind to grasp the transformation he had just witnessed. He noticed the book had been repaired and the subtitle on the cover had disappeared.

When he touched the book, he felt a tingle of pleasure pass through his body. He was tempted to open it, but knew better. The words of the Key of Ban were meant only for the eyes of a benevolent wizard, not the untrained minds of ordinary people. Coaldon placed his sword into its scabbard and the small book into his pouch. The sun was setting in the west when they finished their meal and began to walk. Tiny led the way with long strides. It was midnight when they arrived at the river. They crossed without hesitation and continued their hasty retreat. A sense of impending doom dominated their thoughts.

The light of a new day greeted the companions as they hurried down the stone road. Both men agreed it was necessary to push beyond their physical limits if they were to escape the island. As they walked throughout the day, the ground continued to tremble and shift. They were tired, but did not yield to the desire to take a break. It was late afternoon when they arrived at a deep trench that sliced through the earth from east to west. As they stood on the edge looking down into the hole, the earth shook with a violent quiver. Before they could react, the earth under their feet collapsed into the deep furrow.

Sitting on a pile of dirt in the trench, Coaldon said in an angry voice, "Now what do we do!? The sides of the trench are too steep to climb!"

With patience and assurance, Tiny responded, "We can walk down the channel until we find a place to crawl out. We shouldn't have far to go."

Tiny was correct. After stumbling over the uneven earth at the bottom of the furrow for a short time, they found a wide area with passable sides. With many grunts and groans, they climbed up the side and were once again on level ground. Coaldon walked a short distance before he sat down under a tree. It had been almost twenty hours since they had started the hike. Coaldon promptly fell into a deep sleep. Tiny looked at Coaldon with sympathy. He was surprised Coaldon had walked this far after his ordeal in the mountain. After studying the area, he knew it was only a short distance to the boat. With firm hands and bulging muscle, Tiny easily tossed Coaldon's sleeping body over his shoulder and began the last leg of the journey.

The night was several hours old when Tiny arrived at their first campsite. Tiny gently laid Coaldon on the ground. After a brief examination of the area, he found everything was in good order. He could tell, by the water in the boat that a large wave had washed up onto the shore. He tipped the boat over, dumped out the water, and prepared for departure. With all the preparations completed, he decided to rest for several moments.

He thought, "Should I wait for Coaldon to wake-up before I set sail? During the day, I noticed many birds were fleeing toward the mainland. They must know something that I do not. Also, the number of earthquakes has increased over the past few hours. It would be best to leave now, but I remember the problems we had approaching the island. I do not want to face magic by myself. I must wake Coaldon."

Tiny gently nudged his companion but with no results. Then he resorted to pushes, cold water, and finally carried him around the beach. In spite of Tiny's efforts, Coaldon continued to sleep. Out of fear, he decided not to sail without the protection of his friend.

While waiting, Tiny built a fire to keep warm. He listened with apprehension to the rumbling of the earth. His anxiety was compounded when he felt the presence of something evil. He leapt to his feet, ready to fight any foe that might attack him. To his surprise, he saw a black-mist swaying back and forth over the fire. Tiny had the impression it was searching for him. Tiny remained still while the black-mist drifted toward him. He tried to run, but his body would not move. A finger from the mist reached out and touched his forehead.

Tiny's whole being screamed in revulsion as the mist encroached into his body. The mist began to rip away his consciousness and will power. He would be lost if he did not find a way to flee from the attack.

Coaldon erupted from slumber when he sensed the evil radiating from the black mist. Upon opening his eyes, he was horrified to see it penetrating into Tiny's body. He heard Tiny's panicked voice plead for help.

Coaldon exclaimed, "The black-mist is a spirit used by Crossmore to capture his opponents. You must resist it! I cannot help you with the sword without revealing the location of the Key of Ban, so listen carefully. Look inside yourself. Go to the very bottom of your soul. Do not look at your invader, but rather locate the Pool of Peace. Focus! Focus! Use all your strength to pull your attention away from your fears. Now, touch the quiet pond. Dip your fingers into the pool, drawing strength and courage from its eternal presence. See yourself being filled with holy power.

Now, command the black-mist to leave."

Paying close attention to Coaldon's instructions, Tiny carefully followed the directions. He found the Pool of Peace, touched it, and ordered the black-mist to leave. At first, the black-mist resisted the command with contemptuous arrogance. A struggle of wills developed between Tiny and the black-mist. Tiny focused his attention on the divine authority emanating from the Pool of Peace. He was not going to allow the poison of fear to control his life. Conquest, not failure, dominated his thoughts. With a mighty explosion of will-power, the large man rejected the foul corruption of the black-mist. To his relief, he saw the black-mist floating away into the darkness. This was a moment of supreme fulfillment and conquest for Tiny. At that moment, a new man was born.

In a burst of happiness, Tiny yelled, "It worked! It worked! It actually worked!"

He looked at Coaldon with sparkling eyes. He had confronted fear, disciplined his will, and successfully rejected evil.

Looking at Coaldon, Tiny commented, "Thank you for your help! I would have been lost without your intervention."

Coaldon sat up and looked around the campsite, "You are most welcome. I am glad I awoke when I did or you might be under the control of a new master. By the way how did we get here?"

Tiny responded, "You needed your beauty sleep, so I carried you."

Coaldon followed, "I awoke when I felt the black-mist. By now, Crossmore knows the Key of Ban has been found. He will do anything to stop it from reaching Topple. Crossmore will continue to search for us. He knows we are on or near the island. We must be careful. He is very dangerous. Ready or not, let's face the unknown trials of the ocean."

Large Waves

They hauled the boat down the beach and launched it without any problems. Tiny set the sails and adjusted the rudder while Coaldon carefully stored the supplies and equipment. Tiny found favorable winds and made steady progress toward Seamock. After several hours of comfortable sailing, both men began to feel secure and optimistic. After their dangerous adventure it was time to relax.

Of course, Coaldon should have known better. When people play with powerful magic they need to be ready to face the results. The two men soon learned their escape from the island did not end its influence over their lives.

As Coaldon basked in the warm morning sun, he felt a ripple pass through the water. He turned to look at the outline of the distant island with curious anticipation. He gasped in disbelief as the island suddenly rose into the air, collapsed into a cloud of dust, and disappeared from the horizon.

In an excited voice, Coaldon yelled, "The island collapsed into the sea. What will happen?"

With a grim expression on his face, Tiny looked at Coaldon and then at the empty horizon. Minutes before there was an island, now it was gone. The large man stared in disbelief. His mouth gaped open and his eyes glazed over with a blank stare. He awoke from his dazed condition when a deep, rumbling sound rocked the boat.

In a shaky voice, Tiny exclaimed, "Again, we are in trouble. A tidal wave has been created. We do not have much time to prepare for its arrival. We need to drop the sails, turn the boat into the wave, and secure everything in case we capsize. When the waves hit, I will control the rudder. You can help stabilize the craft."

Both men quickly prepared the boat for the impending rush of water.

As if the sea was anticipating the large waves, it became strangely quiet and calm. Then, on the eastern horizon, the top of a giant wave could be seen moving toward them. Coaldon gritted his teeth and held onto the side of the boat as the large wave towered over the small vessel.

The boat rode up the front face of the wave, as if the vessel was a small piece of drift wood weathering a large ocean storm. Tiny held the rudder with both hands to keep the craft directly in the face of the wave. Coaldon realized the boat would be destroyed if it ever turned sideways to the wave. Up and up the boat went, climbing the vertical face of the wave. It was so steep, Coaldon thought the boat was going to tip over backwards. He assumed things would improve once the boat reached the crest of the wave. The prince was horror-struck when they dropped off the backside of the wave like a rock falling off a cliff. Coaldon closed his eyes and held on as the boat rushed down the mountain of water. He opened his eyes to see another wave, though smaller, rushing to greet them.

The collapse of the island had created a series of waves that decreased in intensity. Up and down the boat gracefully rode over each crest.

Tiny had always been proud of his boat, but today validated the boat's superior design. He had worked years to plan and construct the vessel.

He commented to Coaldon, "When I get home, I am going to brag to my friends about this boat. They constantly teased me about the ugly boat I built."

With the waves pushing the boat, Tiny anticipated they would be home before night fall. Yet, something was bothering him that he could not identify.

Coaldon finally said to Tiny, "I do not understand why the waves have not receded. I can understand why the waves might continue for a short time, but why do the large swells keep coming?"

Tiny shrugged his shoulders, "I do not understand it myself. I guess the island did not go under with one big splash. Maybe it took some time for it to sink into the sea."

It was late afternoon when Tiny finally broke a long silence by saying, "I have noticed something very disturbing. If you look to the east and to the west, you will see calm seas. Large swells are only located around the boat. We have been heading in a southerly direction for most of the afternoon. We are probably far south of Seamock by now. I will use the rudder to turn the boat in a northwest direction."

Coaldon was in a passive state of acceptance, trusting that Tiny would steer the boat back to the farm. Coaldon had been so intense for the past few days, he enjoyed this time of quiet. He forgot about the island, Doomage, the Key of Ban, and the souls released from the mountain. Having completed the task of acquiring the Key of Ban, it was time to sit back and relax.

As the day moved into evening, Coaldon was lulled into a light sleep by the roll of the boat. This moment of peace was disturbed by a dream in which he saw many eyes looking at him. The eyes were not evil, but radiated caring and eager anticipation. Coaldon felt as if they were looking into his soul. He was afraid his weaknesses and failures would be revealed. As the eyes probed deeper, Coaldon tried to escape from their gaze. In an attempt to flee, the young prince literally leaped out of his dream into the water.

If Tiny had not grabbed him by his shirt, Coaldon would have jumped out of the boat. Tiny laughed as he plucked Coaldon out of the air and sat him back in the boat. Coaldon rested for a long time in a state of confusion. It seemed like an actual event. Where did the eyes come from? Why were they looking at him?

Tiny interrupted Coaldon's thoughts by saying, "All afternoon I have tried to turn the boat toward the northwest, but the waves just keep pushing us to the south. We are in the center of a pocket of waves surrounded by still water. I believe the waves are controlled by an unknown power. I do not like this! I want to go home! I do not want to be stranded in a strange and foreign land."

Coaldon looked in all directions to confirm Tiny's observation about the waves. To his dissatisfaction, Tiny was right. They were heading south under the control of a fate beyond their own control.

In a reflective voice, Coaldon stated, "We may want to go home, but it looks as if we are being invited to an unknown destiny. It is best to allow the waves to take us to our next port-of-call."

PART
2

Back at Rockham

In the early morning light, Noel stood in agonizing apprehension as Coaldon departed on his journey to Seamock with Topple and Pacer. She did not want to be separated from her brother after his near-death experience with the Trogs in the Sadden Mountains. With tears welling in her eyes, she watched as her brother disappeared into the distant haze of the forest.

Noel had little time to be miserable because she had to prepare for her own journey. Emperor Brad, Queen Ingrid, Starhood the Elf, Ripsnout the Dwarf, Brother Patrick the Monk, herself, and a patrol of dwarves were scheduled to leave for the Monastery of Toms the following morning.

The Monastery of Toms was a community of monks dedicated to spiritual growth and martial arts. The monastery was located in the central part of the Empire surrounded by the Wasteland, a barren region of deep canyons forming a concentric labyrinth of rings around the Monastery. This maze of ravines was so complex it was impossible to pass through without a map or guide. Many people died from starvation after becoming lost in the immense barrier. The Wasteland protected the monks from the corruption of the outside world.

Preparing for the trek to the Monastery was no simple task. Supplies had to be gathered, horses loaded, and personal belongings stowed. Under the cover of early morning darkness, the small group left the security of Rockham. The group's departure was made with little fanfare. The travelers did not want to draw the attention of Crossmore's spies.

The abrupt and unromantic exit from Rockham was the final event that thrust Noel into state of gloom. Her sheltered life in the Imperial Palace had not prepared her for the robust uncertainty of war and travel. She felt confused and disoriented by the rush of events.

As the journey began, Noel struggled between her desire for adventure and the need for stability. This conflict created feelings of irritation and frustration. It was not easy for Noel to leave Rockham and Coaldon without suffering the pains of separation and loss. Her traveling companions understood the source of her unhappiness and kept a respectful distance. Grandfather Brad had compassion for his granddaughter, yet realized it was time for her life to move on. The expedition to the Monastery was an important step in fulfilling the lofty goal of rescuing the Empire from the foul hands of Crossmore.

Noel's focus of attention was on her immediate anguish. She struggled to push away the uninvited mood, but was unsuccessful. For several hours, she was unaware of the passing sights and sounds of the journey. The surroundings were only a fuzzy background to her misery.

Then, mid-morning, her mood cracked when her senses were invaded by the song of several birds. The warble of the birds' voices penetrated her cloud of dejection like rays of sunshine. A glow of warmth touched her sadness with the infectious power of hope. The gorgeous song of the bird ate away at the darkness dominating her life. Small bits of healing pierced her consciousness, slowly opening her awareness to the immediate events. The sight of a deer, the sound of the wind through the trees, and the touch of a cool breeze gently stroked her being.

The cleansing of her spirit continued as the purifying power of nature seeped into her. Her down cast eyes rose from self-pity to the exquisiteness of life. Sunlight welcomed her with the warm caresses of peace. The disappearance of gloom from Noel's face was greeted with relief by her fellow travelers. The glow of her soft smile elevated the mood of her companions.

The end of the first day's journey was spent in a cove of trees next to the Slownic River. The towering mountains, of the Sadden Mountains to the north, were bathed in the orange light of the setting sun. The tranquility of the evening matched the reflective temperament of the traveler. After the evening meal, quiet conversation blended into the hush of the night.

An uneventful night awoke to bright sunshine. The travelers looked west over the vast hill country leading onto the grassy plains. Over many centuries, the hill country had been carved into broad gullies and rounded hill tops. Groves of trees, thickets of brush, and meadows blended into the intricate pattern of creation.

As the travelers plunged into the new surroundings, they were watchful, but not overly concerned about danger. The dwarf scouts led the group with a cautious eye for any unexpected dangers. They stayed away from hill tops and traveled under the canopy of trees. There was no use taking unnecessary risks.

Being people of rock and dirt, the dwarves refused to ride horses, but rather, choose to trot ahead of the horses. Being people of the earth, they wanted to draw strength from the earth by keeping their feet on solid ground. Plus, they wanted to have solid footing in case the company was attacked.

As the evening sun dropped into the western sky, the companions saw the wide expanse of the grasslands unfold before them. They beheld the grassy plains radiate an orange hue as the sun dropped low on the horizon. The orange yielded to pink and finally to purple.

The members of the troop stood in quiet reflection at the openness of the grasslands. The broad expanse of the landscape revealed itself with naked truth. The ability to hide was no longer available. Each person's anxiety increased as they observed the reality of their new vulnerability.

Brad was the first to respond, "I have been concerned about this part of the trip. When we cross the grasslands we can be seen from great distances. I suggest we travel by night. Let's take a short rest and continue the trek after sunset."

The encroachment of darkness announced the time for the group to depart. With stars as their guide, the small group ventured into the broad sea of grass. Even at night the prairie was alive with activities. The pulse of life did not slow down with the setting of the sun. Creatures of all sizes and shapes continued to respond to the call of life. The rhythm of the horses' plodding hooves was accompanied by the majestic concert of nature. In the Sanctuary of Night, the concert master and members of the orchestra produced beautiful music. The buzzing of insects, hooting of owls, rustling of rodents, barking foxes, and grunting of large animals, created a symphony of unusual character. The melody was escorted by a cool, refreshing night breeze.

The night passed quickly with no signs of danger. It was assumed the evasive action of traveling by night was enough to provide safe passage. The morning light revealed an isolated grove of trees on the horizon. Brad decided the trees would provide the needed shelter from searching eyes during the daylight hours. Upon arriving at the grove a day camp was setup, a quick meal consumed, and followed by a day of slumber.

On the Horizon

During the early evening, Ripsnout, who was on guard duty, awoke Brad from a deep sleep. In hushed words he whispered, "I hate to bother you, but I want you to see something."

Brad rolled over with a moan. Sleeping on the hard ground had cramped his body into bundles of achy muscles. In a laughing voice, he responded, "If I lay on the ground much longer I may never get up again."

Emperor Brad, grumbling about his sore muscles, followed Ripsnout to the edge of the tree line. The setting sun sharply contrasted the sky and earth on the eastern horizon. Ripsnout drew Brad's attention to a point illuminated by the boundary created between the earth and the rays of the evening sun. At first the Emperor did not see anything out of the ordinary. Then, with a gasp, he saw an unusual bump on the flat landscape. It was not a normal part of the prairie. He instantly knew they were not alone.

Brad lowered his head in frustration. In a firm voice he finally stated, "It looks like we have company. Why would anybody be traveling in this section of the grasslands? I anticipate the worst. I believe trogs are following us."

Brad invited Starhood to join them to gain his perspective of the new development. After a brief observation, the elf commented, "My elfin vision allows me to see for a great distance. I count about 25 trogs and several geks. They are trotting like the fires of hell are chasing them. This does not look good. I suggest we quickly break camp and make a hasty retreat."

The camp was aroused by Brad's alarming news. Little time was wasted before the group broke camp and set a rapid pace across the grasslands. After an arduous all night journey, the rising sun offered the opportunity to observe their surroundings. To everybody's dismay, the outline of their pursuers was more distinct. This meant great peril was fast approaching. It was time for the group to decide how to deal with the new threat.

Starhood stated, "At the enemies' present speed, they will catch us in about half a day. It looks as if we have only one choice. We must fight."

After Starhood finished his grim assessment, Brad declared, "So be it! No use wasting our breath on debate. We only have one question to answer, 'How do we fight the beasts on this flat landscape'?"

A serious expression drew across Ripsnout's face as he said, "Our experience of fighting the trogs has taught us that a surprise attack is the best strategy. Yet, how can we surprise them in this vast ocean of grass? We do not have anywhere to hide."

Noel suddenly squeaked in an excited voice. "We can only use what has been given to us! Grass! We can hide in the grass!"

Brad burst out laughing. "Yes, you are correct! Grass it must be! This is our only choice, but I have never attacked from such a hiding place. How do we conceal ourselves in the grass?"

Brother Patrick in a slow, confident voice responded, "The Warrior Monks have learned to fight in many unusual situations. I have a few ideas that might help. I suggest we travel for several more hours before we setup an ambush. The breaks, dropping into the Rolling River Basin, are only a short distance from here. The land will become more hilly and broken. This will offer the opportunity to find good hiding places."

Brad concluded, "Let's follow Brother Patrick's suggestion. I will leave to it our venerable friend to locate the right ambush site."

Using the quick-step march, the company rushed ahead. As Brother Patrick predicted, the flat land of the high prairie gave way to the low hills descending into the river basin. On the western horizon the dark outline of trees could be seen.

With a tone of despair in his voice, Starhood declared, "We only have several hours before the trogs overtake us. We make our plans now or we will pay the price."

Brad followed, "I have been thinking about what we should do. I suggest the warriors prepare the ambush while the remaining group, led by me, continues toward the river with the horses. We want our trail to continue as normal. If you properly hide yourselves, the trogs will not detect your ambush. Brother Patrick, do you have any particular location you want to set up the ambush?"

The monk looked with a critical eye toward a grassy meadow directly ahead of them.

He responded, "The grass in the broad bottom land is just right. We have room to spread out and can find adequate cover. Let's take a closer look."

Upon arriving in the meadow, Brother Patrick was all smiles.

He proclaimed, "This is a great location. We need to hurry if we are going to be ready."

In a firm voice Brad decreed, "I hate to divide the company, but it will be necessary. Starhood, Ingrid, Noel, and myself will take the horses and proceed toward the river. We will rendezvous on the Neverly Road north of the Village of Grandy. May the One Presence guide and protect each of us."

After Brad's group departed, Brother Patrick showed the warriors how to construct woven mats from the tall grass. Even though the woven covers were crudely constructed, they provided the needed camouflage. The covers looked like bunches of tangled weeds. The mats were large enough to cover each of the crouching bodies. Great care was taken not to trample the grass in the area of the ambush. Brother Patrick placed the warriors along the trail created by the passing horses. He made certain each attacker was carefully hidden. He assumed the trogs would be in such a hurry to catch the enemy that they would not look to the side.

It was not long before deep guttural shouts were heard in the distance. A sense of excitement could be detected in the voices of the trogs and geks. The object of their long journey was now close at hand. Their blood lust to kill increased with each step.

The regular rhythm of heavy feet approached the ambush site. The anxiety of the warriors increased when they heard the deep, raspy breathing of the trogs. Several loud shouts erupted from the passing group. The hidden warriors cringed in fear they had been discovered. To everyone's relief, the steady pace of the trogs continued.

Then, with a savage cry, Ripsnout signaled the beginning of the ambush. With sweaty hands and high emotions, the attackers rose from the grass in an explosive assault. The terrifying screams of the dwarves ripped panic through the hearts of the trogs. The beasts paused in a state of confusion. Before the Trogs could adequately defend themselves, the warriors struck with a coordinated assault. Many beasts fell under the wave of flashing swords.

Watching the carnage, the gek masters realized it was necessary to rally the disoriented trogs. With loud shouts, the gek masters formed the bewildered trogs into a tight defensive circle. In a precision counterattack, the trogs rushed the weakest dwarf position. The dwarves were caught unprepared. One dwarf was killed while several more were wounded. Once the trogs had broken through the dwarf offensive line, they ran in the direction they had just come. They did not stay and fight.

The dwarves were shaken by the quick and lethal assault by the trogs. With a loud shout, Brother Patrick declared, "After them! We do not want any of the beasts to escape. They will return and make our lives miserable!"

The dwarf archers were first to respond. They released a lethal cloud of arrows. Half of the beasts crumpled to the ground. While the archers attacked, the swiftest dwarves raced after the retreating trogs. The beasts, with long strides, easily out distanced their short legged pursuers. After a short run, it became apparent the dwarves could not catch the Trogs. Once the dwarf warriors ended their pursuit, the trogs stopped and remained just out of striking distance.

The warriors regrouped at the site of the battle. In a sad voice, Ripsnout moaned, "We have been successful, but we pay a terrible price. One person dead and several wounded. Even though we defeated the enemy, they will not give up. There is no use fretting; we need to catch up with our friends. We do not want to leave them unprotected."

Hoisting the dead and wounded on broad shoulders, the warriors set off at a rapid pace. After several hours of marching, the warriors approached the trees bordering Rolling River. The trogs made several attacks from the rear, but were soundly defeated. The few remaining beasts soon melted away into the tall grass.

Unfortunately, the warriors' eyes were so focused on their destination that they did not observe the surrounding area. The strain of battle reduced their vigilance. If the warriors had been more alert, they would have noticed the unusual motion of the grass. It was not until the movement was directly in front of them that they realized a new danger had arrived.

Ten large, ugly wolves leaped in front of the group. Their large heads had heavy eye ridges which dominated huge, circular eyes. The long, broad, wrinkled noses lent emphasis to their outsized mouths and large teeth. Broad foreheads were bordered by long pointed ears. These were not ordinary animals, but spirit wolves. These impure creatures were Crossmore's pets and attack dogs.

The beasts talked to each other in a series of howls and then spread out across the path of the travelers. The warriors heard the wolves' deep raspy breathing and smelled their foul odor. This was not the scent of nature, but the product of a corrupt existence. The spirit wolves snarled with deep growls while saliva dripped from their gnashing teeth.

In response to the new threat, the warriors formed offensive lines and advanced toward the beasts. When Ripsnout gave the command to attack, the dwarves rushed ahead. The spirit wolves did not fight, but retreated. When the warriors paused, the beasts stopped and faced the warriors. The attack and retreat continued over and over. The beasts were not interested in fighting the warriors.

Brother Patrick finally declared, "Let's stop playing this cat and mouse game. I get the feeling we are being delayed."

Ripsnout responded, "I do not understand the purpose of their strategy. Maybe you are right. Yet, why would they want to delay us?"

Brother Patrick continued, "Maybe the spirit wolves do not want us to catch up with the advanced party. I wonder if our companions are in danger. If so, then we must push ahead and hurry to their rescue."

The monk ordered, "Form your lines! Attack at quick march! Be ready for counter-attacks from all sides!"

Without fanfare or shouts the dwarves advanced at a fast pace. The wolves, just out of sword range, continued to lope ahead of the warriors. Out of frustration, Ripsnout ordered the soldiers to stop. The warriors then barraged the beasts with a shower of arrows. Five spirit beasts were destroyed before the remaining wolves disappeared into the tall grass. As the warriors continued their trek toward the river, the beasts began to lope along side the group. They came closer and closer, forcing the warriors to stop and confront the assault. After a spirit wolf was killed the remaining beasts dissolved into the grass. This touch and go tactic was repeated over and over. It forced the dwarves to slow their pace in order to protect themselves. The few remaining spirit wolves disappeared when a howl was heard in the distance. The warriors hurried toward the river to offer assistance to Brad and his companions.

Learning to Swim

With anger contorting her attractive face, Noel grudgingly left the warriors behind. She wanted to stay and fight, but out of respect for her grandfather, she honored his request to leave. While in Rockham, Noel had frequently attended weapons practice with the warriors to learn the basics skills of combat. During these practice sessions, the princess fed her youthful self-image by pretending to be a great fighter. Using her creative imagination, Noel often visualized herself leading attacks and winning battles against great odds. In her day dreams, she often visualized adoring crowds honoring her as a great warrior.

Yet, the reality of the moment, soon dominated Noel's emotions and fantasies. Motivated by a sense of urgency, the group traveled for many hours before arriving at the banks of Rolling River. Brad decided to rest the horses and eat before continuing the journey. As the sun dipped into the western sky, Grandmother Ingrid lit a fire and prepared their evening meal. While waiting, Noel decided to walk to the banks of the river and enjoy a few moments of quiet reflection. Sitting on a large rock, she became absorbed by the smells, sights, and sounds of the river. As a life long captive in the capital City of Neverly, she never had the opportunity to experience the joys of outdoor life. Even though trogs stalked the company, the escape to the river offered the refreshing aroma of freedom.

As she relished the beauty of the river, a cold chill passed through her body. The forest became deadly silent and an evil cloud flowed over her spirit. She heard her Grandfather give a shout of warning. Then a numbing sense of isolation struck her with paralyzing fear. The innate sense of closeness with her grandparents was severed. Panic gripped her. As she ran toward the encampment, she was confronted by five very large and ugly wolves. The beasts' penetrating eyes burned with hatred. With deep snarls and flashing teeth, they slowly approached her. Their powerful

muscles rippled in anticipation of attacking this helpless victim.

Noel stood in absolute fear of the terrible creatures. Then, out of the depths of her spirit, a power suddenly erupted. She felt a warm glow of confidence and strength possessing her body. Without thinking, she raised her hands, allowing a mysterious surge of energy to radiate from her. Unknown to her, she had inherited the elfin Gift of Resistance. She could freeze an enemies' advance by projecting this power toward them.

The spirit wolves stopped moving and looked at her with confused anger. They tried to move but were unable to advance. Noel realized this was only a temporary fix to a big problem. It took large amounts of energy to hold the creatures at bay. As her fatigue increased, the spirit wolves began to slowly move forward. She looked up and down the river to find a way to escape. The only direction she could go was into the water. Without any thought of danger, she turned and leaped into the river. This was a desperate act because she did not know how to swim.

The fast current of the river gripped her and dragged her down stream. She sank like a rock into the deep water. Opening her eyes, she saw murky-colored water surrounding her. The quietness of the liquid tomb sounded to her like the impending arrival of death. Facing the possibility of death, she felt the overwhelming desire to live. She desperately wanted to return to her family and friends.

In her mind, she cried, "Swim! Swim! You can Swim!"

Her lungs began to burn with the need for air. She had to do something or death would claim another victim. Then, with a fledgling attempt, she started to move her arms and kick her feet in a dog paddle. To her surprise, she moved to the surface of the river. When her head rose above the water, she took a big gulp of air. She once again sank, but resurfaced after vigorously paddling. It was not long before she was able to swim with awkward, primitive strokes. She got her orientation and began to flounder toward the opposite side of the river.

As she breathed in deep, gasping breaths, her muscles began to cramp with fatigue. She struggled to keep moving, but exhaustion finally took control. Her arms could no longer move, causing her to sink. Yet to her delight, her feet touched the bottom of the river. With concentrated effort, she walked through the shallow water. Upon reaching the opposite bank, she crawled upon the shore and collapsed into a deep sleep.

Noel lay on the bank of the river for several hours before the sound of voices brought her back into awareness. She listened carefully to determine the direction, distance, and nature of the voices. At first she hoped it was her grandparents, but soon realized the guttural, crude language came from people of lowly conduct.

She slowly rose to her hands and knees to get a better look at her surroundings. She was located in a large clearing on the bank of the river. The ground was covered with sand, small river rocks, and bunch grass. The young half-elf could not find a place to hide. The noise of the approaching group grew closer with each passing moment. Noel had to act now or she would be captured. For the second time that day, she plunged into the river. She remained close to the shore and floated downstream until she came to a backwater filled with cattails and reeds. The large clump of plants had a small, narrow channel leading into its center. Noel followed the passageway, and found a hiding place under the collapsed cattail stems.

She did not wait long before she heard the approaching sound of many feet.

A gruff voice declared, "We have been ordered to search the river bank for a dangerous elf. I am tired of your complaining. You are soldiers. Orders are orders. We will search this area and then head back to the village."

A voice responded, "I think we are wasting our time. I do not believe in elves, yet alone an elf hiding in the weeds. This search is ridiculous!"

A round of voices agreed with the comment.

There was a quick reply, "One more word of protest and I will use my sword to motivate you! Now start looking!"

Noel heard the group of soldiers spreading out over the area. Several soldiers walked past her hiding place, grumbling about being drafted into the army.

After a short pause, a dominate voice commanded, "Let's head back up river to the village. We can search on the way back."

A rousing cheer greeted the decree.

A hostile voice yelled, "I would rather search for elves at the Inn while drinking a cold tankard of ale!" Laugher and hoots erupted in response to the comment.

After the soldiers departed, Noel stayed hidden for a short period of time before deciding to return to dry land. It took several moments for her to push through the thick, gooey mud of the bog. She walked into the river to rinse off the sticky mud clinging to her clothes. While bathing herself, she noticed unusual bumps under her clothing. She pulled up her dress hem to investigate and found many leeches attached to her skin. The primitive creatures had long, slimy bodies with large oval mouths. With a scream of horror she fell to her knees, sobbing in uncontrollable spasms. She was all alone, chased by the enemy, had no food, and covered with hideous blood suckers. Her youthful idealism of being a great warrior was being tempered by the raw realities of life.

After a long, tearful cry, she felt the emotions of fear and anger drain from her body. She raised her head from dejection and made a firm resolution to deal with the tragedy. The young princess decided it would be a heroic act to just survive the challenges facing her.

She thought to herself, "What do I do now? First, I must deal with the leeches before I can take the next step. I could cut them off, but I might slice myself in the process. I wonder if I have some elfin power that would remove then? Maybe the answer is not to hate the worms, but to treat them as if they were friends."

So, with this idea in mind, she gently touched a leech and tried to push energy into the creatures. At first nothing happened, but then she felt a warm glow of power flow down her arm and into the leech. The creature gave a shiver, released its grip, and fell to the ground. Noel realized it would die if she did not return it to the water. So, with respect for life, she tossed the leech back into the swampy water. She removed the remaining creatures in the same manner.

Her body was covered with many red, irritated round wounds. At first, she was repulsed by the marks, but after some thought, she began to view them as badges-of-courage. If this was the price she had to pay to fulfill her destiny, then so be it. Rather than resent the wounds, she would treat them with pride. She viewed the sores as part of her initiation into a new life.

The Village

The pangs of hunger brought Noel back to the present moment. The call to take action was upon her. She could either make things happen or hide in fear.

With a sense of determination, she proclaimed loudly to the rocks, trees, and river, "I will not just sit here and do nothing! I will go to the village. I can contact Coaldon's friends."

With long strides she followed the path left by the soldiers. It took an hour to reach the outskirts of the town. Noel remembered Coaldon telling her about a deserted cabin located on the river, south of the village. In the fading light of day she walked along the river until she found the old river house. She pushed aside the weeds and brush blocking the door and entered the dilapidated building. Even though it was nothing more than a primitive shelter, it was a palace to her. The room was filled with several old wooden chairs, a table, and a trunk decorated with elfin runes.

The young woman remembered Coaldon talking about the Village of Grandy and his old friends Raff and Paggy. Raff was a large man who worked as a blacksmith. Paggy was an attractive young woman with a beautiful singing voice.

In addition, her brother talked fondly about Rosa and her parents, Dod and Doria. The family had moved to the village after their farm had been attacked by trogs. Coaldon seemed to have had a special interest in Rosa. Noel smiled at the thought of her brother having a secret girlfriend.

Noel debated what to do next. She was hungry, lonely, and tired. Yet, where would she find food and bed? She considered trying to find Paggy or Raff, but she had no idea where they lived. The other possibility was Dod, Doria, and Rosa. Coaldon had told her that they lived in a house on the river just west of the ferry. This sounded like the best choice. Yet, she could not enter the village dressed in her present clothes. She needed a robe and hood to cover her long hair. A hooded gown was acceptable night wear in the rural areas.

The young princess realized it would be difficult to find a robe in her present situation. A sense of despair clouded her mind as she considered her options. Then, she felt a strange premonition attracting her to the old trunk. With hesitant steps she approached it, all the time trusting her sense of intuition. As she touched the lid, a jolt of electricity nipped the tips of her fingers. Opening the lid, she was surprised to find an old, weathered garment lying on top. It was as if the trunk knew what she needed. With a sense of adventure, she put on the robe. She felt a mysterious sense of confidence wrap around her.

She thought to herself, "I may be hungry and alone, but I will find a meal and a warm bed. I was taught to trust in the power of the One Presence in times of great need. So, I will claim the authority of my faith."

With self-assurance, she walked out of the old cabin and into the night. Elfin night vision made it easy for her to navigate over the uneven ground and through the maze of trees. Beacons of light, radiating from houses, guided her toward the community. The village consisted of a cluster of stores and the random assortment of buildings. Houses were constructed from wood cut in a local saw mill. The houses were surrounded by out-buildings, small pastures, and large gardens. Tall oak trees spread their branches over the town like a protective shield. Broad dirt streets provided channels for residents to move throughout the community. Wooden sidewalks, in front of the stores, kept people out of the mud during wet weather. Rolling River flowed passed the town to the north. A ferry crossed the river on the northeast border of the village.

Noel stood on the outskirts of the village with an uneasy feeling. She knew she would be treated as a stranger in the tight-knit community. Outsiders were often viewed with antagonism by the local population. It would be necessary for her to play the role of a male because women would never be found on the streets after dark unless escorted by a man.

After some thought, she decided to construct a story to provide cover for her presence in the village. If stopped, she would claim to be a friend of Doria, Dod, and Rosa. If questioned, she knew enough about the family to tell a likely story. With a smug attitude, she threw her shoulders back, pulled the hood over her head, and walked into the village with long strides.

She nearly made it to the north side of the community before being confronted by a group of men. The three individuals were unshaven, wore dirty clothes, and moved with false boldness. Noel decided to approach the group with assertiveness. She walked directly toward them without hesitation.

Using a husky male voice, she declared, "Greetings, I have just arrived after a long trip from Neverly. I have traveled a long distance to visit friends. Would you please give me directions to the home of Dod, Doria and Rosa. I am anxious to find them."

A tall man crept forward to get a better look at her. She had the impression he was a snake slinking toward its next victim.

The surly man declared, “I am a royal Vigilante of Crossmore. I do not know you. You are not welcome here. Dangerous criminals have been seen in the area today. You might be one of them.”

Noel responded, “I am only a traveler looking for friends.”

The man yelled, “I do not believe you! Tell me something about your friends.”

Noel continued, “Last year they moved to the village from their farm. Dod and Doria are an older couple. Rosa is about my age.”

The unsavory man moved closer, saying, “I think we should place you under arrest for further investigation.”

In anger, Noel flashed, “I am a traveler looking for friends! I did not come here to be harassed by you! Now just tell me where I can find my friends!”

At this point, she gently projected the Gift of Resistance to push the vigilantes away from her. The men did not sense the power, but only felt uncomfortable being close to her.

The man finally decreed, “Move along! We will be watching you very closely. You can find your friends by following this street. They live at the end of the road. I do not want to see you again tonight.”

Without looking over her shoulder, Noel walked toward the river. When she arrived at the house there was a light in the front window. Several sharp raps on the door created a stir in the house and a woman peaked out the widow to investigate the visitor. The door slowly opened, outlining a large man with a black beard. He stood with his legs spread apart and a sword in his hand.

In a gruff voice he demanded, “Who are you? Why do you bother us at this late hour? Do not try anything or I will attack!”

Noel did not move, but only offered a gentle smile.

Then she stated, “I am a friend of Coaldon. May I please enter your home?”

At Coaldon’s name the expression on the man’s face changed from a scowl to a broad smile. The woman rushed to the door, saying, “Young man, please come in. You are most welcome.”

After Noel entered the house, everybody stood in a state of uncertainty. Rosa lingered at a distance, afraid to say anything. The mention of Coaldon’s name caused her to freeze in a glow of excitement.

Noel broke the silence by asking, “Are your names Dod, Doria, and Rosa?”

Dod replied, “Yes, we are. You look most familiar to me. Have we met before?

Throwing the hood off her head, Noel declared, “My name is Noel. I am not a he but a she. Coaldon is my twin brother. My grandparents are Brad and Ingrid. I need your help.”

Rosa was the first to reach Noel with an excited hug. Both young women bonded without saying a word. Their friendship was instantaneous. All her life Noel had prayed to have a special friend and to feel the warmth of caring parents. She melted into the arms of this wonderful family.

She was not alone in feeling the significance of the moment. A radiant glow of happiness filled the house. A meal was hastily made and a deluge of questions were directed at Noel. For the rest of the evening she shared information about her life of captivity, her rescue from Neverly, and the events leading up to her present situation. She explained that her grandparents were to rendezvous with the warriors north of the village. Noel ended her long presentation by stating her desire to meet Paggy and Raff.

After Noel finished her story, Dod stated, "That is one of saddest, yet exciting stories I have ever heard. I would not have thought it possible for such events to happen in the Empire. How did Crossmore ever gain such power? Oh well, we can discuss this later. Now, we must rest. I am sure tomorrow will offer you new challenges and opportunities. The vigilantes will either put you in jail or run you out of town. We can expect a visit from them tomorrow morning. We need to make plans before they arrive."

The Boathouse

As Noel lay in bed, she felt a satisfying blush of peace. Meeting Rosa was an extraordinary event. All her life she had been isolated from the general population of Neverly. Emperor Wastelow had not allowed her to meet young people her own age. She had never had a best friend. The excitement of meeting Rosa filled her with exhilaration. She wanted to stay in the village and be a part of her new-found family.

The first light of dawn did not bring the anticipated sense of comfort, but rather a cloud of despair. Noel erupted from her sleep with the sensation that something evil was looking for her. Her skin shivered in fear at the unidentified danger. She did not know what to do. Should she scream, hide, run, or seek help? Gaining control of her emotions, she dressed and woke Rosa. With a shaky voice, she whispered, "We are in great peril. Something foul is near the house. I must talk with your parents."

With cautious steps, the two girls moved through the house and woke Dod and Doria. After Noel explained what she felt, Dod carefully moved from window to window, looking for any sign of danger. The investigation did not reveal anything, yet Noel continued to experience the impending sensation of danger. The weight of an unknown presence covered her with a blanket of dread. Her thoughts became confused. Her stomach gagged in repulsion. Her body trembled in terror. She sagged on the floor, closed her eyes, and struggled to gain control of her emotions.

As the sun rose in the eastern sky, the sense of evil melted away. When the burden diminished, Noel looked at her hosts with a sagging face and sad eyes. All her youthful dreams of being a bold and gallant warrior had been challenged. The frightened princess realized she was not an island, but rather needed the support of friends and family. This sense of frailty was transformed into a humble acceptance of her limitations. As she sat on the floor holding her head, courage began to fill her with a sense of hope. She was frail, yet she would not allow herself to yield to the dark presence. With the grit of certainty, she vowed not to fail. Unpleasant memories of Crossmore only deepened her commitment to end his reign of evil.

Noel's hosts looked at her with compassion. They understood that she was confronting the rough side of life. As they watched, the young princess's face slowly changed from a frown of helplessness into a calm resolution of success. A smile crossed Dod's lips as he recognized that a conversion was taking place in Noel's life.

He stated to himself, "The future of the Empire is in good hands."

Raising her head from the empty pit of despair, Noel looked at her new friends, saying, "Now what do I do? Evil creatures are searching for me. How do I escape? Where do I go?"

With the warmth and caring of a father, Dod responded, "We could hide you somewhere, but then you would be trapped by the limits of your confinement. You could try to meet your grandparents on the North South Road, yet, you will need to use the ferry to cross the river. The vigilantes will be watching for you."

With alert eyes, Noel followed, "I must leave the village. You cannot be placed in danger by having me stay here. If I cross the river by the ferry, Crossmore's henchmen will know my location and I will be at their mercy. No, I need to find a different way to escape."

Rosa injected, "Maybe Raff and Paggy might be able to help you."

After some thought, Noel stated, "That is a good idea. I do not believe Crossmore's agents found me last night. Again, I ask the question, what will be my next step?"

Dod suggested, "You can hide in the old boathouse. We can have Raff and Paggy meet with you. They can communicate with us. We cannot go near your hiding place because the vigilantes will be watching us very closely."

Doria concluded, "We will give you a pack full of supplies. I suggest you leave from the back of the house, go to the river, and follow the trees to the west. Then, circle around the village and return south to the boathouse. You should leave immediately. We can not take the chance of the vigilantes finding you. Rosa will visit with Raff and Paggy this morning."

Preparations for Noel's departure were quickly completed. Her farewell was short but emotional. The time with her new family had been special. After hugs and mumbled words of best wishes, she hiked into the trees behind the house. The young princess had to control a surge of anger at being ripped from her new family. Yet, she knew anger would only limit her ability to survive. She needed to celebrate, not flounder in self pity. She would be reunited with them someday.

As Noel walked around the village, in the early morning light, she felt alone and vulnerable. She constantly looked over her shoulder to see if someone was following her. Upon arriving at the boat house, she scouted the area looking for anything suspicious. When Noel determined no one was observing her, she slipped into the old building. At first, she paced the floor constantly looking out the windows for signs of danger.

After several hours of tense anticipation, the power of nature finally offered a means of relief. The murmuring sound of the passing river muttered an invitation. The gurgling swish of water was soon joined by the chirping of birds and buzzing of insects. These voices soon dominated her attention. Walking to the waters edge, Noel found a doorway into a new relationship with life. Taking a seat in the lush grass, bordering the river, she allowed her elfin character to bond with the powers of creation. She had never sensed this depth of harmony with life. The mesmerizing hum of creation soon lulled the tired traveler into peaceful slumber.

Visitors

Noel slept soundly until she heard a noise. The sound drifted in and out of her dream-like consciousness without creating a response. She began to toss and turn as her mind struggled to recognize the sound. Through the dense fog of deep sleep, the young princess became vaguely aware of steps. Slowly it registered that someone was standing near her. Then, the memory of spirit wolves and trogs flashed into her sluggish mind.

She awoke, but lay perfectly still and kept her eyes closed.

The princess began to tremble in terror when she heard a rough male voice declare, "Who do we have here? Maybe this is a lost sheep that has strayed from the flock."

At the sound of the voice, Noel catapulted off the ground and started running. To her great surprise, she ran directly into what seemed to be a brick wall. The tall, powerful man grabbed her with giant arms. Kicking and fighting, she tried to escape. Even though she fought with all her strength, the strong arms did not let go. When Noel finally looked up she saw the happy, smiling face of a young man.

He declared, "Noel, you are safe with me. Relax! My name is Raff. Stop fighting. I did not mean to scare you."

The frightened young woman realized she was safe. She was with a friend.

After letting go, Raff laughed loudly. Of course, Noel did not find the situation funny.

She yelled, "What is so funny! You scared me! I thought I was going to die!"

Raff finally stopped laughing when Noel playfully punched him in the stomach.

The young blacksmith giggled, "My, you are a feisty one! I can tell that Coaldon is your brother. Noel, I want you to meet Paggy. She has been Coaldon's friend since childhood."

At this introduction, Noel realized that another person was standing at a distance. Turning, she saw an attractive young woman with black hair, a slender body, and a narrow face. Her gentle eyes greeted Noel with caring and kindness. Noel could not contain her emotions. With open arms and a broad smile, she hugged her new acquaintance with youthful enthusiasm.

Even though Noel was ecstatic about meeting Coaldon's friends, survival soon returned to her mind.

With steely eyes, a straight back, and a grim face, Noel declared, "I need your help! What did Rosa tell you about my situation?"

Raff responded, "It is so great to meet you. We did not know Coaldon had a sister, yet alone a twin sister. It is amazing how much you look and act like him. To answer your question, Rosa told us you had been attacked. She also indicated there is an evil creature stalking you. How can we help you?"

In a strong voice, Noel responded, "At this point, I do not know. It depends on the enemy. I was hoping to meet my grandparents north of here. I do not even know if they are still alive. They were attacked by spirit wolves."

With a curious expression on his face, Raff questioned, "What is a spirit wolf? I am confused."

Noel patiently described the events of the past few days. She gave a vivid description of the trogs, geks, and spirit wolves. She ended with an emotional narrative of her escape from the spirit wolves, learning to swim, and the encounter with leeches. When Noel finished the story, she noticed Raff's face was red and his body trembled in agitation.

Paggy responded, "This is a frightening story. I never imagined such creatures existed. What is your role in this adventure?"

Uncertain of what to say, Noel was slow to respond.

She finally stated, "The following information may seem unbelievable to you, but it is true. My grandfather Brad is the deposed ruler of the Empire. He lived in the Outlast for many years, hiding from Emperor Wastelow. My parents were killed in the Battle of Two Thrones when Coaldon and I were one year old. I was held captive in Neverly by Wastelow. Coaldon was raised in the Outlast by my grandparents. On Coaldon's 18th birthday, he was installed as heir to the throne. He is now recognized as Prince Coaldon. My grandfather is leading a rebellion to free the Empire from Crossmore's evil power. The spirit wolves, trogs, and geks are the wizard's soldiers."

Paggy could only stare at Noel with a gaping mouth and wide eyes. She finally sputtered, "This is astonishing! It does not seem possible that Coaldon is a prince and you a princess. I did not realize Crossmore used evil to control the Empire. To say the least, I am bewildered."

Raff jumped to his feet, threw his hands in the air, and started to pace around the beach. His body trembled with anger as he mumbled to himself. Numbness passed though his body as he struggled to control his temper.

Paggy stated, "Raff, settle down. It will do no good for you to lose your temper."

Paggy's words of wisdom filtered into Raff's mind in small doses. It took several moments for him to stop pacing. He looked at Paggy, then walked to the edge of the river and abruptly sat down.

In a hushed voice he stated, "It is difficult for me to hear this story and not get angry. Many people have and will die because of Crossmore's greed. Something must be done."

As the blacksmith stared into the churning water of the river, he became oblivious to his surroundings. He quivered as he felt a sense of destiny flow through his being. The young man realized that he had already experienced Noel and her story. The memories of a past dream paralleled the current events. He understood that this meeting with Noel was not just a chance event, but an act of fate.

An eerie shadow of foreboding drifted though his mind. He realized there was much more to Coaldon and Noel than met the eye. It became apparent to him that he would soon face a difficult choice. Raff looked at Paggy, then at Noel. Unbeknownst to him, his face was contorted in tense rows of wrinkles. The quiet routine of his life had been interrupted by the silhouette of a future filled with uncertainty and danger.

Raff mumbled, "I must do what is right. I cannot turn my back on the Empire or myself. I must let go and follow my destiny."

Noel and Paggy listened to Raff's unusual words with curiosity. They knew that he had made a major decision when his eyes cleared and his body relaxed. The young man would never be the same. He had been touched by the finger of a holy calling.

Enter Cackles

The group's attention shifted from Raff when they heard a squawking sound over their heads. Before anyone could speak, a large bird swooped out of the sky and landed on Noel's head. She gave a loud squeal of fright and stood perfectly still. Not knowing what to do, she slowly raised her hands to feel the bird's feathery legs.

The bird erupted into a screeching laughter as Noel touched him. In a shrieking voice, the bird yelled, "Stop tickling me! Stop! Stop!"

When Noel removed her hands, the strange visitor stopped its uncontrolled giggling.

With tears running down its face, the relieved bird shouted, "Thank you! Thank you! I am so ticklish!"

The bird lowered its head into an upside down position and looked directly into Noel's eyes. Raising its head and shifting its feet back and forth, the unusual creature gave a loud cackling call. The large bird had dark brown feathers with white tips on its wings and a head crested with a golden feathery crown. Its tattered feathers gave the impression of a long life. The bird's drooping exterior was sharply contrasted by its keen alertness. Its intelligent eyes looked at each person with piercing intensity.

Raff and Paggy could only stare in disbelief. They felt as if the bird could see through them. Their thoughts seemed to be vulnerable to the bird's penetrating gaze.

In a cackling voice the bird declared, "Noel, you have been difficult to find. I thought you had performed a disappearing act."

In frustration, Noel responded, "Would you please get off my head! You are heavy."

The bird spread its wings and landed on a tree branch above their heads. The sagging creature waited several moments before saying, "Maybe you are right. I have put on some weight over the winter. You know, living the good life. I guess it is time for me to go on a diet."

After the shock of the birds appearance, Raff questioned, "I do not believe my eyes. Are you real or just a figment of my imagination?"

With a pompous flip of its head, the indignant bird declared, "I am most certainly real! I am Cackles of Dumpford. It is my pleasure to join you today. There are times when the famous, meaning me, must join the common people, meaning you, to offer assistance. Noel, you and Coaldon have a lot in common. Both of you bubble with potential, but are such slow learners. My, oh my, both of you seem to stumble into such unique situations. It must run in the family. Oh yes, I must tell you that I am a very important bird. I am of noble birth and need to be honored with appropriate homage. So please refer to me as Lord Cackles. In this isolated area it is not necessary to bow or genuflect to me. We can bypass customary formalities."

The bird paused for several moments before continuing, "I know I have been sent to you for a reason, but what is it? My memory is not what it used to be. Am I supposed to tell you to wash your clothes? No, that is not it. Or, you are to stop chasing frogs! No, not right. Now I remember, Noel, you are in great danger. Trogs and spirit wolves are searching for you. Please be careful."

The bird glowed with conceit at the completion of the message.

Noel stared at the bird with a puzzled expression on her face. "I already knew this information. You are late in delivering the message. I remember Coaldon telling me about you. He said you helped him escape from the trogs."

With a look of arrogant contempt, the bird responded, "So, I am late! Well, I am most sorry for not meeting your high expectations. I guess I am just a failure. Oh, why do I keep trying? Maybe I should become a sheepherder."

The bird then hung its head, closed his eyes, and gave a loud mournful cry.

Noel knew she had been too abrupt and critical. Magee, her guardian, had taught her to always be kind and respectful. Rudeness never gained anything.

So, in a repentant voice, Noel stated, "Lord Cackles, I apologize for my rudeness. You need to be thanked, rather than criticized for your efforts."

Cackles peeked out from under half-open eye lids to make sure his act of grief had gained the appropriate results. Then with an abrupt change in mood, the old bird threw its head back and gazed at Raff and Paggy. Both young people backed away several steps under the intense gaze of the bird. They did not know if they had done something wrong.

Cackles ruffled his feathers and shifted into the condescending pose of a great lord. With stately dignity he cleared his voice in preparation for a grand announcement. The bird finally declared in an imposing tone, "Both of you have been called to serve the Empire. You are to leave Grandy with Noel tonight. Your destiny has been cast unless you wish to stand against the flow of history."

The bird ended this declaration with an arrogant toss of his beak and a cold look of authority.

Raff and Paggy could not believe what they had just seen and heard. In a state of confusion, the two friends stood in shock. Their minds struggled to comprehend a talking bird and the possibility of leaving the village. Both young adults looked at each other to make sure they were not dreaming. Their very normal day had been turned into a perplexing dilemma. Their mundane lives had been intersected by an extraordinary event. The common and ordinary had been replaced by the mysterious and intriguing.

In a quavering voice Paggy stated, "Lord Cackles, you must be mistaken. We are just simple people. There is nothing important we can do for the Empire. You must be looking for someone else, maybe a great warrior."

Without showing any sign of compassion, Cackles continued to stare at them.

Finally, the bird gave a robust laugh before stating, "Change is often difficult to accept. You have been preparing for many years to fulfill the demands of your future. Now, no more quibbling and hesitation! Hurry home, gather the needed supplies for a long journey, and return here after dark. Great danger is lurking nearby. The forces of evil are rapidly moving to capture Noel. Now go! Shoo!"

At the end of his commanding performance, Cackles leaped into the air, spread his wings, and flew toward the gaping young villagers. The two trembling individuals moved backwards with unstable steps, turned, and made a mad dash back to the village. No words could describe how they felt at that moment. Insecurity and excitement blended together to form a dynamic emotional state.

After the two villagers disappeared into the distance, Cackles landed on the ground and gave a humorous chuckle.

His eyes gleaming with mischief, he clarified, "Nobody in their right mind would dare follow you. I hope you are far from here before your new friends realize the consequences of their decision. By the way, how did I do? I enjoy giving orders."

Noel smiled at the strategy used by Cackles to convince Raff and Paggy to join her.

She answered, "Lord Cackles, you are most convincing. Your noble heritage was obvious."

Her expression changed when she thought about Cackle's statement. In a loud, anxious voice she questioned, "Why would they not want to go with me? What do you know that I do not?"

With sparkling eyes, the aloft bird chirped, "My, my, you are alert today. I was hoping you would not catch what I said. Let me explain a few things to you. Your grandparents and company honorably destroyed the attacking spirit wolves. They are presently rushing to escape the pursuit of a trog army. The group is heading toward the Monastery of Toms. Warrior monks will join them and defeat the enemy. In simple terms, you are now on your own. The northern countryside is crawling with trogs and spirit wolves. Yes, my dear, you find yourself in a difficult situation."

The somber young woman stared at the ground, shaking her head. "I was hoping my grandparents would be able to help me. I feel helpless."

The bird suddenly leapt into the air with a robust burst of energy. It spread its wings and flew into the sky. After making several loops it dove toward Noel and landed with flapping wings, screams, and commotion.

In a pompous voice, he declared, "Cackles to the rescue. Your famous neighborhood hero has arrived to save the damsel in distress. Never fear, I am here, offering my courageous assistance."

Noel's dejected mood collapsed in the face of Cackles' outlandish behavior. She erupted into spontaneous laughter. Then, with a twinkle in her eyes and her hands gripped in a begging position, Noel pleaded, "Oh, great one, I am a poor lost child needing your assistance. I turn to you for guidance and protection. Please help your lowly servant! Oh, please help me!"

Strutting across the ground with noble steps, the bird declared in a regal voice, "It is only through my great wisdom that I can offer the following advice. I recommend you and your trusted companions go south. The enemy will not anticipate such a bold and clever move. Follow the river until you come to Brags. You are to travel by night and remain hidden at all times. You must not allow anybody to see you. Wait in Brags for guidance. Also, the evil creature searching for you is Scaric. It is Crossmore's pet and a thing of the night. It flies through darkness like a mist, looking for its prey. Beware of the fiend's power to swallow you into its corruptive nature. Victims are no longer victims, but are dissolved into the shadow of its evil. So, with these encouraging words, go in peace, my child."

Cackles then flew into the darkening sky, trumpeting its departure with loud squawks.

Noel gazed at the bird with respect and appreciation. The eccentric character of the noble bird was entertaining and heart warming. In spite of lurking danger, she found comfort in having a path to follow and companions to share her burden.

OFF WE GO

Raff and Paggy spent the afternoon buying supplies, gathering equipment, and making last minute arrangements. They tried to restrain their excitement, but were not successful. Their glowing eyes and quick steps drew the attention of many people. The two young adult's actions fell outside the accepted standard of the village. Members of the community expected all citizens to act in a somber, subdued manner. Whispers could be heard in every corner of the village speculating the reason for their unusual behavior.

The villagers looked with great suspicion at anything outside the ordinary. The idea of leaving the security of the village was incomprehensible. Nobody in their right mind would ever leave. Paggy and Raff were aware of this attitude. Leaving the community unannounced would create a major disturbance. They might even be shunned for being rebels, malcontents, and mentally incompetent. This burden weighed heavily on their minds as darkness smothered the light of day. The call to fulfill their destiny was clouded by the fear of leaving all they had ever known. Once they departed, they might not be accepted back into the community. Walking out the door of their homes would be a giant leap of faith. The prospect of leaving was both exhilarating and frightening.

Raff and Paggy left short notes explaining that the reason for their departure was to help a friend. With heavy hearts and queasy stomachs they turned away from the village and walked to the river house.

Noel found it difficult to wait for the return of her two new companions. She was afraid they would remain in the village. The thought of being alone was terrifying. Her heart raced when she heard footsteps approaching the old building. She was greatly relieved when she saw the two familiar faces enter the door. Tears of joy filled her eyes. Noel realized her new friends were making a major sacrifice to join her.

She burst out, "I am so happy to see you. I was afraid you would not come back."

Paggy declared, "We could not let you down. We are meant to be together. So, what do we do now? I am anxious to get started. Oh, I talked with Rosa and told her about our plans. She was upset, but understood the reasons."

Noel responded, "I think we should leave immediately. It is best to travel at night to hide from searching eyes. Cackles said we were to go south to Brags."

With heavy packs, clear skies, and each other, the small expedition departed. Noel used her elfin night vision to lead the way into the unknown. The road south was full of pot holes and wagon ruts after a recent rain. In spite of the road's condition, the travelers made good progress.

It was not long after departing that the heavy packs began to tear at Noel and Paggy's weak shoulders. Being a blacksmith, Raff's powerful back easily carried the burden of the pack. At first, only infrequent complaints were issued from the two young women. Yet, as the hours passed, an outcry of pain and protest punctuated the still night. Several hours before sunrise, their discomfort became so intense that the travelers decided to stop. The glow of the adventure was soon tempered by the realities of physical limitations. A shelter was located and complaining bodies soon yielded to the need for sleep.

The hot afternoon sun awoke the group. Both Noel and Paggy groaned with pain when they tried to move. Their backs, shoulders, and necks were knots of stiff and sore muscles. Raff had to gently pull each young woman to her feet.

With a sly smile, Noel stated, "Paggy you look absolutely pathetic. You walk like an old lady."

At first Paggy was caught off-guard by the comment, but then realized just how pitiful she must appear. With a grand wave of her arm, she responded, "Woe is me. How can I possibly continue? I have been struck down in the prime of my life by such a heavy burden. I need the assistance of a strong back."

With a twinkle in her eye, Noel caught the jest of Paggy's comment. Looking at Raff, she hinted, "The weak and fragile need the help of a big, strong man. I wonder who that could be? Paggy do you have any idea whose strong back could assist us?"

While Noel and Paggy struggled to walk, Raff smiled with a smug sense of arrogance. He was proud of his strong body and the ability to carry a heavy load with little fatigue. He was so focused on his own self-glorification that he was slow to pick up on the conversation. Then, with a burst of awareness, he realized he was the center of the discussion. He looked at his companions with wary eyes.

He asked, "What are you talking about? Did I hear a tone of sarcasm in your voices?"

With an innocent look on her face, Paggy responded, "I do not know what you are talking about. My pack is too heavy for me to carry. I need your help."

Assuming the poise of a helpless child, Noel complained, "We are tired and sore. We need the help of a strong man."

At first, Raff puffed with pride at being praised for his strength, but then realized he was being manipulated by two playful young women.

Raff bowed and declared, "I offer my services to the delicate and physically inferior. I accept the burden of traveling with such fragile and frail creatures."

The girls' reaction was instantaneous and aggressive. With a scream of frustration, they ran toward Raff. The pain of their sore muscles did not limit their ability to take revenge. As Raff stepped back, he tripped and fell backward with a heavy bounce. This allowed his two opponents to jump on him with good-natured retaliation. He could have easily handled the two assailants, but chose to yield to the lighthearted encounter. The struggle ended when the three jovial contestants celebrated with hearty laughter.

With a broad smile, Raff proudly declared, "I will be happy to help you. I know you are not prepared to carry a heavy load. I can bear most of the weight of your packs until you are ready."

After eating a hasty meal and loading Raff's pack with additional supplies, the night's trek began. The extra weight on Raff's pack soon began to wear on this strength, but out of pride he did not complain. By traveling at night, the group did not meet any travelers. The distant sound of Rolling River was a constant comrade. The next three days passed without incident or concern.

ᚱᛏᚢᚹᛣ

BRAGS

It was early morning when the small group finally reached the ferry crossing the river to the City of Brags. This was the first time any of the travelers had visited Brags. The city was much larger than they had anticipated. It spread over the top of a low mound surrounded by thick, defensive walls. Black flags flew over the city in the morning breeze. A long, narrow road snaked up the side of the knoll to a large gate. Horse drawn wagons and people could be seen entering and leaving the city. A patchwork of orchards and farmland spread out in all directions from the walled city. Numerous farms were abandoned and choked with weeds. In a large, flat open area in front of the gate, idle crowds lingered. People moved with defeated, lethargic steps.

Noel was the first to speak, "I get the impression the city is infected with a disease. While living in Neverly, I saw how evil can suck the life out of a community. I have been looking forward to arriving at Brags, but now I am having second thoughts. I was hoping we would escape from the stain of Crossmore. No such luck."

Raff responded, "No matter our feelings, we are here. We must make the best of whatever we find. I suggest we spend the remainder of the day in the hills."

With a nod of approval, Noel answered, "I agree with you, but we must be careful. It is obvious to me Crossmore's disease has cursed the area."

As they set up camp, the excitement of arriving at Brags was soon replaced by the reality of their situation. They were trapped in a foreign land with a dangerous enemy lurking nearby. Crossmore's vigilantes and troops would be on the lookout for strangers, especially a half-elf. The need for secrecy was essential.

As the sun dropped into the western sky, the companions huddled around a warm fire. The quest to reach Brags had been replaced by quiet emptiness. A sense of loneliness dominated their thoughts. For many days the goal of reaching Brag had consumed their full attention. Now a void of purpose and direction filled their minds. The future stood before them like a black hole.

All three travelers looked into the flames of the fire with haggard faces and hunched bodies. This gloominess continued until Paggy decided it was time to intervene. In a soft, gentle voice she started to sing a popular folk tune. It was difficult for her to push aside her own feelings of despair, but it was not long before she was drawn into the enchanting melody. Closing her eyes, she allowed her spirit to flow freely in the rhythm of the song. The beauty of her voice filled the evening like the song of a nightingale. It was not long before Raff and Noel joined her in song. Even though Raff croaked like a frog and Noel sang off key, the three castaways found peace in the gift of music and each other.

The companions talked late into the night. Long after midnight, each traveler finally drifted into peaceful slumber. As the eastern sky hinted of the new day, Noel awoke with a feeling of dread. Her body constricted into bundles of tight muscles. She searched the area for any signs of danger. Her attention was soon drawn to a shadow slowly gliding overhead. The image of a large bird with long black wings was outlined by the light of the moon. A bone chilling scream cut through Noel with foreboding. She dropped to her knees and covered her ears. The sound filled her head with disorientation and a feeling of helplessness. The creature soared in wide circles high over their camp and then dove toward the city.

Raff and Paggy were awakened by the dreadful shriek. Raff erupted, "What was that?"

In a subdued, voice Noel answered, "Cackles told me about an evil creature that was searching for me. Its name is Scaric. It might have detected us and flown to Brags to report our location. If that is the case, we must leave without delay."

Raff reacted, "I agree, but where do we go? They will expect us to move away from Brags in order to escape. Maybe we should go in the opposite direction they would expect. I suggest we go toward Brags."

Paggy declared, "I would rather stay close to the river than wander lost in the wilderness."

Noel followed, "Paggy, that is a good idea. The river offers us a good escape route."

In great haste the group broke camp and walked to the river under the shelter of trees and heavy brush. The companions selected a hiding place next to the river and in view of the ferry. This location offered the group the ability to monitor the activities of the ferry. The light of dawn revealed singing birds, lush green foliage, and the rushing river. Noel felt a pang of guilt, thinking she might have over-reacted to the presence of Scaric. Her doubts were answered by the eruption of activity at the ferry. A column of soldiers rode the ferry crossed the river and marched toward the group's old camp site. The three escapees responded with both sighs of relief and anguish. The hope of a carefree journey had abruptly ended.

Raff was the first to speak, "It is amazing how fast things can change. At least we were not caught unaware. Where do we go from here? To make things worse, we are running low on food."

Noel's experience in dealing with dangerous situations helped her respond with a clear head.

In a confident voice, she stated, "Raff you need to go to Brags, buy food, and gather information. We have no choice."

With a hasty voice, Raff reacted, "I think that is a good idea. If I enter the city as a blacksmith looking for work, I will be able to move freely."

Raff grabbed his pack, walked in a wide circle around the area, and arrived at the ferry from the west. Upon reaching the ferry he was met by a slender, hunchback man with a scowling face. He greeted Raff with a look of contempt. The man's unhappiness was like an infection oozing with poison.

In a hostile voice he demanded, "What do you want!?"

Raff responded politely, "I am a blacksmith looking for work. I have just arrived from Grandy. I need to cross the river. By the way, why were the soldiers in such a hurry?"

The grumpy ferry attendant growled, "I hear there are dangerous rebels lurking in the forest. Get on the ferry while I am still in a good mood!"

Raff followed the directives of the unsavory man without question. After leaving the ferry, he promptly walked up the hill and entered the city without any problems. The area outside the gate was surrounded by beggars looking for a free meal. This wave of poverty did not end at the gate. Many dirty and hungry people lined the streets, punctuating an environment of misery. The large man began to visit different blacksmith shops to establish his cover. To his surprise, he was treated with hostility. Several times, Raff had to retreat to avoid a fight.

Finally, at the Iron Horse Blacksmith Shop, Raff stood his ground after being confronted by several employees. In a strong, authoritative voice he demanded, "Why are you angry with me? I have done nothing to you."

At this point, a large man entered the shop from an office in the back of the room. His round, clean shaven face glowed with a gentle smile and sparkling eyes. He looked at Raff with curiosity and a gleam of humor.

In a deep, husky voice the man stated, "I am the owner this business. If you must know, spies are constantly causing us problems. To protect ourselves, we do not deal with strangers. You might be a spy."

Raff was surprised at the openness and honesty of the large blacksmith.

The man continued, "I can tell you are a blacksmith by trade. Your skin has been tempered by the heat of a forge. Your rough hands, broad shoulders, quiet nature, and hard muscles tell me all about you. Yet, I get the impression you are not looking for a job."

Raff's mind choked in confusion at the man's insights and truthfulness. He tried to speak, but only a meaningless drivel of words stumbled from his mouth. His face blushed in three different shades of red at his inability to adequately respond. He could not control the embarrassment of being caught off guard. Raff decided it was best to escape from the shop before he said or did something stupid.

Turning, he made a hasty retreat from the shop. He had only walked a short distance before a giant hand grabbed his shoulder. Raff froze in fear. He was afraid he had been discovered by the local authorities. He lowered his head, believing he was under arrest. Should he run or face the person with the strong hand? The grip of the hand became so firm, he knew he could not escape without a major conflict. If he ran, he would be admitting guilt. Thinking quickly, the young blacksmith decided self-control and confidence were his best allies.

As Raff turned to confront the individual holding him, he said in a calm tone, "Why did you grab me? Is there a problem?"

To his surprise, he was facing the smiling blacksmith. The large man stated, "Cackles sends his regards. He said you would be coming our way. I have been on the look-out for you and your companions."

Raff could only stand in stunned silence.

He thought to himself, "Could this be a trap? Maybe, I should just play along with him."

Raff responded, "I do not know what you are talking about. I am a blacksmith looking for work."

The large man laughed, "I now know why you were chosen to accompany the princess. Please follow me before we attract the attention of the vigilantes."

Raff floated in a cloud of bewilderment as he accompanied the man. He always believed he could handle most situations in a casual manner. Now however, everything was flying out of control.

Raff thought, "I felt like a child looking for support from somebody strong and wise. I remember a Monk of Toms talking about yielding to the One Presence. Maybe, this is what he was talking about. When I need help, I can depend on divine providence to be of assistance to me."

The big man led Raff to a small room in the back of the blacksmith shop.

The shop owner looked at Raff for several moments before saying, "It is important for you to trust me. So let me share several things Cackles told me. First, you found Noel sleeping on the bank of the river near an old house in Grandy. Second, our friend Cackles landed on Noel's head. It is a little known fact that our distinguished and noble friend is very ticklish. Finally, this morning Scaric located your old camp site. An all out search for you is now underway."

In faltering words, Raff responded, "Only Cackles could have told you this information. I believe I can trust you. I am just a simple person who has lived a quiet life. I do not know why I was chosen to accompany Noel. I feel like a minnow swimming in a vast ocean. I am totally lost. I feel so small."

The big man laughed at Raf's honesty, "My name is Rosko. I am a close friend of Topple. I have been given the responsibility of helping you. It will be necessary for your group to venture into the swamps of the Southlands to complete your task. This will require courage and endurance. "

Raff interrupted, "How can we possibly survive?"

Rosko gazed at Raff, declaring, "It is not a matter of if, but how. You must be successful. In simple terms, you have an important task to complete. The people of the Empire are depending on you."

After a pause, he continued, "Return to your friends. Be strong and resourceful."

In an assertive manner, Raff declared, "I accept the challenge. I will follow your guidance."

Rosko smiled, saying "We do not have much time. Search parties are already scouring the countryside looking for you. Tonight you will need to escape. You must construct a raft to carry you down Rolling River. You are to go to the abandoned City of Mazz. You will be offered assistance along the way. You will have many obstacles to overcome. It is now time for you to go. Before you leave, I will give you enough provisions to get you to Mazz. May the One Presence bless you and your companions."

After giving Raff the supplies, Rosko escorted Raff to the door and shut it behind him. Raff had the cold sensation of being shoved out on his own. He knew it was up to him and his two friends to overcome challenges facing the group.

Down River

While Raff was in Brags, the two young women hid in the center of a dense thicket of brush. To pass the time of day, they shared stories from their lives.

Noel stated, "I spent most of my life in the palace with my guardians, Magee and Norbert. I was isolated in my chamber in the East Tower of the Palace. I was constantly surrounded by guards no matter where I went. Emperor Wastelow limited my contact with people to eliminate any possibility of escape. I spent many lonely hours wishing I had friends. Being the granddaughter of the beloved Emperor Brad, I was used as a pawn to enhance Wastelow's power. I hated being forced to attend grandiose royal events. The parade of pompous and arrogant people was difficult for me to tolerate."

Paggy gagged in disgust when Noel told of Crossmore's desire to marry her. The young villager cheered when Noel described how she escaped from Neverly. Noel finished by sharing the story of the war with the trogs and her arrival in Rockham. Paggy had a difficult time comprehending how Noel could have experienced so many events. In a trance of disbelief, Paggy gazed wide-eyed into empty space. She thought how exciting it would be to live a life of adventure.

Paggy was brought back to reality when Noel began to ask questions about her life. The young singer felt embarrassed in telling about her simple, quiet life in the village. Paggy told how she was able, as a child, to wander freely in the village. She talked about the excitement at discovering a big yellow bug, listening to the songs of beautiful birds, swimming in the river, playing house with her sisters, and attending school with friends. Noel was surprised to detect Paggy's unhappiness at living such a simple existence.

Noel responded, "You are very fortunate. I am jealous of you. You had the privilege of living a normal life, in a normal family, with normal friends, and in a normal village. I have always dreamed about living your life."

The two young women were so preoccupied by their conversation that they became oblivious to their surroundings. Noel was first to become aware of two human shadows cast in front of her. She gasped in horror. Her body became rigid and her eyes darted back and forth. She assumed they had been discovered by the soldiers. The only way they could escape was for her to use the Gift of Resistance. As Noel released the spell, she jumped to her feet, and pulled out a knife.

As she turned to face her opponent, she heard laughter.

A confident voice declared, "That spell will not work on us. Please put your knife away before somebody gets hurt. You have been negligent in protecting yourselves. You will need to do better in the future."

Noel was stunned to find two stately elves standing before her. Both individuals had tall, slender bodies. Their soft brown eyes were outlined by long faces and black shiny hair. They wore dark green pants and tan colored shirts. The clothes turned to different shades of green and brown to blend into the surroundings. Gazing into their eyes, Noel saw the image of her grandfather, Starhood, looking at her. She had to step back in order to allow the shock of the encounter to become real. It seemed to her the extra-ordinary was becoming ordinary.

The older elf stated, "It is my pleasure to greet you and your friend. I am Willowwalk and this is my companion Riverstone. I am your cousin. Your mother was my father's sister. We have been sent to help you."

Noel was quick to recover her wit. She was learning to adjust to her unpredictable new life.

In an energized voice, she proclaimed, "Nobody ever told me I had a cousin. I am so happy to meet you. I hope you have time to tell me about our family."

Willowwalk gave a deep bow, saying, "I am also honored to meet you. I have never had the privilege of meeting a princess. I will share the family history with you as we travel. I believe you will be impressed."

She exclaimed, "This is like a dream come true! I just hope I do not wake up and find myself back in Neverly."

Willowwalk smiled, "You are not dreaming, but we must hurry, or you might be returning to Neverly. Crossmore wants you for his bride. We have much to do before dark. A raft must be constructed to carry us down Rolling River. The craft needs to be completed before dark."

The two elves walked away with dignified and graceful strides. They began to cut the logs into sections and drag them to the river. During late afternoon the logs were strapped together with leather bindings. The raft was six square strides with a tarp hung over the center to provide protection from the sun and rain.

It was late evening when Raff arrived at the camp with a large bundle of supplies. In excited voices, Paggy told Raff about the arrival of the elves and the building of a raft. Raff glared at Paggy with a sarcastic grin.

Shaking his head, he declared, "Where did you come up with such a wild story? It is entertaining, but we have work to do. Elves no longer exist. No more silliness. We must build a raft before night fall. Soldiers are starting to search the area."

Raff lowered his pack, grabbed his axe, and prepared to start cutting trees. As he turned to begin work, he came face to face with the two elves. He could only stare in disbelief at the two individuals watching him.

He mumbled, "I wonder if I am capable of handling any more surprises. This is like a fairy tale come true. I am either going crazy or I have been invited to join an adventure beyond all imagination. Noel, what have you gotten me into?"

The two elves laughed with delight at Raff's confusion.

The older elf bowed and stated, "We are real, not a fairy tale. It is my pleasure to meet you. We can talk later. You are in great danger and we must depart immediately."

As the sun set, the two elves led the way to the raft, loaded supplies, assisted the companions aboard, and pushed the craft into the river. The two guides jumped onto the raft and used poles to guide it into the center of the river. It was not long before the raft was swept downstream. The tree-lined shore rushed by, leaving Brags far behind. The excitement of the escape soon mellowed into the quiet passage of time.

The three companions sat spellbound by the impression of living a fantasy. A dreamlike atmosphere was created by the passing shoreline, the churning water, the peculiar image of the elves, and the eerie chamber of night. The companions had the queasy feeling that their lives were racing out of control. The security of familiar places, people, and events had been ripped away. The disappearance of their past lives was replaced by the inevitability of an unknown tomorrow. Events were moving so quickly the companions needed to turn to each other to find stability.

The raft drifted freely down the river, sometimes turning, twisting, and pushing up against the banks. The night passed in silence. The elves spent most their time looking at the night sky. Their bodies shimmered with a warm glow as they absorbed energy from the distant stars. The two elves pointed in excitement at different locations in the heavens. At first, Noel's attention was focused on the two guides. Then, a strange sensation drew her eyes to the night sky. A bright star on the southern horizon captured her attention. As the young half-elf stared at it, she felt a surge of strength enter her body. The energy from the star filled her with a warm sense of peace and satisfaction. With a burst of understanding, she realized her elfin nature could gain power from the heavens. Never before had she been aware of this gift. Searching the sky, she discovered each star offered a unique presence. Each speck in the sky contributed a distinct musical tone to the formation of the grand melody. The music blended into intricate patterns of pulsing harmonies. The wavering melodies changed with the delicate interaction of creation. Noel's elfin temperament basked in the beauty of the star-song. She found her spirit weaving and dancing in the substance of the stars. The music soon lulled her into a quiet and peaceful sleep.

The dawn of a new day revealed that the landscape had changed from forested hills to open grasslands. The river continued to surge at a brisk pace. Then, over the course of the next few days, the river spread out and slowed to a sluggish flow. The elves had to push the raft with long poles through the still waters. The grasslands disappeared, replaced by swamps and patches of thick foliage. The air became hot and humid. Insects of all shapes and sizes swarmed around the raft. Some bugs bit the travelers, yet others formed dense clouds of irritation. The annoyance caused by the insects was compounded when a warm, misty rain started to fall. A veil of gloom covered the three escapees. As the humidity soaked the travelers' clothes, they lost track of time within the maze of the river channel. The elves steadily pushed the raft toward a desired destination.

As the long, lonely hours past, Willowwalk shared with Noel the family history. She eagerly held onto each word. The elf told of heroic leaders, peaceful lives, great magic, forest homes, and ugly wars. The lineage of her family could be traced back into the mists of time to the legendary Nightstar. The famous lord stepped out of the shadows of time to lead the elves from the Land of Hellennor. Willowwalk explained that the elves entered the history of mankind to reawaken a knowledge lost to the pursuit of self- glorification. The race of men had become consumed by greed and the quest for power. The noble standards of human creation had been lost to the desire for material pleasure. The elves had been called to guide the human race back to the Truth.

After a long presentation, Willowwalk concluded, "This elfin heritage is alive in you. You must search to find it. All your ancestors were commissioned to fulfill the same mission. You have been given a special assignment to help revive the honor of mankind."

Noel smiled at Willowwalk, saying, "Thank you for sharing the family history with me. Yesterday, I felt limited and narrow. Today, you have given me insight into myself. I am not just a person of the moment, but possess a history reaching back to the Land of Hellennor. I am more than just myself. I am a part of you and all my ancestors. I am a part of the past and the future."

Everyone listened to Willowwalk's story with interest. The magic of the elf's story was soon lost to the reality of a changing landscape. The small group continued to go deeper into the foreboding swamp. Tall, overhanging trees blocked the sun and provided a dense curtain to the outside world. It was not possible to see anything further than the thick undergrowth of brush, moss, and trees. Barks, howls, groans, and screams could be heard just beyond the screen of foliage.

The three companions grew anxious as they traveled deeper into the strange and imposing terrain.

It was midday when a large stone dock appeared on the west side of the waterway. It was covered with brush and tall grass. Skeletal hulls of rotting boats stuck out of the water next to a crumbling dock. This graveyard of the past offered an introduction to the decay of a lost civilization. It represented a page from a haunted history, cursed with the residue of a fallen people.

With long poles, the elves pushed the raft between two decaying ships and up against the old dock. With hesitant steps the three companions, carrying their packs, wearily stepped onto the stone platform. They immediately became aware of the foul odor of decay that permeated the air.

Joining the companions, the two elves looked at the three adventurers with sad, down cast eyes.

In a somber voice, Willowwalk said, "We can go no further with you. This land has been corrupted by man. It is the responsibility of humans to purify it. Here is a map to guide your steps. An ancient road goes from here, west through the swamps, and onward to the deserted City of Mazz. We offer you our blessings. Remember, you can survive this forbidden land by faith, courage, and cooperation.

The two elves bowed in respect, returned to the raft, and pushed the craft away from the docks. With steady strokes, the elves disappeared into the mist of the swamp.

Through the Fog

The three castaways stared in disbelief at the departing elves. They could not move, speak, or think. A spell of disillusionment froze their spirits. The reality of being deposited in this desolate location gripped them with fright. They were on their own, unable to depend on anybody else to make their decisions.

A drenching downpour of rain finally brought them back to reality.

Noel broke the silence, "We can stand here in a stupor, or find shelter. I believe common sense should rule over panic."

The initial shock of being isolated was soon replaced by the need for self-preservation. Drawing courage from each other, they searched the area. A small stone building, with a sagging wooden roof, was located at the end of the dock. Even though the building was unbearably hot and dirty, it offered an escape from the rain.

In a somber voice, Raff declared, "My old grandfather once told me that when things got tough, I could either hide or hike. In other words, we can either be paralyzed in doubt or accept the challenge. There is no better time to forge metal than when the fire is hot. I propose we start our journey as soon as possible."

In a firm tone, Paggy responded, "I agree, but we do not want to blindly rush ahead. I believe we need to wait until the rain stops before we do anything. Let's study the map and make a few plans. We will get into trouble if we get in a big hurry."

The young half-elf looked at her two companions with delight. Their initial shock of being isolated was being transformed into youthful enthusiasm for adventure. They were not sagging in defeat, but ready to push ahead.

After studying the map, the group sat in the rat-invested building with a growing sense of frustration. The old building was a good shelter, but it was too small for their energy and motivation. Youthful impatience soon demanded that the team begin their journey.

Noel declared, "We have a map! We have a path to follow! So, in spite of the rain, let's go! We still have several hours before dark."

Supporting each other's doubts and fears, they enthusiastically marched out of the building. The road to the west was a weed-choked path, blocked by small trees and brush. Raff decided to lead the way. He used his short sword to cut through the dense foliage. Progress was slow, but the three travelers were happy to be doing something productive.

Even though they walked with high heads and sure strides, the claustrophobic confinement of the dense jungle wore on them. The constant sound of unseen creatures in the underbrush dominated their thoughts. A rush of feet and the scream of a wounded animal filled their imaginations with unseen threats. After an hour of hiking, the rain stopped, but it was replaced by a soupy fog. They could only see a few steps in front of themselves. By early evening the dense brush receded, giving way to stagnate, smelly ponds.

As the last light of day gave way to approaching darkness, the travelers arrived at a collapsed bridge. The bridge had once spanned a waterway about twenty five strides wide. It would be necessary for them to cross this unexpected barrier.

Raff proclaimed, "I believe we should wait until tomorrow before going any further. We need to set up camp and eat before it gets too dark to see."

Even though the travelers were hungry, the depraved odor of the swamp limited their appetite. It was impossible to start a fire with the rain soaked wood, so the group ate a cold meal and sat in complete darkness.

The gloom of night was punctuated with the sounds of mysterious creatures. The travelers' imaginations began to create scenarios to match the night sounds. In Noel's mind, a deep, noisy growl created the vision of a huge, furry beast with a big mouth and sharp, gnashing teeth. For Raff, the loud, screeching cry of a bird created the image of a large, black, sinister creature flying overhead looking for humans to eat. Paggy visualized the noise of the churning swamp water to be a monster waiting to eat unwary creatures straying too close to the water.

Raff finally declared in a frustrated voice, "I am going to scare myself to death if I continue to fantasize about swamp sounds. Are either of you having the same problem?"

Paggy laughed as she responded, "We must be thinking along the same line. We have enough problems without creating our own monsters. Let's think positive thoughts."

Noel, trying to keep her mind free of negative thoughts, decided to watch fireflies buzzing around her head. This pleasant pastime was interrupted when a cold finger of hatred chilled her spirit. Closing her eyes, she saw two large, round eyes piercing the shadows of her mind. The yellow eyes had tiny black pupils that penetrated the swamp like a beacon. To Noel's alarm, the eyes stopped scanning and turned to gaze at her. In order to protect herself, she jerked her attention away from the searching eyes.

In a panicked voice she exclaimed, "I just saw eyes searching the swamp! It is not one of Crossmore's servants, but something different. I have the feeling that some foul creature rules this horrid place."

To everybody's misery, the night remained hot and humid. To add to the discomfort, clouds of insects swarmed across the swamp. The travelers swatted, slapped, and yelled in frustration at the unrelenting invaders. The unhappy victims tried to escape the insects by hiding under their sleeping blankets. Yet, the heat under the blanket became unbearable. It was not long before each traveler threw off their covers. After some experimentation, they found the best way to repel the relentless insects was to smear cooking lard on their bodies. With the grease protecting their skin, they soon fell asleep.

The Sin Monster

The morning greeted the group with more of the same: heat, humidity, rain, fog, and bugs. The first task of the day was to cross the water channel. The remains of the collapsed bridge protruded from the water like the skeleton of a large creature.

Raff's practical nature guided his eye to the foundation that had supported the old bridge.

He commented, "It looks like the bridge had been attacked. The large oaken beams of the abutments have been shattered. Only a powerful blow could have caused such damage."

Noel looked at Raff with great interest.

She responded, "If you are correct, I wonder if the bridge had been destroyed to block the road? My vision last night indicates a creature inhabits the marsh."

Paggy did not enter into the conversation between Noel and Raff, but rather, stood on the edge of the swamp, gazing into the water with a penetrating stare. It was as if her attention was being held in a trance by something in the pond. While fixated, the young woman began to probe the pool with a stick. The longer she looked, the closer she was drawn to the murky water. With her head bowed, she began to step into the pond.

She awoke from her spell, when Raff yelled, "Paggy, what are you doing? Are you all right?"

Stepping back, Paggy gave a scream of terror. In front of her, a giant head the size of a large boulder slowly rose out of the marsh. The head was round, with two large yellow eyes. A flat nose, with large nostrils, was located over a huge mouth that opened the full width of its face. Two ears, the size of a table top, flopped wildly up and down. The beast's leathery skin was the color of gray swamp slime. Two long human like arms, with three stubby fingers, slowly reach out of the water toward Paggy. Paggy was so petrified she was unable to move. When Raff saw Paggy was in danger, he made a diving tackle, forcing her to fall away from the creature. His powerful arms pulled her a safe distance from the creature.

The monster screamed in frustration at failing to catch its prey. The travelers covered their ears to protect them from the mournful shriek. The beast's massive body churned wildly in the water, as it raced through the bog. After releasing its rage, the monster calmly returned to the shore line in front of the three huddled spectators. It raised its ugly head above the water and examined the group.

The monster opened its mouth, revealing many rows of sharp, pointed teeth. Its black tongue licked its lips in nervous twitches.

In a deep, resonating voice, the creature declared, "Now, what do I have here? I have not seen humans or elves for many centuries."

By this time, Noel had regained her composure and was ready to talk with the creature.

She stated, "It is my honor to greet you. We are explorers traveling to the old City of Mazz. We come in peace. Please excuse us. We have a long distance to travel today."

The monster threw back its head and laughed with robust enthusiasm. "So you want to pass through my kingdom! My, you are funny. All living things within the swamp are mine. As your ruler, I do not give you permission to leave!"

Noel barked, "We are not your subjects! We are citizens of the Empire! Now let us pass!"

After several moments of reflection, the beast looked at the three captives with curiosity.

In a quiet voice it responded, "I feel your kindness. Your presence disturbs my thoughts. I am a creature created from the sins of humankind. The vile plague of evil committed by the ancient people of Mazz infected the Empire like a disease. The elves interceded by gathering the Sins of Mazz into a seething bundle. This black tar of immorality was then cast into a body. I was created. As you look at me, you see sin made manifest. I have killed, hated, and smashed in the fulfillment of my hideous creation."

The beast paused before continuing, "I both love and hate you for your virtues. I want you to lower yourself to my wicked state of selfishness. But at the same time, I want to elevate myself to your goodness. Over the centuries my evil nature has created its own human counterpart. In order for sin to have presence, it was necessary to establish its opposite character. I have slowly developed a sense of righteousness. In a mystical way, I have become human and formed a soul. Sometimes, I have the desire to do what is good. Other times, I am possessed by my wicked creation. Recently, I am no longer satisfied with my depraved life. After all these centuries, I desire to do what is right and find peace. Maybe you can help me gain freedom."

Without warning, the beast erupted with a change in personality. It lost its pensive appearance and raised its body straight out of the water. The top of its massive torso was supported by two deformed, frog-like legs. Its hostile yellow eyes seem to grow to the size of oak barrels. The monster towered over the helpless travelers. The beast's face grew into the image of iniquity. Laugher rolled out of its large mouth at the sight of the three tiny people cowering in fear.

The raving monster yelled, "Power! Power! I love my power. You are only spineless creatures. I will crush you with my awesome strength."

Even though Noel was trembling with fear, she found a hidden reserve of confidence and courage. She stepped toward the monster with an aura of authority.

She thrust the Gift of Resistance at the beast and commanded, "Stop! You are sin and hence have no authority over us. You only have power over us if we yield to you in fear and corruption."

Noel's words cut deeply into beast's mind. A look of doubt crossed the monsters face as it slowly sagged back into the water. Noel watched the beast's face twitch as it considered her words.

Throwing its head in frustration, it declared, "You are right. Righteousness has dominion over sin. I always thought I had absolute control over my kingdom. I now know you are more powerful than me. Being sin, I only look to myself to find guidance and fulfillment."

The creature slowly retreated from the shore and disappeared into the haze of the swamp.

In a relieved voice, Noel declared, "I am glad that is over. I do not know where those words came from. I felt as if somebody else was talking through me. Whoever it was, I extend my thanks."

Raff responded, "Noel, you were great. Thank you. I suggest we cross the channel before our new friend comes back looking for us."

In a weak voice, Paggy injected, "I have never been so scared. I want to get out of here. While I was poking the water with the stick, I discovered that the waterway is not deep. We might be able to walk across."

Raff did not hesitate to test the theory. Holding his pack high over his head, he walked into the dark, murky water. He discovered that the ground under the old bridge had a solid rock base. To the relief of the group, Raff crossed the channel without any problems. It was not long before the three travelers were on the opposite side and hiking down the narrow road. Even though it was still hot, humid, and oppressive, they did not complain. They were happy to be alive.

The roadway was covered with grass, thickets, and brush. In spite of these conditions, the travelers set a rapid pace for the remainder of the day. The swamp, on either side of the road, continued without end. Insects were a constant irritation.

The group stopped at the arrival of darkness. When their meal was completed, the exhausted travelers talked in quiet voices.

Raff stated, "I believe our new friend has decided to leave us alone."

Noel responded with a playful smile, "Oh, I do not think so. The creature has been challenged by our presence. I do not know how it will respond, but it will do something. The creature is frustrated and looking for answers."

At daylight the group was awakened by a terrifying scream. The ground shook and the creatures of the swamp became still. The companions heard the rush of the giant creature approaching through the water. In the morning light, the group saw a massive body racing toward them. The creature's mouth was open and continued to scream. Before the friends could move, the beast thrust itself on the road bed, landing several strides from their camp.

The ugly, slimy creature gasped in deep raspy breaths. Its eyes sagged with large bags of fatigue. Long lines of anguish drew its face into a grimace of apprehension.

It yelled, "I was afraid you had already escaped my kingdom. I do not want you to leave."

It looked directly at Noel, declaring, "The elves made me into this profane creation. You, therefore, being an elf, will release me from this horrible sickness. I want to find peace. I am ashamed of the evil that permeates my being. You may depart my kingdom as soon as I am free. I will wait for you to complete your task."

Noel's face turned pale; her eyes bulged; and her mouth dropped open. Her mind was numb with uncertainty.

With a desperate look on her face, she said to her friends, "How can I possibly free the monster from its captivity. It took the greatest elf lords in history to create the Sin Monster. I am only a simple half-elf with limited wisdom or power. What am I to do?"

She hung her head and began to cry. She mumbled, "This is just too much for me. This is impossible."

Paggy sat next to Noel and placed her arm around her shoulder.

In a soothing voice Paggy said, "Everything will be all right. There is an answer; we just need to find it."

After several minutes, Raff responded, "Willowwalk told us we would survive if we worked together. I trust him. He would not lie."

Noel raised her head revealing a face smeared with lard, covered with dirt, and streaked with tears.

In sobbing spasms, she whispered, "You are right. I can not allow despair to win. So, let's talk. What can we do to get ourselves out of this mess?"

A long silence allowed each person to consider ways to free the beast from sin. Every so often they looked at the beast lying in front of them. The monster did not move, but only stared at them with unblinking attention. There was no way to escape.

Having composed herself, Noel said, "I believe we have been given this challenge as part of our fate. The answer to the problem is waiting for us. We only have to find it. Let's look at the dilemma from a simple perspective. We must somehow free the beast from sin."

Raff did not know what to say. He looked at Paggy, waiting for her quick mind to find an answer. Paggy tilted her head to one side while she searched for an answer.

Then with a burst of insight, she declared, "Evil creates division, hurt, and anger. It would be my assumption that the monster represents the collective residue of greed and injustice."

Again a long silence allowed their thoughts to ferment.

Noel then responded, "A wise man once told me the best response to sin is forgiveness. Maybe we need to forgive the Sins of Mazz."

Paggy's back straightened as she looked wide-eyed at Noel.

She proclaimed, "You are right! Somehow the crimes against humankind must be forgiven before the monster can be freed."

Noel quickly followed, "Yes, clemency is the answer. I believe this is my burden and responsibility. Yet, how do I do it?"

Raff responded, "Sometimes we make things too complex. You need to assume the authority of your heritage and just do it."

Noel hesitated and then stated, "I guess there is only one way to find out if you are correct."

Noel stood, approached the beast, and bowed. The monster looked at her with amazement. Nobody had ever freely bowed to it.

Noel raised both arms in the air, declaring, "I understand the great weight you have carried all these years. I accept your humble plea to be set free. On behalf of all people of the Empire and the One Presence, I declare the sins of your creation forgiven. Go in peace."

At this statement, the creature gasped in pain. A black substance began to ooze out of its skin. As the amount of black substance increased, the body of the beast began to shrink. It was not long before only a pile of black tar remained. This unclean substance began to bubble and secrete a foul odor. The three adventurers stood in dread as the black mass began to flow toward them.

At this point, a small white bird appeared out of nowhere. It landed on top of the ugly, seething substance. It cocked its head to one side and examined the mass. The bird carefully scratched the surface to stir up the top layer. The delicate creature looked at Noel, raised its beak, and sang a beautiful song. After this benediction, the fragile bird began to eat the black substance with rapid pecks.

A strange lapse of memory quivered in the minds of the travelers, as they became mysteriously suspended in space and time. In a strange and eerie manner they saw the bright colors of goodness being assaulted by a cloud of darkness. As they watched, a black arm projected from the darkness and attacked the light of righteousness. The glorious colors of goodness began to flow into a void of gloom. To the horror of the friends, darkness soon consumed the realm of virtue. Hopelessness gripped their minds as the power of fear filled their hearts.

Then, a single firefly fluttered into the dark expanse. The flickering light of the tiny insect became a beacon of goodness, radiating from the vast emptiness. The blinking illumination of the firefly began to grow in size. At first, its glow was soft and warm and then intensified into a blinding light. With pulsing energy, the brightness began to eat the darkness. It was not long before the blackness had been consumed. The beautiful colors of goodness soon returned in glowing radiance. A healing power had washed away the foul presence of impurity.

A sudden shift in time allowed the three friends to return to the present moment. To their surprise, the black substance was gone, having yielded to a far greater power. The small white bird stood quietly grooming its feathers. The tiny creature looked at the travelers, nodded its head, and flew away.

In a reflective mood, Noel stated, "It seems that great power comes in small packages and simple actions."

SURPRISE PACKAGE

The departure of the healing-bird was followed by a deafening silence. Life, of all shapes and forms, sensed the lifting of the beast's curse. The shock of being freed from the monster's bondage was accepted with uncertain anticipation. As the shackles of bondage were discarded, a crescendo of excitement began to pulse through the surrounding canopy of life. An awakening filled the void of the monster's demise.

The foul smelling fog evaporated, having no source to maintain its presence. The skies cleared, revealing bright sunshine and blue heavens. The aura of corruption yielded to the cleansing power of nature. An eruption of energy suddenly blasted through the fading cloud of wickedness. Centuries of repression were replaced by the rush to fill the emptiness. A swell of exhilaration could be felt in the soil, air, and water.

The three adventurers watched as birds soared in the sky; small creatures scampered in unrestrained freedom; fish leaped wildly from the murky water; frogs hurled themselves, in explosive hops, across the path; and larger animals leaped in uninhibited elation. An upsurge of activity spread across the swamp like a flood. The eruption of life from the restraints of oppression was celebrated in the uniqueness of each creature.

Noel, Raff, and Paggy sat for a long time absorbed in the explosion of energy. It was noon when they decided it was time to continue the trek. The thrill of the morning was replaced by the desire to complete their mission. As the group stowed away supplies in their packs, a shrill cry came from the underbrush. The companions stared in the direction of the howl of distress. For the past several hours only the sounds of joy had permeated the marshes. Now a voice of agony invaded their senses.

The source of the noise came from thick brush about 20 strides up the road. Raff drew his blade and approached with caution. Noel and Paggy followed close behind. Pushing aside the undergrowth with his sword, he peered into the deep shadows. He gasped in shock when he saw the source of the cries. Raff signaled for his two companions to observe his discovery.

Noel looked into the brush, declaring, "Oh no! This is unbelievable!"

Paggy stated, "We cannot just stand here. We must do something."

Noel was the first to react. She stepped into the brush and dropped to her knees. She reached out and touched the tear stained face. The small, naked child looked at her with fear and apprehension. The little boy sprang to his feet and raced away. Noel was quicker than the child, grabbing him by his shoulders, and pulling him into her arms. The child fought Noel's clinched arms until he realized there was no way to escape. He screamed for several moments, but soon yielded to the tender caress of Noel's arms. The boy slowly raised his head and stared into her face with curiosity. The contact of their eyes locked them into an instant bond of intimacy. His eyes softened as the grip of fear melted from his face. The boy lowered his head onto Noel's shoulder and dropped into a sound sleep.

The three spellbound companions could only look at each in bewilderment. Noel gently rocked the child back and forth. Paggy stared at the boy with a growing sense of caring and concern. Raff could only shake his head in frustration. He did not know what to do with a child in the middle of a large swamp.

Paggy commented, "He looked so frightened."

In a quiet voice, Noel questioned, "How did he get here? How old is he? Does he have a name? Where are his parents?"

Raff injected, "Now what do we do? How can we possibly take care of him?"

Paggy's reaction was instantaneous and abrupt, "What are you talking about? He needs us. We have no choice but to take care of him."

Raff knew he had said the wrong thing. He stepped back and allowed the mothering instincts of his two companions to lead the way. Wisdom told him he had stirred up a hornet's nest of sentiment.

Paggy continued, "I brought a sewing kit and have an old cotton dress. I can make him pants and shirt. I will get started right now. Noel, I think it is best you continue to hold him. He needs your reassurance."

Paggy's swift hands quickly cut and sewed the cloth into rough clothing.

Noel kept looking at the child with wonderment. Never before had she felt such a strong desire to nurture and protect a human life.

She commented, "I think he is about 6 or 7 years old. How did he ever end up in this swamp?"

Raff responded, "I believe there is only one possibility. He must be the human remains of the Sin Monster. After the beast was freed, its humanity took the form of a child."

Paggy followed, "If this is true, he has no parents. I guess this means we have become his parents. This is a big responsibility."

The sound of the conversation caused the little boy to stir. With sleepy eyes he looked at all three companions.

He then grabbed Noel around the neck, saying, "Mama, where are we? I am confused. Please do not leave me again. I was so scared."

At first, Noel froze in shock. She could only look at the young boy with blank eyes. It took several moments before the boy's words register in her perplexed mind. Finally, she grasped the unique circumstances in which she found herself.

Looking at her friends, she stated, "Oh my! This is unreal! I do not understand what is happening to me."

Then it occurred to her that she was facing her destiny. This was not a factor of choice, but a reality imposed on her. She knew without a doubt that she had truly become the boy's mother. To deny the boy would be to deny herself.

Honoring the truth of the boy's existence, she said to him, "Will you please tell my friends your age and name."

The boy peeked at Raff and Paggy from the shelter of Noel's chest and smiled. He looked up into Noel's face with an expression of absolute trust and comfort. Shifting his attention back to the two villagers, he took a deep breath.

Holding up five fingers, he said in a robust voice, "I am five years old. My birthday is next month. My name is Dregory."

He paused to make sure everybody was listening before continuing, "I want to have a birthday party. You can be my guests. It will be such fun!"

With a wiggle, Dregory escaped from Noel's arms. He stood with a straight back, a high head, and alert eyes. He saw the clothes Paggy had made. He looked at Paggy and questioned, "Are these my clothes? I must have left them in the brush. I am glad you found them."

Without hesitation, he put on the clothes, and began to explore around the camp site. He looked into each pack with curiosity. Seeing packets of food, he suddenly became aware of his appetite.

He proclaimed with youthful innocence, "I am hungry. What's for dinner?"

This request broke the ice of the spellbound group. With a rush of activities, the companions accepted Dregory as their ward without further thought or concern. He had been adopted as a part of the group. For the remainder of the day, the travelers lingered in camp and became familiar with their newest member.

After a restful night, the travelers returned to their journey through the swamp. Dregory raced ahead of the group with excitement and curiosity. The discovery of a large yellow bug, the sound of a bull frog, the sight of a blue-necked crane, the touch of a grasshopper, and the smell of wild flowers were events requiring his investigation. At first, the interruptions were irritating, but the adults soon adjusted. The enjoyment of watching Dregory's enthusiasm outweighed any other concerns. His broad smile and bright eyes helped time pass quickly. Moments passed into days as the little group bonded into a family.

Mighty Words

Noel found it easy to become mother to the loving and respectful orphan. The youngster was in perpetual motion. The gifts of nature offered him a constant series of events and objects to keep him occupied. He eagerly bounded from activity to activity until exhaustion forced him to sleep. Paggy and Raff soon became his aunt and uncle. Dregory's broad smile and warm personality were a joy for the three companions.

* * *

Yet, the mood was quite different in Neverly, the capital of the Empire. Crossmore the Wizard impatiently prowled the floor of his chamber at the top of the West Tower. His flowing black, silken robe floated behind him as he vigorously paced back and forth. His tall, lean body twitched in spasms of frustration. Lines of stress bordered his eloquently shaped beard. His hunched shoulders and bowed head were in contrast to his usual stately decorum. He no longer strutted with arrogance, but brooded in anguish. Shadows of doubt were tainting the Emperor with dark moments of depression. Crossmore felt he was losing control; the forces of the rebellion were working freely against him. His lack of control was creating growing anxiety.

From his chamber he could see the East Tower. This had been Noel's prison before she had been rescued by Coaldon, her brother. A flash of anger ripped through him at the thought of losing the young woman.

He mumbled to himself, "I will get her back. I will marry her. Her strong will needs to be tamed by my gentle hands. Ha! Ha! Ha! I will make her pay for rejecting me. She will learn to love me. Ha! Ha!"

Crossmore's mind drifted to the recent events. Information had come to him about unusual events happening in Seamock, the Island of Death, Brags, and the Swamp of Grief.

In a whisper, he speculated, "I believe it was Coaldon who was seen in Seamock. He must have gone to the island to find the Key of Ban. Without any doubt, the destruction of the Island of Death was caused by the magic in the Key. If I am not mistaken, Coaldon has the Key of Ban. Yet, where is he? I must find him. I want the Key and its magic."

He then shifted his thoughts to the news coming from the southern Empire.

With growing irritation, he continued his self-dialogue, "The bungling fools allowed Brad, Ingrid, and Starhood to escape to the Monastery of Toms. They will pay for this failure. How did Noel escape from the Village of Grandy and end up in Brags? I believe there is a relationship between Noel's escape and the destruction of the Sin Monster. I must send Scaric to investigate the events in the swamp. I have spent enough time thinking about my problems. I need to return to my daily routine as Emperor. I must maintain my image as a great and terrible ruler. Ah! Ah! Hatred and fear are the tools of my power. I take such pleasure in seeing the citizens cower to me."

Crossmore left the tower in a foul mood. The burden of fighting the war against his enemies was turning out to be more demanding than he had anticipated. He was irritated because the rebellion was pulling him away from his life of luxury.

* * *

Back in the Swamp of Grief, Noel and her companions journeyed through the bog for several days without any change in the landscape. The small group was relieved when the swamp finally gave way to open areas of grass, brush, and trees interspersed with large marshes. Flocks of birds, of all shapes and sizes, filled the skies. The noise of the screeching and squawking birds was a constant backdrop. Furry creatures, of differing descriptions, flourished on the abundance of the land.

It was easy for the travelers to become preoccupied by their daily routine and the beauty of nature. Pleasant hours of companionship melted into a diminishing concern for danger.

Noel found it a full time job keeping track of her new ward. The young boy's uninhibited sense of adventure constantly put him in danger. Snakes, spiders, and giant insects were targets of his curiosity. She had to continually keep him out of trouble.

On the eighth day after entering the swamp, the group stopped at the junction of several roads. They did not know which route to take. While Paggy and Raff studied the map, Noel prepared the evening meal. Dregory wandered off into the tall grass to chase frogs.

* * *

Meanwhile in Brags, Scaric sat on a perch in a tower on the east wall of the city. Its long bat-like wings were wrapped tightly around its black body. Two pointed ears crowned a round head dominated by two beady red eyes and a large mouth. The down turned facial features formed into a constant scowl. The creature's hairless

head was large compared to the rest of its body. Its spear shaped tongue licked its face with repetitive flicks. Its long, leathery wings had huge, sharp claws at the ends. These weapons had ripped the life from many victims. From evil it was created and in evil it found fulfillment.

Even though the beast appeared to be relaxed, tension boiled through its body. The creature had been created to seek and destroy the enemy. Its heightened scent of smell made it a lethal bloodhound. Recently, Scaric found Noel's scent in a boathouse near the Village of Grandy. Her trail led to Brags and then disappeared. This dead end caused impatience to permeate through the beast's whole body. It was a creature that relished the chase and capture of its victims.

Scaric waited in frustration for Crossmore's visit. The beast was relieved when the image of its master suddenly appeared in the room.

The creature growled, "I have been waiting for you. My hunger for human flesh grows by the moment. I await your command."

Crossmore laughed, "Oh, it is good to see that you are hungry. Your annoyance makes me feel good. Remember, if you find Noel you must not harm her. She is mine. You may keep the others for your own pleasure."

Scaric reacted, "Let's get started. I followed Noel's scent to the river and then it disappeared. I found the foul odor of elves in the area. They probably helped her escape."

Crossmore could not help smiling at Scaric's determination. The beast was like a son to him. He had groomed his cherished subordinate to relish the blood of conquest. With admiring eyes, Crossmore stated, "I have detected a shift in the balance of power in the Swamps of Grief. Find out what has happened to the Sin Monster. If you find Noel, be gentle with her. She is precious to me. I want the pleasure of bending her to my will. Ha! Ha! Now, go with my blessing of death and violence."

With a leap of excitement, the black beast burst from its hiding place into the chilly night air. With the rapid beating of its large wings it followed the river south to the swamps. At midday, it landed at the old docks leading to Mazz. It shrieked in triumph when it found Noel's scent. It hopped up and down on its scrawny legs anticipating the rewards of capturing its next victims.

It proclaimed, "Now, it is simple. The end of my quest is near. Their escape is now futile. Oh, I will relish the sight of my victims cowering in my presence. Their fear will feed my hunger for power."

Scaric flew into the sky with a sadistic smile on its ugly face.

* * *

Noel, Raff, and Paggy had no warning. It all happened so fast that they could not defend themselves. Out of the sky, a black creature suddenly descended onto their small campsite. The three companions could only stand and watch as the bat-like creature landed in front of them. Running away would be useless on the open expanse of the marshes. The large beast spread out its large wings as a show of arrogance. In a slow, deliberate manner, it carefully folded its wings next to his body. The creature's small, red eyes looked at its captives with a piercing intensity. In excitement, the beast opened and closed its large mouth, revealing a cavernous space lined with many pointed teeth. With a smirk of contempt, the beast grinned in sweet satisfaction at finding its prey. Stepping forward in haughty strides, it flexed its rippling muscles in a show of conceit. The display of strength had its desired effect. The three friends cringed in fear at the vicious creature.

This brought deep, rumbling laugher from the creature.

He bellowed, "I am Scaric the Grand. I have been sent to capture you. Noel, you will return to Neverly. Your two friends will be my playthings. This is such a special day for me. The chase is fun, but the capture is ecstasy."

Angry words burst from Noel's lips, "Leave us alone! We have done nothing to you! Go back to Crossmore where you belong!"

Scaric's response was instantaneous. With a broad sweep of a wing it knocked the three prisoners to the ground. With bloodied faces and aching bodies, the companions looked at the beast with renewed respect. The creature then reached forward with a clawed wing, grabbed Paggy around the neck, and lifted her high into the air. The young woman gave several loud gasps for breath before passing out. Scaric laughed with delight as it threw Paggy on the ground. The beast showed only contempt for the humans.

Raff could not contain himself. He grabbed his sword and rushed at the creature with uncontrolled rage. Before he could take two steps, Scaric struck him a glancing blow with the other wing. Raff fell unconscious to the ground.

Noel knew she could do nothing to escape from the beast. She only hung her head in submission to Scaric and her return to Neverly.

Scaric bowed, commenting, "My dear, Crossmore sends his regards. He awaits your return. I will not harm you. You will be my queen."

Noel looked at the beast with anger and defiance.

She proclaimed, "You may capture my body, but you cannot control my spirit!"

While all this was taking place, Dregory watched from his hiding place in the brush. The boy was horrified to see the attack on his mother, aunt, and uncle. A swell of anger erupted in his small body. As the emotional rage increased, the small child drifted into a trance. All his senses became muted at the sight of his family being assaulted.

Unknown to anybody, a lingering presence of the Sin Monster still resided in Dregory. Over centuries of being held captive by sin, the monster had created a pool of goodness that had been transferred to the small boy to protect him from evil. The good side of the monster had wanted his human life to live and prosper.

Scaric's violence against Noel, Paggy, and Raff opened a hidden door in the boy's mind, accessing this turbulent power. Churning within the boy's body was the desire to strike back at evil. A pool of repressed energy thirsted for retribution.

With this power dominating Dregory's body, the boy stepped out of the grass and faced Scaric.

Noel screamed, "Dregory, go hide! This creature will hurt you!"

In a nonchalant manner, the boy looked at Noel and then at the beast.

Scaric laughed, saying, "Now what do we have here? I know, a small boy. Yes, you will be just right for my afternoon snack. Ha! Ha!"

The small child did not move. He only stared at the beast with hostility and contempt. Scaric paused with uncertainty when Dregory did not react in fear. In order to establish its authority, it reached out to grab the child with a claw. The beast abruptly stopped when a booming, resonating voice projected from the boy's small mouth.

The voice rumbled, "Scaric, you have terrorized your last victim."

The beast laughed at the unusual event of hearing a deep, loud voice coming from the mouth of a small child.

Scaric responded, "You humor me with your grandiose threats. A mere child is no challenge to my awesome power!"

Again, Scaric extended a wing to grab the boy. As the claw reached the child's neck, the boy opened its mouth and spoke mighty words. The words roared and growled with such force that the beast was knocked to the ground. Scaric rebounded to its feet and leaped at the child. With saliva foaming from its mouth, its claws reached for Dregory's heart.

As the beast flew through the air, the boy spoke more mighty words in a deafening, thunderous voice. When the blast of the words hit Scaric, the beast screamed in pain and dissolved into a yellow mist. Scaric was no more.

Noel watched the display of power in disbelief. She questioned how such power could emit from a gentle child. As Scaric disappeared, she felt the power of Dregory's voice lift her off the ground and throw her many strides away. After hitting the ground, she remembered nothing until a hand touched her. Opening her eyes, Noel looked up to see Dregory.

With a worried expression on his face, he asked, "Are you all right, mama? What happened? I do not remember anything."

Noel looked at him and smiled, "Everything is all right. The foul creature has been destroyed."

Noel thought to herself, "The source of the power in Dregory must have come from the remains of the Sin Monster. I hope it will not infect him with evil."

As Noel sat up, she saw Raff and Paggy nursing their bumps, scratches, and bruises.

She said to them, "That was close. I thought we were done for."

Paggy asked, "What happened to Scaric?"

Noel answered, "I think it best we never talk about it. It is over and should remain a mystery."

She looked at her son, stating, "I want to change your name from Dregory to Dreg. I think it fits your new life."

The boy grinned, saying, "I like my new name. Mom, would you please make dinner? I am hungry."

PART 3

Coaldon and the Unexpected Guest

The waves kept pushing the boat south throughout the night and into the next morning. Tiny was the first to spot the faint outline of land to the west. Both men were happy to see landfall even if they did not know their location. Birds soared overhead on their perpetual search for food. Squawking seagulls drew Coaldon's attention to a flock feeding on a school of fish near the boat. The birds swooping over the boat were focused on their next meal, not the two men sitting in the vessel.

As the sight of land grew on the horizon, the mysterious waves decreased in size. By late afternoon the rhythm of the waves died away to an uncomfortable stillness. The setting sun, shining through scattered clouds, outlined the land with shades of bright orange. A gentle sea breeze from the west rocked the boat in a steady cadence. By the end of the day both men felt trapped by the isolation and quietness. Their freedom had been severely limited by an unknown fate.

Coaldon broke the silence, saying, "This has been another unique day. I remember my grandmother telling me there would be times when I would want to return to the peace of the farm. Right now, it would be wonderful to be a simple farmer in Lost Valley. As a youth, I would sit on mountain tops dreaming about going on great adventures into far off lands. Now that I am here, I do not find it nearly as glorious as I originally thought."

Tiny laughed, "It seems that each new adventure is blessed with insecurity and danger."

Coaldon echoed, "Right now a hot meal of roast beef would be great. Alas, I guess we need to wait for such a gift. By the way, shipmaster, what do we do next?"

Tiny was slow in answering, "I suggest we wait until morning before we do anything. I would like to see what greets us with the new day."

Coaldon continued, "Oh, I have a question for you. When did you first meet Topple?"

Tiny responded, "Tipsy, the old sailor who brought you to my farm, is Topple's friend. Tipsy never told me how or when he met Topple. I always knew there was more to Tipsy than what he told me. He knows too much about everything to be just an old sailor. Whenever Topple was in Seamock, he would visit the farm. He seemed to float in and out of my life like a phantom wind. I never met a person so oblivious to the events of life, yet more in harmony with the flow of nature. His faith in the One Presence radiates a deep sense of trust and peace."

As Coaldon fell asleep, his thoughts were on friends, family, and, of course, Topple. Loneliness accompanied him throughout the long night. After an uncomfortable night in the boat, the new day did not offer any improvement. The air was still; the sun was hot; and the breeze had blown them further out to sea.

Tiny commented, "I think it is best to row to shore before we lose sight of land."

So with a heave ho, the two men began to row with steady, long strokes. By midday the two men were motivated, to continue rowing, by the approaching sight of land. In spite of their sore muscles and blistered hands, they continued to pull on the oars. With the sun hanging low in the west, they could clearly see the shoreline bordered with a solid band of tangled brush and trees. Long beaches, covered with white sand, stretched in both directions.

With only a short distance to go, the water around the boat began to boil and churn. Air bubbles ruptured the surface of the water giving off a rank odor. The men quickly pulled in the oars while watching the water swirl in wild agitation. The boat then rose out the water and flew across the surface in a graceful arch. The craft landed with a jolt, forcing both men to hold on or be thrown into the water. Coaldon only shook his head in the disbelief at the new turn of events.

In frustration, he commented, "Enough is enough! What now? I suspect the Blade of Conquest has attracted an uninvited guest to play with us. I can hardly wait to greet our visitor!"

It did not take long before Coaldon's curiosity was satisfied. As the water stopped churning, he could see a huge creature approach the surface. A large, round head covered with orange warts slowly arose from the water. The black head was about half the size of the boat, meaning a massive creature was underneath the craft. The beast's body shifted back and forth in a steady rhythm. Two large, green eyes were located at the end of long appendages protruding from the head. The eyes moved independently in a random fashion, with one eye looking at Coaldon and the other at Tiny. Coaldon was uncomfortable when both eyes began to examine him from side to side and top to bottom. The eyes, about the size of large buckets, gazed at Coaldon with a penetrating stare. The young prince returned the gaze with an expression of authority and confidence. Coaldon decided to remain still, but was ready to strike if the beast made a false move.

The relaxed movement of the beast's eyes did not indicate any immediate hostility. Coaldon's heart leaped into his throat when three large tentacles reached out of the water and moved toward him. Coaldon pulled the sword from its scabbard and prepared to defend himself. When one of the tentacles touched the sword, a burst of fire from the blade struck the beast. With a yelp, the beast withdrew from the boat and watched Coaldon with inquisitive eyes. It then opened its oversize mouth revealing a row of outsized teeth and a long, pointed black tongue.

Coaldon sensed the beast was evaluating how to respond to the unusual presence of the two men in a boat, plus a mysterious sword. The casual, focused movement of the creature's eyes displayed awareness and intelligence.

In a quiet voice, the beast whispered to itself, "I believe I have read about him in an ancient book of prophecy. Let me think, a sword of magic carried by a young man in this remote place. Why would he be here at this time? What does this mean?"

Coaldon decided to respond by reciting a poetic verse. He stated, "One evil, one good, one gate, one song, one sword, one book, one key. Great challenges confront the path of conquest. The key will unlock the door to justice."

The beast laughed, "So, it is a game you want to play. It has been many centuries since I have been so entertained. Yet, I find your verse full of meanings beyond my understanding. I seem to remember an ancient prophecy telling about a time of calamity, when a young man of royal destiny would wield a sword of great power. Your riddle may tell an interesting story, but there is something more important that I must do."

The beast continued, "I have a great desire to share my story with you. I have not had the opportunity to talk with anybody for many ages. I have been lonely living in the prison of my creation. My body is the image of my evil life. As a youth, I lived a life of greed and selfishness. One day Topple the Wizard gave me a choice, either repent or face the consequences. I did not believe him until he changed me into my present form. I wish I had listened to him. By the way, you smell of magic. What magic do you carry?"

Coaldon smiled, "It is interesting to find an intelligent beast living in such an isolated place. To answer your question, magic is as magic does. In the beginning, true magic was only used for good. Yet, it was not long before the forces of evil learned how to twist it for their own wicked purposes. The power I possess is of the ancient source of goodness."

The beast responded, "Your magic is familiar to me. It has surrounded me for many centuries, holding me in the form of a sea monster."

Coaldon reflected, "Why are you in such a remote location? How did you find us?"

The creature continued, "I have remained hidden in these deep waters because of my shame and grief. During the many centuries of seclusion, I have found new meaning in my life. My old ways have died. I have been reborn. Even though I may look hideous, I have been transformed inside. I have paid a terrible price for my past sins. In response to your second question, I believe you have been guided to me. Hopefully, it is time for me to be resurrected."

Coaldon lowered his sword in a slow, deliberate motion. "What is your name? Did Topple provide you a way to escape from your entrapment?"

The beast drifted away from the boat to reflect on the questions.

He finally said, "It has been a long time since I was cast into my present form. I must go deep into my memories to find a name and Topple's words. Please do not leave before I return."

The creature then sank into the water leaving the two humans to wait for his return. Then with a burst of awareness, Tiny remembered sitting, as a boy, beside a fireplace on a cold winter day listening to tales told by his grandfather.

Tiny said to Coaldon, "I want to share with you a story told to me by my grandfather. During the Second Quarter Age, Philo of Rocknee was Emperor. His father, Emperor Jarro, had been killed by Doomage in a battle so terrible few men lived to tell the tale. Jarro was a ruler loved by his people and a man of honor. In contrast, Philo, who assumed the throne after Jarro's death, was a contemptuous young man who loved wealth and control. He was concerned only with satisfying his craving for luxury and power. Under his rule, the people of the Empire suffered great grief and pain. Controlled by greed, Philo came under the influence of Doomage. The charm and wit of the wizard pulled the young Emperor into the trap of pride. Legend tells how Topple the Wizard told Philo to reform his life. The wizard threatened to change Philo into a monster. With contempt, Philo laughed at Topple and ignored his warning. The wizard fulfilled his promise by changing him into an ugly sea creature. The wizard then told him to spend his life offering penance for the wrongs he had committed against the Empire."

Tiny continued, "I wonder if Philo is the sea beast? As a child, I thought the story was only a tale without fact, but now I am not so sure. I think we should confront the beast with the story."

Coaldon responded, "Your story triggered the memory of a similar tale told to me about an ancestor in the Rocknee family. He was a wicked and corrupt emperor.

He had also been changed into the form of a sea beast."

At this point, the beast returned to the surface. The water gently parted as the beast's head appeared. The beast remained at a respectful distance from the boat. As the monster quietly floated in the water, he watched Coaldon with modest hesitation.

Coaldon was the first to speak, "As a youth, I was told a story about an emperor who was changed into a sea monster because of his wickedness. His name was Philo!"

The creature looked at Coaldon with a humble and repentant expression. The creature's black skin turned white as a violent shutter ripped through its body.

The beast sputtered, "I - I - I am so ashamed to respond. Yet, I must make a confession to you. Yes, I am Philo of the House of Rocknee. Yes, I was changed into my present body for the sins I committed against the people of the Empire. Yes, I shamed the name Rocknee by my many foul deeds."

In a demanding voice, Coaldon ordered, "Tell us about your encounter with Topple."

In a somber voice, the beast murmured, "I remember when Topple confronted me. I was eating a lavish dinner when he appeared in my private chamber. I did not know how he got past the guards. He approached me with his staff in his left hand; his right hand pointed at me; and his eyes burned with unbelievable distain. I tried to attack him, but I could not move. Before he released the spell on me, he said that one day I would have an opportunity to escape my imprisonment and once again serve the Empire."

With a growing sense of compassion, Coaldon responded, "I question if I should help you? You might still be under the influence of your past life. I could jeopardize our mission and the welfare of the Empire if you betray us."

The sea monster followed, "You can trust me. I am a servant to my destiny. I have much to lose if my life has not been reformed."

In a strong voice, Coaldon declared, "My name is Coaldon of Rocknee, son of Rodney, grandson of Emperor Brad, and heir to the Throne of Rocknee. I am the Hand on the Sword. I carry the Blade of Conquest, the Gem of Watching, and Strong Edge the elfin knife. I am on a mission to save the Empire from the foul deeds of Crossmore the Wizard."

Coaldon paused for several minutes to create a climate of suspense. Then with a swift motion he lifted his sword, pointing it at the beast.

He continued, "You are my uncle by ancient lineage, a scourge to the memory of the Empire, and a sin against the people. Your disgrace sears in my mind with anger and disgust. I must decide if you should live or die. Can I trust you to be loyal to the Empire? Are you a blessing or a curse? How do you plead your case with me?"

Looking at Coaldon, Philo remained motionless in the water. With a drooping face and sad eyes, he finally responded, "I understand your dilemma. I believe we have been brought together for the cause of righteousness. I can offer you my service, reclaim my honor as a man, and right the wrongs I have done against the Empire. I humbly submit my service to you. I will swear to you an oath of allegiance."

The Blade of Conquest suddenly surged with power, emitting a burst of energy into Philo's bloated body. Philo raged in pain as the energy passed through every fiber of its fishlike body. With both eyes wobbling wildly in panic, Philo looked at the sword with wonderment.

Coaldon stated, "I wanted you to taste the power of the blade before I accept your oath. I pray your life will offer joy, not agony. I will place the sword upon your head as the channel of your loyalty. Violate the terms of your vow and this sword will cast you into a hell more foul than you can possibly imagine."

Coaldon touched the Blade of Conquest on the beast's head and asked, "Do you, Philo of Rocknee, give your loyalty to Coaldon of Rocknee, Emperor Brad, and the people of the Empire in selfless service?"

Philo declared, "I swear my allegiance to you, Emperor Brad, and the people."

Coaldon continued, "Do you understand you will be plunged into the hell-of-hells if you break this vow?"

Philo responded, "I understand and accept this punishment for violation of my promises."

Coaldon continued, "Do you vow in the name of the One Presence to honor only good and to claim faith as your shield?"

Philo responded, "In the name of the One Presence, I vow to do only good and claim faith with dignity."

A pulse of energy shot from the sword, encompassing the beast with a bright light. As the light faded, an old man with white hair floated in the water gasping for air. Tiny scooped the old man from the water and nestled him in the boat. Coaldon pulled a blanket from his pack, and covered the old man's nakedness. Philo only looked into the bottom of the boat without making eye contact with Tiny or Coaldon.

Few words were said as Tiny and Coaldon rowed the boat to shore. The boat glided onto the beach as the sun was setting in the western sky. Tiny carried Philo to the beach and laid him against a large piece of driftwood. The frail old man was completely disoriented by the rapid change in his physical form. Philo stared at his surroundings with shock and amazement. A vast number of stimuli flooded his confused senses. Trees, wind, birds, sky, sand, light, bugs, and ocean overloaded his ability to assimilate his new world. Coaldon gave Philo a set of his clothes. Philo accepted the clothes with a weak smile. Coaldon and Tiny pulled the boat into the underbrush, made camp, and prepared a warm meal. The cool night air forced the three men to huddle closely around the fire to keep warm.

The pounding cadence of the surf added a pleasant rhythm in the minds of the companions. Even though the men were on an unknown beach, in an unknown land, and facing unknown dangers, the peace of the moment washed away many disagreeable memories. Accepting the providence of the moment added peace in the midst of chaos and peril.

Little was said during the evening. Finally, in a feeble voice Philo asked Coaldon, "Would you have killed me?"

Coaldon did not respond but allowed the question to swim in Philo's thoughts. A vacuum of doubt grew in Philo's mind as the evening passed in silence. Philo looked at Coaldon with growing annoyance.

Out of frustration, Philo demanded, "What is your answer? Would you have killed me?"

Coaldon smiled at Philo saying, "You will never know if I would have killed you. In order to avert justice you must submit to my will. The past is history; tomorrow belongs to the One Presence; but now we can achieve great things together. Rest in peace, ancient uncle, for tomorrow will offer you a new future."

Now What?

Upon awakening the next morning, Coaldon was welcomed by the rumbling cadence of the waves, the screech of sea birds, hazy blue skies, and a refreshing sea breeze. As the sun peeked over the eastern horizon it exploded into a blaze of burning orange colors. This burst of beauty provided nature the opportunity to show off the elegance of her majestic clothing.

While Coaldon was caressed by the gentle hand of nature, his mind struggled to remain in the present moment. The uncertainty of their situation burned in his mind. They were secluded in an unknown land with little sense of hope. Pangs of fear raged through his mind like waves of barbaric invaders. His stomach twisted into knots as he started to create negative images of what might happen to them. Images of death, pain, and hunger permeated his thoughts. The young prince realized he needed to control his thoughts or he would become lost to pessimism and doubt. He desperately struggled to control the wild horses galloping through his mind.

In order to cancel the images, Coaldon directed his attention to the birds wheeling overhead. He decided to follow the flight of a single bird to fill the universe of his mind.

With hundreds of birds to choose, he selected a particularly large bird flying directly over the camp site. The bird's gray feathers were darker than the rest of the flock. The bird drifted on its long wings, suspended in perfect control and motion. Coaldon floated in tranquility as he watched the bird dip, swoop, and turn with no seeming effort. Then, with a roll, the bird dove into the ocean with simple grace.

Coaldon's thoughts were reawakened when the bird reappeared on the surface of the water with a fish in its beak. With an upward flip of its head, the bird swallowed the fish in a single move. The bird kicked its legs, flipped its wings, and once again soared with the grace of divine inspiration. Coaldon realized the bird was not worried about catching another fish, but only waited for the gift of the next fish to be made available.

The bird reminded Coaldon of his own role in the Empire. As the bird yielded in harmony to the events of its life, so Coaldon realized he must also submit to his destiny. Coaldon remembered his grandmother telling about the power of faith. She explained that by trusting in the providence of the One Presence, he could find freedom from concerns and worry. Now, he understood the gift of his grandmother's words. He could either live in fear or soar in the hands of faith. The bird symbolized how he could find peace in a dangerous world by learning to trust more deeply.

Coaldon's reflection ended when he heard Tiny starting to move. The large man slowly rolled out of his sleeping blanket, gave a groan, and crawled to his feet. His eyes were puffy from deep sleep. His hair looked like a tangled mass of jungle undergrowth. His staggering steps were a sign of mind fuzz. Tiny stumbled with unsteady steps to the edge of the ocean and plunged into the surf. He floundered in the waves like a baby whale frolicking in carefree bliss. Tiny's large body splashed, kicked, and rolled in lighthearted play. Coaldon laughed at the sight of a grown man acting with such youthful freedom. After Tiny had completed this ceremony of greeting the new day, he pushed himself through the waves, walked up the beach, and sat next to Coaldon.

The sound of Coaldon's laugher awoke Philo from his deep, comatose sleep. Philo slowly raised his head, looking at his surroundings with wonderment. Then out of exhaustion, he dropped his head back to the earth. He was unable to respond to his new environment. He tried to say something but could only wheeze and rasp. Both Tiny and Coaldon realized they had to intervene if Philo was to survive. So with gentle hands, Tiny lifted Philo, propping him up against a log. Philo offered his thanks by a gentle wave of his hands.

With Philo planted in place, it was now time to prepare the morning meal. Tiny decided to cook a special feast to celebrate their safe voyage. He splurged by adding dried meat and honey to the usual bland mixture of trail food. He even went above and beyond the call of duty by cooking the meal into a hot bubbling, brown porridge. Coaldon found the enriched meal to be tasty and, more importantly, filling. Philo had to be hand fed because of his weakened condition. He gagged and sputtered when swallowing the food, but did not hesitate to accept the next spoonful with appreciation. After eating a large meal he fell into a quiet sleep.

Coaldon commented, "Last month we enjoyed steaks and potatoes, now brown thick gruel is a taste delight. It is amazing how hunger can change our taste for food."

After finishing the meal, Tiny and Coaldon talked briefly, but found it more comfortable to be alone. So much had happened so fast, it was necessary for each man to allow his mind to process past events into a meaningful perspective. Quiet and reflection was the order of the day. As day drifted into night, the three found sleep a welcome host.

The following morning, Coaldon decided to talk with Tiny about making plans for the future. Coaldon began the discussion by questioning, "What do we do now? I have no sense of direction."

Sitting with his back against a piece of drift wood, Tiny listened to Coaldon's question with passive interest. He glanced at Coaldon several times but found his words distracting. The large man did not want to be rude, but he found it necessary to delve into his own presence. After several moments, he was no longer aware of Coaldon's voice, but was held bound by the rhythm of the waves. Tiny soon found himself floating aimlessly in a cloud of white mist. He felt as if he was losing control of his life.

He then saw a small book burst out of the nebulous composition of time and space. The book rushed forward, stopping directly in front of him. He immediately recognized the Key of Ban. The hovering book opened, revealing ancient elfish letters on the page. The script began to waver loosely in fluid motion. Tiny's body trembled in alarm when words drifted off the page. The jumbled text danced wildly in front of his face. As Tiny took a deep breath, the floating letters were sucked into his lungs. He struggled to resist, but was unable to stop the words from entering into his body. The power of the words reached into his mind. Tiny felt as if he was being infused with a gentle and noble character. His thoughts were flooded with new insights into the purpose of his existence. The desire to serve people grew in strength. His self-indulgent life was cast aside. The power of goodness filled him with a calm caress.

He relaxed when the vision disappeared into the void. Then with a burst of light, the emptiness was filled with a turbulent cascade of letters. The letters tumbled in a baffling rush of confusion. Order grew as the letters began to form words, and then words into sentences. Tiny felt comfort as order replaced the bewildering jumble of chaos. His field of vision was filled with a mysterious verse.

With excitement, he read:
"The beast to guide by setting sun,
with rays to lead the run.
A storm to lift a mighty tide,
with watery crest to ride.
Across the mourning murk to go
with mired steps so slow.
To crawl upon the Isle of Shy,
with many souls to let fly.

A new companion to meet and greet,
  with fire to heat the feet.
In halls of deep to carefully walk,
  with the presence of friend to stalk.
On roof to stand as danger search,
  with soaring ride to perch."

Tiny reread the words over and over. While drifting in the trance, he sensed something evil coming closer and closer. The large man gasped in horror as he saw the reaching-hand of Crossmore rush toward him with blinding speed. With a sense of helplessness, he darted back and forth within the vast expanse of his vision. The endless span of his trance did not provide a means to flee from the danger. He found no way to escape except a small crack within a wrinkle of the emptiness.

Without thinking, he leaped head first into the small opening. He plunged into a heaving and rolling tunnel. The pulsing motion of the passageway pulled him into a nebulous roar of words and ideas. He did not identify his new location until he recognized his own thoughts. It seemed incomprehensible, yet he was in the very center of his own being. At first, he experienced isolation, followed by the warm acceptance by his own spirit. Tiny felt Crossmore's hand brush passed him. With a jerk of fear, he pushed through the fiber of himself. He forcefully clawed his way through the surface of his consciousness and returned to the present moment.

When Tiny erupted from his trance he jumped to his feet, waved his arms, and ran for the cover of trees. Terror was etched on his face. He abruptly stopped when he realized Crossmore was not chasing him. Upon closer examination, the large man saw Coaldon sitting on the beach laughing at him. Tiny slowly realized he was back to reality and the danger had passed. Coaldon's confident smile helped him relax and regain his orientation.

In an emotion laced voice he stated, "I have been in a trance! Crossmore's hand was reaching for me! I was scared! I am glad to be here! I have a verse to share with you!"

H

ᚱᛋ ᛏᚢᛘᚨ ᚨᛏ ᛚᚺᚢ

By Land or Sea

Without hesitation, Tiny began to chatter in an excited voice.

In rapid-fire words he declared, "I never experienced anything like this before! At first, I was afraid, but when I finally let go, wahoo, it was unbelievable! Let me tell you about it!"

Coaldon raised his hand in an effort to gain Tiny's attention. "Tiny, you need to slow down. I want to hear the story, but I need to hear all the details. If you are in such a hurry you might miss something important."

Tiny's eyes rolled back in frustration at Coaldon's suggestion, but he listened with respect. He felt he was going to explode from exhilaration if he did not share his experience. The pressure of his enthusiasm was difficult to control.

He finally declared, "All right! All right! I know I must slow down, but the information is important. I find it difficult to hold back."

Coaldon and Tiny were surprised when Philo suddenly raised his arms high in the air. Both men could not believe the energy radiating from the fragile old man. His sunken eyes and hollow face were beaming with keen awareness and mental alertness. Philo's interest in Tiny's experience radiated from every pore of his body.

Philo stated, "At this point, I might be insignificant to you, but I do possess a vast knowledge about life and the history of the Empire. Please include me in your discussions and decision making."

With hesitation and doubt, Coaldon carefully considered Philo's request. The image of Philo as a beast was still fresh in his mind. Coaldon needed to transform Philo from a sea monster into a walking, talking, and thinking person. He knew Philo had entered his life for a reason. It would be a mistake to overlook his talents.

With his eyes on Philo, Coaldon answered, "I extend to you an invitation to join us. I have no idea what you can offer, but you might be a valuable resource."

Coaldon continued, "Okay Tiny, let's hear your story."

Tiny's exhilaration had been somewhat dulled by waiting. With his large body and gentle character as the backdrop to his presentation, the story was made vivid by the interaction between his words, emotional expressions, and sincerity. Tiny's detailed explanation made it possible for the two men to join him on his adventure. At the conclusion of the story, Tiny quoted the prophecy without making a mistake.

Coaldon responded, "You have had a grandiose experience. I hope Crossmore did not detect our location. After listening to the prophecy, I believe it was meant for us. The future of the Empire depends on our ability to decipher the hidden meanings of the words. Where do we start?"

Tiny was first to respond, "If this prophecy is like the Verse of Fate, it will be a step by step progression of events over time. So, the first line of the verse will be the first issue for us to consider. The second would be next, and so on."

Coaldon answered, "I agree with you. So let's begin with the first line, 'The beast to guide by setting sun'. What does this mean?"

Tiny answered, "The word 'beast' has many different implications to me. The first images that come to mind are Crossmore, the island, Doomage, and our new friend, Philo. The first three do not seem to fit our present situation. Maybe it has something to do with Philo. Philo was a beast several days ago."

Coaldon responded, "Philo, you seem a likely candidate to fulfill this part of the prophecy. You have returned to the history of the Empire in a most unusual manner and at a critical time. You could be an important part of the war against Crossmore. Do not underestimate what you can do for the Empire. I observe more strength in you than you see in yourself."

Tiny was eager to add to the conversation, "Let's give your idea a test. Philo, what enters you mind when I say, 'The beast to guide by setting sun'?"

Philo looked at his two companions with hesitation and doubt etched on his face. He stated, "I believe being a sea monster was easy. As a fish, I did not have any responsibilities or duties. Yet, I did pray to be given the opportunity to pay penance for my wrongs. Maybe this is the way I can help gain reconciliation."

Coaldon injected, "Philo, we need your help. What does the phrase mean to you?"

Philo closed his watery eyes to focus his full attention on Coaldon's statement.

He responded, "I will give it a try. Please give me the rest of the day to reflect on the words. My human thinking skills have grown dull over the centuries."

Philo then gazed at the ocean and lost himself in thought. After Philo withdrew from the group, Tiny and Coaldon turned their attention to the immediate circumstances of the expedition.

Since arriving on the beach they had experienced warm temperatures, blue skies, and mild breezes. They had set up camp in a small grove of trees next to a dense barrier of undergrowth. A small stream of clean water flowed from a high plateau rising steeply in the west. The rocky cliffs on the face of the plateau provided an intimidating barrier.

At first Coaldon and Tiny were happy to relax around the campfire, waiting for Philo. They placed several tarps over ropes to provide shelter from the hot afternoon sun and evening rain showers. After taking an inventory of supplies it was determined that they had ample food for several weeks of wilderness living.

Coaldon and Tiny decided to spend the rest of the day exploring the area. The two men explored the beach in opposite directions. They made brief incursions into the undergrowth in search of a path that would allow them to travel overland. It was not long before it became apparent that the western boundary of the beach was blocked by impenetrable foliage and the rugged plateau. It was early evening when the two men returned with long faces and heavy hearts. They knew they were trapped on the beach with only one way to go – the ocean.

Philo was sitting in front of a small fire when the two men returned from their tour. They were happy to see that Philo's strength had improved during the day. As the sun set, a cold sea breeze demanded a larger fire.

With yellow flames reflecting off his ancient face, Philo was the first to speak. "It has been a most interesting day for me. A flood of memories roars through me like a hurricane blowing across the ocean. At first, it was difficult to confront the images of my failures; yet, I was able to shift my attention from past failures to finding hope in the present moment. To my surprise, my creativity is returning without much effort. I must be making progress."

With a smile on his face, Coaldon responded, "I am happy you have improved. We were productive also, but in a different way. The land to the west is blocked by trees, brush, and high cliffs. Our only means of escape is by way of the sea."

In confidence, Philo continued, "Your report does not surprise me. If I am correct, the land to the west is known as the Badlands of Mob. In my time, the Badlands were notorious for being inhospitable and impassable. It is best not to venture into these forbidden lands."

Pausing, he continued, "I am happy to announce I have interpreted the verse. At first, I tried to make the obvious too complicated. Once I stopped searching for profound inferences, I started looking for the straight forward meaning. The verse states, 'The beast to guide by setting sun'. Not to mince words, I believe we are to follow the setting sun into the west."

Philo looked at Tiny and Coaldon and waited for a response.

With a smile on his face, Coaldon declared, "Philo, I find your interpretation delightful. All day I have been searching for some weighty insight into the meaning of the verse. You cut through all the mental jargon and found the answer. Thank you for a job well done. Tiny, what do you think?"

Tiny thoughtfully looked at both men, and then stared into the flickering flames of the fire.

With hesitation he said, "Coaldon, you scare me the way you jump to conclusions. Our future depends on making good decisions. I believe the 'setting sun' refers to a prominent symbol at the Monastery of Toms. The large crescent of the setting sun is displayed on the west wall of the chapel. It has been a powerful symbol to monks for many years. I find it difficult to accept the prophecy to mean we are to travel to the west. I will need some time to think about this. Let's make our decision in the morning." Both Coaldon and Philo nodded in agreement.

The following morning greeted the three travelers with low-hanging clouds and a chilly wind blowing out of the west. They huddled around a fire, ate cold bread cakes, and waited for someone to start the conversation.

It was Coaldon who finally broke the silence, "Well, there is no use putting off the discussion any longer. I will start. After a great deal of thought, I believe we are to go west."

Philo followed, "I agree with you."

Tiny gave a frustrated groan before he began to speak, "My mind keeps weighing different factors against each other. This thought process has taken me nowhere. So, I have decided to take a more direct route. I believe the answer to my dilemma is found in the prophecies we have already encountered. If you remember, past prophecies have been hidden in vague terms, but eventually reveal straight forward solutions. With this in mind, I have decided to agree with Philo's interpretation. With this settled, we must decide how and where to go."

Coaldon was happy to get past this hurdle. He reflected, "Often times, we reach hard won decisions only to come face-to-face with even more difficult choices. Tiny has challenged us to go to the next step. So, let's begin. What does it mean, 'A storm to lift a mighty tide, with watery crest to ride?"

Tiny injected, "The words 'tide' and 'water' provide the answer. I believe we are to travel by sea. I do not like the idea of facing a storm, but if we are to follow the prophecy, there is no choice."

Coaldon concluded, "So be it. We will travel west by way of the sea. Now let's consider one more verse, 'Across the mourning murk to go, with mired steps so slow'."

Both Tiny and Coaldon were surprised when Philo started laughing.

With a twinkle in his eyes, Philo declared, "I know what it means. During my last years as emperor, I traveled extensively throughout the Empire. I remember journeying through the Swamp of Grief when I became stuck in the deep, sticky mud. It took me many hours of hard work to free myself. I believe we are to journey through the Swamps of Grief to reach our destination. If the swamp has not changed, we will truly become mired down in grief. I would rather not accept this interpretation, but it is the only answer that makes sense to me."

Philo paused for several moments, allowing past memories to emerge from some hidden recess of his mind.

He continued, "Furthermore, I would speculate our destination would be the City of Mazz. From my perspective, there is no other location of value in the southern part of the Empire. Many years ago, Mazz was the center of learning. The city collapsed when wickedness infected the whole population. It was a sad ending to a most beautiful and prosperous city. When I was young, I enjoyed the peace in Mazz. I feel great sadness that this gem has been lost to the foul odor of evil. I think it is best for me to stop talking. I need to rest before continuing our discussion."

Philo withdrew into a state of misery and remorse. Shortly afterwards, the rain started as a mist, but progressed to a steady downpour. Philo's grim mood, plus the gray skies, cold wind, and rain added to the dismal disposition of the trio. Philo remained wrapped within the cloak of his own memories and regrets. His wrinkled face was cast in stone, and his sad eyes stared through the rain into the past. Philo's body jerked as the passage of his failures rolled across the stage of his mind. After all the centuries of dormancy, he was being called to reconcile the sins of his life.

After eating a warm noon meal, Philo's disposition suddenly changed. His stony face melted into a warm glow and his eyes were transformed into pools of deep peace. As the sunshine of forgiveness drenched his soul, Philo's gentle smile blossomed. The healing power of clemency allowed him to resolve his past and be reborn. A mystical sense of hope flowed from him in an unexplainable expression. It was like the renewal of life through the miracle of spring.

Philo's uplifted spirit indicated he was ready to proceed with the discussion. Tiny and Coaldon found their own moods elevated by Philo's new spirit of peace.

Philo smiled, "It may seem strange but something special has happened to me. I feel as if centuries of despair have been washed away. I like it! Even though my body is frail, I am ready to go. It will not take long for me to regain my strength."

Tiny followed, "This morning you talked about the Swamps of Grief and the City of Mazz. I have read many horror stories about the swamp. For me, it would be simpler and more logical to go north to Seamock. It is closer, and without the threat of the obvious dangers."

Coaldon studied Tiny's suggestion before responding, "You might be correct from a logical point of view. Yet, logic does not always provide correct answers to real life questions. I would hate to go north and not follow the prophecy. We may face more risks by traveling north, rather than going west. The easy way might turn out to be a disaster."

Philo injected, "I stand by my first interpretation. We are to go west and meet the challenge of the swamp. I contend we are to go to the abandoned City of Mazz. We will find the pieces of the puzzle by following the prophecy."

Tiny smiled, "I was thinking about being home, eating a steak dinner, and enjoying a peaceful evening in front of the fireplace. So much for my fantasies. I need to come back to the words of the prophecy. OK! I cast my vote with Philo. Let's do what needs to be done."

Coaldon declared, "We will travel by boat and follow the shoreline south until the continent turns west. Then we can sail west until we reach the mouth of Rolling River. We can decide what to do at that point. Tiny will be captain of the boat. Philo and I can be the crew."

In a mature voice, Philo finalized, "I suggest we begin tomorrow. Hopefully we will find good sailing and pleasant seas. We must not waste time, but press on with the journey."

Water Wings

As the last remnants of the storm hung on the eastern horizon, the morning sunshine warmed the chilly air hanging over the beach. With loud grunts and straining muscles, Coaldon and Tiny pushed the boat down the beach and into the calm coastal waters. The three travelers were excited to get started on the next leg of their journey. Tiny gently picked up Philo, staggered through the surf, and sat him in the center of the vessel. As Tiny and Coaldon leaped into the boat, it rocked wildly before settling into the natural roll of the surf.

The three adventurers were in a light hearted mood. Tiny stood up with great dignity, pointed his finger to the south, and commanded, "Crew, take your stations! Prepare the boat to sail! Man the oars! Stroke! Stroke! Stroke!"

Philo laughed with unexpected pleasure at Tiny's comic show.

Then, with a look of self-satisfaction at his great theatrical performance, Tiny sat down next to Coaldon. Neither man had to say a word. With the expertise of seasoned sailors, they rowed with long, even strokes. It did not take long for the boat to reach the open seas and escape the land breezes and currents. With swift hands, Tiny set the sail and manned the rudder. With sharp eyes on the prevailing winds, he set a southerly course.

All three men were pleased with the progress made by the sleek little boat. Some boats are made to carry supplies, others are built to handle fishing nets, but Tiny's craft was constructed to cut through the water with ease. It did not take long for the crew to settle into a daily routine. It would be a long journey, so it was essential for the three adventurers to work together in harmony. Each man assumed a different responsibly, such as preparing meals, maintaining the sails, steering the boat, and panning water.

Tiny and Coaldon were impressed with Philo's physical recovery. Philo gained new strength each day they were at sea. He consumed large amounts of food and established a regular exercise program. It was a challenge for Philo to exercise in the small boat, but his companions cooperated by giving him the room to stretch, wave his arms, and practice leg presses. Over and over, Philo would submit his body to increasingly difficult movements. The old man was determined not to be a weak link in fulfilling his duty to the Empire.

For many days, the weather held a pattern of warm days, clear skies, and mild winds. Day after day they sailed south. Tiny kept sight of land on the western horizon to maintain a correct course. It was late in the afternoon on the fifth day when the sight of land disappeared. Tiny instinctively knew it was time to change their course to the west, or possibly become lost at sea. With a shift of the sails and firm hand on the rudder, Tiny steered the boat around the southeast tip of the continent. The boat was no longer protected by a western land break, but had to face the rough water of the open sea. The new strain on the boat caused it to roll precariously as it cut through the large waves.

Tiny decided to train Philo and Coaldon to handle the rudder. It did not take long for the two apprentice sailors to master the fine art of maintaining the proper course while confronting rough seas.

During the early days of the voyage, the men had regular conversations about past experiences and daily events. Yet, as one day led to the next, the discussions dwindled into minimal communications. The loneliness and isolation of the sea slowly saturated each person. A quiet pool of self-reflection permeated the souls of the travelers. The roar of the past was transformed into a quiet time for each person to prepare for the challenges of the future.

It was on the ninth day of their journey when an outline of haze appeared on the southern horizon. The day began with calm breezes, but by midday a strong southern wind started to blow. Tiny was first to state his concern at the change in the weather. He kept looking to the south until his suspicions were confirmed with the appearance of churning, dark clouds.

In a grim voice, Tiny stated, "We have had it too good for too long. This looks like a nasty storm. I want each of you to secure everything to the hull, tie yourself to the boat, and be ready for a wild trip. I believe we will soon be at the mercy of a strong gale. I remember my grandfather talking about storms called 'water wings'. He told me how these blows suddenly churn out of the south with strong winds, feeding into the face of the storm. These gales form an abnormally dark, flat storm front, with columns of twisting clouds bellowing ahead of the tempest. Granddad said water would be sucked up by the strong cyclone-shaped winds to form sheets of water taking on the appearance of 'water wings'. He said these killer storms caused the death of many good sailors. From the looks of things, we may be meeting a 'water wing' much sooner than we want to."

As columns formed in front of the gale, Coaldon groaned in anguish at the potential of disaster. With haste, he secured the sails, tied all their supplies in the bottom of the boat, and sat next to Philo. Coaldon shut his eyes to calm his fears.

He wanted to be in control of himself, in case he needed to act in a decisive manner. He opened his eyes to see a wall of storm rushing toward the boat with flat sheets of water forming in front of the surge. It looked like the wings of a bird.

The young prince laughed to himself, saying, "And I thought Tiny was joking about the tale of 'water wings'. In the future I will believe Tiny's stories."

As the leading edge of the storm struck the boat, Tiny braced his legs against the sides, while holding the rudder with both hands. Coaldon gritted his teeth in anticipation, as the violent blast of water and wind hit the boat.

Coaldon looked to his right to make sure Philo was all right. To his astonishment, he discovered Philo was casually watching the storm. It seemed Philo was more fascinated by the power of the gale than fearful of the dangers. He did not grip the side of the boat but just casually rolled with the violent jerks and twists of the craft. Coaldon noticed a smile on Philo's face when the boat was nearly flipped over by a huge wave. Philo was totally lost in the magic of the wind and waves. It was as if the old man was an actual part of the grandeur of the storm. Coaldon had the impression Philo viewed himself as conducting the orchestra of sea and storm. The magnificence of the sea and wind seemed to have raised Philo to the height of splendor and happiness. The old-man-from-the-sea was observing the beauty of nature presenting its greatest performance. Philo was so mesmerized by the tempest, he was oblivious to everything except the glory of creation.

Coaldon's attention shifted when Tiny gave a loud cry of desperation. As much as Tiny tried to keep the boat facing into the waves, it had become crossways to the front of a wave. Unless something happened, the boat would capsize and all would be lost. Just as the large wave was about to crush the small craft, the mast broke, causing the sail to pop open. As the wind caught the sail, the boat was lifted out of the water and flew over the crest of the wave with a violent jerk. Coaldon watched as the mast and sail were ripped from the craft and disappeared into the gray mist of the storm. He crashed onto the bottom of the boat when it smashed into the churning, raging sea. Coaldon raised his head to see Philo sitting next to him, observing the storm like a child watching the performance of a circus.

To Tiny's relief, the vessel did not sink or capsize. Tiny handled the rudder with the strength of a giant holding back the waters of a flood. To everyone's relief, Tiny successfully guided his precious vessel through the bowels of the storm. Coaldon watched Tiny with admiration as the big man faced the blasts of water and wind with courage. With his head high, shoulders back, and chin thrust forward, Tiny's face was molded into a rock of determination.

Then, without warning, the boat suddenly shot between the tops of two large trees. The storm surge had reached land and was pushing the water far inland. It assaulted the coast with such force that large trees were up-rooted and tossed

around like match sticks. The small boat was carried inland, accompanied by a tangled mass of trees, brush, and debris. Tiny struggled to protect his vessel while it danced among the unbelievable carnage of nature. A large tree branch suddenly shot up through the floor of the boat, tearing a large hole. As quickly as the limb appeared, it was yanked out, allowing water to foam up into the bottom of the craft. Coaldon grabbed a large burlap sack from a storage bin and shoved it into the open wound. As the men struggled to keep the boat from overturning, a wall of willow branches attacked them. The violent slap of the tree limbs tore flesh and raised large welts all over their bodies. Coaldon pushed Philo to the bottom of the boat to protect him from any further abuse.

As the surge of water pushed over the land, it crushed trees immediately in front of the boat. It did not take long for the resistance of the trees and land to slow the advancing water to a shallow stream. With unbelievable good fortune the boat floated to a stop on top of a large pile of brush. Tiny assumed the worst was over. Of course he was wrong. Hurricane force winds battered the three men with a cloud of limbs, debris, and water. Tiny knew they would be blasted to death if they did not act quickly.

He yelled at Coaldon over the scream of the storm, saying, “Grab Philo, jump out of the boat and help me turn it over. We do not have much time.”

With heightened survival instincts, the men acted with uncommon strength by turning the heavy vessel over and crawling underneath. Several times the boat was lifted into the air by the winds, but Coaldon and Tiny held it down, using their powerful arms and body weight. To everyone’s relief, the storm finally blew itself out. The overturned vessel had been a life-saving shelter. As the storm subsided, Tiny and Coaldon shifted their focus from surviving the storm to treating their wounded and bruised bodies. Soon thereafter both men slumped into a deep, restless sleep.

Mud and More

Philo wasted no time in assisting his new friends. Even though Tiny and Coaldon were asleep, he proceeded to make their situation as comfortable as possible. Philo was happy the boat rested on a pile of branches, rather than float on a murky pool of black mud. This was not just ordinary mud, but the type that crawled with large bugs, slithered with worms, and produced a nauseating odor. Broken trees, piles of debris, and tangled patches of tall razor grass formed a barrier in all directions. As the wind and rain decreased, the drone of insects increased. A cloud of insects descended on the camp with unrelenting persistence. Most of the intruders did not attack or bite, but only formed a buzz of misery and irritation. It was not long before Philo had bugs matted in his hair, crawling down his shirt, and invading his ears, nose and mouth. In addition to the insects, he was quickly reminded of the muggy heat of the swamp. As emperor many centuries ago, he never got use to the swamp's unrelenting heat and humidity.

Philo searched the storage areas of the boat for anything to help set up camp. He spread blankets on the pile of debris, which helped make them more comfortable. He spread out the food, clothing, and survival equipment in piles according to their usefulness to the group. Using his survival experience, Philo considered what would be needed to complete the trek through the swamp. He knew Tiny and Coaldon were young and strong, yet they could only carry so much weight. Hiking through the mud would quickly drain their strength. Philo was concerned about the group's ability to escape the entrapment of the wetlands.

Philo provided some relief from the insects by draping tarps over Tiny, Coaldon, and himself. He did not know which was worse, the insects or enduring the heat under the tarp. To his disappointment, the setting sun did not offer any escape from the oppressive heat. During the night, Philo was only able to sleep for short periods of time. He was constantly awakened by the growl of unknown creatures and the screech of a large bird roosting on top of the boat.

Philo rejoiced when the light of a new day illuminated the misty cloud hanging over the swamp.

After enduring a difficult night, he declared, "Oh well, I am still alive. I have two good friends. I am not churning in the mud on the ocean floor looking for food. I best not complain too much, things could be worse."

With sweaty faces and soaked clothes, Tiny and Coaldon awoke to greet the smothering heat of the new day. As they crawled from underneath the overturned boat, they looked in despair and frustration at the vast expanse of the swamp. All they saw was murky water, clusters of trees, mounds of grass, and piles of storm debris. It was not long before they realized they were in a difficult position. Just being lost was bad enough, but being lost in the middle of a treacherous swamp was something else.

Tiny commented, "I assume we are in the Swamp of Grief. I do not think I want to be here. Matter of fact, I know I do not want to be here. I suggest we cancel yesterday and start over. I want to sail to Seamock."

Coaldon laughed, "This does not look like a good place for a picnic. I doubt if any of our invited quests will attend. I suggest we stroll back to the ocean and catch the next boat to Seamock. I would enjoy a dinner of shrimp and lobster."

Philo was in no mood for banter or jokes.

In a tired, hostile voice, he grumbled, "I am not interested in talking about picnics, shrimp, or sailing to Seamock. So, do not waste my time by discussing the weather or the price of bread in Neverly. Now, eat! I want to get out of this horrible place!"

Both Tiny and Coaldon wanted to talk about the events of yesterday, but knew it was best not to tempt the foul disposition of their ancient friend.

After a meal of trail bread and dried meat, Coaldon opened the conversation, "Philo, do you have any suggestions about what we should do? I am looking to you for guidance."

With a long face, Philo answered, "I am sorry for my burst of anger. I had a bad night. I believe the ocean is too far away to return. We were carried far inland by the storm. If we were close to the ocean, sea birds would be seen on the horizon. So, I suggest we travel toward the northwest. My intuition tells me the City of Mazz is in that direction. We need to make an educated guess and evaluate things as we go along."

In a relaxed manner, Tiny commented to Philo, "It sounds as if you had a miserable night. Coaldon and I missed all the fun. We must have a lot to look forward to. By the looks of our surroundings, mud will be our constant companion. Maybe I should write a poem entitled, 'Marching through the Murky, Mushy Mud'. It could start, 'Marching, marching in muddy clothes, with mucky mud squeezing through my tiny toes'."

With a look of disbelief, Philo threw his hands in the air and giggled at Tiny's innocent sense of humor.

Coaldon laughed, saying, "Tiny, you are too much. I assume your presentation was the literary portion of our vacation."

With a shy smile, Philo declared, "Tiny, before we leave this swamp, you will have the opportunity to see mountains of mud ooze between your toes. You will also be able to write many verses from your experiences in the swamp. I am looking forward to reading your masterpiece."

Tiny bowed to Philo, saying, "I will be most happy to share it with you. I might even include you in one of the verses. I will be watching you closely to find an interesting story to tell."

Coaldon interrupted, "Let's get focused. I say we go north until we are given a better offer. Philo, it looks as if you have been busy getting ready for our trek."

Philo nodded, "My plans are simple. We will only carry what is essential for our survival. The rest can be given to the creatures of the swamp. One of the most important things we must do is find solid ground. This cursed mud can be dangerous. The mud will suck the life out of us."

Tiny reacted, "I have an idea! One of us should climb a tall tree and take a look around."

Coaldon reacted, "I will do it! I used to be the best tree climber in Lost Valley. Just give me some rope and up I will go."

Without any further discussion, Coaldon grabbed a length of rope and waded through the swamp to the nearest tall tree. It did not take long for him to reach the top. Most of the leaves had been blown off by the violent winds. This made it easy for Coaldon to see in all directions. Philo and Tiny watched with anticipation as Coaldon studied the surrounding area with keen eyes. Tiny had the impression that Coaldon was an eagle scanning its domain. Something to the north held Coaldon's attention for a long time. After a careful examination of the area, Coaldon quickly descended the tree. Using his strong arms, he lowered himself with rapid hand-over-hand extensions.

When Coaldon returned to the camp, his sparkling eyes and a broad smile offered a sense of hope to his companions.

In a confident voice, he stated, "Even though we may be in trouble, I am happy to announce that I have spotted high ground just north of us. It looks like an island with a section of land trailing off into the west. The land mass has a low, rounded mound in the center. I do not understand how a hill could exist in the swamp, but I guess that is for us to find out. It is difficult for me to estimate how long it will take us to get there. The mud and the debris from the storm will make it a tough walk. I suggest we get started as soon as we get organized."

Philo had a concerned look on his face as he responded, "During my time as Emperor, I heard rumors of an island, hiding great danger, in the middle of the swamp. This may be the island."

Shortly, the small group loaded their packs and started the journey to the island. They found it unbelievably difficult to trudge through the deep mud, debris, and undergrowth, plus fight the cloud of insects. For most of the day, Tiny and Coaldon had to take turns carrying Philo. Philo made a gallant effort, but did not have the strength to endure such a strenuous trek. It was late evening when they finally stopped for the night. Coaldon selected a large, floating pad of weeds and brush on which to spend the night. The floating cushion was nothing more than a mat of vegetation, but it provided a dry place to rest. They had to wiggle and scramble to get on the limp, wavering pad.

After a short rest, Coaldon was the first person to notice movement underneath his clothes. Pulling up his pant legs, he found his skin covered with black, slimy leaches. Tiny was especially disgusted by the presence of these large, slippery creatures. He yelled in anger at this violation of his body, yet this did not change the situation. So, finally, he pulled out his knife and proceeded to scrape off the invaders. Philo and Coaldon joined him in cleansing their bodies of the trespassers. Their legs were a mass of round, irritated sores.

During the night, the swamp was filled with strange noises, but the men were so tired nothing interrupted their sleep. Coaldon awoke before sunrise with the desire to get an early start. Even with Coaldon pushing, Tiny and Philo were in no hurry to jump into the nasty water and be greeted by more leaches. Tiny suggested they tie their pants leg at the bottom to stop the leech attack.

Tiny and Coaldon again took turns carrying Philo's small, frail body. The further they journeyed to the north, the easier it was to walk. The ground became increasingly solid, with a decreasing amount of debris from the storm. By noon they could see the outline of the island directly in front them. Coaldon encouraged his companions to keep going. With the end in sight, it was easier to go beyond exhaustion to achieve their goal. The shadows of evening were upon them when they arrived at the island. Their celebration was short lived, however, when they discovered an impenetrable mass of undergrowth surrounded the land mass. The dense barricade of thorn bushes stopped them from reaching the island. They stood knee deep in water, staring in frustration at the snarled wall of brush. Dry land was only several strides away. The rush of darkness descended on the swamp without showing any concern for the three stranded travelers.

just say hello

The three travelers stood before the barrier with growing anxiety. They did not want to spend another night in the open swamp. Tiny was the first to react. He drew his sword and made a mighty swing at the thick wall of thorn bushes. To his surprise, the sword came to a jarring halt, rattling his whole body. The sharp weapon did not cut through the foliage. He stood gaping at the impenetrable wall.

He finally declared, "I do not believe what just happened. How is it possible that I could not even cut one branch? Those thorns must be infused with magic."

Coaldon responded, "It is not normal for any plant to resist such a powerful blow. I wonder if we should answer magic with magic. Maybe, I should use the Sword of Conquest against the barrier."

He pulled his sword from the scabbard and released energy into the blade. He stepped forward, raised the weapon over his head, and made a firm downward stroke. To his amazement, the sword easily cut a swath through the undergrowth.

As the blade sliced through the brush, a loud scream of pain came from the island. Coaldon ignored the sound and continued cutting until he had opened a passageway. As the three men scrambled onto the island, the intense shrieks of agony diminished. They were relieved when the howl of anguish quieted to a soft whimper.

Philo raised his head to look around, "Unless I am wrong, the cries of pain came out of the earth."

Tiny followed, "I believe you are right. Is it possible that something in the island actually experienced the pain of the brush being cut?"

Coaldon commented, "After all we have been through, anything is possible. It will soon be dark, so let's get a quick meal, scrape leaches, and get a good night's sleep. We will have plenty of time to deal with the island in the morning."

After a peaceful slumber, the morning greeted the small group with low, gray clouds producing a misty rain. Tiny hoped the rain would cool the air, but to his disappointment the temperature and humidity only increased.

Coaldon stated, "In spite of the rain, we will need to start our journey north. I believe the humidity and heat will be our companions for many days. So, let's eat, load up, and move out. Sitting here will only prolong our expedition."

With hopes of having a productive day, the men started walking in a northerly direction. The sandy, rocky ground was solid in spite of the rain. The landscape was dominated by tall stands of grass, groves of trees, and thickets of thorny bushes. As the morning passed, Coaldon had the sensation of being lost in the midst of familiar surroundings. Looking back, he had the impression they had not moved away from their last location. Even though they tried to walk past the low mound in the center of the island, the hill remained straight ahead of them. It seemed to be a magnet drawing them toward its presence. Coaldon felt as if an invisible path was guiding them toward some unknown destiny.

When the travelers stopped hiking for the day, the mound still remained in front of them.

Tiny commented, "We have not made any progress. We keep walking, but have gone nowhere. How could this be possible?"

Philo looked at Tiny with curiosity, "It is possible we have ventured into an empty space in time. A scholar of Mazz once told me about an island in which people entered but never escape. It was described as walking in a circle and never being able to find the start or finish. People caught in this void, ultimately dissolve into the emptiness."

Coaldon followed, "If Philo is correct, then it would be worthless for us to go anywhere. Effort would only cause enslavement to the goal of providing more meaningless effort. If our attention is focused on getting off the island, then we would be following a path to nowhere. We can only make progress by going nowhere. I believe we should concentrate on solving the mystery of the island."

Nightfall put an end to the discussion. Philo's story created a major stir in Coaldon's mind. As he reflected on their present situation, he lay on his back, gazing into the vastness of the universe. As the night sky filled his elfin presence with power and insight, he was infused with an unusual message. The celestial energies urged him to respond to the island with gentleness. Somehow, he knew the solution to their dilemma would be found in soft steps, not an aggressive assault. The rays from the rising moon touched him with a warm embrace of confidence and peace.

The following morning, an eerie feeling of disorientation clouded the camp site. The companions had the impression they were trapped by several unseen and unknown power. They were ensnared by the demands of the prophecy, plus the added burden of the island.

In a subdued voice, Tiny was the first to speak, "I am frustrated. It seems we are being confronted by one new challenge after another. Sometimes, I believe I cannot keep going."

Philo responded, "I am having the same feeling. Yet, we cannot allow our emotions to direct our behavior. We are blessed with the guidance of the One Presence. We are to look to the light, not the darkness. Trust and faith are to be our friends."

In a quiet tone, Tiny stated, "You are right. Our emotions can be false guides. We are to accept the Truth no matter the situation."

Philo declared, "It is time to face our present situation. I believe we have entered into a great mystery. I agree with Coaldon, we can walk forever and never reach anywhere. We are better off to sit here rather than waste our time and energy wandering aimlessly toward nowhere."

Coaldon nodded, "It seems we are dealing with two mysteries at one time. Besides being a prisoner of the island, the island seems to have a life of its own. From outward appearances, it also shows signs of intelligence. This is most extraordinary."

Philo injected, "It would appear the whole island is tied together into a living network. If it can communicate within itself, I wonder if it can converse with us."

Coaldon stated in an excited voice, "Those are good points. I do not believe we are dealing with a hostile life form. Therefore, we might be able to open communications with it. This sounds promising, yet what could we use as a common language? The intelligence within the island might be of ancient origins. We may not have anything in common."

Philo followed, "As long as we have something in common, we have the potential to communicate. For example, if we both experience suffering, then suffering can be used to establish a connection. We need to discover a common link and then use this commonality to find a way to dialogue. Can we exchange information by touch, sound, sight, thought, or maybe taste? I believe we have the ability to solve this mystery."

Both Tiny and Coaldon looked at Philo with new admiration. They realized their new acquaintance had a sharp mind and a good understanding of life. Innately, Coaldon knew Philo was correct, yet he did not know how to solve the problem.

Finally, Coaldon said, "Philo, how do we proceed?"

With hesitation, Philo injected, "My experience with life has taught me to allow solutions to come to me. The mind has the ability to assimilate large amounts of information and then develop logical conclusions. This can be a slow process. In other words, we need to sit back and allow the answer to grow out of us."

Coaldon reacted, "So, let's get started with the waiting game. I propose we spend the day in camp and wait."

With a nod of approval, Tiny and Philo agreed. After many days of travel, they found it important to catch-up on domestic chores: clothes to clean, torn fabric to mend, supplies to sort, wounds to treat, food to inventory, and time to rest. In addition, they discovered clean water, berries, and fresh fruit near their camp. The abundance of food and water seemed unusual for such an isolated location.

After the evening meal, Coaldon opened the discussion by asking, "Is it possible to become too comfortable on this island? I feel so pleasant. I can see myself getting lost in the soothing tranquility of this place."

With sleepy eyes, Philo stated, "Every muscle of my body is relaxed. For some reason the heat and humidity are not bothering me. I get the impression my body is melting into folds of bliss and serenity. I feel good!"

Tiny also enjoyed the peaceful caress of the moment. His shoulders slumped forward as he relaxed. Then, without warning, Tiny's body suddenly jerked into an alert posture. His sleepy eyes popped open, revealing the shock of an unexpected revelation.

He yelled, "We are falling under the spell of an enchantment!"

With an abrupt start, both Coaldon and Philo were ejected from their pleasure binge. The warm glow of comfort passed into the night air like a fleeing phantom. This passage marked the return to an awareness of the heat and humidity. The raw certainty of their current situation returned with a vengeance. The glow of the emotional high was followed by feelings of despair and discouragement. Their smiles were replaced by grimaces of unease.

Coaldon yelled, "What is happening to us? First, we feel trapped on what seems a hopeless journey, then we felt good about being hopeless, and now we feel completely hopeless about feeling good. This does not make sense!"

Philo injected, "Maybe there is more to the enchantment than meets the eye. This could be a strategy used by the island. What we are experiencing is unnatural; therefore, I would assume magical. Why are we being subjected to these emotions?"

Tiny reacted, "I believe we are being manipulated. Something is deliberately attempting to confuse us! But why?"

At this point, a sense of irritability consumed the three men. They looked at each other in anger and frustration. They sensed a vast difference of opinion, and an instantaneous dislike of each other. This caused them to feel paranoia. A cloud of distrust forced the companions to sit in separate parts of the camp site with arms crossed. Angry words and hostile threats escalated into growing antagonism.

Finally Coaldon groaned, "Enough! Enough of this foolishness! Why are we angry with each other? I cannot believe us. I think children can do better than this. We are being drawn into a trap and stupid enough to go along with it. This is not very smart."

The wings of night covered the island as each man looked at one another in childish embarrassment. Something was successfully playing a game with their minds and emotions. The intrusion did not feel evil, but more like a mischievous child tormenting its parents.

A sense of innocence permeated the night air, causing Tiny to giggle, "This feels like a naughty child trying to gain control. I believe it is time for us to think before reacting."

With a sheepish look on his face, Tiny continued, "I believe we are dealing with something blameless and innocent. I do not sense any malice on the part of our opponent. It is more like a game of hide and seek. If evil was the intent, we would be dead by now. Sometimes children seek attention by striving to manipulate people. I believe our communication with the island needs to be simple, direct, caring, and honest."

Coaldon responded, "Tiny, where do you get these ideas? You make perfect sense. Maybe, we just need say 'Hello'. We should view ourselves as being guests on the island. Our host has provided us with a bounty of food and water. I believe kindness and understanding will be the best tactic."

Philo stated, "I accept your conclusion. Without wasting a lot of time on idle words, I suggest we say 'hello'."

He placed both hands on the ground saying, "Hello. Thank you for your generous hospitality."

For several moments, each traveler tried different ways to send greetings to their unknown benefactor. Yet, no matter what they tried, nothing brought a response. Finally, the need for sleep outweighed any more attempts to communicate.

Coaldon was the first to take guard duty. He sat near the edge of the camp with his full attention on the sounds of the night. These included the bark of a fox, the chatter of squirrels, the hum of insects, and the hoot of an owl. While he listened to the voice of nature, he heard a gentle whisper in his ear. At first he ignored the voice, assuming it was a bug with a broken wing, or maybe a figment of his imagination. Then he clearly heard a fleeting voice whisper, "Hello." The word was not spoken in the dominate voices of a conqueror, but rather, the shy murmur of modesty. After this introduction, the whisper floated away like the flutter of a butterfly.

The Willow Wraiths

While Coaldon watched the stars, events were unfolding in another part of the swamp. In a hidden cave, on an uncharted island, the chants of guttural voices could be heard. Roars and grunts blended into a chorus of shouts, creating an image of primitive savagery. Slender, supple man-like creatures, called willow-wraiths, danced around a blazing fire. Their bodies were covered with green alligator like skin. The facial features of their oversized heads were small and recessed. Their small, beady eyes and flat noses had a bug-like appearance. Long spindly arms and legs loosely flowed in graceful motion. Snot and slime dribbled from their tiny mouths and noses. The drool ran down their faces and dripped off their wide chins. The creatures' wild dancing was a ritual in preparation for a raid into the swamp.

The willow-wraiths had detected the repulsive scent of human flesh for several days. Returning scouts reported that three humans had cut their way onto the Island of Shy. To their great satisfaction, the inaccessible island had been mysteriously breached by the humans. It was time for the creatures to attack the island and destroy the detestable humans. Tonight, a raiding party would pass through the new opening in the island's defenses and claim the land for the tribe. This raid was unusual because it was to be performed at night. The willow-wraiths had a fear of darkness, yet they decided to venture into night in order to surprise the humans. Small torches would help cut through the threat of darkness.

* * * * *

Back at the camp, Tiny and Philo sat in relaxed positions next to the fire. While talking about the mystery of the island, a large net fell over their bodies. They yelled and fought, but to no avail. The two men were quickly bound with strong ropes.

Tiny's shouts gave Coaldon ample warning to defend himself against the attack.

With sword in hand, Coaldon sliced through the net thrown over him, allowing him to escape. Without hesitation, he attacked the first creatures he encountered. The willow-wraiths were no match for Coaldon's sharp, lethal sword. Coaldon quickly dispatched several creatures before retreating into the darkness. He was followed into the night by a mob of raging beasts. It was not long before the willow-wraiths' fear of darkness overcame their desire to capture the human. They slinked back to the camp to claim the security of the camp fire.

Coaldon spent a restless night in a wooded area not far from the camp. At dawn, he advanced to the willow-wraith's camp site. As Coaldon approached the encampment, he was driven away with a cloud of stones. This was a warning to stay away. The creatures did not chase him out of fear of his dangerous sword. The beasts were not concerned about Coaldon's presence; he was no threat to them. He was only an insignificant bug.

The young prince saw a group of wraiths lounging around a large fire eating their breakfast. Tiny and Philo lay next to the fire bound with ropes. He saw several willow-wraiths poking at them with sticks and laughing. After watching this treatment, Coaldon realized his friends were in great danger. In hopelessness, he sat on the edge of the camp for the rest of the morning, watching the beasts prepare for a celebration.

As the day passed, many willow-wraiths arrived on the island. By early evening, hundreds of creatures danced around a large fire.

Coaldon was absolutely powerless in attempting to save his friends. It would be suicidal to attack the large number of enemies. He had never felt so helpless and lonely in his entire life.

As he watched the dance grow into a frenzied pace, Coaldon knew something had to be done or his friends would die. He decided it was time to ask for assistance.

In a simple request, he stated, "Please help me."

Then he heard the whisper of a gentle voice say, "Hello."

Coaldon knew this was the voice of the island. He responded, "Hello, friend. Can you help us?"

At this point, the wraiths grabbed Tiny and Philo, tied them to wooden poles and carried them around the fire chanting grotesque incantations. The shouting and dancing stopped when an elderly beast stepped forward, sprinkled a liquid over the two companions, and raised his hands into the air. He then shouted a loud command to the crowd. Instant excitement exploded from the large group.

Coaldon just sat and watched in despair; but then jumped in surprise when the soft male voice again spoke into his ear.

The voice stated, "I have been invaded by these foul creatures. They come to corrupt and destroy, not heal and nurture. Up to this point, I have been patient, but no longer."

Coaldon heard the island voice continue to talk as it moved toward the willow-wraith's camp. When the voice-of-the-island entered the camp, its whisper grew into a roar. Coaldon watched as the voice was transformed into a white cloud that expanded from the size of a small ball into a giant dome over the camp. The wraiths casually accepted its presence without concern.

As Coaldon watched, the color of the cloud shifted from white to gray to black. The cloud began to swirl and throb at an ever escalating pace. The sides of the cloud rapidly pulsed in and out, creating a bone-rattling thunder. Then, from out of the center of this churning mass, a light started to grow. As the brightness expanded, it rapidly consumed the black vapor. The cloud slowly changed into a clear, glowing liquid. This undulating mass flowed freely within the bounds of its nebulous contours. It hung heavily over the willow-wraith's camp, sagging under its own massive weight.

The willow-wraiths looked with contempt at the undulating reservoir of fluid hanging over their heads. The creatures' arrogance would not allow them to yield to threat of another power. The island was now theirs to rule. No pathetic demonstration of magic would detract them from their celebration. They responded to the churning reservoir with curses and laughter.

Suddenly, the clear mass fell onto the group of vile beasts, enveloping them in the shroud. Coaldon saw the forms of the creatures floating within the pool of fluid. The creature's bodies were changed from their normal shape into formless blobs of matter.

Then, without grace or nobility, two human forms were suddenly ejected out of the mass. As they sailed through the air, their arms and legs flopped wildly. Coaldon heard groans when the two bodies landed on the ground in awkward piles of flesh and bones.

The pulsating liquid suddenly exploded into a fast burning fire. The flames leapt high in the air, burning hot and intense. A greasy odor filled the air as black smoke rose high into the evening sky. After the fire had burned out, nothing was left of the foul creatures.

Coaldon rushed to assist his two friends. Their bruised and battered bodies lay in a patch of tall grass. Tiny gasped wildly in an attempt to gain his breath. Philo lay whimpering in pain and misery. After examining his two companions, Coaldon happily announced that the two men had no broken bones. He carefully helped each man to roll over onto their sides and sit up. In spite of their pain, Tiny and Philo smiled at Coaldon in gratitude. The three adventurers spent a restful night in the comfort of each others company.

The Joining

The following morning, Tiny and Philo were slow in responding to the voice of the new day. The throb of sore muscles limited their desire to move. It was only through the stern application of will-power that they were able to push their aching bodies into motion. The first task was to investigate the events of the previous day. The three men found no signs of the willow-wraiths or their camp site.

In an eerie dream-like state, Tiny questioned, "Did they really exist? If it was not for the rope burns on my arms and my sore muscles, I would question if yesterday was only a dream."

The group was happy to find their supplies and equipment in a pile near their original camp.

In a subdued voice, Philo followed, "The island is such a riddle. I am having a difficult time convincing myself that it is alive. It looks like ordinary earth, but I know it is much different."

Coaldon laughed, "This place is a puzzle unto itself."

Philo followed, "Mystery or not, we need to do something. Let's consider some of the facts. First, the island spoke to Coaldon. So, we were correct in assuming it can communicate. Second, it shows human like emotions, as demonstrated by its anger with the willow-wraiths. Third, the island is powerful. The liquid cloud was more than a simple hand trick. This indicates it will act with authority if its values are violated. Fourth, the island thinks logically. So, we can rationalize with it once we establish communication. Last, for some reason, our fate is tied to this unusual place. I believe we must complete an important tack before continuing our journey."

Coaldon nodded in agreement, saying, "I just realized something. If you remember, the only direction we could walk was toward the mound in the center of the island. I believe we should honor this invitation. Let's go to the mound and find out what is waiting for us."

Philo and Tiny looked at each other in agreement. Without hesitation, the little group loaded their packs and hiked toward the mound. With long easy strides the adventurers rapidly approached their destination. At times they had the impression of being pulled and tugged along the way.

The pleasant trek ended at the base of the large mound. The trees and underbrush ended at an unseen boundary circling the mound. Inside the border, the hill was covered with waves of lush grass. Tiny and Philo casually crossed onto the grasslands without incident. Both men sensed a great sadness infecting the area of the mound.

When Coaldon stepped onto the grass, he was overcome by an uncomfortable heaviness and with each step, he was burdened with an ever-increasing weight. At first, he thought the load would be lifted, but after a short walk, he could hardly move his legs. A heavy weight had been cast on him from some unknown source. Coaldon finally collapsed helplessly onto the ground, unable to move. Tiny was first to notice something was wrong with him and rushed to help.

In a weak voice, Coaldon said, "I have been afflicted by a great burden. I cannot move my body. It is as if an ancient sorrow has been heaped on me. I believe I must go to the top of the hill and complete an important task. Would you please carry me?"

Tiny grabbed Coaldon with his massive arms, but could barely lift him off the ground. Tiny's knees nearly buckled as he threw Coaldon over his shoulder. With unsteady steps, Tiny labored up the mound. He could only take four or five steps before he had to rest and catch his breath. After a long struggle, Tiny finally reached the top. As the big man carefully placed Coaldon on the ground, he saw the earth sag under the weight of the prince. Tiny's movements caused the mound to quiver. A jelly-like trembling resonated back and forth through the hill until the energy had been absorbed by the surrounding earth.

Philo joined Tiny and Coaldon on the hill top. He sensed something important was about to take place. Without any doubt, he knew the grass was a disguise covering a crime of immense evil. The vibration of the mound only reinforced his belief that it was not a normal physical feature. It was something created by man and would need to be healed by man.

Philo looked down at Coaldon, stating, "You have been given a responsibility to complete."

Coaldon nodded to Philo in agreement. The prince found it difficult to concentrate on the surroundings. He felt something was pulling him down into the soft earth. When he closed his eyes, he saw a legion of faces looking at him from the mound. The hill was a fusion of innumerable human bodies compressed into a nebulous mass. The voices of the captives formed a single, unintelligible roar.

The culmination of their voices reverberated within the gelatin-like mass of the hill. Coaldon saw anguished faces desperately pleading for something. Thousands of reaching hands grabbed him, pulling him into the hill. Their grasp on Coaldon was so strong he felt as if he was being ripped apart.

Out of desperation, he shouted, "Back off! Give me space!"

A gasp of recognition shot through the compressed mass of humanity. In collective understanding, they realized it was against their best interest to destroy their champion. The hope for a miracle was held in Coaldon's hands. An instantaneous silence encompassed the hill. Tiny and Philo felt a calm enter the quivering mound.

Philo was first to notice the rush and swirl of transparent images hovering over the mound. At first, he thought it was the mist rising off the swamp, but changed his mind when he saw the vague outline of faces within the vapor. The wave of translucent souls began a clockwise flow around the mound. The blur of the transparent images could be seen rushing in and out of the trees and brushes surrounding the hill. As the agitated cloud of souls intensified, he detected a growing pool of energy.

With his eyes still closed, Coaldon grew increasingly uncomfortable as thousands of eyes eagerly stared at him from inside the hill. To escape from their haunting presence, Coaldon opened his eyes. To his frustration, he then encountered the gaze of many souls swirling in the sky.

At this moment, the bodies in the mound and souls in the sky began to pulsate in excitement. The massive cloud of energy covering the hill increased in strength as the two opposite forces clamored for union with the other. The nebulous lake of energy became so intense that Philo and Tiny were forced to race off the mound in fear of being consumed by the power.

Coaldon could only lie on the ground, watching the faces from both directions draw closer and closer to him. As Tiny and Philo watched from the bottom of the mound, they saw the souls in the sky form into a bright red band of light over Coaldon's body. Then, out of the mound, a radiant green light began to glow. The bright green light formed under Coaldon, slowly lifting him into the air, compressing him between two dazzling bands of light.

Coaldon felt immense heat as each band grasped for the other. Hands from the opposite sides hopelessly grabbed for their counterpart. Their inability to join together created deep moans of anguish. A collective climax of grief was released through agonizing screams of distress.

In compassion, Coaldon extended one hand to each side of the pole-of-grief. As his hands made contact, Coaldon experienced a raging surge of heat pass through him. Unknowingly, he had provided a conduit for the bodies and souls to be joined. As the power passed through him, Coaldon's body glowed. The blast of energy was so intense he lost consciousness.

Philo and Tiny stood in awe as they watched Coaldon's body illuminate into a blinding light. The transference only took several seconds. The resulting union of the bodies and souls formed into a swirling cloud. Thunder and lightning discharged from the cloud, filling the sky with a magnificent display of grandeur. Then with an explosive force, the cloud shot into the north-western sky. A trail of luminous sparks followed the cloud into the distant horizon.

As suddenly at it started, it was over. The throbbing tension was replaced by a peaceful calm. Philo and Tiny were spellbound by the rapid occurrence of events. As the two men pulled their eyes away from the receding cloud, their attention shifted to Coaldon. They found the mound had shriveled into a low grassy knoll. Its surface had the appearance of a wrinkled prune. In the middle of the knoll, they saw a large black area of scorched earth. In the center of this burnt area lay Coaldon's body. Even from a distance, they could see his clothes had been badly burned. With long strides the two men stumbled across the uneven landscape to reach their friend.

Tiny and Philo huddled around Coaldon, expecting the worst. When Tiny touched Coaldon his clothes disintegrated into dust. Tiny covered Coaldon with his shirt to protect him from the ever present cloud of insects. Coaldon slept deeply, showing no signs of bodily damage. His skin had turned a golden brown and his head was once again completely bald. Tiny picked up Coaldon and carried him to the edge of the grassy mound where they set up camp. In excited voices, Tiny and Philo talked late into the night about the events of the day.

Walty

It was mid-morning when Tiny and Philo awoke. With their minds full of cobwebs and eyes matted with sleep, they peeked out from underneath their sleeping blankets.

Coaldon's brown, smiling face greeted them with enthusiasm. He laughed, saying, "It's about time you gentlemen face the new day."

Tiny answered weakly, "I have not slept this good in weeks."

Coaldon commented, "We must have found where Doomage hid the bodies of the souls imprisoned in the Mountain of Death. It was my destiny to be the channel that allowed the bodies and souls to be joined. I felt their great joy when the joining took place."

Coaldon looked at his body, commenting, "I wonder if my skin will remain brown? The way things are going, some wizard will say, 'Now, let's turn Coaldon purple!'"

In a joking tone, Philo interjected, "I think red would be a better color for you. And maybe a few white strips down your side would add some distinction."

Coaldon smiled, saying, "You are right, but I would like several yellow stars on my forehead."

Tiny interrupted, "OK! OK! Let's get serious! First, we need to get off the island. How do we accomplish this great feat?"

Coaldon questioned, "Before we start planning, do either of you have any idea where the cloud might have gone?"

Philo responded, "The cloud headed into a northwest direction. I assume it had a destination. The 'joined' could not have gone far before the weight of their physical bodies would have brought them to earth. It is possible we will meet them on our journey."

Tiny broke in, "Since we are heading into the northwest, we might find their trail along the way. That would be exciting!"

Pausing, he continued, "We still need to deal with the problem of the island. If we start hiking, will we end up walking in circles?"

In an assertive voice, Philo declared, "I believe we can walk for hours, but will accomplish nothing. We need to go to the source of this mystery. I suggest we simply ask our host for help."

In a somewhat joking manner, Coaldon stood up and threw his arms apart, saying, "Hello, friend. We need your help."

Before Coaldon could take a breath, a vaporous figure flowed out of the earth. The mist took the wavering shape of a boy. The shape floated over the ground in flitting, fluid movements. With sudden bursts of speed, the mist shot from point to point around the camp. It finally stopped in front of the group. The eyes of the little boy looked at the three men with respect, then an adult voice spoke out of the boy's mouth.

The voice stated, "Greetings. Welcome to the Island of Shy. Hopefully, my enslavement to Doomage is about over. I need your help to gain my freedom."

Coaldon responded, "How can we help you?"

Looking at Coaldon, the image answered, "You have assisted in the reunion of the Lost. Their lives can now be completed. I am the only remaining soul not to be made whole."

Philo questioned, "Would you please explain to us why you are here and how you gained your powers?"

The voice paused before responding, "I was made guardian of the island by Doomage. He separated my soul and body, forcing me to protect the island from trespassers. He promised to reunite me if I successfully protected the Prison of the Lost. I was to guide intruders into the vast emptiness of canceled time and space. By using the powers given to me by Doomage, I was able to confuse people into following me to their destruction."

The vapory form vanished and then reappeared. He looked with anticipation at Coaldon, before he continued, "I always hoped a champion would someday come to free me from my captivity."

In a firm voice Tiny asked, "Why do you have the body of a child and the voice of a man?"

The voice continued, "Do not be deceived by my body. Doomage limited my ability to rationalize by making me into a child. My child's body does not have the powers of an adult. Let me introduce myself. I am Walty, Counselor to the Court of Philo. As his counselor, I lived a life of corruption. My foul life made me susceptible to the whims of darkness."

In a gasping tone, Philo croaked, "I thought I recognized your voice. I am Philo, your Emperor. I was recently rescued from the imprisonment of my sins. It is a pleasure to once again meet you. I believe we have much to talk about and many adventures to share. To be certain, we must answer the call of the Empire to fight Crossmore. We know first hand how the power of evil can infect the heart and soul of people."

Looking at Philo, Walty responded, "I am not surprised you are a member of the group that freed the Lost from their enslavement. You always impressed me as someone who got lost on the way to doing something good and noble. Unfortunately you allowed yourself to be possessed by powers of selfishness and greed. You now have the opportunity to follow the summons of goodness. I offer my congratulations."

Philo bowed saying, "Thank you. I believe we have a great deal to prove. By the way, how can we help you? Your true character is not suitably expressed in the shroud of a child."

Looking at Coaldon, Walty answered, "The young champion will need to form a link between my spirit and body. My body is still in the mound. It can only come out by your command."

Coaldon responded in a sympathetic voice, "I will be happy to help you."

He drew his sword, pointed it at the mound, directing, "I order the body of Walty to come to me."

Coaldon watched as the hazy outline of a body pushed through matted grass and hovered in the air. The body modestly floated toward Coaldon. It began to vibrate in excitement when it recognized its own soul. The translucent image of body and soul rushed toward each other, but were violently repelled. The two halves of Walty were forced apart by an unseen power.

Coaldon reached out his hands, inviting the two parts of Walty to join with him. Walty's body and soul each grabbed one of Coaldon's hands. The power holding Walty's body and soul apart collapsed, creating a flash of lightening and a clap of thunder. A cloud of blue smoke flowed out of Coaldon's mouth as the two aspects of Walty were united.

Materializing out of the smoke, Walty stood like a statue in front of Coaldon. His small, delicate body showed the ravages of time. He could be described as mature, but not elderly. Walty's pale face was outlined with long, gray hair. His alert eyes darted back and forth, feeding on the details of his surroundings. At first, Walty watched with fascination as he slowly raised his hands in front of his face. He then placed one foot in front of the other in an awkward attempt to walk. Tears of joy ran down his face at the thrill of being whole. Taking uncertain steps, Walty stumbled forward, joyfully throwing his arms around Coaldon.

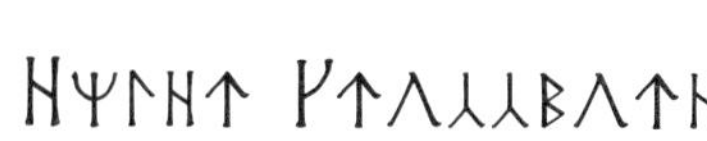

Enter Crossmore

Like many great events, the joy of the moment was short lived. The energy released by the 'joining' of the lost-souls did not go unnoticed in the capital City of Neverly. In the West Tower of the palace, two eyes probed into a crystal ball, desperately searching the Empire to find the source of the massive release of energy. Crossmore could not image what had caused such a giant blast. He knew Coaldon was roaming the Empire, but he did not believe his opponent could create such a force on his own.

A nagging sense of uncertainty caused him to pause. He vividly remembered the pain of his many encounters with Coaldon. Yet, the frantic need to be in control caused him to continue his search. A smile of satisfaction covered his face when he detected the lingering residue of magic in the Swamps of Grief. Crossmore closed his eyes and extended his scarred right hand. The hand had been badly burned by a previous conflict with Coaldon. Not wanting a reoccurrence of that event, he carefully probed the swamps, searching for the source of the disturbance. His reaching-hand was an extension of the power he used to terrorize the Empire.

As Crossmore's reaching-hand swooped southward, Coaldon and his companions enjoyed the peace of a quiet moment. The stress of completing the 'joining' took its toll on each of the companions. They decided to take a well deserved rest. As the travelers casually talked under the shade of a large tree, Walty suddenly became rigid and tense. Terror etched his face, as he searched for the unseen presence.

He stammered, "Something wicked is searchisng for us. I can feel it getting closer and closer."

Coaldon responded, "I think our good friend Crossmore is on the hunt. The power released by the 'joining' has attracted his attention. We can expect him to appear any time. How should we greet him? We could pick a bouquet of flowers or maybe bake him a cake. No, it is best to honor his arrival with my sword."

In the meantime, Crossmore had located the point of the energy surge in the center of the Swamp of Grief.

He thought to himself, "Maybe the stories are true about Doomage having a special interest in the swamp."

As Crossmore extended his reach, he detected the presence of four people on an island. Even more wonderful, he sensed the emotion of fear. The pure, wonderful presence of panic invited him to a feast. Creating and feeding on fear was one of the delights of his life.

As Crossmore's reaching-hand swooped toward the four men, he identified a person cowering in a state of panic. His lust to banquet on fear caused him to only focus his attention on the quarry. Normally, the evil of his depraved presence would paralyze his intended victims. With arrogance and self-confidence, he rushed forward unabated. In pride, he laughed at how easy it was to terrorize the wretched people of the Empire.

Crossmore was about to grab the pathetic, cringing victim when he felt a terrible pain shoot through his being. The pain was not a sting, but a deep, agonizing stab of anguish. He had received a wound from something on the island. He quickly retreated from his victim. The ache of the wound caused a sickening weakness to flow through him. Crossmore gave a loud screech of anger. He staggered back into the center of the tower, attempting to escape from the attack. The pain had not been caused by a physical wound, but by an assault on his spirit.

At this point, Crossmore decided to identify the people on the island. Using his power-of-vision, his attention was drawn to a man standing in a defensive posture with a sword in his hand. He recognized Coaldon, his mortal enemy. Crossmore knew in an instant that Coaldon had grown in strength since their last meeting. He was no longer a youth, but a young man of courage and determination. Pushing back his pain and torment, he decided Coaldon's attack could not go unanswered.

Taking his time, Crossmore wove a powerful spell to cast at the young warrior. Drawing on reserve energy, he sent a blast of fire into the sky. A bolt of flames could be seen arching over the Empire toward the Swamp of Grief.

Coaldon sensed the flames-of-death hurling toward him. Coaldon was thankful he had adequate time to prepare for the attack. Few things in the Empire could withstand the destructive power of Crossmore's magic.

With a confident voice, he commanded his sword, "Defend and protect us. Attract and absorb the power of Crossmore's magic."

Coaldon held the Sword of Conquest in the air, pointing it in the direction of the incoming flare of destruction. The bright inferno of the flames streaked out of the northern sky in a graceful arch. As the raging ball of fire approached the island, the Sword of Conquest sent out a beam of light. Following the shaft of energy, the firestorm rushed directly toward the sword. When the magic struck, it was sucked into the blade. Coaldon's whole body sagged under the pressure of the attack. The blade turned bright orange as the power of Crossmore's magic surged inside the blade. The captive energy heaved back and forth within the metal, attempting to escape. The turmoil within the sword caused it to swing wildly over Coaldon's head. Coaldon had to use all his strength to keep the blade from flying out of control.

As Crossmore's magic attacked the fiber of the elfin blade, it bulged into the shape of a balloon. The sword changed colors, from orange to red, as a war raged within the blade. The heat from the conflict began to scorch Coaldon's hands. He had to do something quickly before his hands were severely burned. With an instinctive response, he used all his strength to point the swirling tip of the sword toward the north.

In a firm voice, Coaldon commanded, "Release the power! Send it back to Crossmore!"

When Crossmore's magic exploded out of the blade, its kickback threw Coaldon backwards onto the ground. The returning trajectory of the fireball followed its incoming path. Instantaneously, Crossmore knew a counter attack had been released. He raised his hand and directed a stream of energy at the incoming inferno. When his defensive shield met the fireball, it created a blinding flash of light and deafening roar.

Crossmore tried to push Coaldon's assault back to the swamp. The more Crossmore asserted his magic, the more he felt an opposite pressure fighting against him. He soon realized Coaldon was also struggling to control the direction of the flames. The fireball darted over Neverly, quivering under the pressure of the opposing forces. Back and forth the battle raged between Coaldon and Crossmore.

Tiny, Philo, and Walty watched Coaldon stand with his legs spread apart, his sword pointing to the north, and his muscles straining against an unseen power. As sweat poured off his face, Coaldon's full attention was focused on the enemy.

The people of Neverly rushed into the streets to watch the bright, blazing sphere flittering in the sky. The heat radiating from the ball became so intense it forced the residents to escape back into their houses. The longer the battle continued, the more Crossmore showed signs of anger. As Crossmore's rage grew, the windows of the tower flashed with angry shades of red.

Coaldon's endurance was waning after the long confrontation with Crossmore. Coaldon knew something had to be done before he collapsed from exhaustion. His goal was not to conquer Crossmore, but only to protect his friends and himself. He knew Crossmore was much too powerful for him to confront in a battle to the death. Therefore, he determined it was best to gracefully exit from the conflict. To escape the battle, he lowered his point of pressure on the fireball. The instant he shifted the point of his attack, it caused Crossmore's forward force to push the fireball into the sky. The mass of flames shot upward like a skyrocket. Once Coaldon and Crossmore's opposing forces ended, the internal pressure on the fireball was released. The resulting explosion created a dazzling display of fireworks over the city. The concussion from the explosion broke windows, ripped off doors, and knocked down trees.

At the conclusion of the battle, Crossmore stood in a state of frustration. He raged, "Someday I will destroy him! My plans for conquest are too important to allow a mere human to interfere with the fulfillment of my dreams!"

Four on the Road

After the battle was over, a great stillness extended over the swamp. Not a sound was made by any living creature. Coaldon stood like a statue. His eyes were closed, head hung down, and arms extended stiffly in front of him. He teetered back and forth before finally falling backward. His rigid body lay buried in the soft-grass. Tiny feared Coaldon had died. With his massive arms, he scooped up Coaldon's body and gently held him.

As Coaldon went limp in Tiny's arms, the young prince opened his eyes. With disorientation and confusion, his blank eyes looked around the camp site. He then looked into Tiny's eyes with an expression of peace. Tiny was relieved when a broad smile spread across Coaldon's face.

Coaldon said, "Thank you for your help. I feel secure in your arms. You should put me down before I start calling you daddy."

Tiny laughed with mirth to discover his friend still had a sense of humor.

Holding Coaldon, Tiny commented, "You are such a cute little guy. Maybe I need to change your diaper. Should I check?"

Coaldon rippled in frustration, thinking Tiny might actually do it.

He stated, "That will not be necessary! I think I am doing just fine! Please put me down!"

Tiny looked at Coaldon with the warmth and caring of a new father. Holding him firmly, he commented, "You look hungry. Do you need a bottle?"

Coaldon tried to escape Tiny's firm grip by squirming and wiggling, but to no avail. With a red face, he finally yelled, "Put me down! I am not a child!"

Philo, Walty, and Tiny roared with laugher at Coaldon's agitation. Tiny finally lowered the angry young prince to the ground. In frustration, Coaldon stood with his arms crossed, casting hostile glances at Tiny. This only fed the laughter of his three companions. It took several moments before Coaldon recognized his childish behavior and joined into the good humor shared by the group.

A hearty evening meal was enjoyed by four men. Walty, the newest member of the group, was quiet as he reflected on the changes in his life. As he ate, he struggled to transcend the gap of many centuries. Walty knew he was a man-from-the-past with no understanding of current events.

After the meal, Walty stated, "What am I going to do? Everything from my past life is gone, except for my friend Philo. I never thought I would feel such despair and loneliness when I returned to normal life."

In a reassuring voice, Coaldon said, "You are welcome to join us. We are on a mission to save the Empire from Crossmore. We do not know where we are going, but I can guarantee you it will not be boring. So, what do you say?"

Without pausing, Walty declared, "I have no plans for the next few days, so I will be happy to join you. I denied my friends once, but never again. I will not be a burden to you. I will carry my load."

Smiling, Coaldon continued, "That sounds good to me. Now we need to get off this island. What should we do? How do we escape the magic?"

Walty paused before answering, "I believe we are free to leave. I am the medium who kept the magic alive. I am the only person able to control it."

With that in mind, Coaldon stated, "I suggest, that tomorrow, we travel north to find a way off the island and out of the swamps."

Noel and Something Odd

While Dreg looked for tadpoles in a pond, the three adults sat near their campfire enjoying the fresh morning air. Raff and Paggy casually questioned Noel about Scaric's destruction, but could not convince her to tell the story. Noel did not want anybody to know about the great power that erupted from Dreg. She would keep the secret to herself. As the friends gazed into the flickering flames, illusive shadows of the future invaded their minds with an unidentified sense of anticipation.

With the image of Scaric still filling their minds, the companions began their daily hike. As the day progressed, the swamp began to yield to grasslands and scattered trees. The tall grass had tough, broad stems, with sharp edges, that cut and tore flesh. At times, Raff had to use his sword to cut swaths through thick patches of foliage. Paggy called the vegetation 'cut grass' to characterize its disagreeable nature.

As the group left the swamp, the humidity decreased, but the temperature slowly increased. The mild northern climate of Grandy was cool compared to the high temperatures of the south. Even though the group suffered from the heat, they celebrated the decline of the insect population.

In spite of the unpleasant foliage and heat, the four companions enjoyed the open spaces. They had found the dense undergrowth of the swamp to be suffocating and uncomfortable. The broad expanse of the grasslands provided a feeling of freedom.

The group decided to stop late-afternoon to allow Dreg time to rest. The young boy was still not use to the rigors of long hikes. His drooping eyes, short steps, and hanging head, signaled the end of the trek for the day. The evening was spent in pleasant conversation and preparing for the next day. Dreg was first to notice a thick column of black smoke bellowing into the southwest sky.

The boy declared, "Look! Look! I see smoke!"

Leaping to their feet, the three adults glanced simultaneously in the direction of Dreg's pointing fingers. Silence was accompanied by a sense of anxiety. Their private world had been invaded by the unknown. The short lived column of smoke rose in a massive cloud on the distant horizon. The group watched as the black cloud dissipated into wisps of gray haze. It was difficult to gauge the distance to the cloud. Yet, it was close enough to draw their attention.

Paggy responded, "I wonder what this means?"

With a serious expression on her face, Noel answered, "The smoke means that there was a fire. Fire in this grass could be dangerous. Hopefully, it was started by an act of nature, not by some vile creature. What ever the case, we need to be watchful. We do not want any surprises."

An uneventful night passed with no hint of anything extraordinary. The trekkers made good progress the following morning and early afternoon. The group decided to take a midday break in a grove of trees. Warm temperatures and tired bodies made it easy for the travelers to slip into quiet slumber.

Noel was jarred awake when a throb of energy rushed through her body. She abruptly sat up searching for danger, but found nothing out of the ordinary.

She yelled to Paggy and Raff, "Wake up! Something strange is going on!"

Her two companions erupted from their naps expecting to face a crisis. Looking around, they discovered Noel intently staring into the southwest. The two friends could not see what captivated Noel's attention. They glanced at each other with puzzled expressions.

Raff quietly interrupted, "Noel is everything all right?"

Noel slowly turned to him with a vacant expression. Her awareness of the present moment returned as she shifted her attention to Raff.

In a sober voice she stated, "I am not trying to ignore you, but a massive blast of energy is radiating from the southwest. This is coming from the same location we saw the smoke yesterday. Something strange is happening."

As the three companions focused their attention to the southwest, a bright flash of red and green light filled the sky. The display was followed by a piercing scream of agony from thousands of desperate voices. Then a bright, luminous cloud appeared on the southwest horizon. Lightning flashed from the cloud and claps of thunder rumbled in the distance.

The three observers were held in spellbound fascination as the mysterious occurrence infused them with an unexplained flood of calm. This emotional rush was climaxed when the cloud shot into the western sky. They stood in awe as the large cloud, moving with unnatural speed, quickly disappeared over the horizon. The event was so marvelous, few words were spoken for the remainder of the evening.

As the travelers continued their trek on the following day, the mystery of the previous day dominated their thoughts. The events seemed more like a dream than an actual event. The flash of red and green lights, the agonizing scream of many voices, and the glowing cloud floated eerily in their minds.

Midmorning, Noel's thoughts were once again interrupted. She felt a burst of energy emanating from the same location as the day before. A short time later, a feeling of disgust smothered her senses. Looking up, Noel saw a fireball arching through the sky from the north into the southwest. Instantly, the young half-elf cringed as the evil presence of Crossmore passed overhead. The young woman's knees turned to jelly as she sagged to the ground in fear and trembling. At that moment, she made a resolution to never again allow the presence of Crossmore to dominate her. She needed to stand up against the power of Crossmore or always be subject to his corrupt nature.

After Crossmore's power had disappeared, Noel gained control of her emotions. She stood up and waited in expectation for the next event. A lurking sense of fore-knowledge indicated there was more to come. Minutes later, a fireball erupted from the southwest and shot into the northern sky. As the fireball disappeared, a vibration filled the air. Noel felt the air tremble in shock waves. It was as if two great powers were battling each other to a stalemate. As the force of the encounter increased, she had a hard time breathing and moving. To her surprise, Raff and Paggy were not affected by the raging battle. The young princess questioned why she was able to sense the conflict and not the others. She concluded that her elfin character allowed her to perceive things beyond human awareness. To her relief, the battle abruptly ended. The pressure of the stalemate disappeared, leaving only questions. Why? Who? What?

The following morning Noel awoke before anybody else. She enjoyed watching the sun slowly rise in the eastern sky. She allowed the tranquility of the moment and the beauty of the new day to massage her whole being.

While in this peaceful state, Noel began to examine the change that had taken place in her life. She looked at Dreg sleeping next to her. His gentle, caring, trusting character had a profound effect on her. She remembered the first time he looked into her eyes and called her mom. Something changed inside her. The feeling was far greater than any wizard's magic. She remembered how she truly became his mom and formed a lifelong bond with the little boy. A deep sense of caring and love grew in her heart. She smiled at the thought of being a mom. She vowed to care for him as if he was her own flesh.

Drums

While Noel sat watching the sunrise, Coaldon also enjoyed the same early morning splendor. He awoke before his traveling companions to find a few moments of personal meditation. The events of the past days dominated his thoughts. He did not understand how so many different events could happen to him in such a short period of time.

Coaldon's attention soon drifted to thoughts of his grandparents, Noel, and his friends. He wondered what had happened to them. He assumed his grandparents and Noel were safely residing in the Monastery of Toms.

As the warm morning sun caressed his body, Coaldon drifted into an uneasy sleep. His slumber was disrupted by a dream filled with the images of wavering faces and the pounding of high-pitched drums. He saw a swirl of narrow faces with beady eyes watching him. The willowy faces twitched with anger. Within the folds of his dream the tap, tap of the drums grew closer and louder. Coaldon's body thrashed wildly until he awoke with a start. He abruptly sat up and looked around. The faces disappeared from his mind, but the sound of the drums could still be heard.

He immediately identified the faces, in his dream, as willow wraiths. With a burst of recognition, he put the drums and faces together.

He asked himself, "Is it possible that the willow wraiths are the source of the drum beats?"

As he stared into the direction of the drums, his three traveling companions awoke. The steady thumping brought the camp to full alert. Even though they could not see the source of the disturbance, they believed that peril was fast approaching.

Tiny was the first to speak, "The drums sound like the beat of the willow wraiths."

Coaldon responded, "I just had a dream in which I saw the faces of the wraiths and heard the beat of the drums. I wonder if the willow people are planning to visit us. They are probably enraged by the destruction of their clan members and are seeking revenge. I do not want to wait around to find out if they are pursuing us. I suggest we pack up and move out."

The desire to avoid another encounter with the willow wraiths was a powerful incentive. With long strides, Walty lead the travelers in a northwest direction. The throb of the drums continued to draw closer with each passing hour. As the team traveled, the island became a series of small bushy mounds and boggy channels. Clumps of tall bunch grass and thickets of thorny bushes made progress increasingly difficult. Low hanging tree limbs offered a wall of resistance. Fingers of the swamp began to encroach into the island. The further they hiked, the deeper their feet sank in the soft soil. The murky water of the swamp violated their sense of smell. The stress of struggling through the undergrowth and mud soon sapped their strength. By mid-afternoon, heavy breathing, sweat, and fatigue reduced their progress to slow, labored steps. Walty's unique relationship with the swamp allowed him to move through the mire with ease.

As everyone struggled, Walty declared in a loud voice, "This wasteland was created to keep northern invaders from the island. A secret path was built by magic to allow friends of Doomage to easily pass through this barrier. We need to cut across the island to find the trail. Follow me!"

With limp bodies, Walty's tired companions followed him without question or hesitation. He assumed the leadership role with a strong sense of determination. His many years as master of the island made it possible for him to intuitively locate the hidden trail.

With an excited smile and sparkling eyes, Walty rushed ahead searching for the path. His focus on finding the trail was so strong that he was unaware of the difficulties confronting his companions. Like a bird dog, he aggressively pursued his quest. With his head high and eyes darting back and forth, he quickly moved forward, sensing the approaching magic of the path.

When Walty paused to catch his breath, he suddenly felt the sensation of being alone. Looking around, he realized he was by himself. In the distance he heard weak voices calling his name. He suddenly remembered that his old magic allowed him to flow through the tangled foliage with ease.

In a loud tone, he yelled, "I am over here! Follow my voice!"

After a short wait, his three companions joined him on the top of a small hill. A clearing on the top of the mound gave them the opportunity to view the surrounding area. To the south, the lowlands spread out before them. This was the area in which they had spent the past several days. Looking to the north, they saw the island narrow to a ribbon of dense green foliage. Beyond the jungle a broad expanse of grasslands spread across the horizon.

In a frustrated voice, Tiny declared, "This is both good and bad news. We are offered the hope of reaching the grasslands, but the area between here and there will be difficult to pass. I do not know if I can make it through the dense blockade."

Walty was quick to respond, "Do not fear, Walty is here. I will save the day, you just wait and see. I will find the path to the north."

At this moment, the sound of drums drew their attention to a small clearing just south of the hill. A long line of willow wraiths could be seen easily striding across the bog.

Walty responded, "The swamp is the homeland of the wraiths. Their shadowy bodies can go through the quagmire as if it was dry land. They could be here in less than an hour."

The faces of Tiny and Philo drooped in frustration. Their tired bodies sagged under the weight of desperation. Lowering their heads, they stared at the ground, entertaining thoughts of defeat and death.

Walty, in a burst of enthusiasm, declared, "Follow me! I believe we are near the trail. Do not give up hope."

Walty's zeal added energy to their heavy feet. Following Walty, Tiny used his size and strength to push through the barrier of undergrowth. Tiny, Coaldon, and Philo were soon lost in the dense underbrush. Only by focusing on Walty were they able to find orientation in the sea of foliage. No matter which way they turned, everything looked the same. Leaves, branches, small trees, and vines provided the same backdrop in all directions. The tomb of foliage deadened noise to an eerie stillness. The sound of their voices and steps only carried several strides ahead before being consumed by the underbrush. Coaldon had the impression of being lost in the unending folds of a bad dream.

Tiny suddenly declared, "I heard foot steps."

The group stopped to respond to Tiny's observation. To their horror, they heard the steps of many feet sloshing through the soggy soil. Turning, they saw the shadow of many wispy figures approaching through the underbrush. The travelers could hear the whisper of voices coming from the wall of foliage.

In an anxious voice, Walty proclaimed, "We are near the path. I feel the magic just ahead of us. We must keep going."

Coaldon drew his sword and faced the invaders. With a wide sweep of the blade, he released a blast of fire into the foliage. The plants absorbed most of the heat from the blast, but several screams indicated his challenge did not go unnoticed. Coaldon's attack created panic among the ranks of the pursuers. A commanding voice pierced the stillness of the jungle like a sharp knife. Its authority created a stir of movement. The wraiths melted away like a mist dissolving before the morning sun.

Walty commanded, "Let's go! I do not believe we have much time before our new friends return for a repeat engagement."

As the group pushed ahead, Coaldon felt the gentle pulse of magic. He cried, "Walty, I sense the presence of the path!"

Walty responded, "Yes! So do I! When we reach the trail, we must not waste time. We need to escape before the willow wraiths overwhelm us.

Coaldon felt a flutter of power brush against him as he stepped onto the path. He looked to his left and right detecting the outline of a tunnel through the foliage in both directions. The power surrounding the path created the sensation of being encased in a cocoon.

Walty declared, "We have arrived! I am pleased to announce the wraiths cannot see or use the path. The magic protecting the path is invisible to them. Let's go! The creatures may not be able to use the trail, but this will not stop them from chasing after us."

Walty lead the way down the trail. The further they traveled, the more they felt a sense of speed. The travelers had the impression of being carried forward in an effortless manner. Their steps rushed ahead as if floating on an invisible cushion of air. Like a flash in time, they suddenly found themselves standing on the edge of the grasslands. Looking back they saw the impenetrable boundary of the jungle. They could not see the opening that they had just departed.

With dazed minds, they shifted their attention to the sea of grass stretching out before them. The chest-high vegetation grew in large bunches, interspersed with groves of small trees. With occasional glances over their shoulders, the group quickly moved into the grasslands. The thought of battling the willow wraiths motivated their progress.

A Column of Smoke

As Coaldon stood before the grasslands, he felt energy drain from himself. For the first time since departing Lost Valley, his desire to continue had evaporated. His long list of battles and adventures had finally sapped his strength. His eyes were lack-luster, feet heavy, and steps unresponsive. He had to force himself to move.

Tiny was the first to notice Coaldon's change in attitude.

The large man quietly said to Philo, "Coaldon is tired. The stress of his many exploits has taken a toll. I am not surprised the young lad is having a difficult time. He has been through a lot. I hope something happens to lighten his dark mood."

The group set a brisk pace into the grasslands. Coaldon labored to keep up, but managed to stay with the group. As the travelers ventured forward, they soon discovered the unpleasant characteristic of the unusual grass. Its blades were lined with rows of sharp teeth that would cut and tear skin. The lethal grass forced the group to carefully pick their way northward. Occasional clearings in the vegetation and animal trails offered the travelers the opportunity to make steady progress. Ponds and water channels were scattered randomly over the vast landscape. Birds of all kinds populated the area. Ducks and geese flew overhead, while smaller birds fluttered among the reeds and groves of small trees. Deer, fox, rodents, and wild dogs could be seen in every direction. The abundance of life reflected the rich bounty of nature.

As the group moved north, Coaldon kept looking over his shoulder to watch for the willow wraiths. After many observations, Coaldon declared, "I see the outline of the wraiths emerging from the swamp. I wonder if they will pursue us."

Walty responded, "They might, depending on the strength of their desire for revenge. The beasts are swamp creatures, therefore the grasslands are foreign to their way of life. The creatures may follow us, but not too far. If they are going to attack, it will be soon."

After several more hours of steady progress they arrived at an old road. It was constructed of rocks, cemented together with a black substance. The road bed was about seven strides wide and still passable. Occasional bunches of grass grew from between the stones.

Tiny commented, "I am surprised the road is still intact after all these centuries."

Coaldon asked Philo, "Do you remember this road?"

With a nostalgic smile, Philo stated, "I have passed over this road many times. It goes from the Rolling River in the east to the City of Mazz in the west. From what I remember, it should take us about fives days of travel to arrive at the Highlands of Mazz."

As Philo gazed at the road through the eyes of past memories, Coaldon's attention was on current events. The young prince abruptly stopped, dropped to his knees, and carefully examined the old roadbed. His three companions gazed at him with curiosity.

The young half-elf slowly looked up, stating, "As a child I was taught by the wood elves to read the signs of passing creatures. It may sound strange, but someone has recently walked passed here going toward the City of Mazz. As far as I can tell, there were several adults and a child. This seems strange. Why would anybody be in this lonely and desolate land, especially with a child?"

Tiny listened to Coaldon, but his thoughts were somewhere else. The memories of the willow wraiths were fresh in his mind. As he looked around the vicinity, he noticed a tiny whiff of smoke rising from a small grove of trees to the west.

Pointing with his hand, Tiny declared, "I see smoke coming from those trees. Matter of fact, I can actually smell it. It is drifting in our direction."

Showing no emotion, Coaldon slowly turned to look at the smoke.

In a sterile voice, Coaldon responded, "You are right. The rays from the setting sun clearly outline the small column. From this distance it appears to be a campfire."

Tiny commented, "I suggest we investigate. I do not like surprises. The sun will set in several hours. We have time to reach the grove before dark."

After a short conference it was decided to proceed with caution. The group left the road and approached the grove by creeping through the tall grass. After a half hour of slow, careful stalking they arrived at the trees.

The companions held a conference in a shallow ravine just east of the grove. As Coaldon began to speak, Walty gave a gasp of horror. Unable to speak, he pointed to the south. A billowing cloud of black smoke filled the southern sky. All four men instantly knew what had happened.

Philo declared, "The willow wraiths are seeking their revenge in the simplest and most efficient manner. The creatures have set the grasslands on fire. Fire will get the desired results without any risk to themselves."

With an unusual burst of energy, Tiny declared, "We have no time to waste! We must act now! Let's rush to the trees and take our chances. If we find friendly people, we can help each other. If foe, we will take the appropriate action. Let's go."

Coaldon and Tiny drew their swords and ran forward. Walty and Philo followed carrying knives. As the four men hurried into the grove, they saw the backs of three adults and one child. The four people were so focused on the approaching fire that they were unaware of the four men standing behind them. As the intruders watched, they recognized the shapes of two women, one man, and a small boy.

After sheathing his sword, Coaldon quietly stated, "Hail to you. We come in peace."

With a sudden jerk the three adults turned, saw the four men, and ran toward the cover of the tall grass. As the tall, young woman ran, she suddenly stopped and noticed the boy was not at her side. She stopped, whirled around, and stared in horror. The small boy had not tried to escape, but rather stood looking at the men. With unusual confidence, he casually walked toward the new arrivals. He stopped in front of Coaldon, tilted his head to one side, and stared with an inquisitive expression on his face.

The young boy finally stated, "Welcome to our campsite. You are the only people we have met in this lonely land. Where did you come from? You look familiar to me. Have we met before?"

Coaldon laughed at the little boy's boldness.

Coaldon followed, "Thank you for your welcome. We come in peace. I do not believe we have met. We offer our assistance in this moment of danger. Please ask your companions to join us. We are no threat to them."

The young boy turned in a relaxed manner, taking several steps towards his companions.

Waving, he shouted, "Everything is all right. Come and meet my new friends."

The tall young woman with long black hair, ragged clothes, and dirty face slowly approached the four men. Her hair hung loosely over her face in a ruffled and unkempt manner. Stopping just behind the small boy, she stood in a defensive stance with both hands on her hips. As she stared at Coaldon, an obvious ripple passed through her body. A subtle look of joy and relief replaced the cloud of hesitation and caution. A sly smile crossed her face with a haunting cast of mischief. Then she erupted into a soft laugh.

In a raspy voice she stated, "What has happened to you? Your hair is gone and your skin has turned brown. You must have had some unusual experiences."

Coaldon stood in disbelief. The abruptness of the young woman caught him off guard. Coaldon was overwhelmed by the woman's self-assurance. The clarity and crispness of her words, plus her erect posture indicated a noble character. The young woman's familiarity totally disarmed him. The hero of many dangerous conflicts was tongue-tied.

Realizing Coaldon's distress, she teasingly continued, "This is my son Dreg. He has heard many stories about you. He has been so eager to meet you. By the blank look on your face, you still do not recognize me. Shame on you!"

The young woman's sense of intimacy caused Coaldon to take several steps back. Then, out of curiosity, he looked at her two traveling companions. At this point, he was once again caught off guard.

As he recognized the two people, he declared in an excited voice, "Raff and Paggy, what are you doing here!? I never imaged you would ever leave Grandy!"

The two young adults looked at Coaldon with curiosity and puzzlement. After a short pause, Raff erupted into a broad smile.

He declared, "Coaldon, I cannot believe my eyes! I never expected to meet anybody in this deserted land, yet alone you. What ever happened to your hair and skin?"

The three old friends hugged each other in joy. After an emotional reunion, Coaldon turned to the young woman questioning, "And who might you be? I have met you somewhere, but in my dazed state I do not recognize you."

She responded with a broad smile, "I am your sister, you big ox. I guess you do not recognize me in my palace finery."

Coaldon could only stand in disbelief. When the truth finally sank in, he grabbed his sister in happiness.

With tenderness, he looked into her eyes, questioning, "I am sorry I did not recognize you. How did you get here? Who is the boy you call your son?"

Before Noel could say anything, Tiny declared, "We could spend days sharing stories, but we have more important things to do. If you have not noticed, a wild fire is fast approaching us."

With a guilty look on his face, Coaldon, stated, "You are right. We can talk later."

The orange and red flames from the approaching inferno could be seen leaping high in the air. Animals of all sizes and shapes retreated past the eight observers. The still evening air slowed the fires advance, but it would only be a short time before the small group would be consumed by the blaze. Everybody was so mesmerized by the giant force of nature that they could not speak, run, or think.

Raff finally broke the silence, by clarifying, "If we run, the fire will catch us. If we stay here, the fire will destroy us. How do we escape?"

As the remainder of the group groped for a solution, Philo's thoughts regressed to his past life. As he stared at the approaching fire, he heard the sound of water splashing in the hidden recesses of his being. He remembered waves washing over his fish-like body. He had pleasant memories of water comfortably wrapped around him. The secure womb of the ocean had been the home that fed, protected, cleansed, and healed him. The unrelenting flow of watery images continued to drift through his thoughts as if searching for a response to the fire. Then it hit him.

His body became ridged, as he yelled in an excited voice, "Fire and water do not mix! Water does not burn! We will be protected by submerging ourselves under water!"

His voice brought everyone back to reality. Each member of the group looked at Philo with a dazed expression.

H

ᛚᚦᚺ ᛟᚢᛚᚺᛏ ᛟᚢᚼᚼ

The Water Wall

Coaldon's melancholy mood had been washed away by his reunion with Raff, Paggy, and Noel. His eyes sparkled. He stood with his shoulders back and his head elevated into an erect position. Animation filled his whole being with a radiant glow of energy as the fire approached the group.

He yelled, "Follow me! I remember seeing a pond to the west."

Without hesitation, he grabbed Dreg into his arms and trotted out of the grove. He did not look back to see if anybody was following, but rather focused his full attention on reaching the water. To his distress, he discovered the pond was further away than he first estimated. Looking to the south, he also realized the fire was fast approaching. He increased the length of his strides in hopes of beating the flames.

Glancing over his shoulder, he yelled, "We must move faster if we are going to survive. Hurry up!"

Pushed by a gust of wind, a finger of fire jumped across the path between the group and the pond. Without pausing, Coaldon lead the group to the right, away from the flames.

Coaldon was at a full run when he heard a cry from behind him. Looking back, he saw Paggy lying on the ground. Everyone stopped and waited for the young woman to regain her footing. This interruption allowed the giant blaze to draw ever closer. The sound of choking and gagging erupted when a dense cloud of smoke covered the struggling group. Through the smoke, he saw each member of the group sprawled on the ground trying to escape from the suffocating smoke.

The young warrior stood in desperation. He knew all was lost unless an escape route was found. He had learned from past experience that when all else failed he always had final recourse. In reverence and trust, he asked, "Please help us."

At this moment, he felt a strange energy wrap around him. Time suddenly slowed down to a crawl. He looked behind himself to see the flames moving in slow motion. Even though time had slowed down, he could still move freely.

In the blink of an eye, the smoke cleared from around him, leaving an open space in the cloud. Through his irritated eyes, he beheld a sight nearly impossible to comprehend. A flat wall of liquid formed in front of him. It appeared to be composed of water. He looked up and down, examining the watery surface of the wall. The half-elf could not understand how a barrier of liquid could stand upright. Stepping forward, he touched the rippling, undulating mass of fluid. To his surprise, the barrier felt like water but stood in a vertical position. Coaldon sat Dreg on the ground so he could investigate the strange new phenomenon.

Reaching forward, he pushed his hand into the wall and then pulled it back out. He shook his head in confusion at the mystery facing him. Again, he thrust his hand into the wall. His arm easily went forward until he reached all the way to his shoulder. To his surprise, his hand went through the water barrier and poked out the other side. He felt sunshine warming his fingers. Moving his arm back and forth he felt leaves rub against his fingers. Out of curiosity, he grabbed a small branch. Yanking, he ripped the small limb from the tree and pulled it back through the barrier. He stared in disbelief at the branch in his hand. He knew the leaves of this variety of tree were not found in the grasslands.

Glancing around, he saw flames slowly crippling towards him.

Looking down, he saw his companions lying in a deep slumber. His head swam in dizziness at the absurdity of the situation. His mind could not comprehend the incredible sequence of events unfolding around him. His legs grew weak and collapsed under the weight of his body. Falling to his knees, he closed his eyes, hoping to clear his mind of confusion. The young prince had to discover a way to save their lives. Feeling the heat of the advancing fire on his face, he knew the end was near if he did not do something soon.

As he knelt, he heard an unusual noise in front of him. A loud squawk and the flutter of wings caused him to open his eyes. To his surprise, Cackles the Bird stood in front of him. The large creature spread its wings and casually glanced around the area. Coaldon noticed the ancient bird did not seem to be concerned about the flames.

Giving a loud cackling call, the bird said, "You do get yourself into some unusual situations. Why are you acting like a helpless child? If you know it or not, you will die in several minutes if you do not act immediately. You have been offered an escape route. Now get busy!"

In exasperation, Coaldon stared at the bird. Finally, he forced himself to speak, "What are you talking about? How can we escape?"

Shaking its head, the bird responded in a screeching voice, "It does not take much to bewilder you. You are such a slow learner. All right, I will explain things to you. It is your destiny to be here. The reality of the fire cannot be altered, but the presence of hope offers the opportunity to survive. In other words, the heat of the flames is a physical fact, whereas, the power of faith offers a solution. What seems miraculous to you is just a simple manipulation of the physical world. What appears to be the unchanging nature of time and space is, in reality, subject to a higher Truth. The hand of creation is offering you and your friends a means to escape. So, get going!"

With dazed eyes and the appearance of helplessness, Coaldon responded, "I guess I understand what you just said. Yet, I do not know how to save us."

The bird slumped forward in disbelief. Slowly, the old bird raised its head. In a sarcastic tone, the old creature declared in disgust, "Listen carefully to what I say. Pick up each person and carry them through the water-wall and leave them on the other side. Hurry! Hurry! The energy holding the timelessness in place will soon collapse."

The bird then spread its wings and leaped toward Coaldon. The rush of flapping wings awoke the young warrior from his trance. Looking around he saw the blaze was several strides away. Without pausing, Coaldon rushed to assist his friends.

As the young prince moved, he heard nothing. The surroundings, except the wall, were a fuzzy image of the physical world. Colors blended together into a bland mesh of overlapping layers. He tried to touch a bush, but his hand passed through the limbs. He felt as if he was walking on a soft, puffy cloud. His mind spun in disorientation as he tried to place order to the fluid, nebulous world.

Looking down, Coaldon saw the bodies of his companions lying on the ground. Their eyes stared into space with an empty gaze. Reaching down, he grabbed Tiny under his shoulders, lifted, and dragged him toward the wall. Taking a deep breath, the young warrior backed into the barrier. As he stepped into the liquid, a chill passed through his body. He felt as if the liquid was flowing through him. His vision was filled with a swirling collage of people, trees, houses, rivers, towns, farms, and landscapes. He wanted to stay and look, but realized it was necessary to save his companions.

With a burst of energy, he pulled Tiny through the wall with a jerk. On the opposite side, he stepped into a different environment. The warrior stood in a green meadow with bright sunshine flooding his body. Lowering Tiny's body to the ground, he turned to face the wall. Its fluid surface filled his field of vision. He wanted to stay in the meadow, but the lives of his friends depended on quick action. Stepping back though the wall, he once again entered the time lapse. He sensed the energy holding the void in place was eroding. Without paying attention to the contrast between the different sides of his reality, he quickly dragged the remaining bodies through the tenuous barrier. As the last person was laid on the ground a brilliant flash filled his mind. Turning, he found the water-wall had disappeared, being replaced by the meadow. As his friends awoke from their trip into timelessness, Coaldon heard loud shouts of astonishment.

A Time to Rest

Coaldon patiently listened to a string of questions from his companions. "How did we get here? Where are we? Where is the fire?" The rush of questions was interspersed with bouts of coughing. The strong odor of smoke filled the air. Everybody's clothes were layered with soot and ashes. Runny noses and red eyes confirmed the group's recent encounter with fire.

Not knowing what to say, Coaldon did not respond to their inquires. He only smiled, allowing his silence to provide its own answer. After the initial burst of excitement, the travelers focused their attention on the immediate surroundings. The meadow stretched several thousand strides across, ending in a border of pine trees. A stream flowed through the center of the meadow. The creek was lined with brush and small trees. To the south, a road followed the boundary of the trees. The northern horizon was outlined by a range of tall, jagged mountains. The snow-covered peaks looked like the teeth of a large saw. Long ridges descended from the mountains, forming rocky spines and deep canyons. These ridgelines flattened out creating the gentle slope of the meadow. The humid atmosphere of the swamplands had been replaced by cool, dry mountain air.

The exhilaration of escape soon melted away. Elation was replaced by fatigue and hunger.

As the long shadows of evening pushed across the land, Noel proclaimed, "I smell like smoke. My clothes are dirty. I need to wash away the trail dust. I am going to take a dip in the stream."

Her proclamation was followed by a robust round of agreement. The men and women took off in different directions to enjoy a refreshing scrub. Upon returning, a camp site was selected and the evening meal prepared. As the group sat around the warm campfire, Coaldon shared the account of their escape from the fire. Then each person told stories about the adventures they had experienced over the past several months. Laughs, groans, cries of disbeliefs, angry shouts, cheers, and whispers-of-awe interrupted the stories.

After a long evening, many yawns announced the end of the gathering. The companions approached sleep with minds filled with incredible images and a new respect for the power guiding their journey. The obvious involvement of the Father of Life offered renewed hope in defeating Crossmore. Peace caressed each person into deep sleep.

The following morning, a short meeting was held to decide the group's next step. Coaldon stated, "We are no longer a few travelers lost in the wilderness, but a small army following an unknown destiny."

The young prince paused, pulled the Key of Ban from his traveling pouch and lifted it into the air for everybody to see.

He continued, "I never imaged I would be here with you. Yet, the hand of fate has somehow guided us together. This book is the Key of Ban. The goal of our quest is to unite the Key of Ban and Topple the Wizard. Crossmore can be defeated by the power originating from this elfin book. In order to complete our mission, we must follow the path laid out before us."

Tiny interrupted, "I also believe we have been brought together for a reason. Yet, what path are you talking about? What direction will this trail take us?"

Before Coaldon could respond, Philo declared, "We are on the Highlands of Mazz. The towering mountains to the north are the southern shoulder of the Black Mountains. As emperor, I have been here many times. It is only a half days march to the City of Mazz. You must be warned of the great danger facing us in the city. The people of Mazz destroyed themselves by their own evil. The lurking residue of sin has poisoned the city to this day. It is inhabited by an evil army of spirits. We must proceed with caution."

Philo's gloomy words cast a dark cloud over the mood of the group.

Noel's face twisted in frustration as she questioned, "Do we need to go to Mazz? How do we find Topple?'

Silence answered her questions. Coaldon's eyes darted back and forth as his mind searched for a response.

He finally projected, "I believe we have been guided from one crisis after another for some unknown purpose. We have been focused on surviving, not on the long term goal of defeating Crossmore. The immediate reality of the City of Mazz has forced us to ask tough questions."

Walty followed, "It is best not to go to Mazz without good reason. Maybe, we should wait here until we find direction. It appears we have a goal, but no way to get there."

To everyone's surprise, Paggy burst into quiet laughter. The reserved and modest young women looked around the group with a broad smile lighting her face.

With a giggle, she commented, "We have an old village saying, 'It is a fool who runs in the forest on a dark night'. I believe it is foolish for us to rush ahead without any thought of purpose."

Everybody looked at Paggy with growing respect. She helped clarify the obvious in simple and direct terms. Her burst of insight was refreshing.

In her usual, abrupt manner, Noel concluded, "I suggest we stay here until we find guidance. It is not necessary to endanger our lives without just cause. Anyway, we can use a rest. We still have enough food, so let us relax and allow our journey to unfold."

Nods of approval confirmed her suggestion.

The Mouse Message

After several days rest, impatience began to grow among the companions. It did not take long for the restlessness of youth to begin its search for the next dose of adventure.

On the morning of the third day, Noel and Coaldon decided to examine a large out-crop of rocks north of the meadow. As they casually walked through the lush meadow, they enjoyed the concert of birds and parade of wildlife. As the early morning sun danced through the dew, the grass sparkled like diamonds. Dreg raced ahead throwing his arms in the air as he chased after elusive rodents and colorful insects. The brother and sister spent this time quietly talking about their earlier lives. Upon arriving at the rocky mound, they watched the antics of Dreg with delight. The little boy busily poked his head into different openings of the hill in search of the next great mystery.

Noel's and Coaldon's attention shifted when they found a narrow channel extending into the heart of the large mound. Coaldon noticed the vague outline of elfin script on the wall next to the opening. Its weathered appearance indicated its ancient origin. Upon closer examination, Coaldon saw the outline of a path leading into the rocky knoll. As he was studying the ground, Dreg came running up to him.

In an excited voice, he declared, "I have a new friend. I just talked with him. I like him. He is funny."

Coaldon looked at him, not knowing what to say. At first, he thought the boy was playing imaginary games. To join the fun, Coaldon responded, "What is your friend's name?"

In a matter-of-fact manner the boy answered, "Topple. He said he knows you."

Coaldon could only stare in disbelief at the boy.

Finally, he questioned, "What did he look like? What did he say to you?"

Watching a line of ants crawling across the ground, Dreg mumbled, "He is an old man wearing a dirty robe. Yet, I think he is a ghost. I could see through him. Oh yes, he wants to talk to you. You can find him inside the hill."

With this said, the busy boy rushed off to tell Noel about Topple.

Upon hearing the story, the princess joined Coaldon saying, "How could Dreg know anything about Topple? He must have talked with him. Yet, how could Topple be a ghost?"

Coaldon's face contorted into lines of concern. He projected, "Something must have happened to him. No matter the situation, we must enter the rock to find him."

Taking his leather water bag, Coaldon poured water over the ancient elfin symbols written on the rock face. As he vigorously rubbed the rock, the letters slowly grew in clarity. The elfin script was written in High Elf. He remembered his grandmother Ingrid teaching him the difference between High and Low Elf. High Elf was a complex series of symbols written in delicate script. Low Elf used block letters with heavy lines.

At first it was difficult to read the complex text. Yet, as he combined what he had learned from his grandmother with the actual writing on the wall, it began to make sense. It read, 'This is a safe haven for those unfulfilled in death. Enter at your own risk. You will be tested according to the Truth. This challenge will determine your fate'.

Noel and Dreg stood behind Coaldon as he slowly read the text out loud.

Looking at Noel, he asked, "According to this message, it might be dangerous to go inside. Should you and Dreg go into the rock?"

Noel gave a snort of disgust, "My dear brother, you need not ask such a dumb question. Of course we will accompany you. I would not miss this for the world. This could be very interesting. Let's go!"

Coaldon lead the way into the narrow channel of rock. The walls towered high over-head. The narrow passageway forced them to turn sideways to squeeze forward. After a short distance, the passage opened into a wide tunnel. Their casual attitude changed when they saw piles of human bones lining the tunnel. The number of bones increased the further they walked. A dull glow from the end of the passage provided enough light to guide their steps.

The three explorers stopped when they entered a large cavern. The cave was illuminated by sunlight flowing through large windows in the roof. The trail led to several large statues standing on both sides of the entrance. On the right was the statue of a man wearing pants and shirt with his right hand raised in greeting. His smiling face projected gentleness and peace. On the left was the statue of a woman wearing a flowing robe. Her hand was raised with the palm facing forward. It indicated they were to stop. The authority of her stare demanded submission to her presence. The statue's face radiated an image of power and judgment.

Between the two monuments a wavering wall of energy pulsed back and forth. They could not enter the cavern without passing between the two statues and through the barrier.

Coaldon commented, "The piles of bones indicate many people died trying to enter this holy place. I assume they were not judged adequate to be admitted. According to the message on the rock, we must pass a test before entering. If we fail, I believe our bones will also litter the floor."

Before Noel could respond, Dreg rushed ahead, passing between the two statues. A bright light flashed when he went through the energy field.

A loud rumbling voice announced, "Welcome to the Haven of Protection. You have passed the test. Be at peace."

With wide eyes, the little boy looked around, searching for the source of the voice. Turning, he smiled at Coaldon and Noel. He waved his arms in excitement and rushed ahead to explore the mysterious cavern.

Noel yelled at him, "Come back! Stay with us!"

Dreg smiled saying, "I am all right. I am safe. Come on!"

With that proclamation, the small boy disappeared into the shadows of the cavern. Noel's whole body gripped in panic. She ran forward, not thinking about herself, but the safety of her son. When she ran through the power field she froze in place. Her mind was suddenly filled with the image of Crossmore standing with his back turned to her. Looking down, she saw a bright, shiny knife in her hand. The shriek of Dreg's voice brought her attention back to Crossmore. She saw the wizard lift the little boy high over his head. The wizard laughed in sadistic delight as he looked at the child. The boys face twisted in horror at the sight of the wizard.

The child screamed, "Mother, help me! This man scares me! Oh, please help me!"

As motherly instinct dominated Noel's thinking, she boiled in hatred of Crossmore. She had vivid memories of being Crossmore's prisoner in Neverly. The image of the wizard's corrupt and foul nature dominated her thoughts. She shivered in revulsion at the idea of his unclean hands touching Dreg.

Standing behind him, she slowly raised the knife over her head and walked toward the evil wizard. Thoughts of killing him controlled her thinking. The blade began to move forward when she abruptly stopped her attack. The princess became aware of tears running down her face. She realized hatred was guiding her. With her arms high over her head, she struggled between the desire to kill the wizard and the knowledge that it was wrong.

She thought, "The wizard is evil, but it is not my role to destroy his life. His fate belongs to another. I must not allow anger to govern my life."

As she dropped her arms, a bright light flashed and she fell forward. She heard the rumbling voice welcome her to the cavern. Looking around she realized she had been tested and survived. Staggering to her feet she turned to face Coaldon.

She stated, "It is difficult, but you must also cross the barrier. Take courage and join me."

Coaldon hesitated as he stepped forward. When the power gripped him, he saw a large black monster standing before him. The massive beast stunk of death, smiled with arrogance, breathed whiffs of fire, and stared at Coaldon with cold contempt. Its round, human like body was wrapped in leathery skin and supported a huge head. The beast's ugly face scowled between two huge ears. It had large round eyes, a sausage shaped nose, and a wide, gaping mouth. From past experience, Coaldon knew the monster's only motivation was to kill, destroy, consume, and create fear.

Coaldon had never faced such a challenge by himself. He reached down, pulling his sword from its scabbard. To his great surprise, he held a wooden blade used in children's play. As Coaldon looked in horror at the object in his hand, the monster laughed in glee. While the young prince stared at the wooden toy, the monster gracefully lumbered forward and hit Coaldon with a glancing blow. The half-elf was taken by shock as he rolled across the ground. Before he could clear his head, he was struck again and again by the agile beast. With a loud roar of victory, the creature backed away from Coaldon allowing him to regain his strength.

The monster rumbled, "This is like a cat playing with a mouse. You are so pathetic. I was told you were a great warrior. You are just a baby in my presence. I will continue my fun when you have recovered."

The beast sat down next to Coaldon, watching his every move. The cat was ready to pounce on its prey if the mouse tried to escape.

Coaldon felt throbbing pain in every part of his body. Looking down, he realized he was still holding the wooden sword.

Then, in a quiet voice he pleaded to an unseen presence, "Please help me. Guide me."

As these words drifted from his mouth, the young prince heard a whisper in his ear. Glancing over he saw a mouse sitting on its hind legs, looking at him. The little creature twitched it whiskers and sniffed the air.

Opening its tiny mouth, it squeaked, "You are to listen carefully, or die. Any sword, whether metal or wood, is no more powerful then the spirit filling it. Allow the power of your destiny to energize every fiber of the wooden blade. Confront the beast with faith in the power of Providence. Trust in the Master of Life. Face your doubts with boldness and fortitude. You will be given as needed."

The little creature looked at the monster, squeaked, and dove into a hole in the ground. Coaldon took several moments to allow the message to sink into his confused mind. He tried to force himself to stand, but fear would not allow his body to move. Several times he tried to push himself to a sitting position, but with no success.

Finally, he thought to himself, "I can either conquer my fears or die. I can claim my destiny or suffer a miserable death. What is my choice?"

With super-human effort, he staggered to his feet, holding the wooden sword high in the air. In a weak, trembling voice he stammered, "I am ready to fight you. Be prepared to die."

Never in his life had Coaldon done anything more courageous. He went beyond the limits of reason by assuming the power of trust. Doubt had to be defeated in order for faith to rule.

The monster gave a roar of laughter as it stood up. With its hands resting on its hips, the foul creature raised its foot to step on Coaldon. The prince darted to his left to avoid being crushed. When the giant foot hit the ground, Coaldon turned and buried the wooden sword deep into the beast's foot. The creature responded by violently jerking its foot away. This sudden movement ripped the wooden sword from the half-elf's hand. The prince was surprised to see the beast dancing around in great suffering. Its foot began to swell. The beast responded to the pain with fits of anger. It began to chase Coaldon, trying to step on him. The agile young prince darted back and forth, successfully escaping. The encounter ended as quickly as it had started. The monster's whole body bloated into the shape of a large bubble. Gasping for breath, the beast fell to the ground. The creature flailed until it exploded into a foul smelling smoke.

Coaldon awoke to find Noel holding him in her arms.

With a broad smile, she happily stated, "You have survived. I knew you would find the courage."

Dust in the Wind

Noel and Coaldon stared in awe at the cavern. The vaulted ceiling had large windows which allowed sun light to filter into the room. The domed surface of the roof was perfectly smooth with streaks of red, green, yellow, and orange colors flowing into patterns and images. These colors blended together, forming scenes from different places in the Empire. Pictures of cities, farms, and sea life merged together into a collage of indescribable beauty. The dark brown colors of the smooth floor were illuminated by soft sunlight.

Several doors entered the room from opposite directions. The large room was bare of physical objects. As Coaldon and Noel talked, the sound of their voices did not echo. The noise in the room was deadened by an unseen presence. The barren rooms radiated a feeling of warmth and caring.

After absorbing the unique character of the room, Coaldon finally commented, "I believe we are being watched by many unseen eyes. We must be the center of attention."

Noel interrupted, "The elfin message at the entrance said that this is the haven for the unfulfilled. These lost souls must be waiting to return to the physical realm to finish important tasks."

Coaldon followed, "Whatever the situation, we are here to find Topple. Where is Dreg? I last saw him standing by the doorway to our right. Let's have a look."

As they approached the opening, the little boy came running out, radiating a happy smile.

He stated, "I have been talking to Topple. He said he would join us."

With a puzzled look on his face, the little boy turned to search for his mysterious friend.

The lad questioned, "Where is he?"

At that moment, Coaldon felt a gust of air flow out of the opening. Carried by the breeze, a cloud of dust particles drifted into the room.

At this point Dreg proclaimed, "Topple, I cannot see you. Please, stop being silly."

The scattered dust particles then pulled together into a swirling column. The cloud slowly expanded, forming into a wispy outline of a person. The image of Topple solidified out of the drifting cloud. Coaldon and Noel gasped in excitement when they recognize their old friend.

In a thin, delicate voice, Topple said, "I am so happy to see you. I have followed your progress over the past several months with interest. I knew you would ultimately arrive here. I am glad you chose to visit me."

With uncontrolled enthusiasm, Noel declared, "I have missed you! What happened to your body? Did you die? How did you get here?"

The ghostly image of Topple raised its hand to stop Noel from rambling on.

He responded, "I have missed you also. My story is short, yet tragic. But first, I want to tell you how much I enjoy Dreg. He laughs at my dumb jokes. Now, that is the ultimate kindness."

Coaldon commented, "He is a special gift to us. His innocence is delightful. He is so full of life and excitement. What about you? Please, tell us your story. It must have something to do with Crossmore."

Topple allowed his ghostly figure to expand the size of a large, round ball. The wizard's smiling face and eyes were expanded over the top of the sphere. To entertain the small boy, Topple rolled his huge distorted eyes and opened his mouth into the shape of a deep hole. All this was accompanied by red, yellow and green lights flashing from inside his transparent body. At this unusual sight, Dreg gave a loud squeal of laughter, yelling, "More! More!"

Enjoying the attention, Topple shifted his figure into the shape of a tall, narrow tree trunk. The outline of Topple's face could be seen in the surface of the bark. The trunk then sprouted short stubby legs and arms. In robust leaps, Topple danced around the cavern to the beat of an unseen drum. Dreg laughed with glee.

The fun loving old wizard then shifted into the shape of a colorful butterfly. Flapping its wings, he fluttered about the cavern in wide swoops and circles. As the transparent image of the old man returned to his normal shape, the three observers clapped with enthusiasm. Topple threw his hands into the air, bowed with a noble gesture, and assumed an elegant poise.

The old wizard proclaimed, "You must be impressed with me. I am so good. This is just a small demonstration of my many talents. Ha! Ha!"

Dreg declared, "Uncle Topple, you are the best."

With a glow of pride, the old wizard continued, "So, now I have become an uncle. I like this new honor."

With impatience, Coaldon continued, "Please tell us your story."

Topple took several moments to gather his thoughts before responding, "After you left Rockham the trogs captured a group of dwarves. The dwarf army attacked the enemy in the high meadows. Cando and I planned a special welcome for Crossmore when he arrived to assist his foul army. Upon his arrival, Cando and I attacked him at the same time from two different locations. Things went well until I released a huge blast of energy at Crossmore. It defeated him, but it was so massive it pulled the life force from my body. I allowed my desire to win to go beyond my strength. I assumed my present form at that moment. Oh, well, at least I fried Crossmore's bacon. I was brought here by the power of life. I have been waiting for you to come and help me."

With a surprised expression on her face, Noel stated, "I never imaged you could be hurt. Life is full of surprises. How can we help you?"

Topple responded, "When my body was separated from my spirit, it was sent to the Healing Hall in Mazz. My wholeness can be returned to me if you complete a simple task. Well, it may not be simple, but it should be interesting. It will require you to go to Mazz. The evil in Mazz is powerful. It is both dangerous and clever. Yet, you will have the power of the sword to assist you."

Coaldon went stiff as he declared, "We will do anything to help you. You are a friend in need. Tell us what we must do"

Topple smiled with an expression of guilt clouding his face. "You will need to enter the Hall of Powers in the College of Magic. You must open the Cage of Life and claim my body. It should be healed by now. Your task may appear to be impossible, yet for the sake of the Empire you must be successful."

Without hesitation, Noel declared, "We will do what is necessary."

Topple concluded, "Now, you must return to your friends. You are needed. Good bye."

Again, a strong breeze blew through the cavern. As the wind disturbed Topple's visual presence, his shape turned to a puff of dust. His spirit floated away in a nebulous cloud of particles.

Noel and Coaldon walked away from their meeting with a strong sense of purpose. They radiated a glow of excitement at the challenge of a new adventure.

The Joined

Turning away from Topple was difficult, but necessary. The call to complete their mission was of far greater importance than personal feelings. Upon leaving the mound, the small family started back to the camp. Noel and Coaldon were so engrossed in discussing their meeting with Topple that they lost track of the surroundings. With eyes cast down, the two young adults discussed Topple's situation and the goal of entering the City of Mazz. They were lost in conversation when Dreg gave a loud shout.

The happy little boy came rushing to their sides, proclaiming, "Look! Look! We have company. This is wonderful!"

The ring of Dreg's words brought them back to reality. They were surprised to be so near the camp site. Upon closer observation, they saw a large crowd of people surrounding the camp. The sound of shouts and loud voices could be heard at a distance. The crowd appeared to be demanding something. The mob was so focused on the companions in the camp that they did not notice Noel and Coaldon approaching.

When the two half-elves arrived at the outskirts of the throng, they listened to the dialogue of the participants.

One person shouted, "Where is he?"

Another demanded, "I thought he would be here."

Yet, another yelled, "When will he return?"

Out of curiosity, Coaldon ask a woman on the outside of the group, "What is happening?"

In an excited voice the woman declared, "We are looking for Lord Coaldon. He is supposed to be here. We need his help."

Out of curiosity, the woman turned to Coaldon, asking, "Who are you?"

Then with a gasp, she gave a loud scream. "He is here! He is here!"

At this proclamation, the mob became deathly quiet. All the faces in the crowd turned to look at Coaldon. At his sight, a wild stampede of people raced toward him.

Coaldon was afraid of being crushed by the approaching mass of people.

He suddenly raised his hand in the air and shouted, "Halt!"

At his command the whole crowd came to a sudden stop. In a quiet procession, they slowly formed a tight circle around Coaldon and Noel.

A hush grew over the crowd as a shriveled old man, with a white beard, shuffled forward. He stopped when he stood directly in front of Coaldon and Noel. Without saying a word, he slowly shifted his gaze from one to the other.

Clearing his voice, the old man declared, "Yes, you are the prince and princess. We are happy to greet you."

Coaldon, responded, "Greetings to you. I hope I am not being too bold, but who are you? I assumed this part of the Empire had no population."

With a kindly smile, the old man responded, "I am sorry for being so impolite. I am Wisemont, the spokesperson for the group. You assisted us in the reunion of our spirits and bodies on the island. The wrongs of Doomage have been reconciled. Thank you. You are a person of special honor to us. We are a varied people brought together by accident, not by design. After the 'joining', we were cast into this isolated land. To date, nature has provided for our needs. The fruits of life have been bountiful. Yet, we are concerned about the future. The City of Mazz stands before us as our new home, yet we cannot enter. The power of evil blocks our way. You are the only person who can help us."

Coaldon glanced at the crowd with a broad sweep of his eyes. He then began to look into each person's eyes. It was not long before he felt the souls of the people. Their desire to find a new life was honest and sincere. Coaldon knew he had to honor their plea for help.

Coaldon stated, "I am honored to have played a part in your 'joining'. Doomage's wrongs have been corrected."

The old man responded, "Since the 'joining', we have struggled to find our place in the Empire. We have lost our families, friends, and history. We are lost sheep in a new land, new era, and new life. We have chosen to release the past and look to the future. We beg you to assist us."

The young prince stated, "I never imaged I would ever meet you. I am overwhelmed by this turn of events. How did you find us?"

Wisemont continued, "We hear voices in the night. Our journey is guided by an invisible hand. We know and trust that life will provide for us. The voices told us where to find you.

In a stately manner, Coaldon declared, "I, Coaldon of Rocknee, son of Rodney, grandson of Brad, and heir to the throne, grant the City of Mazz to the Joined. All present are witness to this binding decree."

A loud cheer erupted from the community. Smiles, tears, and handshakes followed Coaldon's proclamation.

Coaldon paused before continuing. "I will travel to Mazz with you, but do not celebrate too soon. We face a great danger. Be prepared to earn the right to claim the city as your own."

After Coaldon finished talking, a somber quiet drifted over the meadow. Dreams came into contact with the harsh reality of life. The group had to confront the power in Mazz before they could gain the city.

In silence, the joined-community set up camp on the western end of the meadow. The companions maintained a separate camp on the east border of the forest. After a hot meal, Coaldon eagerly shared the story of their meeting with Topple.

He stated, "Topple is the only wizard who can control the power of the Key of Ban and conquer Crossmore. Before he can use the Key, it will be necessary to release his body from healing. We must go to Mazz and defeat the evil power controlling the city."

The small group agreed to join Coaldon and Noel on their journey to Mazz.

When the new day greeted the residents of the meadow, a long procession followed Coaldon on their hike to the city. By early afternoon the city appeared on the horizon. Tall, white granite walls gleamed in the heat of the afternoon sun. On each corner, towers soared high into the sky. Each tower was capped by a dome with oval windows. The huge, black metal gates were closed. Large, black flags, hanging over the gates, whipped in the wind. An aura of hatred emitted from the city, forming a defensive barrier.

Gasps of despair gripped the crowd as they approached the walls. The hopes of the Joined were dampened by high walls, as well as the obvious barricade of hostility. Long faces and downcast eyes revealed the fear created by the malice radiating from the city.

Coaldon slowly walked forward by himself. He stood before the metal doors with his arms crossed. He examined the walls, gate, and the surrounding area. As his eyes returned to the metal doors, he felt his sword begin to rattle in its scabbard. He was caught off guard when a surge of hatred hit him like a club. He staggered backward, drew his sword, and held it firmly in his hand. The sense of evil dissipated when the power of the blade was activated.

Coaldon's eyes were drawn to the top of the wall. On the rampart, he saw a black shadow outlined by the blue sky. The being was covered, from head to toe, with a black silky robe. It cast its unseen eyes at Coaldon, then to the crowd waiting in the distance. The black being raised its head, emitting a haunting, mournful cry. The howl created an image of terror in the hearts of the listeners. The crowd standing behind Coaldon covered their ears to escape from the penetrating howl.

Coaldon bowed to the black shadow and raised his sword into the air.

In a loud voice, he proclaimed, "I am Coaldon of Rocknee, son of Rodney and heir to the throne. On behalf of the Empire, I claim the City of Mazz. I order you to depart. This I decree, and so it will be."

The creature did not move or respond. Coaldon had the impression the beast was studying his opponent. For several moments the creature dropped into a deep trance, looking beyond the immediate and focusing on an unseen reality.

The spirit finally stepped forward in slow, deliberate steps. The creature's erect body swayed back and forth as it raised its right arm in a gesture of authority. In an eerie voice it erupted into an uncontrollable bout of laughter.

After a long episode of frolic, it declared, "My name is Emnot. I have ruled this city for many centuries. It is humorous to watch a child trying to play adult games. You make me laugh. It takes great stupidity for you to approach me, yet alone to challenge my powers. Who might you be? I remember reading about a pathetic weakling who fantasized about possessing a powerful sword. Now, here you stand, leading a flock of cowering sheep. Look at them tremble. You have an army of fools. I am so scared. Ha! Ha! Please gather up your toys, go home, and play with children. Ah! Ah! I offer you the opportunity to leave my domain without facing death. Now, go away! I am tired of looking at you. Children should obey the commands of their superiors."

A ripple of anger rolled through Coaldon. Yet, the lessons of the past had taught him not to do something stupid out of anger.

In a clear resonating voice, Coaldon announced, "Do not be deceived by the appearance of the simple and common. I have stated my intentions. I claim what belongs to the Empire. You are counterfeit. Your power is like emptiness supported by emptiness. I offer you the privilege of leaving the city in peace. I recommend you depart before I take action."

The black creature suddenly dropped its head, lifted both arms, and cast a bolt of fire at Coaldon. The prince responded by raising his sword and released a burst of energy. When the two forces met, they clashed, neutralizing each other. The impact created a loud clap of thunder that echoed off the nearby hillsides.

The creature loudly proclaimed, "It has been many centuries since my army has feasted upon human spirits. We are eager to fill ourselves with your tender souls."

Coaldon followed, "You are the fool, not me. Your arrogance has created its own delusions. You are not what you pretend to be. You are false. In hopelessness you exist and into nothingness you will return."

The Evil-Eye

As Coaldon prepared himself for the next assault, he took several steps back and stared at Emnot. The evil spirit returned Coaldon's gaze with intense concentration. Under its hood, the creature's eyes turned bright red as it released an attack by using the power of the evil-eye. Emnot's attack burned as it passed through Coaldon's eyes and reached into his mind.

The young prince felt the force of evil groping to gain control of his thoughts. A sense of defeat and despair began to fill his mind. Images of death clouded his thoughts with fear and misery. The portal of Coaldon's eyes was being used as a gateway into the very essence of his being.

As Coaldon began to slide deeper into a sense of hopelessness, he became conscious of the danger he faced. At first, he tried to push the gloomy thoughts from his mind, but found Emnot's power overwhelming. He realized he needed additional help so, without thinking, he reached into his coin pouch and grabbed the Gem of Watching. The Gem had been given to him on his 18th birthday. The stone possessed the Power of Grace, offering Coaldon assistance in times of great peril. As he touched the stone, a tiny warm glow ignited in the center of his being. The smoldering ember slowly grew in strength. The power of the stone soon expanded into a raging inferno of energy. Fingers of flames leaped from the fire, consuming the evil injected into Coaldon by Emnot. Then, with a twist, the power of the Gem blazed out of Coaldon's eyes. This counter-attack pushed the power of the evil-eye out of Coaldon and toward the evil creature.

This assault upon Emnot soon escalated into a battle of minds. The clash created a muffled roar and a throbbing vibration. A bright white light emitted from the area where the two powers met.

Coaldon was amazed to find that he could direct energy through his eyes. He knew he was not the source of the power, but an instrument allowing a greater power to flow through him.

As the conflict continued, Coaldon felt his strength beginning to wane. He also noticed that the black figure, on the wall, started to sag. The stalemate ended when Emnot slowly withdraw from the confrontation. Coaldon sensed the black figure did not want to make itself vulnerable to defeat. Emnot would let his army be its tool of destruction. With a sudden release, Emnot vanished from the wall, postponing the battle to another time and venue.

Deception

With weak knees, Coaldon turned and staggered back to his waiting companions. He soon realized the price required to challenge Emnot. The young prince stopped in front of the group, gave a sigh of relief, and hung his head in exhaustion.

In a quiet voice, he stated, "I am glad that is over. I am tired. I need to rest."

Noel was first to speak, "We need to get away from the wall and find protection from the hot sun.

The companions set up camp near a stream in the bottom of a shallow ravine, while the Joined rested in a nearby wooded area. Coaldon slept for several hours while the travelers prepared a meal and discussed the unusual battle between Coaldon and Emnot. The prince awoke refreshed and ready to talk.

Looking around the group, he noticed everybody was waiting for him to begin the conversation.

In order to break the silence, he stated, "That was an unusual battle. I was not ready for the attack by the evil-eye. After this conflict, I can honestly say we have a big problem. The enemy is strong. We are in great danger unless we can find a way to defend against such a wicked force."

Tiny followed, "Your words offer a grim appraisal of our situation. What type of army waits for us behind the walls of the city?"

Philo responded, "As emperor, I remember when this force grew into power. It is the by-product of human evil that over time assumed a life of its own. As a matter of fact, the wickedness of the people of Mazz actually created the evil power. That may sound strange, but it is true. In this situation, evil consumed its creator. The people of the city were destroyed by their own sins."

Coaldon continued, "We have much to talk about but first things first. The joined-community must setup a camp site in a protected area away from the city. Lookouts need to be stationed to warn us in case the army of Mazz departs the city. A war council, with representatives from the community, must meet with us tonight. Last, I need to get away, for a while, to evaluate our situation. We must find a way to defeat the forces occupying the city. So, please excuse me. I will return this evening."

Without looking back, Coaldon disappeared into the underbrush. He walked up the stream, passed a meadow, and climbed to the top of a hill. From this location, he could see in all directions. The gleaming white granite walls of Mazz, the green grass surrounding the city, and the calm pastoral appearance offered a pleasant image. At first glance, the city radiated an image of innocence. Coaldon smiled at the irony of how appearances can hide the truth.

The top of the hill was barren except for an ancient tower built of cut stone. Out of curiosity, the young prince decided to examine the building. Upon further investigation, he found that the wooden door into the tower had endured the ravages of time. Yet, with a gentle push, the door collapsed forward into a heap of rotten wood. Stepping inside, the young prince saw the decayed remains of furniture and the residue of wild animals that had entered through high windows.

Looking around the room, he found a dilapidated stone staircase leading to the top of the tower. With careful steps, he climbed the crumbling flight of stairs. At the head of the staircase a doorway opened into a small room. Coaldon observed that after many centuries of weathering the large hardwood beams still supported the tower's floor and roof. Sunshine filtered into the room through large windows. The room was bare except for a large mirror hanging on the south wall. A rusty metal ladder allowed access to the roof.

Coaldon climbed the ladder and stood on the roof. A strange sense of peace filled his troubled thoughts. He sat down, in a crossed legged position, and gazed at the distant city. Warm sunshine and a gentle breeze caressed him into ever deepening waves of relaxation. As he dropped into deep meditation, his subconscious mind opened. In order to find the answer to his dilemma, he planted a question in the fertile soil of his intellect.

He asked in a soft voice, "How can we defeat the powers controlling the City of Mazz?"

He allowed the question to freely drift in the substance of his being. At first nothing responded to his request. Then, one vague idea after another began to dart through his subconscious mind. Coaldon tried to grab the passing ideas, but only unrecognizable whispers were heard. The flitting glimpses of a solution remained an allusive reality.

Then he heard a whisper declare, "Deception can hide the truth".

This statement resonated in his thoughts as he struggled to interpret its meaning. He thought, "I wonder how deception can hide the truth? More importantly, what is the deception? What is the truth?"

The wavering, fluid image of Emnot then filled his mind. Coaldon had the impression that the creature did not have a physical form, but rather, its appearance seemed to be an outline of a void covered by false pretenses.

The young prince stated to himself, "Is it possible that Emnot is wearing a robe to give shape to its spirit? If so, then the creature is using the deception of the garment as a means to show its presence. But, what could this have to do with the truth?"

Pausing, the warrior's eyes glided over the landscape surrounding the tower. He suddenly realized that nature had physical form. Nature obeyed the laws of creation. Looking back at the city, the prince concluded that Emnot and his army did not have physical form. They were the essence of evil, functioning as spirits.

Lowering his eyes, Coaldon glanced at his hands.

He whispered, "It takes hands for me to hold a sword. It takes hands to eat, lift, write, touch, wash, and harvest. I remember the story about the 'fearnumb' under the palace in Neverly. The spirit killed by creating fear in the victim, not inflecting physical damage."

As hard as Coaldon tried, the answer to his problem would not materialize. It only floated out of reach on the perimeter of his consciousness. Coaldon suddenly stood up and began to pace around the top of the building. His frustration increased as the solution floated like a shadow hiding from recognition. Twitching with annoyance, he climbed down the ladder and glanced around the deserted room. Looking at the mirror, he noticed a wave of movement in the glass. The thought of Crossmore attacking him through the mirror created a swell of alertness. Pulling his sword, he approached the mirror, ready for combat.

To his surprise, the face of Topple appeared. The happy wizard gave a loud shout, "My, you do get around! Why are you carrying your sword? I am just a harmless old man. How did you ever find my home? I see the mirror still works."

Speechless, Coaldon stood staring at the image of Topple.

With a choke and a sputter, he finally responded, "It seems our paths keep crossing. To answer your question, I am here searching for a way to defeat the enemy in Mazz."

With a mischievous smile, Topple continued, "How can I help you?"

Shaking his head in aggravation, the young prince responded, "I am irritated because I cannot find the answer."

Topple smiled at Coaldon's youthful seriousness.

In a peaceful voice, the old wizard stated, "The answer is waiting for you. Your doubts delay the solution. You cannot hurry that which will be. So relax, sing a song, go for a walk, smell a flower, or dance in the meadow. The solution will arrive just in time."

With a playful smile, Coaldon asked, "How can I find the answer by dancing?"

The old man laughed, "Just be patient, it will come to you. By the way, put your sword away before you hurt yourself."

At this, the mirror went blank. Coaldon knew the old wizard was correct, yet impatience dominated his being. He wanted results right now. The warrior felt as if the answer was like giving birth to a child. The delivery was difficult, requiring endurance and resolve. He wondered how Topple could be so casual about solving such an important problem.

Following Topple's suggestion, the young warrior forced himself to sit down and pull his thoughts together. Again he asked the question, "How does deception hide the truth?"

As if struck by lightning, Coaldon leaped to his feet.

Raising his arms into the air, he yelled, "I got it. The power of the army of Mazz is not physical. It cannot be seen, felt, heard, or touched, unless the victim grants it authority. We can become its power and expression. If ignored, the evil spirits will pass through the material world without causing damage. Like the 'fearnumb', we grant it power through recognition. It has no physical presence or strength."

With long strides the young warrior loped off the hill, singing a happy song. He was now ready to face the Army of Mazz. Success depended on the ability of each person involved in the war to ignore the false image created by Emnot's army. Victory depended on the mental discipline of each person. It would be a battle of minds, not swords.

Mind Over Deception

Before arriving at camp, Coaldon's cheerful mood was replaced by a sense of gravity. As he walked through the shadows of evening, he became painfully aware that many people could die in the war against Emnot. It would be difficult for each person to resist the power of fear. He realized humans were conditioned to respond to the sights and sounds they perceive in their environment. The Joined would be required to deny their basic instincts in order to survive.

When Coaldon entered camp, he was greeted by a curious silence. The companions sat around a fire in deep thought. Dreg poked a dried stick into the flames to catch the end on fire. He then ran around the camp, waving the branch around his head. The flames created wide circles of red lines against the night sky. Coaldon found the innocence of youth refreshing.

He thought to himself, "I should assume the same sense of freedom as Dreg. I need to stop focusing on fear. I need to be like a child by trusting in the promise of the One Presence. Of course, that is much easier said than done. Oh well, I will do my best."

Coaldon only had time to eat a plate of food before a small group of the Joined approached the campsite. With hesitant steps and down cast eyes the small contingent stood on the outskirts of the camp. Noel greeted the representatives of the Joined community with warm smiles and handshakes. After a period of informal conversation, the Joined began to show signs of discomfort. Casual words helped break the ice of social uneasiness, but did not deal with the impending battle. With searching glances, Wisemont looked at Coaldon.

Coaldon soon realized the group was expecting him to provide leadership.

In a clear voice he stated, "Please be seated around the fire. I have information to share with you. I spent the afternoon searching for a way to defeat Emnot's army.

I believe we must use our minds, not muscles, to win the fight. The evil warriors are spirits created from the foul residue of the ancient citizens of Mazz. This afternoon I recognized that these spirits do not possess physical form."

In an excited voice, Tiny interrupted, "Are you saying that if I sliced through one of the creatures with my sword, it will not die? If so, how can we kill the enemy!?"

A gasp of despair rippled through the small group.

Raff commented, "Do you mean that we cannot hurt them!? This would be bad news! Maybe we should leave here while we are still alive!

Coaldon reacted, "Wait! Wait! Listen! There is a way we can defeat the enemy. I want each of you to raise your arms and swing them in front of you."

With hesitation each person waved their arms. Puzzled looks challenged Coaldon's odd request.

In a frustrated voice, Philo questioned, "So, what does this prove?"

Coaldon smiled, "If a spirit stood in front of you, your hand would pass through it."

Paggy frowned as she responded, "If these creatures do not possess bodies, then they cannot hold a sword, yet alone swing it. So, how can they kill us?"

Coaldon laughed in satisfaction, "You are getting the picture. The spirits cannot use physical strength, so they must depend on the power of evil to do their work. The enemy can inject images of fear and doubt into the minds of their victims. These images are not real, but can be perceived as being true. The enemy's power of suggestion can be lethal. The victims do not die from a real wound, but from what they believe to be wounds. In fact, the victims kill themselves. They are not cut, but believe they are cut."

The group remained quiet for a long time. Each person took time to allow Coaldon's words to sink in. One after another, each member of the group raised their eyes to Coaldon. He knew they recognized the truth of his statement.

After a long pause Coaldon continued, "The enemy will use mind tricks to win, therefore, we must use a similar strategy."

After a short pause, Tiny questioned, "This sounds good, yet how do we destroy the enemy? We might be able to resist the call of Emnot's army, but for how long?"

Coaldon responded, "Good question. I do not know the answer. Does anybody have an answer to Tiny's inquiry?"

People glanced around the group, waiting for someone to come up with an idea. Then, in a deep raspy voice, Wisemont injected, "An ancient saying may be appropriate at this time. It states, 'Evil only has life when it has food to feed upon'. The spirits of Mazz have a limited amount of energy to maintain their existence. The evil spirits gain strength by creating fear in the hearts of people. The food of fear and suffering is like a great feast to them. Like gluttons, evil will gorge on the distress of their victims. It requires a great deal of energy for the foul spirits to maintain a fear-attack. If they do not gain strength from suffering and death, they will dissolve from a lack of energy. I believe we can defeat the enemy by not giving them the power to continue the battle."

Noel reacted, "Wow! I believe you have found the answer. How did you figure this out?"

The old man responded, "I don't know. This interpretation came from an unknown source. I do not strive to understand why, but I only speak the words that come to me."

The position of the moon in the sky indicated the night was growing short. The discussion had taken much longer than anticipated. The fire had died down to a hot bed of embers. Dreg was sound asleep in Noel's arms. Yawns and drooping eyes indicated it was time for everyone to succumb to the need for sleep.

Coaldon concluded, "We have learned a great deal this evening. Tomorrow morning we need to decide how we are going to defend ourselves against the enemy. Rest in peace, for hope has been offered to us."

The hot morning sun awoke everybody from a short night's rest. After a hearty breakfast, the small group once again gathered around the campfire.

Coaldon opened the discussion, "Yesterday, we determined the enemy could be defeated by not giving them the power of our fear and suffering. The question for this meeting is, 'How do we ignore the enemy's power of suggestion?'"

Philo responded, "I have been thinking about your question. We have many options. We could sing, dance, run, hide, sit, talk, or have a party. Whatever we do, we must force ourselves to completely focus on an activity and ignore the call of the foul spirits."

With her eyes burning with enthusiasm, Noel proclaimed, "We can win this battle. We need to figure out how to push away the enemy's suggestions."

Walty stood up in a slow, confident manner.

In a soft voice he stated, "Since the spirits have no physical bodies, they can only attack the victim's mind. Therefore, we will need to keep the thoughts of the community busy with some type of activity."

Paggy responded, with a broad smile on her face, "I suggest we have a contest. We can divide the community into teams and have rousing games of kick ball. Every person will need to offer full attention to the game. This sounds like fun, plus it will force each individual to focus on the game. What do you think?"

Before anybody could respond, Coaldon, in a formal tone, declared, "As the prince of Rocknee, I declare a kickball contest. The champions will carry the glory of great honor. It will be necessary for each person to participate to their full potential.

Teams will be selected by lot. Playing fields can be laid out in the large open area in front of the city gates."

After a pause, Coaldon continued, "Each team will need to make their kick balls from woven grass. Also, remember we must educate the people concerning the danger of letting the enemy control their thoughts. It will be important for each person to maintain total focus on the game or die a miserable death. Before separating, remember that the lives of the community depend on our leadership."

The Wisemont followed, "There are many ways to occupy our minds. It does not matter what it is, but rather how we use it to escape from the enemy."

Coaldon laughed at the old man's enthusiasm.

He declared, "When you return to the Joined, you are to share this information with the community. Be ready for the games to begin at any time. Let's move our camps closer to the city, so we can begin the games quickly. I never thought a simple game of kickball could be a battle strategy."

ᚾᚺᛚ ᛚᚦᚺ ᚹᚢᛒᚺᛣ ᚱᚺᚹᛁᛘ

Let the Games Begin

The Joined community representatives returned to their camp with grim faces and hurried steps. It was not long before meetings were held to educate the community members on the nature of the enemy. Kickball teams were selected and the campsite was moved to the outskirts of the city. Numerous playing fields were marked off and the waiting game began.

Coaldon and his group also made preparations for the battle. It was decided that Noel and Dreg would be sent away from the city. The companions determined that the young boy should not face the enemy's call to death.

Coaldon made regular trips to the city to challenge the enemy. Each time he approached the wall, he felt a growing level of energy emanating from the walls. A foul aura of hatred pulsed in ever-increasing waves. Coaldon had the impression that the enemy was starting to use an ancient reserve of energy in preparation for battle. The crescendo in activity was a sign of the enemy's impending attack.

Upon returning from his latest visit to the wall, he called a meeting of his companions.

He began, "I believe the enemy is ready to attack. I am concerned the spirits will strike with a massive blast of fear. The initial assault may be intense."

Philo responded, "While Emperor, I remember the spirits gaining control of the people by a sudden and deadly attack-of-dread. The victims were often incapacitated by a massive discharge of fear. The weakened individuals would then be vulnerable to the negative power of the spirits. I believe people need to be prepared for the opening strike."

Coaldon questioned, "How can we withstand this attack?"

Walty stated, "I believe understanding is half the battle. If people know the strategy of the enemy, it will be easier for them to push away the initial blast of evil."

Noel abruptly interrupted, "I suggest all teams stay together for mutual support. When the assault begins, we can draw each other's attention away from the fear-attacks."

Coaldon concluded, "I will take this suggestion to the council of the Joined. We want to do everything possible to withstand the first assault."

The barrage of fear increased for the remainder of the day and night. The following morning, people had become irritable and grouchy. Arguments increased and people were showing signs of hostility toward one another. To help relieve the tension, Coaldon approached Wisemont to discuss the problem.

The stately gentleman looked at Coaldon and then at the irritated community.

In a quiet voice he responded, "I know just the thing to solve the problem."

He then pulled a large drum out from under a blanket.

Wisemont stated, "I built this instrument, over the past few days, for such an occasion. It is easy for people to lose track of what is important. I think the rhythm of my drum will reach deep into the soul of each person. Music is a powerful tool in the healing of souls."

The old man closed his eyes and began to beat on the drum with expert hands. He soon lost himself to the rhythm flowing from his heart. It was not long before a small group of musicians gathered around him. Using homemade flutes, horns, and stringed instruments, they began to play beautiful melodies.

As the music drifted across the camp, the members of the community started to relax. The tension created by the pulse of fear was replaced by the quieting presence of the music. Coaldon realized the gentle stream of music was slowly eating away at the foul energy infecting the community. He felt as if an innocent child was defeating an ugly giant. This peaceful wall of resistance pushed the power of the enemy away from the camp. Smiles and pleasant words accompanied the stream of music.

This mood was suddenly interrupted by a loud, savage scream of anger coming from inside the walls of the city.

Coaldon stated, "It seems Emnot does not like the sound of music. I would assume the spirits of the city have been challenged by the melodies. Evil can only find fulfillment by inflicting pain, suffering, and fear. Our defiance will force the enemy to strive to establish its dominance. I believe we will be attacked at any moment.

Looking up, Coaldon saw the gates of the city violently slammed open. A foul burst of evil images slashed at the minds of each member of the community. The music faltered, but soon regained its original rhythm. Screams of horror could be heard coming from the Joined.

A host of black robed creatures flowed from the city. The clothed spirits drifted across the ground in a fluid motion. Terrifying blasts of hatred preceded the arrival of the enemy. The attacking creatures sucked up the sunshine and created a black hole. The shimmering black hooded figures could be seen moving inside the emptiness of the dark cloud. The wavering black void was like a gap in the middle of the normal view of the area. The impenetrable mass of black gloom rushed forward to consume the community.

The horrifying images, created by the enemy, injected instant terror in the hearts of the victims. Each member of the community reeled in fright. Human cries of suffering and dread penetrated the area. Yet, a small spark of hope clung to the desolation of the moment.

One voice, then another, began to yell, "Ignore the spirits! They cannot harm us! Let the games begin! Form your teams! Keep your eyes on the ball!"

The movement of the community was slow at first, but soon exploded into a burst of activities. The game of kickball had never been played with such enthusiasm in the history of the Empire. Teams began to move up and down the fields with shouts of support and eagerness. As the dark cloud arrived at the playing fields, it appeared to devour the teams within its blackness. When the music group, who watched from a distance, saw the community disappear into the black hole, they erupted with a renewed explosion of music.

Noel watched the assault from a hilltop north of the city. She gasped in panic as the community was veiled by the darkness. The black hole of evil seemed to absorb everything in its presence. She gave a mournful cry of anguish as she lowered her head in misery. She could not bear to watch the destruction of the community.

When the darkness surrounded the Joined, the people could no longer see beyond the black enveloping them. Even though the cloud imposed complete darkness, a warm glow of light radiated from their bodies. The darkness was confronted by the light of goodness flowing from the people. This glow provided enough light for the players to see the field and each other. The teams played kickball with the devotion of people struggling to survive.

The spirits, covered with robes, flowed among the teams playing ball. The sight of black robes drifting across the playing fields was mind bending. The players rushed up and down the field, while forces of evil tried to divert their attention. It was not uncommon for a team member to run into a spirit floating across the field. This encounter ended with a robe falling to the ground like an empty shell. Even though many of the enemy lost the form of the garment, they still continued to project images of defeat at the community.

Wave after wave, the enemy continued to project images of destruction. It was not unusual for team members to scream in horror and collapse to their knees. At this moment, all team members would gather around the infected person and encourage them to focus on victory. Each victim of the attack struggled to push away the haunting voices and images. With the help of friends, each victim was able to return to the world of hope. No member of the community was lost to the call of the Spirits of Mazz. As the teams members pulled closer together, in mutual support, Emnot's army began to lose power.

Noel continued to look at the ground under her feet, rather than the black hole. After excruciating moments of anguish, she heard Dreg's voice penetrate her thoughts.

He declared, "Look Mom, something is happening!"

Noel looked up to watch an unbelievable event. Small flashes of light emitted from the dark shadows of the emptiness. One after another, black robes drifted to the ground under the hole of darkness. Slowly, the black cloud began to dissolve. The enemy started to disappear. Sunlight filtered through the darkness surrounding the community. To her great surprise, she saw the hazy outline of people playing kickball. Up and down the fields the teams rushed after the elusive grass ball. The dark cloud slowly cleared away to reveal a crystal clear day. The enemy had been destroyed due to a lack of energy. She no longer felt the presence of defeat. She leaped to her feet, picked up Dreg, and jogged down the hill toward the city. Tears of joy ran down her face as she gave thanks for the victory against the enemy.

The Storm

Before the attack, Coaldon and his companions decided not to play kickball, but rather to station themselves near the gate. When the enemy attacked, the spirits were focused on the teams playing kickball, not a small group huddled in a circle near the wall of the city. Coaldon had placed the Key of Ban in the middle of the gathering to act as a catalyst of positive thought. Even though the group was not swallowed into the black hole, they still received violent mind images. Many times the companions had to fight to escape the intense call of death. With the aid of meditation and the support of each other, they were able to fight off the enemy.

Coaldon watched with delight as the black hole dissolved. He saw the community members reappear, playing robust games of kick ball. The young warrior watched as the members of the community realized their victory and stopped playing kickball. Coaldon expected the crowd to cheer and show great joy, but rather, the Joined stood in silence with dazed eyes and stoic faces. An eerie silence was cast over the playing field. Then, in slow motion, the members of the community turned toward the city gates and started walking. The people moved in a lethargic and mechanical manner. Coaldon had the impression they were hypnotized.

Coaldon suddenly remembered why the companions decided to stay by the city gates.

He called to the companions, "It is time to take our position at the gate. We cannot allow the Joined to enter the city. Danger may lurk within its walls. We must stop the community from entering the city until we have a chance to investigate."

The closer the crowd came to the gate the faster they walked.

A few loud voices began to shout, "It is ours! We have earned the right to the city! We must claim what is ours! Let's hurry!"

The once pleasant group of people turned into an uncontrolled horde, as it pushed forward. The small and weak were shoved aside without care or concern. Coaldon saw crazed looks in the eyes of the people running toward the gate.

As Coaldon and his companions stood in the gateway, they realized the crowd had turned into a mob.

Tiny yelled at Coaldon, "Their minds must be spellbound. The community is out of control! You must do something to stop the mob!"

With great hesitation, Coaldon pulled out his sword and pointed it at the sky over the approaching throng. Not knowing what would happen, he released a blinding flash of energy from the blade. The bolt of lightning ripped through the air creating an ear piercing scream and ending with a loud clap of thunder. The energy exploded into a huge cloud of silver sparks. The sparks were instantaneously transformed into drops of moisture. The suspended droplets rapidly formed into a black churning cloud. Within moments the cloud had grown from a small disturbance to a massive thunder storm. A frenzy of lightning and thunder announced the arrival of a cloud-burst. Raindrops fell from the convulsing cloud in torrents. The rain hit the rushing mob with such force that everyone was washed off their feet. It turned the once dry ground into a sea of mud. As each person tried to regain footing, the clay soil held them fast in place. The rage of flailing bodies mired the community members ever-deeper into the sea of muck. Angry shouts wailed until exhaustion quieted the crowd into whimpering voices of defeat.

The rain ended and the skies cleared, revealing bright afternoon sunshine. The storm had been isolated to the area directly over the community. The ground surrounding the quagmire was dry. Coaldon and his companions stood on solid ground.

A sparkle of humor fluttered through Coaldon as he watched the mass of people floundering in the sea of goop.

Smiling, Coaldon commented, "It will be a while before the Joined will escape from the pit of sludge. They look like moving blobs of mud. Maybe they should be renamed 'the muddies'."

Tiny responded, "I like the name. I suggest we allow the people to find their own way out of the prison of muck. They need time to think about their irrational behavior. I wonder why they turned into a mob."

Coaldon continued, "The community must have received suggestions from the enemy during the battle. They may have been hypnotized to take over the city. The enemy planned to defeat us 'one way or another. "

Noel reacted, "The city might be filled with many dangers. I recommend we take great caution as we walk through the gates. I assume that Emnot and the remainder of his army still lurk within the walls."

In a serious tone, Coaldon injected, "I believe you are right. If the community had entered the city unprotected, they might have been destroyed. We need to enter the city with respect for the power of the enemy."

The Abyss

The old man and the music group had not been affected by the enemy's spell. The musicians walked around the mud pit, approaching the city gate at the same time Noel and Dreg arrived. The three different groups greeted each other with enthusiasm. A round of congratulations was interrupted by the spectacle of the muddy field. The bog was a sea of people struggling to break free of the prison of sticky clay. People on the edge of the mud pit were starting to crawl onto dry land.

Coaldon commented, "It will take hours for everybody to escape. By the time the whole community is free, they will be too tired to do anything except sleep."

Turning to the old man, the young prince continued, "Please advise your community not to enter the city without my permission. I assume great danger prowls within the walls."

Turning to his companions, Coaldon stated, "It is now time for us to pass through the gate. We must be ready for anything. I assume Emnot is waiting for us, so let's not disappoint our host."

Noel followed, "I believe all of us should go in together, including Dreg. We may need all the strength we can muster."

The small group turned away from the freedom of open space and passed through the gate into the prison of tall walls. As they entered the city, the gate suddenly closed behind them with a loud boom. This sound filled their hearts with the uncomfortable feeling of entrapment. Looking back, they realized their only way of escape had been removed. Tiny and Raff ran back to the gate and found that it did not have a latch. Together the men pushed and shoved the doors, but were unable to open it. Seemingly, the gate could only be opened and closed by an unknown power. Now, the group had no choice but to fulfill the mission placed before them.

Even though the city walls showed no signs of aging, the interior had decayed through many centuries of non-use. Most of the buildings were piles of rubble, clogging the dilapidated streets with mounds of bricks and refuse. A large courtyard separated the group from the remainder of the city. A statue of a man wearing a long robe stood on a pedestal in the middle of the square. The loose-fitting cobble stones covering the court yard were buckled and uneven.

After the initial shock of being trapped in the city, Coaldon led the way with caution. He stopped when he saw the ground in front of him begin to change shape. The solid earth was transformed into a flowing, quivering mass. The fluid ground separated into a wide canyon. This transformation created a gulf between them and the city.

Foul odors and flashes of red light emitted from the deep crevice. A mist boiled up from the bowels of the fracture, forming a haze over the surrounding area. A rumbling sound rattled the earth with a deep penetrating disturbance. Wailing shouts of agony drifted from the fissure. These calls were accompanied by the roar of many beasts. The growls and shrieks of the unseen creatures created a vision of cruelty and violence.

The group inched forward to the edge of the fissure and gazed into the vast hole. As they looked, a burst of heat and stench blasted their faces. A sense of foreboding filled their minds. Only Coaldon and Dreg escaped the imprint of dread. The group staggered away from the crevice and retreated to the closed gate. Their grim faces revealed the anguish consuming their thoughts. The members of the grouped sagged to the ground and covered their faces in panic.

Dreg walked away from the abyss, as if it did not exist. He looked at his companions with puzzlement. He shook his head in confusion, but soon lost interest in the group's strange behavior. To entertain himself, he began to build a tower from the rocks littering the ground.

Coaldon looked at his companions and then at the seething crevice. He soon realized that not everything was as it appeared. As he watched the mist bellow from the fissure, he saw the figure of Emnot floating in the haze. From under its hood, the spirit of Emnot laughed at the cowering group of humans.

In a loud and hateful voice, the spirit declared, "Now look at my powerful enemies. You were never opponents, just frail and defeated humans. You live in the fantasy of your own minds. I will defeat you. I only need to wait until you destroy yourselves. I will soon attack you with my best weapons. So until then, tremble in the certainty of your deaths."

Coaldon shifted his eyes, from the outline of Emnot, to the cowering huddle of his companions. After hearing Emnot's words, the group moved closer together and pulled their clothes tightly around their bodies. Fear was slowly consuming their minds.

Coaldon knew he had to do something to save his companions. He closed his eyes and within the depths of his mind, the memory of an early event filled his thoughts.

He remembered walking in a tunnel under the palace in Neverly with Brother Patrick and Pacer. The passageway suddenly ended. He recalled Pacer and Brother Patrick walking through what appeared to be a solid stone wall. He later learned that the wall was not made of stone, but rather, the creation of ancient magic. His mind perceived the stone barrier as being real and would not allow him to pass through the facade. He remembered trying to walk through the illusion, but without success. It was only when his willpower conquered the false image that he was able to pass through the veil.

It suddenly became apparent to him that Emnot was using another trick to control his enemies. With assurance, Coaldon knew the crevice and all the images were a false reality. Jumping to his feet, he walked to the edge of the fissure.

As the warrior stood before the abyss, he heard Noel cry out, "Coaldon, what are you doing!? Come back here before you get hurt!"

Without hesitating, Coaldon stepped into the mist rising from the crevice. It was as he believed, only the product of his mind. On the other side of the illusions, he walked onto the city square. Turning, he looked back through the false wall and watched his friends rush to his rescue. They only saw the false image of the abyss.

He heard their shouts of misery and cries of grief. He witnessed Noel fall to her knees and begin to sob. Coaldon could not allow his companions to suffer needlessly. As he stepped back through the illusion, he stood in the middle of the small group. Shouts of amazement greeted his reappearance. Dreg came running up to his uncle with excited shouts.

The little boy proclaimed, "That was great! How did you do that trick?"

Then, without warning, the impulsive young lad darted through the veil. Noel screamed in hysteria. All she could see was Dreg being consumed by the crevice. Without thinking, she leaped forward, through the illusion, to save him from death. By this time the remaining companions erupted into wild shouts of alarm and desperation.

This agitation was quelled when both Noel and Dreg walked back through the wall of illusion. Stunned silence greeted the pair. Noel, Dreg, and Coaldon looked at each other without responding. They knew words would not explain what they had experienced. Holding each others hands, the three again passed through the image of the crevice. They knew that each companion needed to confront their own test of courage.

Coaldon, Noel, and Dreg watched as pandemonium broke loose on the other side of the false vision. Anxiety caused the companions to run up and down the edge of the abyss yelling in unrestrained confusion. Philo was the first person to understand what had taken place.

With a loud shout, he ordered, “Stop! Stop! We are being foolish! We have been tricked by Emnot!”

At these words, everybody stopped in their tracks. Each person suddenly realized they had lost control. They knew the enemy had successfully injected the poison of fear into their minds. One by one, each person hung his head in shame.

Philo declared, “We do not have time for self-pity. We must find a way through the abyss. If Coaldon, Noel, and Dreg can pass through it, so can we. The fissure is an illusion. We must find the courage to step through what appears to be real.”

The foul sights, odors, and sounds of the crevice raged against their senses with unrelenting attacks. Paggy was the first to step forward with trembling steps. Even though her mind screamed in terror, she made several attempts to step through the illusion. Each time she was unable to overcome the power of the false image. Then, with a burst of fortitude, she leaped forward into the abyss. To her relief, she stood in the city square. With a shout of joy, she greeted Coaldon and Noel.

Then, one by one, each member of the group overcame their uncertainty by stepping across the barrier into the unknown.

jusme

After the journey through the illusion, the companions looked at each other with sheepish grins.

Tiny was first to speak, "I am embarrassed. I actually looked with contempt at the Joined for their mob behavior. I could not figure out why they rushed the gate. Then, I did the same thing, yet even worse."

Walty responded, "Yes, we failed, but that is part of being human. We need to put aside ideas of failure. The enemy can use our negative thoughts to attack us. We should view our failures as opportunities."

Coaldon followed, "Let's get started. It will be dark in several hours. I would like to find a secure place to set up camp."

The small group walked to the center of the courtyard to observe the statue. From a distance the sculpture looked normal size, yet when standing below it, the figure towered over them. The metal statue was covered with layers of grime and the residue of many birds. As each person gazed at the sculpture, they began to glance at Philo.

Finally Tiny commented, "Philo, the statue looks like you."

With a glow of pride, Philo responded, "The statue is of my grandfather. If you look closely, you will also see similarities with Coaldon and Noel. The Rocknee family facial characteristics are strong."

With a nod of agreement, Coaldon stated, "It is strange to actually see the resemblance between my ancestor and me. Oh, well, we need to find the School of Magic before dark. Philo, do you remember the location of the building?"

Philo answered, "Yes, I do. It is on the southern edge of the city. We should be able to arrive before dark if we start now."

The old emperor led the way through the wasteland of dilapidated buildings. It was frequently necessary to go around or over the rubble blocking the streets. The small group soon learned that the city was much larger than it appeared from the outside. After an hour of slow progress, they entered a row of buildings that had not collapsed. The street was clear of debris and well maintained. Looking around, Coaldon noticed the lawns surrounding the building were trimmed and bushes pruned. The large courtyard in front of the buildings was clean and repaired.

At the end of street they saw a large, windowless, square building. It was constructed of multicolored bricks placed at random. At regular intervals the brightly colored blocks flowed freely to form varying patterns. One moment the walls appeared to be solid, the next it was a fluid blend of floating bricks. The movement caused the observers to occasionally lose their balance and orientation. If anybody stared at the wall too long, they felt themselves being drawn into the mysterious power of the building. Paggy became so mesmerized by the wall that she staggered sideways and fell to the ground.

Philo declared in a loud voice, "Do not look at the wall. Its enchantment is a defensive weapon to keep people away."

After a pause, Philo continued, "If you have not already figured it out, this is the College of Magic. As you can see, we will be challenged before being allowed to enter. Be prepared for the unusual."

As the group approached the building, everybody, except Coaldon and Noel, felt a force pushing them away from the structure. The further the group advanced toward the college, the harder it was for them to continue. In the middle of the court yard, the companions were finally forced to stop. They could not take another step forward.

Coaldon stated, "Since Noel and I are not affected, we will ago ahead."

As Coaldon and Noel approached the double doors into the building, they noticed an old woman sitting in a rocking chair to their right. The ancient lady wore a white linen dress, a pink apron, and red shoes. Her gray hair was pulled back into a tight bun. Sparkling blue eyes radiated intelligence with a hint of mischief. Her skin appeared soft and warm. As she rocked back and forth, her frail body moved with slow, graceful movements. An eccentric aura of nobility dominated her presence. A delicate smile projected an aura of peace and confidence.

The elderly woman did not seem surprised at their arrival. With the elegance of a dignified woman, she gracefully waved for Coaldon and Noel to approach her.

In a firm voice, the woman stated, "I extend my greetings. I have been waiting for you. This is a most memorable day."

Noel bowed, stating, "Thank you for your gracious welcome. Would you please share your name?"

The old woman's eyes twinkled with a sly expression of humor.

She responded, "My name is irrelevant. After all these eons of waiting, I have yielded my presence into the wholeness of life. I am no longer me, but an outward image of totality. I have submitted to a far greater presence. I walk in the Light. As you look at me, you see yourself. As you listen to me, you hear the voices of the past, present, and future."

Noel and Coaldon stood in silence as the mystical words of the old woman slowly filtered into their minds. They drifted in wonderment at her quiet power and delicate wisdom.

The woman continued, "Yet, for your sake, I should have a name. So, let me come up with something. Oh, yes, Jusme. I am Jusme.

Noel giggled with delight. "You appear to be much more than what the name might indicate, but so be it."

Jusme continued, "I have been anticipating your arrival. You are the first people I have talked to in many centuries. My mission is about over."

Coaldon stated, "I am Coaldon of Rocknee. My companions and I have been sent on a long and dangerous journey. We have been directed by Topple the Wizard to enter the College of Magic."

The ancient lady stared at Noel and Coaldon with casual curiosity. They felt the power of the matron gently searching their minds.

The noble lady smiled as she stated, "It is my pleasure to meet you. I extend my congratulations for a job well done. I take great delight in your defeat of Emnot's army."

Noel stated, "Thank you. Emnot is a dangerous opponent. I expect we will face him again."

Coaldon had a difficult time focusing his attention on the lady. He kept staring at the doors leading into the building. His body twitched with the desire to complete their mission. Jusme's casual attitude was irritating to his youthful drive for action.

With tension in his voice, the young prince declared, "We must enter the College of Magic. The fate of the Empire depends on our success. It is very important. Can you help us?"

In a relaxed manner, Justme paused before responding, "You are most impatient. I have learned to wait for the right time to fulfill my destiny. Hasty actions create hasty results. It is best to allow time to create the desired outcomes."

Noel turned and stared at Coaldon with a look of disgust.

She responded, "What is your problem, little brother! We have just arrived, met a very special person, and you want to rush off! Cool your heels!"

Coaldon reacted, "Little brother! We are twins! How can you claim to be my big sister?"

Noel laughed with the satisfaction of achieving a major victory. "Oh relax! Many years ago, Maggie told me I was first born. So, little brother, I can claim to be your elder."

Coaldon paused and hung his head as a red flush covered his face.

He looked at Noel, then Jusme, with guilty glances. In a quiet voice he mumbled, "I am sorry for my rudeness. I am so consumed by the mission, I sometimes lose track of what is most important."

Jusme laughed in a robust explosion, "You need not be concerned. Your enthusiasm is contagious. Your passion speaks of your devotion to the people of the Empire. In this situation, intentions are more important than results. Be at peace my friend."

Coaldon responded, "Thank you for your kind words."

The noble woman extended her arms in a slow deliberate movement. Her hands invited them to join her. With hesitation, both young adults slowly touched Jusme's fingers. In a quick movement, she grasped their hands with a firm grip. Before they could react, they were held by a powerful binding spell. Unable to move, they were trapped in a trance. To their fright, the image of the gentle woman was transformed from something beautiful to grotesque. The face of an ugly hag replaced the image of the kind and gentle woman. Screeching laugher erupted from her mouth.

Coaldon and Noel tried to escape, but they were paralyzed by the magic possessing them. Fear dominated their minds, as the old hag stood before them with a broad, toothless smile. She cocked her head from one side to the other.

With unrestrained glee, she stated, "Many things are not as they appear. Take me for example, you thought I was a gentle-woman. It is possible I am not what you perceived. If I was evil, you would be dead right now."

As the power of the trance melted from their bodies, the gentle lady once again reappeared before them.

In a soft voice, Jusme stated, "You trusted me. That was a mistake. I could have been Emnot in disguise. Emnot would have destroyed you. Coaldon, your desire to hurry ahead is a dangerous characteristic. Patience is a virtue you must strive to achieve. Also, once I changed form, fear gained control of you. You created your own prison. You were in my power."

With wide eyes, Noel and Coaldon stared at Jusme in disbelief. The shock of being so naïve paralyzed their ability to respond. Their mouths gaped open, bodies froze, and minds rushed in panic.

With downcast eyes and a trembling voice, Noel declared, "I cannot believe I was so stupid. I did not realize I was so vulnerable to believing the outward images of the world."

Looking at Jusme, Coaldon followed, "The pleasantness of your personality lulled me into a false sense of security. Evil can be wrapped in attractive packages."

With a soft smile, Jusme stated, "Please, do not be concerned about falling into my trap. It was necessary to teach you a lesson. Sometimes it is best to allow people to feel the intense pain of failure. These lessons tend to be remembered much longer."

At the assurance of Jusme's words, both Noel and Coaldon visibly relaxed.

With a burst of laughter, Coaldon declared, "It is not often I am tricked with such skill, caring, and honesty. You did a great job. Thank you!"

Without speaking, Noel giggled in agreement.

Jusme followed, "Once you enter the college, you must defend yourself against following false images. Awareness will be your weapon of defense. The College is protected by the power of deception. You and your acquaintances will need to be ready to battle against both negative and positive images."

The sound of footsteps and loud voices drew Coaldon and Noel's attention away from Jusme. Turning, they saw their companions approaching from the courtyard. Upon the group's arrival, Jusme stood and bowed in a deep formal manner.

The gentle lady declared to the whole group, "I have been waiting for you. The ancient books have predicted your arrival. My mission is now over. I will soon melt into the curtains of time, never to be seen again. I am here to assist you on your journey. Many centuries ago, the prophets saw the great importance of today. I am only a small voice helping you in fulfilling your mission."

With a gentle gaze, she looked in the eyes of each person. Dreg was the last person she observed. She was shocked when she discovered the truth of his existence.

Looking at Dreg, she stated, "I never imagined such a miracle was possible. Young man, you are living proof that the raw power of evil can be transformed. Hope, even under the worst conditions, has the ability to penetrate the wall of corruption with healing. New life is possible in spite of the magnitude of the evil."

Returning her attention to the group, she declared, "Go in peace."

With this statement, Jusme disappeared with a bright flash of light. The fragrance of roses filled the air. At the same time, the double doors into the building swung open.

Me, My, and Mine

Jusme's disappearance happened so quickly that the small group was slow to respond. The sense of security offered by Jusme was gone. The warmth of her caring personality was replaced by the haunting sounds drifting from the building. As the group watched, a dense cloud of fog flowed through the doors and dissipated into the cool evening air.

Coaldon was the first to respond, "At this point, I am not ready to enter the building. I suggest we wait until tomorrow."

Philo stated, "I agree with you. I am in no hurry to face the unique challenges awaiting us. As emperor, I learned that the College of Magic has a defensive system that protects it from unwanted visitors. I never entered the building because of the peril of failing the test. The founding fathers established the college on the standard of goodness. Deviation from this standard is met with judgment. I know of many people who thought they could endure the trial, but were consumed by the fires of their own selfish desires."

With wrinkles of concern distorting her face, Noel followed, "If you are correct, we must seriously consider Jusme's words before entering the college. She demonstrated how easy it is to become entrapped by a web of deceit. I have the uncomfortable feeling that the college will offer us the supreme test."

Without further discussion, the group found a sheltered camping site to spend the night. Even though few words were spoken, each person's attention was focused on the doors leading into the college. Apprehension about the unknown challenge awaiting them, created an uneasy tension within the group.

The light of the new day revealed bright sunshine, cloudless skies, and the multicolored building. The companions gathered together for a cold breakfast and to discuss plans for the day.

After a time of quiet reflection, Coaldon began, "For obvious reasons, I am uncomfortable about entering the building. But, we must move ahead. This could be a most interesting day."

Gripping his hands in frustration, Tiny reacted, "I am not so sure 'interesting' is the right word. Maybe 'dangerous' would be more appropriate."

With a tone of irritation, Noel interrupted, "Let's stop talking about negative ideas. We need to have positive attitudes, clear heads, and open minds."

Walty injected, "It is time to stop talking and start doing."

After a short pause, Coaldon stated, "No wiser words could have been spoken. It is now time to enter the building. I will lead the way."

As the group approached the double doors, flashes of light and a crescendo of shrieks greeted them. Coaldon took a deep breath, straightened his back, and plunged through the doors. He walked with long strides until he realized they were not in an ordinary place.

The young prince stood in the middle of a vast open space. Looking back, he found that the doorway had disappeared. Glancing around, he could see a great distance in all directions. There were no trees, hills, or any physical objects to block his view.

The light gray earth churned with streams of vacillating patterns. The sky was dark blue with puffy clouds randomly drifting overhead.

As Coaldon looked down, the ground under his feet became translucent. Even though he saw the gray earth, the young prince could clearly see through it. There was no bottom to the space underneath him. If he fell through the ground, he would fall forever.

As he stood looking down, a blend of different sounds flooded him. The mewing of kittens was mixed with the roar of a large beast. A savage scream was accompanied by the laughter of a child. The deep rumble of an earthquake was interrupted by the gentle ripple of a small creek. An angry shout was covered by the beautiful song of a bird. Even though there was a cacophony of sounds, each sound could be distinctly and separately heard.

In a like manner, different odors filled his nose. The foul odor of decay was confronted by the sweet fragrance of spring flowers. The stench of unclean creatures was met by the fresh air of a morning breeze. The aroma, from a wide variety of odors, collided in a clash for supremacy. Coaldon was fascinated that he could detect each odor among the multitude surrounding him.

As he absorbed the deluge flooding his senses, he could not determine where the aromas, sounds, and sights originated. Within this blast of sensory stimulation, Coaldon detected a struggle for dominance. Chaos assaulted order, forming a boundary of confusion.

Out of curiosity, he turned to view his companions. Each of his friends, except Dreg, was mesmerized by the overpowering impact of the strange place. Their eyes shifted back and forth in an attempt to place order to the mysterious new world.

Coaldon began to feel isolated from his companions. The vast void of space surrounding him started to pull his attention away from the group and toward the broad expanse of emptiness. With a sudden awareness, he realized he was expanding in size. He maintained his normal shape, but began to fill the space around him. With explosive speed, his body grew in all directions. It increased in size until he filled the void.

At this point, Coaldon had the self-fulfilling premonition that he had become the omnipotent ruler of the void. He was the all-powerful monarch of chaos.

Without thinking, he felt the grip of control enter into his hands. Coaldon was no longer just himself, but a mighty leader. With pride, he saw himself commanding a great army. A smile of contempt crossed his face as he beheld himself sitting on a great throne. A crowd of courtiers stood in humble submission to his great power. He saw people bowing to him with reverence. He relished the sound of his voice declaring judgments on matters of great importance.

The young prince became annoyed when he collided with another being. To his frustration, Tiny moved into his space. One after another, his companions laid claim to the space that was his own. He was no longer the only person alleging ownership of the emptiness. His control of the kingdom was being challenged. As he was forced to yield part of his domain, a slow rage began to grow within him.

A clash of wills forced each of his competitors to draw back into defensive positions to protect their territories from invasion. From an unknown source, defensive walls were built and burly soldiers paraded in defiance. Trumpets blared as each army prepared for battle.

With fascination, Coaldon watched the pending conflict grow from peace to hostility. He realized the soldiers and instruments of war appeared out of nowhere. Even though he could touch, see, and hear the soldiers, he knew they were a distortion of reality. Out of curiosity, he shifted his attention to his friends. They were robed in stately garments and projected the dignity of great rulers. With regal authority, his companions stood behind their armies, radiating contempt at their opponents. The desire for control and power demanded victory.

Looking around, Coaldon spied Dreg playing with toys in an area between the armies. The little boy seemed oblivious to the storm of emotions raging around him. Coaldon had the impression that Dreg was a tiny ant surrounded by giants. The growls and rumble of the armies, preparing for war, cast a dark shadow over the innocence of the little boy. It seemed odd to Coaldon that a child would be playing in the middle of a war zone. The child acted as if the turmoil did not exist.

As Coaldon watched the little boy, Dreg turned to him and waved. The boy's casual attitude caused Coaldon to take a closer look at the child's activities. Out of curiosity, Coaldon walked across the open space to visit with Dreg. Upon arriving, he watched the little boy arrange blocks in separate piles. As Coaldon stared at the stacks of blocks, he saw each pile assume the miniature shape of his companions. The prince heard the tiny, squeaky voices of his friends shouting hatred at each other. Each of the tiny figures held a sword and made threatening gestures at the others. The emotional tempo of each small person grew until only rage controlled their behavior.

Coaldon was dumb-founded when he recognized himself as one of the tiny figures. He was horrified when he saw himself ready to attack Tiny. His miniature self began to run toward Tiny with his sword flashing with deadly intent. Coaldon suddenly realized the bizarre nature of the conflict.

The young warrior was so distressed by the display of hatred, he shrieked, "Stop! This is insane! What are we doing?"

The penetrating blast of his voice created a shock-wave. As the blast of his words moved across the void, it evaporated everything in its path, except his companions. The resulting emptiness was totally black, except for a glow radiating from each person. Within this darkness, the members of the group floated in suspension, unable to move. Complete silence dominated their senses. They were forced to look at each other as they drifted in a state of helplessness.

All eyes were drawn to Dreg, when in a deep male voice, they heard the child thunder, "You have failed! Yet, in life, forgiveness is a great gift. You have the opportunity to choose either jealousy or reconciliation."

At the completion of this proclamation, the little boy closed his eyes and went to sleep.

Only shame and guilt passed through the souls of each adult.

In a disgusted voice, Noel declared, "My, we are such fools! We were warned by Jusme that something like this might happen. How could we have allowed ourselves to be trapped by such a stupid conflict? The power of flesh is very strong."

Paggy responded, "We could have killed each other. It took the innocence of a child to help guide us back to reality. I choose to trust in the Truth, not the power of selfish goals."

The Receptionist

As the companions floated helplessly in the black expanse, the reality of their intense selfishness began to burn like a hot fire in their souls. Their rage had been so extreme, killing had become a possibility. Greed had consumed their minds. Something had allowed their sense of right and wrong to be compromised. Without thinking, each person had allowed the tyranny of greed to control their lives.

Grief soon dominated their thoughts. As the healing words of reconciliation penetrated the darkness, a halo of bright light radiated from the group. That which had been black and selfish soon became warm and caring.

The destruction of selfishness by the power of goodness, allowed the immediate to be revealed. At first, hazy objects swirled in non-recognizable shapes. Then, as the darkness receded, objects began to drift together to form solid patterns. The lines of many doors appeared in a long hallway. Upon further revelation, a room with high walls and many pictures came into focus. A large desk sat in the center of the room with an old man sitting behind it in a straight back chair. The desk was covered with mounds of paper, stacked in neat piles. The old man was so occupied with his work that he did not see the group standing in front of him.

After the initial surprise of entering the room melted away, searching eyes carefully studied their new environment. As each person gazed around the room, their attention was drawn to brightly colored paintings hanging on the walls. These pictures depicted wizards in different settings. The wizards wore colored robes, carried long staffs, and stood in stately poises. Their stern faces and cold stares radiated an unpleasant sense of arrogance and pride. As the members of the group studied the pictures, they gained a different perspective of wizards. Up to this point, wizards, except Crossmore, were recognized as possessing mystic decency. These paintings revealed something different.

With a shiver, Noel declared, "I do not like these pictures. I see only self-indulgence and conceit in the faces of the wizards."

Philo declared, "These paintings give an indication of why Mazz became a forbidden city. The wizards became greedy and used their powers for selfish gains. The quest for possessions and control became the focus of their lives. It is my understanding that just before the fall of the city, all the wizards faced justice as required by the standard of righteousness and the College of Magic. The lack of remorse by the wizards created their demise. The self-destruction of the wizards left a void of power in Mazz, allowing Emnot to gain control. The Age of Wizards ended at that point. Only a few wizards are alive today."

With an abrupt start, the man sitting behind the desk suddenly became aware of the group's presence.

In a formal voice the old gentleman stated, "Welcome to the College of Magic. I am sorry I did not notice you. No one has entered the college for many centuries. Most visitors fail the Test of Indulgence. I am surprised you survived."

After a short pause, the ancient host continued, "How may I help you?"

Coaldon stepped forward and stated, "I am Coaldon of Rocknee. My companions and I have been sent by Topple the Wizard to visit the Hall of Powers."

In a rigid, formal manner, the receptionist declared, "We only admit guests who have an appointment. Let me check the appointment book."

This revelation caused Coaldon to lower his head in frustration. Turning to his friends, he shrugged his shoulders and shook his head in doubt.

In a serious manner, the elderly man opened a large red book and carefully browsed through many pages. As he leisurely looked at page after page, it became apparent that time was of no concern to him.

Then with a surprise expression, he exclaimed, "Yes, here it is! Many centuries ago, you were scheduled to be admitted into the college. You have arrived on the exact date and at the appointed time. This is most extraordinary."

These comments created a stir of conversation among the travelers.

With a relieved look on his face, Coaldon responded, "Thank you for your courtesy. We have never visited the college. Would you please provide us with directions?"

In a crisp, formal voice, the receptionist continued, "Follow the hallway to the end, turn right, and proceed down the stairs. At the bottom, turn left, and you will find the Hall of Powers. Do not be deceived by the spell-of-confusion you will encounter. This is only a slip in the grids of power."

The young prince stated, "Thank you for your assistance. Since we are not familiar with this building, do you have any advice for us before we depart?"

With a cold, blank expression, the old gentleman looked at Coaldon, then the others. He gasped with shock when his attention fell on Dreg. The little boy greeted the old man's stare with a broad smile. The crisp formality of the receptionist abruptly faded. As he gazed at Dreg, his shoulders rolled forward, and his face relaxed. A gentle smile broke through his stony exterior. The mechanical movement of his body was replaced by fluid grace and poise. His icy, indifferent eyes melted into pools of peace and comfort.

It took several moments for the stunned man to regain his wit. With confusion clouding his thoughts, he struggled to put his ideas into words.

Then with an explosion of excitement, he proclaimed, "Little boy, I know you! My nights have been filled with your presence. Dreams have revealed to me your origin and transformation. I sense in you the burden of great failure, as well as the healing presence of forgiveness. You bring great joy and hope to my life."

This burst of emotions was followed by a long period of silence. The elderly gentlemen's face assumed a blank expression and his eyes gaped at an unseen reality. Out of respect for the old man, the companions allowed him to grapple with his thoughts in peace and quiet.

After a long period of contemplation, the gentleman broke from his deliberation. His complexion had changed from a pale white to a soft pink glow.

He looked at Dreg, then at the group before speaking. "My life has been fulfilled on this day. My waiting, for all these centuries, has been rewarded today. Thank you for entering my life."

In a calm voice, Coaldon responded, "It is our pleasure to join you today."

The old man slowly stood and, with shuffled steps, walked around the desk to the small boy. He placed one hand on Dreg's head and mumbled a sentence in an ancient elfin dialect. A soft light flowed from the man's hands and into the boy. The child looked up at the old gentlemen with an expression of surprise and curiosity. The child lifted his hand and touched the man's arm. After receiving this gentle stroke, the receptionist smiled and hobbled out the front doors of the college and disappeared.

In a reflective tone, Noel stated, "I do not know what just happened, but I will accept it as a blessing upon us and our mission. I find courage in the words of the old man. We must be in the right place at the right time. Let's find the Hall of Power."

Down Below

With Noel in the lead, the group walked to the end of the hallway, turned right, and progressed down the stairway. The staircase abruptly ended at a junction. Five passageways branched out, going in different directions. Each hallway looked exactly the same. The walls were constructed of smooth stone with a yellow tint. A soft light flowed from the walls. A fresh, clean odor drifted in the air.

Philo stated, "The old gentleman said we were to turn left. So, I suggest we follow his directions."

With commanding strides, the group preceded a short direction, before an odd sensation twisted through their bodies. A chill of confusion caused the group to stop and look around the hallway in perplexity. A shiver of doubt filled their minds.

In a deep resonate voice, Walty stated, "The receptionist warned us about this passageway. We need to keep moving and not yield to the feeling of uncertainty. This discomfort should pass after we go a short distance."

Even though it was difficult to pass through the bewilderment, it was not long before the shadow of bafflement was released. As the doubt dissipated, the hallway opened into a large, empty cavern with jagged stone walls. The floor was as smooth as glass indicating a high quality workmanship. At the far end of the room, two huge metal double doors dominated the wall.

To every ones surprise, the room was filled with bright light. Sunlight flowed into the room from a large hole in the roof of the cavern. The spacious shaft leading to the skylight was scarred with deep scratch marks and burnt areas.

Coaldon said, "Something unusual has taken place in this cavern. Why is there such a large skylight? What has caused the scratch marks and burnt areas in the shaft?"

Noel responded, "It does seem unusual, but why should we be concerned? We are here to help Topple, not play guessing games. We need to focus our attention on getting through the doors."

Coaldon looked at Noel with an angry look on his face. "What is your problem? I am just curious."

Philo reacted, "All right you two, there is no need to bicker with each other. You both have valid concerns. I believe we will discover the reason for the shaft, plus find Topple."

At the completion of Philo's correction, both Noel and Coaldon looked at each other with sheepish grins.

Noel declared, "It seems I have been a little too brusque. Oh, most honorable brother, please forgive me."

With a look of appreciation, the young prince followed, "I accept your apology. We have more important things to do than bicker with each other. Even though we are brother and sister, we need to be a little less critical."

With these words still hanging in the air, Tiny walked across the cavern and stood in front of the doors.

In an excited voice, he reacted, "The floor in front of the door has the same scratch marks and burnt areas, as we saw in the shaft. Also, look at how the dust has been disturbed on the floor in front of the door. I get the impression something has moved across the floor."

Tiny's observations caused the rest of the group to closely study the floor. Coaldon started to move around the room, as if a dog searching its prey. He dropped to his knees and carefully examined the area just below the shaft. He finally paused and looked at his friends with a curious expression.

With uncertainty dominating his voice, Coaldon stated, "All my life I have lived in the forest and learned to study nature by the clues left by its inhabitants. Up to this point, I thought I had seen most everything nature had to offer. Yet, I have discovered something most extraordinary. Look at this spot on the floor. Something with a wet foot has left a footprint. The outline is vague, but easy enough to see. The print is long and wide. Whatever walked here is a very large creature. Also, notice how the dust on the floor, in front of the door, has been pushed from side to side in broad sweeps. I believe only a large creature with a tail could have created this pattern."

This revelation caused a stir of conversation among the companions. Each person took time to study the footprint and the strokes of dust across the floor. After the investigation, the group gathered in the center of the room to discuss their findings.

As all this was taking place, Dreg found other things to keep busy. As he explored the room, his youthful curiosity drew his attention to the large doors. Standing at a respectful distance, he stared with fascination at the surface of the metal. At first, he thought the surface of the doors was only blank metal, but then he saw the appearance of thousands of tiny lines. These lines scrolled across the door in long beautiful curves. As he gazed in wonderment, he saw the lines blink and reappear in the shape of a tree. He found it necessary to concentrate on the tree to keep it from disappearing. The fragile image was so mesmerizing that he sat down and focused his full attention on it. The tree glowed with a delicate golden hue.

While Dreg basked in the warm glow of the tree, the adults continued their discussion.

Raff stated, "I have studied the door and cannot find a way to open it. I did notice some words written near the bottom, but can not read them."

Philo followed, "It was the practice of the wizards of old to write in a language unique to Mazz. Let me take a look. I may remember the script."

As the comrades looked on, Philo approached the doors and examined the writing. After a long pause, he shook his head in doubt. Closing his eyes and lowering his head, the ancient emperor searched the recesses of his memory. With a sudden movement of his body, he became erect.

He declared, "I got it! It is amazing that I can still read the words after so many centuries. It says, 'The secret glow of the door will reveal the key. Go to the root of the tree'."

Noel stated, "What tree? The door's surface is plain and unadorned."

The companions approached the door and looked for any sign of a tree. Over and over they examined it, but could not find it.

Walty asked, "What does the message mean by, 'The secret glow of the door'? I only see dark, corroded metal."

No one could offer a response to Walty's question.

Noel was the first to notice Dreg staring at the door. She was curious why the little boy was so quiet and peaceful.

Approaching him, she asked, "Dreg, what are you looking at?"

Coming out of his trance, he turned his head towards Noel in a slow deliberate manner.

He responded, "The door is so beautiful. I just want to look at it."

Noel looked at the dark, discolored door and then back at Dreg. Her face twisted in confusion.

She reacted, "Dreg, I can only see a dingy old door, nothing beautiful. What do you see?"

The small boy returned his gaze to the doors. "I see thousands of thin lines glowing with a golden light."

Noel followed, "Do the lines form an image?"

"Yes." Dreg responded. "I see a tree."

In a loud voice, Noel called to her companions, "Come here! Dreg sees the image of a tree on the doors."

A quick shuffle of feet brought the group to her side. The little boy glanced up at his friends, but his attention soon returned to the image of the tree.

Then Noel stated, "Dreg sees the golden shape of a tree on the door. Why can he see it and not us? Something odd is going on."

Paggy looked at Dreg and then the doors. "I think he is seeing the door through different eyes. I believe we are looking through the eyes of logic, not innocence. It is my assumption that the college was created from the powers of caring and kindness. We will need to find a way to commune through these elements."

Paggy's statement was greeted with silence.

Noel was the first to respond. "Paggy, you never cease to amaze me. This journey has awakened you to a whole new understanding of life."

Philo followed, "As emperor, I was so busy ruling the empire, I never took the time to investigate the college. Yet, I believe Paggy is correct. If the college is maintained by the standard of righteousness, then it will be necessary for us to be in harmony with this norm."

Noel followed, "I suggest we allow the simple and gentle to open the door. Yet, how do we do this?"

Paggy suggested, "Let's sit down, relax, and seek the spirit of the college. I believe we will need to quiet our minds to find the voice."

The Librarian

As the group joined Dreg sitting on the floor, silence filled the room.

In a quiet voice, Coaldon stated, "As a child, I was taught by my grandparents to mediate. I learned, at an early age, that meditation could be difficult. It is necessary to quiet the mind from the rush of the world and allow the deeper presence of life to speak to you."

With this said, each person began to meditate. It was not long before the struggles of the past few months suddenly came to life in their minds. Their thoughts were overwhelmed by the images of past trials and situations. These once dormant memories stampeded in uncontrolled streams across their minds. The repressed images rushed on and on with unrelenting persistence.

Dreg was surprised when he became aware of the adults surrounding him. As he glanced at them, he noticed that their bodies were rigid with tension and faces contorted with concentration.

The young boy declared, "Is something wrong? You guys look as if you are upset about something."

At this comment, a burst of laughter rippled through the cavern. The bubble of frustration was released in an explosion of giggling.

Noel declared, "Let's try this again. It seems we have many memories seeking to be recognized. We need to let them go."

The second attempt to meditate was more successful. It was not long before a stillness of mind and spirit yielded the desired results. As the images of the past receded, the quietness of the present moment grew into tranquil reflections. One after another, the members of the group gave quiet gasps, as the golden figure of the tree appeared on the doors. The warmth of the glow touched each person with wonderment.

Paggy was the first to respond, "The tree is beautiful. This is a special time for me."

Noel followed, "I agree with you. I understand why Dreg is so fascinated with the image."

While deep in reflection, Coaldon thought to himself, "The message on the door states that we are to 'go to the root of the tree' to find the key to the door. I believe I should take a closer look at the roots. I hate to move, but we must find Topple."

While the group remained seated, Coaldon stood up and casually walked to the door. His eyes were guided to the broad expanse of roots. With a gentle touch, he moved his hands over the rough surface of the door.

Shaking his head, he said out loud, "This is mind-boggling."

Shifting his focus away from the tree, he began to study the complex pattern of tangled roots. The prince soon discovered that all the roots, except one, branched off to form many lateral chains. This single root swirled in and out of the other roots in what appeared to be an unending maze. After losing track of the line several times, he found it necessary to use his finger as a guide. After a long search, Coaldon found that the line ended at a tiny starburst in the lower right hand corner of the door. The image was so small it was difficult to see.

When Coaldon touched the starburst with his finger, a hole opened in the center of the cluster. The hole slowly expanded until it was about three hands across. The opening was black, except for streaks of light darting randomly through the darkness. The young warrior was surprised when an eye slowly grew out of the obscurity of the hole. The eye was yellow with a slit-shaped pupil. With rapid movement, the eye shifted back and forth, searching the room. It stopped when it saw Coaldon. The eye stared at the young warrior for several moments before it disappeared back into the darkness. The prince had the impression that the eye had examined him and made a decision.

As Coaldon watched the hole, it again expanded in size. Before he could react, an invisible energy attached to him with a powerful grip. He suddenly felt the sensation of movement as he was pulled into the hole. A rush of darkness ended when he found himself standing in a large, brightly lit room. Looking back, he saw a wall with no doors. Turning, he found a room filled with many shelves piled high with countless books.

As he stood in awe of the books, his concentration was broken when he heard a voice to his right. Shifting his attention, he saw an elderly elf sitting behind a large counter. The librarian's wrinkled face glowed with a broad smile and twinkling eyes. His slender body moved with grace and poise. He wore a red shirt, green pants, and a yellow hat with its brim drooping over his face.

With a gentle voice, the elf stated, "Welcome to the library. How may I help you?"

Coaldon responded, "How did I get here? Several minutes ago I was standing in front of a door; now I am here."

The old elf chuckled, "I keep forgetting that not everybody knows how to enter the library. The door you saw is only an illusion. The doorway into this room is through the star cluster. The eye-of-judgment determines if a person is worthy to enter the library."

Looking around the room, the prince asked, "Is this the Hall of Power?"

The old librarian answered, "Yes, this is the Hall of Power, or more simply the library. How else may I help you?"

Coaldon followed, "I have been sent by Topple the Wizard to locate the Cage of Life."

The librarian stated, "You will need to talk to the Keeper if you want to enter the Cage of Life. You will find him at the far end of the library. You will see a large door. Hit the gong to attract the attention of the Keeper. Now if you will excuse me, I have many tasks to complete today."

The ancient elf lowered his head and returned his attention to the papers on his desk.

Marko

With long strides, Coaldon walked to the far end of the room. Upon arrival, a large, imposing door loomed over him. After a short search, he located the gong, grabbed the hammer, and hit the metal disc. This caused a clanging sound to resonate throughout the room.

After several minutes, a deep rumbling voice stated, "This is the Cage of Life. I am Marko. It is wonderful to have a visitor. What may I do for you?"

Coaldon could not see who was speaking, but only heard the voice. "I have been sent by Topple the Wizard to enter the Cage of Life and release his body."

The reverberating voice responded, "Topple has been under my care. His healing has made steady progress in spite of the great damage he did to himself."

The prince stated, "I am happy. Topple is a good friend. How do I claim him?"

In a wavering tone, the voice continued, "I am sorry, but you are not permitted to enter the Cage without Topple's permission. How do I know he has entrusted you to release his body? What proof can you provide me?"

Coaldon was frustrated by this mandate. His mind churned, as he considered different solutions. After a short period of contemplation, Topple's parting words filled his mind.

Coaldon declared, "Topple stated that I would have the power of the sword to assist me."

The young prince withdrew the sword and in a commanding voice, declared, "I am the hand-on-the-blade, carry the Key to victory, and claim the right to release Topple's body."

Coaldon stepped up to the door and lightly touched it with the tip of the sword. A surge of energy leaped from the sword and penetrated the door. The door swung opened so suddenly that the prince was knocked to the floor by its force. Shaking his head, Coaldon slowly got to his feet and stared in disbelief. To his amazement,

he saw a large creature filling the doorway. Coaldon had only seen pictures of this creature in fairytale books.

He was looking at a dragon. The tall creature had a long neck, narrow head, and a huge scaled body. Its large wings were spread open in a threatening manner. Puffs of smoke and bursts of fire shot from its massive mouth. Its skin changed colors from a dull black to a bright red. The creature stood on its hind legs, its yellow eyes staring at Coaldon with an intense glare.

In quick motion, the young warrior raised his sword in preparation for a battle.

Coaldon and the dragon gazed at each other for a long time without moving a muscle.

Coaldon was the first to break the silence, "My name is Coaldon of Rocknee. I have been sent by Emperor Brad on an important mission. It is essential that Topple be reunited, body and soul. I request his release."

The large creature looked at Coaldon with delight. "You are daring and brave. I believe a battle with you would be most interesting. What do you think?"

Beaming with courage, Coaldon laughed, "I am ready to die defending the Empire. Yes, I will fight if attacked. By the power of the One Sword, you will meet your doom."

With a broad smile and a glimmer of satisfaction, the dragon declared, "Stand down, young prince; I desire no battle with you. I was only testing your metal. I am pleased with what I have found. You are truly a bold warrior on an honorable quest."

Coaldon quickly responded, "I do not want to fight you. I have already fought far too many battles. I only want to release my friend."

The dragon looked at Coaldon with concern, "You are most impatient, yet I believe this is characteristic of youth. Before you release Topple, I have a question for you. Are you here by yourself, or with companions?"

Looking directly into the eyes of the dragon, Coaldon stated, "Yes, I have companions. They are waiting for me outside the doors of the library."

The dragon responded, "Thank you for your honesty. By the way, my name is Marko. I am a healer. You are the only person who has ever seen me. I see others, but no one sees me. I am a shadow in the night and invisible to my patients."

Coaldon questioned, "Why can I see you?"

Marko answered, "It is our destiny to meet. I need your courage, and you need my strength."

Coaldon continued, "Why would you need courage? You are awesome. Your size and power are intimidating."

The dragon paused, listened, and glanced up. "We can continue this discussion later. Right now, we have important things to complete. You and your friends are in great danger."

The young prince felt a vibration and warmth radiate from his sword.

Shaking his head, Coaldon stated, "I should have known that Crossmore would find me sooner or later. Before we do anything, we must release Topple."

Marko gave Coaldon a shy wink of an eye, turned around, and lumbered into the Cage of Life. The room was constructed in the shape of a circle with doors lining the walls. The ceiling was vaulted with a small hole leading to the outside. Above each door were signs with names written in large letters. In the center of the room was a large, elevated stage with a huge orb sitting on a stand in the center of the platform. The glass ball was several feet across with blue beams of light directed at each room.

After a short examination of the names, Coaldon saw the name 'Topple' written in green letters. With cautious steps, he approached the door showing respect for the power of healing that filled the room. With the sword still in his hand, he looked over his shoulder to receive Marko's directions.

The dragon had been carefully watching Coaldon to make sure he did not interfere with the healing process.

In a slow, quiet voice Marko stated, "Touch the door with your sword and allow its power to break the bonds of healing."

With modest steps, the young warrior stepped up to the door, raised the blade, and gently touched it. A flash of light outlined the door as it slowly opened. Looking inside, Coaldon saw Topple's body suspended in the air, floating over a glowing light. As Coaldon watched, he saw Topple take a deep breath, open his eyes, and give a loud yawn. Topple's body floated out the room, past the dragon, and drifted to the top of the room. Then, with a sudden burst of speed, the body shot through the opening in the roof. This happened so quickly that Coaldon was at a loss for words. He could only stare in disbelief at the wizard's departure.

The dragon did not seem surprised by Topple's unusual exit from the room.

With a sense of understanding, Marko declared, "It is done. Your friend is once again whole."

As Coaldon gripped the sword, his body became rigid.

Turning toward the dragon, he declared, "I forgot about my friends waiting for me. They might be in danger of attack by Crossmore."

The Unholy Alliance

In Neverly, the capital city, the mood of the people was grim. After the rescue of Noel by Coaldon, Crossmore had imposed rigid military order. A curfew was imposed; citizens were subjected to constant searches; and freedom of movement was limited. Crossmore was concerned that the rebels might try to take over the city.

The evil wizard was still recovering from the wounds he received from the battle with Topple and Cando. During his time of recovery, he constantly received messages from his spies concerning strange activities happening in the southern part of the Empire. His battle with Coaldon in the Swamps of Grief was a grim reminder of his failure to destroy the enemy. Adding to this event, he was aware of the disappearance of the Sin Monster, the destruction of Scaric, the anger of the Willow People, and a disturbance in Mazz.

Looking out his window, his attention was drawn to the eastern horizon where the City of Rockham was located. Very soon, he would order his army of trogs to attack the dwarf stronghold. He relished the thought of this being a glorious victory.

The wizard then shifted his attention to the south. His intuition, plus the trail of evidence, told him that Coaldon and Noel had arrived at the City of Mazz.

In a whisper, he stated, "I must contact Emnot. For many years, I have been at odds with this foul spirit, but I believe it is time for reconciliation. Ha! Ha! I will dazzle the enemy with my charm and wit. The fool will have no choice but to succumb to my enchanting personality. This should be fun! Of course, I will never honor any agreement with this rival. Yes, it will be necessary to destroy the pathetic creature after I have used it to my advantage. "

Standing in front of the Mirror of Power, Crossmore raised his crippled right hand, visualized Emnot, and released the power of the reaching-hand. After several moments, he saw an image of the evil spirit form in the mirror.

In an agitated tone, Emnot declared, "I find it most unpleasant that I am speaking to you. Why are you wasting my time?"

In a soothing voice, Crossmore crooned, "Now, is this the way to greet an old friend? Yes, we have had our differences, but it is now time to let the past rest in peace. Right now, we can support each other. I need your skills of deception, and you can use my magical powers. Together, we will make a powerful team."

Emnot laughed with delight, "You have treated me with contempt for many years. Why would I want to have anything to do with you? I do not trust you."

In a sympathetic voice, Crossmore stated, "You are correct. I am sorry that I have not been a good neighbor. I have decided it is time to turn over a new leaf. Would you please forgive me? It is time to reconcile our differences."

In a hesitant tone, Emnot responded, "I cannot believe you can be remorseful for anything."

In an amiable voice, the wizard pledged, "Let me prove my sincerity. If you work with me, I promise to let you have control of Mazz. I want you as an ally, not an enemy. You are too powerful to have as an adversary. Rather than wasting time and energy fighting each other, we can work together. After our success, we can share the spoils of our conquests. You can have control of the southern part of the empire, I will take the north. Let's make a deal!"

Emnot demanded, "I am reluctant to believe you. I need your help, yet you might turn on me."

Crossmore begged, "Just give me a chance to prove myself."

In frustration, the evil spirit stated, "All right. I may regret this, but I am willing to give you a chance. We can begin our alliance today. A group of trespassers have invaded my city and entered the College of Magic. One of them is Coaldon of Rocknee. I want to destroy him."

With warmth, Crossmore followed, "I am so happy you have changed your mind. You will not regret your decision. Coaldon is our common enemy. I will join you immediately to begin our conquest."

After breaking communications, Crossmore raised his arms in triumph.

He ranted, "I did it! Emnot is such a fool! Now, I must join him in Mazz. First, I will destroy Coaldon, and then claim Noel for my bride. Ha! Ha!"

With confidence, he stepped into the Mirror of Power and found himself rushing toward Mazz. He traveled so rapidly that the trees, grass, mountains, and rivers were only a passing blur. As he approached Mazz, he was surprised to see a large group of people camped several miles west of the city. With a final burst of speed, he found himself standing in the courtyard in front of the College of Magic. Upon landing, he saw the transparent spirit of Emnot approaching him. He greeted the ghostly presence with a broad smile.

In a friendly voice, Crossmore stated, "It is great to see you again. By the way, who are the people camped outside the city?"

Emnot responded in a muffled voice, "They arrived with Prince Coaldon. I do not know their origins. For your information, I claim them as my own. I will feed upon the sweet energy of their souls. Remember, they are mine. Keep your hands off."

Crossmore declared, "I will honor your request. Now, let's make plans to destroy our enemies."

******

As the power of evil surrounded the building, Coaldon and Marko stood silently in the room-of-healing.

After a long pause, Coaldon stated, "Crossmore is waiting for me. I can feel his presence through my sword. I do not understand why he has not attacked us."

Marko stated, "Evil cannot enter the college. He is waiting for you to leave the building. You and Crossmore are at a stalemate. You cannot leave and he cannot enter."

After considering Marko's words, Coaldon stated, "I feel an added level of evil."

The dragon followed, "I assume that Crossmore and Emnot have formed an alliance against you. This might prove to be a difficult battle to fight."

Shaking his head, the young prince responded, "Before we confront Crossmore, I suggest you meet my friends."

Marko lowered his head in frustration. "I am too shy to meet people. I am afraid. No! No! I can not do it."

Coaldon stood back in astonishment. "I can not believe my ears! A big bruiser like you should not be afraid of anything! No more hesitation! Let's go!"

With reluctant steps, the dragon followed Coaldon through the library and to the librarian's desk. The librarian looked up from his work when he heard the approaching steps.

At the sight of the dragon, the old elf jumped to his feet, gave a loud yell of fright, and passed out.

The dragon moaned, "I was afraid of this. The old gentleman is such a nice person. He has never seen me. I hope he is not hurt."

Coaldon looked at the old man on the floor, and nodded. "He will be all right. After he wakes up, he will think it was just a dream. Now, how do we get to the other side of the wall?"

Marko said, "To pass the wall, we just walk through it as if it was not there. I believe it is best if we go together. If I appear on the other side without you, there might be a big problem."

Without waiting, they walked into the wall, side by side.

Tough Choices

When Coaldon appeared in the cavern with the large dragon at his side, the companions were huddled together, deep in conversation. Raff was the first to notice the reappearance of Coaldon, plus the surprise package – Marko. Upon seeing the dragon, his body became rigid, his mouth gaped open, and his eyes froze in fear. He tried to speak, but only bursts of loud squeals erupted from his mouth.

Noel turned to see what caused Raff to act in such an unusual manner.

When Noel spotted Coaldon and Marko, she leaped to her feet and declared in an excited voice, "Look, we have company!"

At this outburst, the remainder of the group turned to see the new arrivals. The added attraction of Marko caused the companions to freeze in uncertainty. Dreg was the only exception.

With a happy shout, he declared, "This is awesome! Uncle Coaldon, who is your new friend?"

Without hesitating, the bright-eyed little boy ran up to the dragon. In an excited voice, he stated, "My name is Dreg. Are you a real dragon? What is your name? This is so great!"

Coaldon was delighted to see Dreg's response to the appearance of the dragon.

In a calm tone, the shy creature responded, "Hi, Dreg. My name is Marko."

Looking at the small group standing on the other side of the room, Coaldon declared, "Come join us. Do not be afraid. I want you to meet Marko. He is the healer for the college."

Moving with slow steps, the companions shuffled across the room and stood in front of the towering creature. They felt a ripple of fear when a puff of smoke and a whiff of fire erupted from the dragon's mouth.

In a shy voice, the dragon alloyed their fear, "I will not hurt you. I come in peace."

Coaldon continued, "Marko was Topple's healer. Topple's body has been reunited with his spirit."

At these encouraging words, the companions relaxed and began to question Coaldon and Marko about the events of the past few hours. After the initial shock of the dragon's appearance, a comfortable atmosphere developed within the group. Dreg was especially enthusiastic about the turn of events.

After the glow of excitement diminished, Coaldon drew everyone's attention by waving his arms.

In a firm voice, he stated, "I hate to change the subject, but I have some bad news. Crossmore and Emnot are waiting for us outside the college. They can not enter the college without being destroyed, but in the same light, we cannot leave without being attacked."

Coaldon's blunt statement brought a chill to the enthusiasm of the group. The positive experience of meeting the dragon and learning about Topple's healing was dashed with the cold blast of reality.

Looking at Coaldon with a teasing smile, Noel declared, "Little brother, why do you have to be so honest? I did not want to hear news about Crossmore. I could have done very nicely without this information."

Philo reacted, "Now, what do we do?"

In response to Philo's question, the group sat in a circle and began to discuss how to deal with Crossmore and Emnot. During the discussion, Coaldon remained quiet, as he studied the face of each companion as they talked. Warm memories caressed him as he remembered the special times he had shared with each friend. The young prince was brought back to the present moment when Tiny cleared his voice.

In a serious tone, the large man concluded, "This looks like an impossible situation. We have talked about many different ways to escape, but nothing will work without facing unbelievable danger. There must be a way to escape."

These words hit Coaldon with the seriousness of their situation. As he considered Tiny's conclusion, a solution began to take form in his mind.

In a solemn voice, Coaldon declared, "I have the answer to our problem. The solution is simple, but will require me to take a risk. I will attack Crossmore and Emnot to provide a cover for your escape. You can flee by riding on Marko's back, while I occupy the enemy in battle."

After a short pause, Coaldon continued, "I believe this is the only solution that will work. Crossmore will wait outside the college for years in order to kill me and capture Noel."

The group sat in silence as they considered Coaldon's proposal. Several people tried to speak, but were unable to put their feelings into words. Paggy was the first person to respond. She jumped to her feet, rushed to Coaldon, and hugged him with deep affection.

With tears welling in her eyes, she mumbled, "I have never had anybody offer to do such a gallant thing for me."

Stepping back, the young lady returned to the group and stood in silence.

Coaldon's proposition was difficult for the group to accept.

Noel stood, looking into Coaldon's eyes, and stated, "My first thought was to reject your idea, but we have no other choice. The future of the empire depends on us fulfilling our mission. We can not just sit here and do nothing. Coaldon, you have defeated Crossmore in the past, and I know you can do it again. We must depend on the providence of the One Presence to protect us. We must have faith and trust. With great reluctance, I recommend we accept your offer."

Coaldon responded, "I am the only person who can confront the enemy. I will give the Key of Ban to Noel for safe keeping."

Philo stated, "I agree with Noel. We must move ahead with confidence. It is best to act immediately. We want to catch the enemy off guard."

Coaldon looked at Marko with searching eyes. "Are you willing and able to help us?"

The large creature did not hesitate in answering, "I would find it an honor to offer my assistance in your time of need. I believe I can safely carry everybody on my back at one time."

Marko's words were greeted with sighs of relief.

PREPARE the WAY

Little time was wasted in getting ready. Ropes were secured around Marko's body; packs were tied to his side; and a route to the roof of the college was located.

When all the preparations were completed, the group gathered to make final plans.

After a brief review, Philo declared, "We are ready. I would like to get started soon, rather than wait. Waiting will only increase our danger. So, unless there is more to discuss, let's say good-bye to Coaldon and begin our flight. By the way Marko, where are we going?

The dragon modestly stepped forward into the circle of the group. "I will take you to my home. It is Dragon Keep and located on the southern wing of the Sadden Mountains. Nobody knows the location of the Keep other than Topple. I will do my best to provide you with a safe, comfortable ride. Be sure to hold on tightly to the harness tied around my body. There might be some rough weather."

Coaldon stated, "I will wait to begin my attack until you are in position. Marko, please yell when you are ready. At that time, I will commence my assault. Marko, after you have completed your journey to Dragon Keep, please return to pick me up. I will be waiting for you."

With this said, a brief, emotional farewell was shared. Coaldon went to the front of the building, the companions walked up the stairs to the roof, while Marko prepared to leap through the hole in the top of the cavern.

Two Against One

The dragon's savage shriek of defiance echoed throughout the empty streets of Mazz causing Emnot and Crossmore to tremble in alarm. The scream of a dragon had not been heard in the Empire since before recorded history. Only folktales rumored of the existence of such majestic and noble creatures.

The fierce intensity of Marko's herald caused Coaldon to stumble as he started to move. Gaining control of his emotions, Coaldon lurched, with uneasy steps, out of the college with the Blade of Conquest clutched in his hand.

Though Coaldon made a feeble attempt to make a grand entrance, the Blade of Conquest was anything but indecisive. The sword raged with such power that Coaldon had to hold onto it with both hands. While the young warrior stood in a state of disorientation, the blade released a blast of energy at Emnot and Crossmore. The sword seemed to have an innate understanding of its mission.

The scream of the dragon and the arrival of Coaldon caused confusion in the minds of the enemy. The attack by the sword forced Crossmore and Emnot into defensive positions. When Crossmore saw the surge of energy approaching him, he erected a shield of magic. Emnot escaped by darting across the city. Even though they escaped the full brunt of the attack, the searing impact of the blast drained their energy reserves.

* * *

While this rapid sequence of events transpired, Marko spread his powerful wings and flew into the northern sky carrying his human passengers. With labored strokes, the dragon slowly gained altitude, soaring high over the trees, rivers, and mountains. With wide eyes and rigid bodies the passengers clung to the rope harness for dear life. The thought of falling off the dragon was an ever present concern.

Noel and Dreg were the only two travelers to celebrate the excitement of flying. Dreg squealed of exhilaration, while Noel glowed with total ecstasy.

The journey was long, but uneventful. As the flight progressed, each of the riders gained trust and confidence in the ability of the dragon to provide a safe ride.

Marko was happy when he felt the bodies of his passengers relax. A smile of pleasure stretched across his long, narrow face when he began to hear words of praise for his smooth traverse.

* * *

Back at the college, the initial attack by the sword had ended. Coaldon and Crossmore carefully watched each other across the college courtyard. Even though Crossmore felt a twinge of fear, he stood tall, posed, and self-assured. The wizard was wearing a coal-black, silken robe with the hood pulled over his head. A neatly trimmed black beard dominated his narrow, lean face.

Crossmore's dark eyes exuded a compassionate expression, while his mouth turned up into a gentle smile. A glow of warmth radiated from him.

An enticing image of Crossmore filled Coaldon's mind. This imprint of empathy was so strong that the young warrior was tempted to trust the wizard. The lulling impact of Crossmore's seduction touched Coaldon with gentle strokes of comfort. The warrior's eyelids started to feel heavy and his body drooped in relaxation.

As the young warrior began to succumb to Crossmore's enticements, he received an electric jolt from his sword. The blade somehow understood that Coaldon was in danger. The discomfort of the shock caused Coaldon to leap backwards, open his sagging eyes, and recognize the alluring power of Crossmore's charm.

In a quiet, exasperated tone, Coaldon mumbled, "Why am I being so stupid? I should know better than to trust Crossmore. I believe Crossmore is trying to lull me into a defenseless state. I cannot allow that to happen."

With a concerned voice, Crossmore crooned, "It is good to see you again. I forgive you for your hasty assault on me. I am ashamed of my hostility towards you in the past. I should not have attacked you. Being the heir to the throne is a major responsibility. I should support and encourage you. You need to be groomed to fill my shoes, not treated as a rival. I admire your determination and courage. Some day you will be a great leader. I am so proud of you. I encourage you to join me in Neverly. Your strength and youthful attitude will complement my maturity and wisdom."

Coaldon was surprised at the power of Crossmore's words. Again, he felt himself being drawn into the wizard's charisma. Without moving or changing his facial expression, the prince regained control of his thoughts.

Again, Crossmore's warm whisper of enticement entered his mind. With a thrust of resistance, Coaldon pushed the attack aside and prepared to respond to Crossmore's invitation.

Coaldon declared, "You are not being honest. I know you want to destroy me. By the way, do you know that Noel and my companions have escaped the college?"

There was a long silence before Crossmore responded. "Oh yes, now it makes sense. The scream and your appearance were a diversion to keep my attention away from their escape. I was so occupied by your attack that I did not see them depart. Why did you do that to me? You must learn to trust me if we are to work together. I am surprised Noel does not accept my love for her. She would make a beautiful queen. By the way, how did they get away from the college?"

Coaldon responded, "It is my secret."

Then with a burst of insight, Crossmore reacted, "The scream is the answer to my own question. Only a dragon could make such a penetrating shriek. Your friends escaped on the back of a dragon. But, where did it come from? I have been such a fool! A dragon has existed in the college for all these centuries and I did not know it."

As Crossmore ended his self-dialogue, he turned to Coaldon with a hostile expression on his face. "You tricked me!"

Another sudden shift in attitude transformed Crossmore's appearance. With a sweet smile, he murmured, "I am sorry for my frustration. I was hoping I could have talked with Noel."

Coaldon declared, "I do not trust you. You only want to gain complete control over the empire. People are only objects for you to use."

The truth of Coaldon's statement rang loud in Crossmore ears. The wizard's attempts to manipulate the young warrior had failed. Coaldon had not cowered to his presence and will. His normal ability to dominate people had failed. His lack of power over Coaldon caused his temper to burst into rage.

With a loud shout, he declared. "I am your emperor! You will follow my commands, or you will die! Drop your sword and bow to me! You are now my humble servant!"

Without warning, Coaldon laughed, raise his sword, and released a fiery blast of energy. The ball of fire sizzled and crackled as it raced toward Crossmore. This sudden assault came so quickly that the wizard was caught off guard. The orb of fire hit the wizard with such force that it tossed him backwards. Crossmore's eyes closed, as his body sagged to the ground. His clothes smoked and gave off a foul odor. The wizard tried to move, but his senses were paralyzed.

At this moment, hundreds of sin-spirits assaulted Coaldon's mind. As the evil apparitions entered Coaldon, the horror of the spirits' wickedness filled his body with unrelenting misery. He gripped his head with both hands in an attempt to curtail the ugliness possessing him. Images of death, feelings of pain, clouds of dread, and pangs of suffering consumed his thoughts. The attack was so intense that Coaldon fell to his knees and dropped his head to the ground in despair. With all his strength, he struggled to push away the negative images attacking his mind.

Then, starting with small successes, he was able to slowly build barriers against the invasion.

As Coaldon fought his battle, Emnot approached Crossmore with smug arrogance. He showed delight at Crossmore's vulnerable condition. The sin-spirit injected his power-of-control into the wizard with unrelenting force. Crossmore felt his mind slowly being consumed by Emnot's evil powers.

Emnot laughed, "Do you think I am stupid? I must kill you before you kill me. You would never let me live and challenge your power."

Watching Crossmore wither in agony, Emnot declared, "Die, you miserable pile of scum! Ha! Ha!"

Crossmore looked at Emnot's gloating face with loathing. His fury toward Emnot ripped through him with such hatred that he erupted out of his paralysis with an unmerciful desire for revenge.

The wizard used his intense anger to pull together every last strand of energy remaining in him. As Emnot drifted in front of him, Crossmore focused his full attention on the spirit. With a jerk, he raised his hands and released a blast of destruction into Emnot. Even though the power of the attack was modest, it was successful. The sin-spirit was destroyed upon impact. The depraved creature dissolved into an empty black mist. This expenditure of energy caused Crossmore to fall into a deep comatose state.

Emnot's death also ended the attack on Coaldon. Without Emnot's leadership, the sin-spirits retreated from the city.

Not knowing what had happened, the young warrior slowly raised his head and looked around. He saw Crossmore's collapsed body on the ground and no sign of Emnot. With the last vestiges of his strength, he slowly stood up and stumbled into the college.

A Change of Plans

With unceremonious awkwardness, Coaldon slowly eased himself into a sitting position with his back against a vacant wall. As he sat, the savage scream of the dragon returned to occupy his thoughts. Even though the dragon was long gone, its penetrating shriek echoed over and over in his mind. The incomprehensible power of the screech had touched a hidden facet in his elfin nature. In the recesses of his being, an inherent knowledge of dragons had been aroused. A feeling of unity with these noble creatures was opened to the young prince from an ancient birthright passed to him from previous generations.

Coaldon was relieved when the assault of the dragon's piercing scream ended. As the dragon's voice subsided, the stillness of the room numbed his bewildered mind. Taking deep breaths, the young prince soon drifted into a comfortable slumber.

After what seemed many hours, Coaldon was awakened by the loud screech of a bird. Opening his heavy eyelids, he saw Cackles standing in front of him with his wings spread wide and his eyes intensely staring at him. Shivering from a sense of improbability, the young prince quickly closed his eyes, doubting he had actually seen Cackles.

Folding its wings, the ancient creature gave a loud cackling cry and declared in a firm voice, "Silly boy, I am standing in front of you. I will not go away."

With this statement hanging in the air, the bird lowered its body into a sitting position.

Coaldon peeked out of one eyelid to see if Cackles was there or only an illusion. The image of the bird filled his being with both consolation and foreboding.

Opening his eyes, Coaldon stated, "I thought I was dreaming, but no, you are real! I never expected to see you again!"

The old bird croaked, "You cannot be so fortunate. You are stuck with me. This is a burden you must learn to accept."

With a twist of melodrama, Coaldon declared, "Oh great one, you are most discreet and honest in sharing the truth. I will strive to accept the obvious with kindness and respect."

With a twinkle in his eyes, Cackles stated, "It is refreshing to know that your young mind acknowledges the whims of reality. By the way, you look a little rough around the edges. I think a change of scenery would be good for you. Yes, a working vacation."

With a look of puzzlement, the young prince declared, "I believe you are trying to make the unpleasant seem pleasant."

With a tone of disappointment in his voice, Cackles moaned, "You sound as if you are questioning my motives. My feelings are hurt. I am such a fragile individual. You know that I only want what is best for you."

Coaldon fell forward to his knees and bowed toward the eccentric bird with reverence.

He held this pose until Lord Cackles declared, "You may rise and face your superior."

The young prince, with bowed head, groveled, "I am sorry for questioning your motives. You are right in all things."

With a smug flip of his head, the royal bird puffed himself into a tower of indignation, declaring, "I accept your apology with humility and benevolence."

Looking at Cackles with cowering appreciation, Coaldon cried, "Thank you, Oh Great One. I will never forget your mercy."

Then, with an arrogant spread of his wing, the pompous bird proclaimed, "Now that you have properly submitted to my nobility, we can now get down to business. Where are Noel and your friends?"

The young prince answered, "They have been taken to Dragon Keep by Marko the Dragon. It was necessary for then to escape from Crossmore and Emnot."

The old creature reacted, "My, oh my, this is good news. I was hoping you would meet my old friend. I am happy Marko is helping you. This makes things easier."

Coaldon challenged, "What do you mean, 'This makes things easier'?"

In an authoritative voice, Cackles stated, "It will be easier for you to travel without your friends. Your grandfather needs your help."

In a concerned voice, Coaldon questioned, "How can I help my grandfather?"

The old bird stated, "You will need to get the details from him. I am just an over qualified messenger."

Cackles continued, "I assume Marko will return to pick you up."

Coaldon replied, "He will come back for me as soon as he delivers my comrades to Dragon Keep."

The bird reacted, "That is great! This will save you many days travel through the

Black Mountains. I assume you are planning to follow your grandfather's wishes. This is a most important mission."

Coaldon sagged in submission, "Of course I will do as my grandfather has requested."

Cackles responded, "Good! We need to get some rest before we begin our journey across the Empire."

And so saying, the great bird sat, tucked his head in his feathered wing, and promptly began to snore. Coaldon smiled and with his mind set on the future, lay down to rest by his friend.

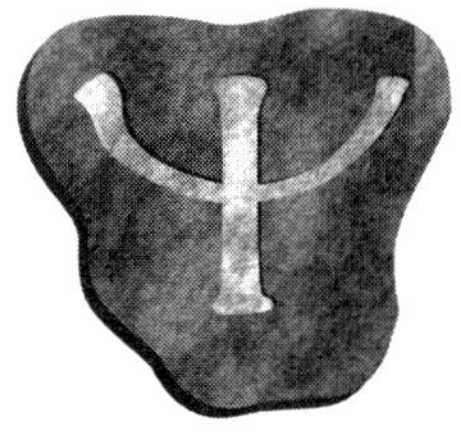

GLOSSARY

Historical Time Periods:

First Quarter Age - Age of Seaborn (Time of Prosperity)
Second Quarter Age - An era of war and evil (Time of Doomage)
Third Quarter Age - A time of peace
Fourth Quarter Age - The era of Coaldon (Time of Crossmore)
Black Mountains - Location of Lost Valley and Dragon Keep
Black Mist - Evil presence controlled by Crossmore
Blade of Conquest - Coaldon's elfin sword with the power of Blessed Acts
Brad Rocknee - Exiled Emperor of the Empire and Coaldon's grandfather
Brother Patrick - Warrior monk from the Monastery of Toms
Cando the Wizard - Wizard whose body and spirit had been separated by magic
Cave of Hope - Location of the Key of Ban
Chamber of Oblivion - Location of imprisoned evil spirits
City of Mazz - Abandoned city in the Southern Empire
Coaldon Rocknee - Grandson of Ingrid and Brad & son of Rodney and Starglide
Crossmore - Evil wizard
Dod, Doria, and Rosa - Friends of Coaldon who lived in Grandy (Duke of Slownic)
Doomage the Wizard - Vile wizard of the Second Quarter Age
Earthkin - Dwarf warrior of the Long Beard Clan of Rockham
Emnot - Sin Spirit who controlled the City of Mazz
Gem of Watching - Possesses the Power of Correct Actions
Hardstone Clan - Dwarf clan from the Northern Sadden Mountains
Ingrid Rocknee - Wife of Emperor Brad and Coaldon's grandmother
Island of Death - Located off the eastern coast of the Empire
Island of Shy - Located in the Swamp of Grief
Joined (The) - Enslaved people united by Coaldon on the Island of Shy
Jusme - Old lady greeting Coaldon and Noel at the College of Magic
Key of Ban - Elfin book with the power to control evil
Long Beard Clan - Dwarf clan in the City of Rockham
Lost Valley - Childhood home of Coaldon located in the Black Mountains
Marko - Dragon
Monastery of Toms - Located in the Wasteland of the Outlast
Neverly - Capital city of the Empire
Noel Rocknee - Coaldon's twin sister

Pacer - Scout for Emperor Brad (Duke of Paulic)
Philo - Ancient Emperor of the Empire (transformed sea beast)
Raff and Paggy - Friends of Coaldon who live in the Village of Grandy
Ripsnout - Hardstone clan member
Rockham - Dwarf city in Southern Sadden Mountains.
Rodney Rocknee - Father to Coaldon and Noel
Rolfe - Head of the Hardstone Council of Elders
Sadden Mountains - Mountain located in the eastern part of the Empire
Scaric - Evil firedrake that attacked Noel
Seamock - Sea port on eastern coast of the Empire
Sin Monster - Culmination of sins from the City of Mazz
Starglide - Mother to Coaldon and Noel
Sid - Coaldon's dog and friend
Shortshaft - Head of the Rockham Council of Elders
Slownic River - River flowing past the City of Neverly
Starhood - Grand Advisor to the Elfdom of Talltree and father of Starglide
Strong Edge - Coaldon's magic knife that bonded him to Starhood
Swamp of Grief - Located in the southern reaches of the Empire
Topple the Wizard - Happy-go-lucky wizard
Trogs and Geks - Crossmore's evil soldiers
Village of Grandy - Located on Rolling River
Walty - Protector of the Island of Shy
Wastelow the Emperor - Emperor killed by Crossmore
Westmore, Land of - Location of the Key of Ban
Willow Wraiths - Creatures living in the Swamps of Grief